The Gravity Box II

Race to the End of the World and Beyond

**A Novel by
Norman Macera**

While journeying through The Gravity Box II. Enjoy along this exciting trip the wonderful concept art used in creating the book covers of both this novel and the first Gravity Box book by Hector J. Ortega.

Date of Publishing 2021
ISBN: 978-1-7375779-0-4

Special Thanks to Hector J. Ortega for still another great cover design with his incredible art.

Special Thanks to Craig Walker for once again riding to my rescue.

Special Thanks to Dorothy Macera for the great photo of Mom.

Special Thanks Joan Klenn for all of her help in pulling this together.

This Book Is Dedicated To:

Cass Macera, Best Mom Ever.
For Your Incredible Love and Support Over the Years.
Will Love You Forever.

Table of Contents

Part 1: How To Save the World in Three Easy Steps 1

Chapter 1: The Comet and How to Dodge It 1

Chapter 2: How Doing the Right Thing Doomed the Earth 6

Chapter 3: Time Travel, and Why You Shouldn't Go On An Empty Stomach 36

Chapter 4: The Three Day Journey Into The Middle Ages 50

Chapter 5: How We Were Mistaken for Witches and How That's Not a Good Thing 59

Chapter 6: The Bringers of Evil, Death, and Destruction, I Think They Were Talking About Us 68

Chapter 7: Basil the Laughing Dungeon Master and Will the Whipping Boy 77

Chapter 8: Lord Hoxley, and How He Got Us Killed 93

Chapter 9: The Bones at the Bottom of the Moat, and How They Were Gonna Be Ours 106

Chapter 10: The Serpent From the Underworld Comes to the Rescue 116

Chapter 11: The Secret Behind the Castle Wall 134

Chapter 12: Hide and Seek in the Tower of Death 146

Chapter 13: How the Psycho Queen Met the Demon from the Underworld, and How Much Fun That Was 161

Chapter 14: Just When Things Couldn't Get Any Worst, How They Did 175

Chapter 15: Altering the Time Space Continuum, or Playing Dodge Ball With the Comet 188

Part 2: Back For the End of the World and Just in Time 221

Chapter 1: In the Belly of the Beast 221

Chapter 2: Sir Sagamore to the Rescue 238

Chapter 3: Home Sweet, Deadly Place 255

Chapter 4: Fe Fi Fo Fum, Here Comes Bobby 267

Chapter 5: How Sagamore Destroyer of All Evil Helped Us Steal the Milk Crates 291

Chapter 6: The Shadow Creature in Jimmy's Room 311

Chapter 7: Will and Kate Up in the Clouds And Not Happy About It 344

Chapter 8: The Last Tuesday On Earth 358

Chapter 9: How the End of the World Ruined Recess 369

Chapter 10: The Shadow Over the Earth 385

Chapter 11: What To Do About Will and Kate 402

Chapter 12: My Talk With Dad, and Other Terrors 412

EPPI-LOG.. **418**

Part 1: How To Save the World in Three Easy Steps

Chapter 1: The Comet and How to Dodge It

Being the two most powerful kids in the Universe isn't all that it's cracked up to be. And that's what the Gravity Boxes had made me and Jimmy. Sure we had all the power, but we also had all the scary stuff that went along with it. Let's start with the black knight, yeah, that's a good place to start.

He was big, and mean, and had come chasing me and Jimmy across time and space. He was a knight from the not so merry old England that had followed us through centuries right into our own backyards. And believe it or not, a crazy knight, with murder on his mind was the least of our problems. It had all been a big mix up, and if me and Jimmy hadn't been trying to save the world none of it would've happened. The truth is that the last time we saved the world we didn't have nearly this much trouble, and it could all be blamed on us finally deciding to do the right thing. Yeah, that's right doing the right thing. I'll think twice before I do that again. But let me tell you first how the planet was about to come to an end, and ruined our Saturday afternoon.

It was the size of our entire town, and could kick this old planet of ours right into the sun. That's what the Professor told us. And from the sound of things it was headed right towards the Earth. That's why me and Jimmy decided to take the afternoon off from our foosball game with some of our buddies, and go and see the Professor.

Yeah, Professor Burkhardt had sounded kind of serious when he called Jimmy, or at least that's what Jimmy had told me. It seemed that the Professor was always calling Jimmy, 'cause he was the smart one. I got the calls when he needed his lawn mowed, and stuff like that. But for this saving the Earth thing, I guess he needed the two of us.

We raced all the way through the woods to get to the Professor's house. As usual he was in the laboratory, cooking up some crazy experiment, and that's when he laid the whole story on us. But to my mind with the destruction of the world just around the corner it didn't make much sense to run out on a good game of foosball, especially if there wasn't a darn thing that we could do about it, or so we both thought.

The Professor walked us out to the yard. That was the place where we talked about the Gravity Boxes, and junk like that. The Professor was still scared that secret agents might have his house and lab bugged. They had done it before, and so he thought that they could still be listening in. And what he was about to say to us he didn't want anybody else to hear.

The Professor questioned us first about the Gravity Boxes, which he had told us to destroy. In case you don't remember the Gravity Box was an invention made by the Professor that allowed me and Jimmy to fly over the city, and levitate junk, stuff like that. It also allowed us to increase the gravity of something so that you could make a feather weigh a thousand pounds. Pretty cool, huh?

Naturally government agents and enemy spies were trying to get their hands on it, and they were willing to kill us all to do it, so me and Jimmy had to defeat them to keep the world safe that time too. With the both of us about to enter the seventh grade, I knew our parents expected us to take on more responsibility, so this saving the world thing would go over good with them. Problem was, like I said, that it was a Saturday afternoon, and I had other plans for that day, and to be honest this whole saving the world thing was getting old.

When the Professor told us that this comet was gonna crash right into the center of downtown Main Street around four o'clock Tuesday, even Jimmy wanted to know what he was telling us for?

"There has been nothing on the television or radio. My thinking is that they don't want people to panic," the Professor said. Although to my thinking, panic was all you really could do at a time like that. "The impact will cause world wide calamity, and then send the Earth hurling into the Sun." The Professor talked about tidal waves, and earthquakes, and with the planet burnt to a crisp by the Sun, that other stuff seemed like the good part.

"But what can we do," Jimmy said.

The Professor turned sadly to us, "I know you boys have been naughty, and not complied with my deepest wishes."

"What are you talking about dude," I said.

"Don't call me dude, I hate it when you call me dude."

And I knew he hated being called dude. Sometimes I think I just did it to see him get all crazy when I said it. It was really funny when he did that, but I guess that this wasn't the best time to be messing with the old guy, I mean with the planet going to be trashed and all.

"Professor," Jimmy said real serious like, "what did we do wrong?"

"One night," said the Professor, "while I was looking out of my telescope. I happened to see a strange sight flying across the forest."

"I told ya' we shouldn't a…" I tried to get out, but Jimmy shut me up quick enough, before I had stuck my foot all the way into my mouth.

"Shut up," he said.

And we both knew at once what the Professor was talking about. He had wanted us to destroy the Gravity Boxes, and we should've, but it was just so cool flying above the clouds, pretending to be Superman, that at first we couldn't do it. One time we must've soared too close to the edge of the woods where Professor Burkhardt lived, and gotten caught by his telescope. Heck, it could spot a comet millions of miles away in space, so what made us think that we wouldn't get caught?

"We're sorry Professor," Jimmy tried to explain, "but why didn't you say anything before?"

"An old man's vanity, I guess," said the Professor. "I had devoted my life to the creation of the gravity machine… in a way it felt good knowing that somewhere in the universe it still existed… Even if it were in the hands of two naughty boys, I thought it would be harmless enough as long as you two were careful, and quiet about your activities."

Jimmy looked down sadly, "I'm sorry Professor… you trusted us and…"

"No, it's a good thing, I'm glad you were naughty" the Professor stopped him in his tracks.

"You are," Jimmy answered, 'cause what the Professor had said had caught us both off guard.

"Those gravity machines might be the one hope for all humanity."

So the way I was seeing it, that in exchange for saving the planet and all the people on it from total destruction, the Professor would let us off the hook for our little white lie. There was only one problem with that, we had finally gone through with what he had wanted, and destroyed the Gravity Boxes. Let me tell you about that.

Chapter 2: How Doing the Right Thing Doomed the Earth

"You did what," the Professor gasped.

"We felt bad," said Jimmy, "and…"

Jimmy never got that "and whatever" out of his mouth. The Professor seemed to be real upset that we had actually done what he had wanted us to do, even if it had been five months after he had told us to do it.

"When I first found out of your little deception, I wanted to take a paddle to the both of you. But part of me was happy. Part of me knew that the gravity machine could be used for the greater good, and so I hesitated to talk to you about it. Part of me, I guess, could not destroy the work of my lifetime, my invention. Even with the precarious possibility that it could fall into the wrong hands. So I guess I cannot fault you boys for wanting to hold on to that too. We were all being selfish. So why did you finally destroy my creation?"

What the Professor was really asking was how did we take the worlds one chance for survival against a giant comet ready to crash into the middle of Main Street on Tuesday, and toss it down the sewer?

The way that came about was like this: It was a cold night for the time of year we were in. Me and Jimmy, we hardly ever took the Gravity Boxes out on cold nights, 'cause at a thousand feet up in the air, it seemed a whole lot colder than on the ground. That was really true with the wind hitting you about a hundred miles an hour.

We sneaked out of our houses as usual, and met late at night when our parents were all asleep, and went to a secret hiding place where we had kept the flying machines. It was easy for Jimmy, the secret hiding place was his garage. It was close to twelve when we finally got together, and I could see that Jimmy was a bit tired. The both of us had made too many trips to the clouds that week, and it was beginning to wear us down. 'Cause after sneaking back into our houses later that night, we'd have only a couple hours of sleep before we had to get back up in the morning for school. It had been so much fun flying that we didn't seem to mind in the beginning, but now after weeks of missing sleep, we were starting to feel it.

"Do I look as bad as I feel," I said to Jimmy.

"Shawn," he said, "you look worse than I feel. Maybe we should only go up an hour tonight, and save ourselves for the weekend?"

"Sounds like a plan," I told Jimmy.

The place where we hid the Gravity Boxes was in the loft inside Jimmy's fathers' garage. There was enough junk in there to hide an elephant, so keeping the Gravity Boxes secret there was easy. No one ever went up to the loft, and Jimmy's Dad hadn't cleaned it in years.

There was window in the loft that we could fly out of, and we now had such control over the boxes that we could do it so fast that it would be hard to spot us. That was unless you were looking for us. And at that time of night, mostly everybody was asleep anyway. Except for old man Betson, who lived down a few doors from Jimmy's house. Being retired I guess all he did was watch television all night. During the day when he came out into the Sun, he would spend hours checking under cars along the street to see if they were leaking oil. The rest of the day was spent clearing the gutters outside of his house, and shooing the birds away from his property. Since everybody thought he was crazy, a story about a couple of flying kids in the neighborhood wouldn't have gotten much more than a polite smile from anybody who heard it.

Let me get back to why we finally did what the Professor had wanted, and how doing that only made things worse. Me and Jimmy were soaring about three thousand feet near a very big, dark cloud when thunder roared, and lightening lit up the sky. We had seen it all before, but we had always been smart about it, and headed right back to the loft before things got too bad. We soared above the clouds to avoid the lightning and the drizzle that had rolled in with the storm that was about to come showering down on the town.

"Maybe we should just stay above the clouds," I called to Jimmy over the wind that was stirring wildly in the air.

"Na," he came back at me, "it's too cold Shawn, and I'm beat."

"So ya' want to head back to the loft," I said.

"Yep back to the loft," Jimmy came back at me. "We'll stay over the clouds until we get near my house."

"How 'bout so I don't get drenched, you drop me off at my house, and you levitate my Gravity Box back to your place?" We had done that many times before. Since the both of us were now experts with the boxes it was easy for Jimmy just to float the extra box back to the loft, and save me the trip home.

"Good idea," he said, and we started heading to my house.

The sky was lit bright that night with lightening sparking off every minute or so. And staying above the clouds seemed like the best idea, even though it was getting freezing cold up there. There were flashes and thunder all around us, and the chill and the wind were getting worst all the time. It seemed like we were heading straight into the middle of a hurricane. So we both figured to get back to our houses as quickly as possible.

As we dipped under the cloud there was another sudden blast as the electrical charge from the lightening filled the air. The light was blinding, and the thunder was so loud that it scared the heck out of me, and caught us completely off guard. So much in fact that for an instant Jimmy left go of the handles on his Gravity Box to cover his ears, and started to fall to the ground. It took a minute to get my sight back, so I only had his scream to let me know that he was in big trouble. He was only a few feet over my house when I shot the green beam from my Gravity Box, and tossed him and his box back into the air. I guess it was good we were up so high, that gave me a chance to think straight before Jimmy crashed through my roof, and my parents would've been sure to find out what we had been up too.

I could see a lot better in no time, and made sure he got his hands back onto his Gravity Box, so that he could continue flying on his own.

Jimmy seemed a little shaken, but it wasn't the first time he had fallen from the sky, and he had always gotten over that fast enough. But there was something else that seemed to be bothering him.

"Let's get back up high," he said like it was real important that we do it right away.

Real quick like we zipped back over the big dark cloud that seemed to be following us.

"What's wrong," I called at him from across the windy sky.

He seemed almost too scared to answer for a minute, and this wasn't one of those I've just fallen a thousand feet and almost got killed kind of scared, this seemed serious. In just a second I was gonna learn just how serious it really was.

Just above the storm, in the now really cold air Jimmy yelled two really scary words at me: "Shadow Creatures!" I knew right away what he meant by that, and I wasn't happy. When we first came across the secret agents that had been spying on the Professor and us, we at first thought that they were Shadow Creatures. It had been dark, they wore all black, and they didn't make any sound when they moved along. So what else were two kids in the middle of the pitch black woods gonna think? It was later when we started spying on them that we realized that what was lurking in those dark woods were enemy agents, trying to steal the Professor's invention, the Gravity Box.

"Where did you see them," I yelled back at Jimmy through the thunder and the wind that had started to toss us around like we were leafs caught in a nasty breeze.

He came closer so we could hear each other.

"I was just about to crash through your roof, when another bolt of lightening flashed and lit up the area. It was only for a second, but I could've sworn I saw one of them run behind the garage."

"But why would they be watching us, don't they know we destroyed these things."

"Maybe they didn't fall for our story, maybe somebody saw two unidentified flying boys soaring over the town. Whatever, we got to find out what's going on before they abduct our families again."

"We can't let that happen. My Mom and Dad got really mad the last time they got kidnapped by enemy agents, and held at gunpoint, and stuff."

"If they are here, there's only one thing that they could want."

And we both knew that what they wanted was the Gravity Boxes. Whoever had the secret of those flying machines could run the world. They could down missiles, crush buildings, crush whole cities in fact, which is the exact reason the Professor had wanted us to destroy them in the first place. We hadn't let any of our friends take rides with us, heck they didn't even know about the Gravity Boxes, so how could the spy guys know that we still had them?

"Are you sure you saw what you saw," I said to Jimmy, 'Cause I really wanted him to be wrong. For one thing I didn't want anything to happen to my family, and the other was a whole lot more selfish, I didn't want give up the Gravity Boxes. Not only was it an invention that could be used for great evil, but it was maybe the coolest toy in the world.

Jimmy looked at me real serious like, "I know I saw something, but maybe we should check around."

Jimmy was being selfish too. Nothing in our lives had ever been so exciting, and given us so much fun as those two flying machines. When you flew with them it actually felt like it was you

11

doing the flying. At night, when our parents went to bed, and the rest of the world was busy sleeping, we could both be Superman. But if the "Shadow Creatures" were back then we knew that trouble was just around the corner, trouble and a whole lot of danger.

We came to a decision that night. First we were gonna check out the area. Maybe the figure of the Shadow Creature running next to my garage was all in Jimmy's imagination, maybe not. If he had seen what he said he saw, then we were putting ourselves, our families, and oh yeah, everybody else in the world in real danger. That wouldn't be cool, so there was only one thing to do, destroy the Gravity Boxes like the Professor had wanted us to do in the first place. First we had to find out if the spy guys were still keeping an eye on me and Jimmy.

"We'll go closer to the ground…" Jimmy said.

"But…"

"I know it's dangerous, we could get caught."

"Then why we going…"

"Because," he cut me off again. It was hard getting a whole sentence in with this guy; "if we stay up here we'll never be able to see anything if they're hiding down on the ground."

"But the lightening…"

"It's a chance we'll have to take…'

"Maybe not," I stopped him this time.

"What do you have in mind?"

"The way the green beam works is by our imagination, right?"

"We already know…"

It was my chance to be rude this time, and I had actually come up with a better idea than Jimmy. True he was the smart one, but every once in awhile old Shawn could top him in the idea department.

"What do you say we shoot anything up into the air that's wearing a black hood?"

He smiled at me. It was only the moon shinning through the dark of night onto his face that let me know that Jimmy was happy with my idea. And so that's what we did.

Closing our eyes we saw the pictures in our heads. In no time the green beams shot from the glass lens in the front of the Gravity Boxes, and cut through the storm, and hit the ground below. It was a bad move in one way, anybody looking out of their window would have definitely seen the whole ground flash bright green. The giant beam spread wide, and covered most of the ground, and definitely did not look like lightening. Seconds later, there were several screams of terror that cut through the thunderous bangs going on all over the place. Three men dressed in black, and wearing hoods flew into the air. Jimmy was right, these creeps were back, and they were looking for us. As they were shot up into the air like rockets, it seemed like they were trying grab hold of the sky, as if that would keep them from falling back to Earth, which of course it wouldn't do. I had learned that the hard way. It was that green beam, and only that that had kept them afloat in that cold April sky.

With the storm going on all around them they also seemed to be trying to dodge the lightening that was going crazy that night. Me and Jimmy got a little scared that they might be hit, and so we brought them up over the clouds as quick as we could.

Once above the clouds the guys in black started to get a little silly. Two of them pulled out their guns, and one guy started making demands right off. These guys never learn.

"Put us down now punks, or…"

"Okay," Jimmy said, when he instantly dropped the guy with the big mouth a thousand feet or so. He then screamed all the way down.

"Go on shoot, you'll be part of the sidewalk in about two seconds," Jimmy yelled to them.

The other two were both scared enough to believe that he meant it, and slowly placed the guns back into their holsters that were hidden under their shirts. Jimmy then brought the other guy, the one with all the demands, back up to hang out with us. He was still acting like he was in charge when he got to our height.

"You little son of…" he called out, but Jimmy cut him off.

"If we fall you fall, if you shoot, then we all crash." That seemed to get through. He lowered his voice, and placed the gun back into his holster.

"You kids are in big trouble," the big mouth said, and when he said that he sounded a little familiar. I wasn't sure that that was such a good thing.

"Who are you," I called out to him, "and why are you spying on my house?"

That's when he removed his hood, and then I really got a sinking feeling. Both me and Jimmy knew at once who we were dealing with. This guy wasn't a foreign spy; he was a government agent that had chased us to the junkyard where we were supposed to have destroyed the Gravity Boxes.

The thing is that me and Jimmy had faked it all. We had used explosives to make it look like the real Gravity Boxes were blown up. Somehow he must have figured out that we played a trick on him, and was now coming to get the boxes back. The problem with that was that the Professor didn't want anyone to have the Gravity Boxes, not even us. They were too dangerous for any one nation, or person to have. But me and Jimmy didn't see any harm with us just keeping them around for midnight joy rides to the clouds. We didn't think that the Professor would have seen it that way, and that's why we didn't tell him. But now that the government agents were here, and wanting to take them back, we knew we were in big trouble.

"I'm the one who ask the questions here kid," the leader of these guys spoke again, still imagining that he was somehow in charge of the whole situation, in the mean time he was looking kind of silly bobbing around in the sky like a beach ball floating on the ocean waves.

"What were you doing at my house," I figured since I had one of the Gravity Boxes it was all right for me to be cocky. I guess power did that to people. On the ground, and without the magic of the Gravity Box, I would have been really scared of these guys. I was still scared, but now I was more worried about my parents and my little sister, and what these guys were back in town for.

"As a representative of the government I am hereby confiscating those levitation devices…"

"I don't think so," Jimmy told him.

And I couldn't believe that he had actually said it. This guy was a real big shot, and he could have us locked up for a long time. You see, like I was saying before, Jimmy was the smart one. Everybody expected me to go off, and do something stupid like argue with a big government agent, but not Jimmy.

"The Professor don't want you to have them," Jimmy told the leader, who wasn't looking happy at all right about now.

"Do you understand the implications of refusing to cooperate with…"And that was all that Jimmy would let him get out.

"Just relax," he stopped the guy right in his tracks.

"Why you cocky, little…" he called out, but Jimmy wasn't listening.

"I'll be back in just a minute," Jimmy said, and then he turned to me. "Shawn, would you join me in my office."

I knew right away what he had in mind, and we traveled a short distance away so we could talk in private. All the time the leader of the agents was calling us names, and I think he even bad mouthed Jimmy's parents. Saying things about the way he wasn't brought up right and stuff.

We had drifted over to that nearby cloud, and Jimmy laid it all on me.

"They're really mad," I said.

"He's gonna get a whole lot madder, but we can't worry about that now," Jimmy told me. But in my head, I couldn't think of a better time to worry about this stuff. Those guys could give us a lot of trouble when they got us back on the ground.

"I'm supposed to be the one who is always… always… what's the word you, and my parents, and everybody is always calling me?"

"Impulsive!"

"Yeah, that's supposed to be me."

"I'm not being impulsive Shawn, I know we're in big trouble, but do you really think that our trouble is worth more than the whole planet?"

I have to be honest, right then and there I was thinking about my own butt. I mean the planet had gotten along pretty good for years before old Shawn came along, so how was I gonna be such a big help?

"Jimmy," I said, and I was having to talk real loud, 'cause the wind was getting strong again, and blowing us around, so that we had to send real strong pictures from our mind to the Gravity Boxes, just to keep from being blown across the sky. And we didn't dare forget about the agents floating on air not too far away. They would've dropped from the sky like paperweights.

"Keep it down," he said, "I don't want them to hear us."

"I can hardly hear me…"

"The thing is Shawn," and now he got real close, "is that we promised the Professor that we'd destroy these gravity machines. What we do tonight will effect the whole world. Do you think that we're more important than the whole world?"

"Maybe they'll just use them to help people," I was looking for any reason to get out of the big trouble that we were swimming in right at that moment.

"We can't take that chance, we have to destroy the Gravity Boxes, and they have to see us do it."

"But," I tried to get out.

"If they don't see it, they won't believe it," he came right back at me.

"How we gonna do that," because I didn't really know how we could do that without getting shot, or whatever these guys were willing to do to get the Gravity Boxes from us.

"I gotta plan," he said. And he always did. That was one of the good things, and one of the bad things about hanging around with Jimmy. There was always something cooking on the inside of his head, and a lot of times that is what got us into trouble. So he came close, and he told me the whole idea, and it seemed like it just might work.

"First we had to destroy the one Gravity Box, while we were still in the air. The tough part was destroying the second one, now that was gonna be a little tricky, but if it worked they would know for sure that the Gravity Boxes were really gone, and that maybe they would stop watching us and our families. That seemed to be the best that we could hope for. Otherwise we were gonna get ourselves killed by these guys, and probably locked up for treason, and what was the other thing the Professor had told us about before, sabotage. Didn't even want to think what my Dad would do to me.

Once we got down all the details of the plan, we flew back to be near the government agents who were still floating around just above the storm. They still didn't look too happy being up there. We were greeted with the usual welcome from the leader.

"You punks, ready to cooperate, or am I going to have to haul your scrawny butts in and…"

That's all that Jimmy let him get out, before he interrupted him again. Jimmy was being kinda bossy that night. That really surprised me considering the kinda trouble we were in right then.

"We're not giving the levitation devices to you or to anybody," Jimmy said, and I swear everybody thought that I was the cocky one.

"Do you know what will happen if you fail to…"

"I won't give them to you, but I promise that no one else will ever get their hands on these levitation machines," and then Jimmy looked to me. "Shawn," he said.

With that word he released his grip on his Gravity Box, and it was now up to me to keep him up in the sky, in fact to keep them all up in the sky.

"What are you doing kid," the Leader called out. The wind was hitting him pretty hard in the face too, so we still all had to yell to be heard that night, and he was looking kinda nervous about now.

"Do it Shawn," Jimmy yelled as he drifted across the air to my side. And do it is exactly what I did. In my mind's eye I saw Jimmy's Gravity Box drop down below the dark clouds, and into the middle of the violent and crazy storm. It would only take seconds, but it seemed like forever, and then it happened. A flash of lightening blasted out of a cloud, and crashed right into the lone Gravity Box out there in the middle of the sky. We could hear the leader of the agents, scream at us: "No!" But at that point there was nothing that any of us could do to stop the box from exploding, and filling the air with a bright green glow. The explosion knocked us all back across the air. And I had to get control of the situation real fast as the agents started to drop like rocks. There was some screaming, but I caught them with the beam from my Gravity Box before they had fallen too far, and brought them back up in the air with us.

That fast the Gravity Box had disappeared. The green glow created by the explosion was beginning to die down. Then like a snuffed out candle it was gone leaving nothing but a puff of smoke that danced in the air for a few seconds, and then was blown away by the strong winds. The leader was still screaming at us from across the sky trying desperately to stop what we were doing.

"You'll kill us all," he yelled at us.

"Not if we do this right," Jimmy tried to quiet him down.

Yeah, he really wanted us not to destroy the boxes, but we both knew we couldn't stop, no one would be safe if these machines fell into the wrong hands. So we were just gonna do it, and the less I thought about it, the easier it was all gonna be. One box had been destroyed, but destroying the second one was gonna be a little more tricky. Jimmy wanted to handle that one. The plan was a dangerous one, and Jimmy said that that would be "our moment of maximum risk." I had heard those words before, and it just meant that that was the time that we were most likely to get killed, or worst. But somehow he wanted to take it on, and being a good friend I handed that "moment of maximum risk" right over to him. The problem with this part of the plan was that we just couldn't have lightening destroy the second box. First of all we were all still too high in the sky, and to do so would mean that we would all fall a couple of thousand feet to the ground below, and kill us all. So we both agreed that a better plan had to be cooked up. And it had to be done in front of the agents, or else they wouldn't believe that we had really destroyed them this time either. Yes, that was the tricky part; they had to see it all. Which meant that they had to be nearby, and they'd still have their guns. A couple of thousand feet in the air they were scared to use them, but once on the ground, I didn't think they would have any problems, not if it meant getting their hands on something as important as the Gravity Box.

As I handed control of the box over to Jimmy, I could see sadness in his eyes. Neither of us was happy about what seemed to us like killing the Gravity Boxes.

"What are you two crazy kids going to do now..." the leader shouted again at us.

We both decided not to look at him. What we were gonna do we had to do quickly. Once on the ground we couldn't give them a second to think about how to stop us before we had trashed the second box. Of course we could've just dropped them from the sky, but that would have probably meant more trouble. Besides Jimmy stopped that idea almost before it came out of my mouth, not actually wanting to kill these guys. Me neither, I guess, and when I thought about it, everybody would've guessed that they just didn't fall out of an airplane or something. Oh and yeah, it would be wrong.

The plan was simple, but needed to be timed right. They had to see what we had done, but at the same moment not have enough time to stop us.

Jimmy had planned to increase the gravity of the large tree outside of my house so that it toppled onto the last box, and crushed it.

It was me who came up with the idea that just might give us all the time we needed, and with no danger to us, until after the box was gone, and all the power we held over these guys with it. First I thought to make them drop their guns, but Jimmy told me that at that height they might go crashing through a house, or go off and shoot somebody. So that idea was out.

Yeah, it was my guess that these government agents were gonna be pretty mad at us when this was all over. What might happen then was too scary to think about. And that seemed to be the real fear running through my body, as we got ready to trash the second box. Not knowing was always the most scary part of any situation. Usually my imagination would see things turning out a whole lot worse than they were really gonna be. And then it happened. It looked like my imagination had not seen how really bad and dangerous things could get.

It was right after I had come up with my great plan that the trouble, and the situation we were in got a whole lot worse. As we were preparing to take the government agents all back to the ground, and crush the last Gravity Box, the air filled with something besides the sound of screaming, and that crazy wind knocking us about like we were rag dolls. It had come up on us all the sudden, and we didn't know till the last minute what was going on.

With the storm lighting up the night sky, we had hardly noticed the distant lights sneaking up on us. And before we knew it they were on top of us. Giant army helicopters had arrived to add to our troubles. We really didn't want the cavalry showing up right then.

It was that quick that they came bursting onto the scene, and stirring up the air even more than the storm. It was blinding at first, and we both knew that we had to act instantly.

"You are surrounded," a loud booming voice came over the loud speaker of one of the choppers, "Put those men down immediately."

Without thinking a minute about it, Jimmy dropped us down like falling stars to below the clouds, us and the agents that is.

You could tell they were pretty upset, and they started to scream out to us. They were scared of being up so high, and now they were scared of the thunder and lightening tearing up the sky all around them, but mostly I think that they were just scared of hitting the ground at a hundred and twenty miles an hour.

That maneuver seemed to slow the choppers down a little, 'cause they were afraid of the storm too.

"You're going to get us all killed," the leader yelled at us.

Another blast from the clouds charged the air, and scared us all. We didn't know if the Gravity Boxes could protect us from the lightening.

"He's right," I yelled at Jimmy.

"Just needed a minute to think," he said.

"There's no time to think," I screamed out at him.

"Do you know what to do?"

"They got choppers Jimmy," I was yelling and shaking all over.

"Nobody will do anything to us till we get them on the ground," he said, and then he asked again, "do you know what to do?"

I knew, but I didn't want to do it. Then I remembered how the Gravity Box could be really dangerous in the wrong hands.

"Let's do it," I said shaking as the words came out of my mouth, and that fast we were all falling back to earth. It must have scared everybody, 'cause I knew what Jimmy was doing, and the kind of control he now had over the Gravity Box, and I was scared.

In no time one of the choppers had dropped down with us, daring to chance flying into the storm, so I guess they all knew how important the Gravity Box was.

The lights were still a little blinding, but he couldn't keep up with us 'cause we were moving real fast, almost as if free falling. The screams from the agents filled the sky again, but with all the other noise going on, I doubt that anybody else could've heard them.

In no time we stopped, and Jimmy had us hovering just above the ground. The leader of the agents wasted no time in pulling out his handgun, and aiming it right at us. And that's when Jimmy brought my great plan into play. He instantly increased the gravity of all of the agents and of their guns. Like rocks tossed into a pond they dropped, and groaned when they hit the dirt.

"Let us up," the leader was handing out orders like he still thought he was in charge.

"It'll all be over in a minute," Jimmy called to him as he placed the Gravity Box down in front of the tree that he was going to use to crush it.

"What if we don't return to normal after you destroy the box, we'll die," the leader cried out. This time he wasn't ordering, this sounded a little bit more like begging.

"When the box is gone, you're gravity will return to normal."

"How do you know?"

Jimmy looked at me, 'cause neither of us had the answer. We had always put things back afterwards, but the box had always been there too. But there wasn't much time to think about any of it, 'cause the helicopter was coming down faster than we expected, and was just above the trees.

"What do we do," Jimmy looked at me, and he was scared, 'cause, if the chopper was almost on top of us, and the agents were close enough to stop us if we didn't move real quick.

"We can't kill them," I said, and Jimmy agreed. We didn't like them, but we didn't want those guys crushed into the ground either.

"We got only a few seconds, no time to think…"

"I got it," I said. "Weigh down their guns, not them, and if they get near you, I'll stop them."

"How you gonna…"

"I'm a pretty good football player."

"Shawn, these guys are commandos, they all outweigh you by a hundred pounds at least…"

"But…"

"There's three of them!

"Guess we say goodbye to the most powerful kids in the Universe."

"Tear those commandos apart Shawn," he said, and smiled at me, "cause we both knew what my chances against those guys were really like.

Jimmy turned back to the Gravity Box, and took the handles. A glow of green light flashed out, and began to surround the tree. At the same time the three government agents felt the weight of their bodies return to normal.

I don't know if Jimmy was having trouble getting the pictures in his head, or if the tree was just being stubborn, but it wouldn't fall.

In no time the three agents were coming after us. The only thing that had slowed them down was that they had stopped to try and pick up their guns, but we had not returned the gravity of the guns to normal, so they weren't going anywhere. I think one guy hurt his shoulder, 'cause he seemed to cry out in pain as he stooped to pick up the gun.

As the leader headed at Jimmy, I went in for my first tackle. It was like brick hitting a windowpane, me being the windowpane. His knee had caught me right in the gut, and I dropped like a lead balloon. And as if he hadn't been tackled at all the leader guy was moving still after Jimmy. Jimmy must've saw him coming, and another blast of green light sent the three agents sailing back. One of them almost hit me as he whizzed through the air.

The helicopter was hovering just above the ground now, and one of the Soldiers inside jumped out to join in. His rifle was ready for action, and not affected by the Gravity Box. He readied to aim the rifle, but the leader warned him: "Don't shoot, you might hit the levitation device." That told me right away what he was really worried about.

But still Jimmy tried to make the tree fall, and still the tree wouldn't fall. It was now four guys going after Jimmy, and I had to try and stop them all. I picked myself up off of the muddy dirt with two scoops of mud in my hands, and I tossed it at them as they too were getting back on their feet. My mud attack had done as much good as my tackle in slowing these guys down. The leader was moving the quickest, and was the first, so I tried to take him out one more time. This time I dived down, and grabbed hold of his leg, and he dragged me along for about a yard before I fell off, and the others just ran over me.

An extra burst of light flashed out of the Gravity Box, and made the tree glow even brighter than before. That fast it had begun to uproot, and now started dipping down towards Jimmy and the Gravity Box.

As the leader got closer to Jimmy he shoved the leader, but the push actually knocked Jimmy back, and away from the tree. Jimmy's push was as good as my tackle, like nothing at all. It was a sudden blast of lightening hitting the tree that drew the leader's attention away from grabbing the box, and halted him in his tracks. The flash had blinded us all for a minute. It even stopped the soldier suddenly in his footsteps who was also going after the Gravity Box. Me being back further could see what had happened. All of them had stopped in their tracks, Jimmy was clear of the tree, and the only one who was in danger at that moment was the leader, who was now right in the path of the falling tree. The lightening had instantly set the tree ablaze, and the flaming tree was falling right into my yard, and onto the Gravity Box. The leader was still determined that he was gonna get his hands on the box, but the tree was falling too quick now, and looked like it was gonna crush him too. He stooped down to grab hold of the handles, and it looked like he was gonna get cooked by the burning tree. Jimmy was looking on in horror. We didn't want them to get hold of the Gravity Box, but we didn't want anybody killed either. Whether he stumbled, or got scared as he saw the tree about to come toppling right down on top of him I don't know, but the leader was moving kinda of slow for a guy who thought he wasn't gonna live through the night. In fact for military guys they were all moving kind of slow, so I decided to take one more shot at this guy. There wasn't much time at all, the tree was half way down, and the roots didn't seem to be holding at all now. From the ground I pushed off as hard as I could, and sprinted past the agents as fast as I could make my legs run. It seemed like a stupid thing to do, but it just happened. In my head, I knew in that instant if I didn't do something that the leader guy would be crushed. And just before the tree came crashing down I rushed in, and tackled him. This time he was bent over so his balance was off, and I could shove him out of the way. An instant later the tree fell squashing the box, and almost getting me. The tree was on fire now from the lightening, and had set what was ever left of the Gravity Box on fire.

The leader got up from the ground, in no time the other agents and the Soldier had us surrounded. I had saved his life, but he still didn't look happy. He walked over to us, and I closed my eyes afraid that he was gonna hit me or something.

"You kid's don't know when to quit," the leader said.

"Should we take them in," the Soldier said pointing the rifle at us.

In no time people had come out of their houses, and the lights in my parent's room had gone on, so I knew that they would be coming outside soon. The crash had gotten a lot of attention. The leader turned real quick like to the Soldier.

"Put that rifle down," he screamed. "And get that chopper out of here."

That quick the Soldier had run off. The leader then motioned to the other agents with him, and they started to move off into the night. The leader wasn't leaving us off the hook that easy though. He looked right at me.

"You saved my life punk, but that won't get you off the hook the next time we cross paths."

"You're welcome," I said. I think he thought that I was just trying to be funny, but I was just nervous, and looking for stuff to say so that I didn't cry.

"Shawn... Jimmy," I heard my Father's voice coming from the back porch.

I looked back for a moment, and the leader said: "Go on, before I change my mind, lock you up, and toss away the key."

The helicopter had already moved away, and would soon be out of sight.

Newsy neighbors had already come out into the rain to gape at the burning tree. They were acting like they'd never seen a fire before, or a helicopter in their backyard. The tree was sparking and sizzling as the rain kept pouring down on top of hot burning wood.

"Shawn," I heard my Father's voice calling again.

"Go," said the leader, and he started to walk off just kind of ignoring the crowd.

Jimmy surprised me when he moved after the guy, 'cause I didn't know what was gonna happen, or what Jimmy wanted from him.

I moved after Jimmy, and acted like I hadn't heard my Dad. He'd a gotten really mad if he knew I had heard him, but if he figured that I was to caught up in the excitement he might not be so mad.

"How did you know," Jimmy asked the leader.

And the leader didn't stop he just kept walking. Jimmy kept right up with him, and I was right behind.

"How did you know that we still had the levitation devices?"

"That's twice you two made a fool out of me," he said.

"The Professor didn't want it to fall into anybody's hands," Jimmy told him.

"Then you shouldn't have done so much advertising," the leader said, and he sounded angry right before he turned back, and looked at us. "One of your neighbors reported an unidentified flying phenomenon, and there was only two punk kids that fit the profile. You are playing games with national security you two…"

"Sorry," Jimmy said. "But now no one will have it."

"My name is Flynn," the leader said to us. And it was strange suddenly having a name to go along with the face and the fear. "Maybe nobody should have those weapons…"

"But now they're weapons," Jimmy stopped him.

"Whatever they are if anybody is going to have them, then I want it to be us. Now we may not be the only one's who know about you two, and you're midnight joy rides. If you see anything suspicious, I want you to call me." He then handed me and Jimmy cards with his name and phone number on it.

"Do you think there are any other…" I tried to get out.

"If that is truly the end of the levitation machines, you should be safe. Unless this is just another magic trick you two cooked up."

"No, I swear," I said.

It was then that my Father came running into the scene. Flynn turned walked away just before he arrived.

"Shawn," I've been trying to get your attention.

I turned back to him, "sorry Dad, didn't hear you I guess".

"What are you two boys doing out here this time at night in the pouring rain," Dad asked us.

Jimmy was the best at coming up with the quick answers, "Hi Mister Malloy, Shawn and I got together to watch the storm. My science teacher said that this type of storm is a rare electrical anomaly, that only occurs… in… and…"

I could tell that Jimmy was slipping. The pieces of this story weren't coming together as fast as they usually do.

"They only happen once in awhile," I jumped in not having any idea what I was talking about.

"Yes," Jimmy came back, happy for the back up, and unusually speedy brainstorm coming from me.

My Dad looked at him kind of strange, and I could tell that he wasn't buying that story. So much for Jimmy's quick thinking in tight spots. Next time maybe I should come up with the whole cover story, I thought.

"It's one thirty in the morning," Dad said. "You boys have school tomorrow." He looked back at Flynn, and the helicopter that had already climbed back into the sky. "Are you going to tell me what that was all about," my Dad asked.

"Just here observing the… the…" Jimmy started to say, but once again he seemed to be fumbling. I think it was all the excitement of the night that had fried his brain.

"That anomaly thing," I jumped to the rescue one more time.

The rain was coming down harder, and I could tell that my Dad was irritated standing out in the downpour, and not buying a word of what we were saying. We all started to move into the house. As we got to the back porch he stopped us both.

"Look boys, I know that was the same man from the Professor's lab."

Both me and Jimmy stood frozen.

"Dad" I started to say, but he cut me off quick like.

"Don't you lie to me, don't you dare lie to me," he looked down at me and Jimmy.

Now we were both out of words to say.

"I want to know what just happened," my Dad's voice got louder, and a little madder.

"The truth is Dad," I cleared my throat, and was hoping for Jimmy to jump in with something.

"Well," said Dad.

"The truth is Dad, it's all over, I promise, it's all over."

"Were you playing with those gravity machines again," his voice kept getting louder. "Because you told me before that they were destroyed."

"They're gone Dad, they're gone for real, I promise". Just then he heard my Mom calling from inside. Dad looked at the door nervously.

"I don't want your Mom to know about any of this, do you understand." Me and Jimmy bobbed our heads nervous like. Then Dad looked back at us. "We're going to have a long conversation about this, both you boys understand?"

Me and Jimmy just kept bobbing our heads.

My Dad could yell at us later, and that would give us more time to come up with a better story, just in case we decided that we needed one. The truth would've really upset him and my Mom, and I had a feeling that Dad already knew that much. After that my Dad drove Jimmy home to make sure he got there safe, and not get hit by lightening, 'cause he was already totally soaked by the rain.

Thanks to the rain the fire of the smoldering tree had begun to die down. I looked deep into the ashes to see if I could see any of the last Gravity Box, but all that remained was the burning mess left by the lightening. In the crackling of those flames was the end of a dream. And I could feel a sort of churning in my stomach, like I had just lost something really important. And that's how I felt about the Gravity Box. Me and Jimmy had gotten so good in handling them that they reacted almost like they knew what we wanted, and before we could think about it. Like a dog that knew when you were coming home way before you ever got there, or when you wanted to play, and the pet was always ready. Me and Jimmy had never had so much fun and excitement in our lives, and with the Gravity Boxes gone we thought that our lives would be much sadder, and never as exciting again. Boy were we wrong.

Concept Art Used In Creating The Cover For The First
Gravity Box Novel.

Chapter 3: Time Travel, and Why You Shouldn't Go On An Empty Stomach

After that night both me and Jimmy were not feeling quite right. We knew that we had finally done what the Professor had wanted, but we both missed the excitement of our midnight flights.

We never guessed that what we had done was gonna cause the Earth to crash into the Sun. But thinking back, we didn't really have much choice in any of it. If we had kept the Gravity Boxes the secret agents would have gotten them, and that wouldn't have been good either. Now Professor Burkhardt seemed mad at us for a whole different reason, that we had finally done what he wanted us to do.

But getting back to the problem that we were now facing, and why the Professor had asked me and Jimmy to the lab that day.

After we had told him the whole story, and how the Gravity Boxes were no longer around, he looked really upset, and I guess both of us boys were really glad that he hadn't had that paddle close by.

He couldn't look at us for the longest time. He must've really been mad, and he just kept pacing back and forth, and staring at the floor.

"Professor," Jimmy tried to break his concentration, but the Professor acted as if he couldn't hear a word. "Professor Burkhardt, we're sorry…" but still Jimmy's words just dangled in the air with no one to catch them. I knew better than to try and get through the Professor's trance, I had never seen him this sad before, even when foreign spies were about to steal the Gravity Boxes. But then I had an idea; it was a good one too, I thought, so I said it out loud, which maybe wasn't a good idea.

"Why don't you just build another Gravity Box?"

And those were the words that stopped the Professor in his tracks. He stopped, and he looked at me, and I thought, I mean I really thought I had hit the jackpot of ideas. I turned to look at Jimmy, but he wasn't so sure that I had said the right thing.

"Do you know how long it took to build the first levitation device... lets not count the seven years in development, and time needed just to gather the materials"?

"Seven years, huh," I said. That had been a little longer than I thought that it would take, and with the world coming to an end in just a few days, it just didn't seem like it could work out.

"Assemblage alone could take nine months," the Professor screamed. Yes that's right, he screamed at me again. I had never heard him like that, and it was kind of scary. He put down his head, and I could swear that he was gonna cry. Neither me or Jimmy knew what to do. And then as fast as he had gotten mad at us he stopped, and looked out the window of the lab.

"There is only one thing to do," the Professor said.

"What is that Professor," Jimmy said. And he said it like he was really afraid to ask.

"The both of you, outside," said the Professor.

And I looked at the door and at the crazed look in his eyes, and I wasn't sure that I wanted to be taken out into the woods by the Professor. True, I had never seen him violent, or even hurt a fly, but I had never seen him like this either.

"Professor," Jimmy tried to get through again, but he did not answer, he just walked to the door, and expected us to follow him. Me and Jimmy we looked at each other, 'cause no one wanted to go outside with the Professor.

But as he walked off, both of us followed. Not too close, 'cause we had given ourselves some running room, just in case we had to bolt.

Outside the Professor turned to us. "Do you know why I have brought you two boys out here," he asked. And the glassy look had left his eyes, so I was feeling a bit safer.

"Professor," Jimmy said, "we want to help anyway we can."

"I know that," said Professor Burkhardt, "that is why we have come out here to talk."

"We're just here to talk right," I said, still a bit scared. I guess you're thinking with the world coming to an end in just a few days, what could anyone do to scare us, but there was a lot fear in the air just the same, and things were just about to get a whole lot scarier.

"What else would I bring you out here for you silly boy, with the world on the brink of total destruction we have to discuss possibilities for survival."

"Then there is a chance," Jimmy asked.

"Just one, I fear, and I'm afraid that you boys will have take that chance, that is if the world is to continue spinning."

"Without the Gravity Boxes, what chance do we have against a giant comet," I said.

"That is why I have taken the precaution of making sure that this conversation is totally private."

"You think that someone may still be bugging your lab Professor," I said, because that's how the spies had found out about the Professor's secret experiments before. The lab had been scanned for bugs, and miniature listening devices were found all over the place. Still the Professor was scared that there might be more, ones that weren't found.

"For months I have been conducting the last of my experiments on my latest invention," he said. "But I was unsure of its dangers, and so I kept my work out here, not only to keep it away from prying ears, but in case of an explosion…"

"Explosion," Jimmy said.

"What I am about to reveal to you can go no further. I know now that you two are the only ones that can be trusted with what I am about to show you."

"Really," I said.

"It took some time for you to do the right thing, but that's what you did. This latest invention was a foolish design of a sentimental old man. The practical applications only became apparent to me a short time ago."

"What is it Professor," Jimmy said.

"There were things in the past that I wanted to see, and places and people that are no longer there…" and as he talked he walked towards the garage.

"That's too bad," I said, "but…"

"To visit loved ones, and just once more relive the golden days of my distant youth," he kept rambling away as if back in that trance once more.

That's when I looked over to Jimmy, and he was all wide eyed, and I could only guess that he already knew what the Professor was talking about.

"Professor," Jimmy tried to get out, but still the Professor kept talking, and not really paying attention to us. "Professor," Jimmy tried again, "are we talking about a..."

And that's all that Jimmy got out before the Professor opened the garage door. And all at once it looked like Christmas coming out of there. Inside there were bright lights flashing on and off, and for a moment it was blinding. I had to look away, but then I squinted, and was able to look back.

"Is that what I think it is," Jimmy said.

"If you think it is a time travel device, then I would say that you were correct in your assumption?" The Professor seemed quite proud as he looked at what he had made in the garage. And when we got in closer I could see what it really looked like. It had a large metal base, and was covered in a glass dome that was shaped like a diamond. On both sides of the contraption that was sitting in the middle of the floor were copper coils venting off steam that seemed to be coming from the inside of the diamond head.

Jimmy just looked and looked, and now he was acting as crazy as the Professor. He wasn't speaking, and he seemed to be hypnotized by the crazy looking thing that was flashing on and off like a thousand photographers taking pictures at once.

I was trying to stand back a little 'cause I was remembering what the Professor had said how this thing might explode.

Finally somebody said something, and it was Jimmy.

"Does it work?" Jimmy asked."

"I have only had it out for a trial run," said the Professor. "I visited tomorrow…"

"It can go into the future," Jimmy yelled out in disbelief.

"Of course," said the Professor, "what is the good of a time travel device that can only go in one direction, silly boy?" Then he let his head hang down sadly, "and tomorrow is when the world comes face to face with the knowledge of its own end. Those who are not fortunate enough to be killed instantly by the collision will be helpless and terrified as their world is crumbling around them and the planet is hurling towards the sun. It was something that the government, the people in charge wanted to keep quiet. Some thought it would be of no use to know that the world was coming to an end. Perhaps better to die in ignorance than to live out your last few moments in total terror."

"You saw this Professor," Jimmy asked him.

"I had only went a day into the future and realized that the comet was coming soon. All too soon. Naturally there were those who wished to bring the truth to light, but at that time, with death just over your shoulder, what was the point." He looked sadly at the ground. "For the most part people were complacent, and there ignorance seemed to be a gift. I escaped back here into the past before the collision, before the death."

"But you came back to save the planet too," I said to him, "ain't that right Professor?"

The Professor looked like he was about to cry, and then he seemed to pull himself together and then answered me. "Yes, yes, that's what we must do."

"But how do they know, how do you know Professor that...," Jimmy tried to get out.

"Before my trip to tomorrow you mean?"

Jimmy nodded his head and looked kinda sad.

"Never before has there been such precise satellite footage to back up such claims global catastrophe," the Professor came back at Jimmy really upset. "The survivors will be going crazy in the streets, trying to run and hide, but there will be nowhere to hide."

"Professor," I said, "what can we do?"

"We can't travel into the future, because there won't be any future," Jimmy said.

"No, the answers to all of our problems lies not in the future, but in the past," said the Professor.

"You think we should all move into the past," I said.

"No a journey of several days should do the trick," he looked at the both of us. And I could see the look in his eyes as my eyes were starting to get use to the flashing bright lights. "To a time and place right before you destroyed the gravity machines."

"You think it will work," Jimmy said.

"You two are the only ones I can trust with this assignment. I cannot let the world be destroyed, and I cannot let the levitation machines fall into the wrong hands. That could prove just as disastrous as the planet hurling into the Sun."

"But you said the time travel machine could be dangerous," I said.

"Shawn," in three days the worlds gonna end, it's not like we got a lot of choices here," Jimmy came back at me.

"I would go in your place, but your control of the devices are far superior to mine, and it will take all the power of both gravity machines to offset a comet of this mass, if in fact they can."

"Professor," Jimmy said, "will we remember all this when we get into the past, remember what to do?"

"The time travel device creates a gap in the fabric of the universe, inside the containment field of the machine, all stays the same, only outside is there change occurring."

"Which is why you can't go back to the past," Jimmy looked back at him.

"True," he said, "back there the people I love, they are all young and beautiful, they would not recognize this old man at their doorstep. So as I said before, the practical applications of this machine only came to light a short while ago."

"We go back in time," Jimmy said, "only this time…"

"This time you don't destroy the gravity machines," the Professor looked at us.

"But what about the agents after us," I said.

"He's right," Jimmy chimed in. "If they don't see us destroy them, then… wait a minute he said."

"You have a plan," the Professor asked.

"We did it once."

"Did what," I wanted to know, 'cause I knew I was gonna be on the tail end of the dangerous part.

"It's like the guy said, a little magic trick."

"But how," I still was thinking about the dangerous part, so I needed details.

"I don't know yet, but we have all the time in world to figure it out."

Then I looked back at the flashing lights coming off of the Professor's latest invention. They were almost hypnotizing the way they flickered on and off.

"Do we go inside that thing," I asked him.

"No it's too bulky," said the Professor, "this is merely the main generator for the time device, as you can guess it must be quite powerful, especially if one wishes to go back to the Neolithic period and such."

"It can travel back that far," Jimmy sounded really excited as if he had already forgotten about how the whole planet was gonna be trashed in just a couple of days.

"Well that is really the problem, people were always trying to figure out how to travel through time. Time travel is in reality misnomer, we are not traveling through time."

"A miss what," I said, but they both just ignored me.

"Then what," Jimmy got really curious, and all I could think about was just how hot it was gonna get right before we crashed into the Sun.

"Time seems to be set up in continuous line with everything throughout history occurring all at once."

"Well how is the…" Jimmy tried to get out.

The Professor was on a roll now, and not gonna stop until he told it all. "Although it is happening all at once we only have access to that moment in time that we are in at the present."

"But," Jimmy just wanted to know it all.

"So technically what the time belt does is it let's you skip over stretches of time to the period that you want to be in. So technically it is not time traveling, as much as time skipping. It is so simple I am amazed that no one has ever thought of it before. People, scientists in particular, are always trying to complicate matters. For clarification what we are doing is time skipping, but for the sake of simplicity we can call it time travel, but we know the truth."

"But when you're skipping along, aren't you also traveling," I said, and the Professor just looked annoyed at me again. He did that a lot.

I think he was trying to make things simple, but it didn't seem that way when he was done explaining it.

The Professor walked closer to the machine, and we followed. I guess he was right, in not being afraid, right then and there we were the only hope for the entire planet, and if anything happened to us, or if the machine blew up, it was all over anyway.

On a table by the machine that was going to let me and Jimmy skip through time were two belts. They were made of thick leather, and on the sides were what looked like small holsters holding some type of batteries. Looking at the belt I didn't see nothing that looked like a control device or anything. Just a round thing that looked kinda like a buckle. The Professor told us that the belts were in fact transceivers that received the directions from the big time machine that was lighting up the whole garage. He handed the belts to us, and we looked down at them.

"How do you make this thing go," I asked the Professor.

"I'll explain everything when you…" that's all the Professor could get out before Jimmy had another thought.

The time belts were kinda big for our sizes. They looked like they had been made to fit the Professor, but would slide right off of us.

"They're kind of big," Jimmy said.

"That is no good," the Professor came back, "you must have a snug fit. If they fall off, or you should lose these belts you would be lost forever in an ever expanding inter-dimensional time warp."

Just what I wanted to hear, and I still had no idea what he meant.

"And what would that be like Professor," Jimmy said.

"Endless blackness, bouncing from time to time, without ever being able to get your foot in the door of any one time."

"And what about eating," I said, 'cause that was a real concern. Suppose you were, like the Professor said, "bouncing from time to time, how would you get your hands on cheeseburgers or fries?"

"Not to worry about that boy, your terror would be too great to think of eating." And that really wasn't the answer that I had wanted to hear. I wanted to be lied to, and told that everything was gonna be just fine. Jimmy was the one who always wanted to know the horrible details, but old Shawn sometimes he just wanted to be lied to.

46

You know when you're a little kid, and your parents take you to the dentist, and tell you that everything is gonna be all right, and that it ain't gonna hurt or nothing. Part of you might've known that they just didn't want to drag you into the office kicking and screaming, but for a little while it felt good just buying into the story that they were selling to you. But I wasn't getting any of that from the Professor. He was letting me know all about the drilling and the big needles before I put my foot through the dentist's door.

Walking over to a big metal cabinet that was at the back of the garage, he pulled out a spool of fishing line. He held it up, and showed it to me and Jimmy.

"This is the good heavy stuff, it should do the trick."

"What trick," I said.

"We will tie the time dimensional transceivers to your waist with some heavy duty fishing string."

I don't think me or Jimmy was happy about that plan.

"Professor, don't you think that maybe we can cut the belts down, make some new holes, and try and make them fit better," Jimmy asked him

Jimmy's idea was sounding better than trusting a piece of old fishing line keeping us from falling into an inter-dimensional time thing, or whatever the Professor had said that we'd be traveling around in terror forever if that belt slipped off of us, or the string became untied.

"Very good thinking Jimmy, not a bad idea at all," said the Professor. "That is why it is good to have another inventor around." Jimmy smiled, and liked the idea of being called an inventor.

"We'll have to head home, before we take off," Jimmy told him.

"Time is precious, and none to waste," the Professor seemed worried about us leaving.

"We'll be right back," Jimmy told him.

"No," said the Professor, "adjustments must be made on the time belts, and you have your own preparations to make. No part of this mission is to be slipshod." Cool, I thought, we're going on a mission. "Be here Tuesday noon right after school. That should give us enough time to fix the settings and make the necessary adjustments."

"Right," Jimmy agreed with the Professor, "if we're going to fool the agents into thinking that the gravity machines are really destroyed, than I have to retrieve some special equipment from my own lab."

Did I forget to tell you, if you didn't already know, Jimmy considered himself a scientist? A while back he had designed a lot of neat stuff. There was briefcase that turned into a skateboard, incase we had to make quick getaways, a parachute that would slow down our bikes, incase we were going off the edge of a cliff, or something like that, and a lot of other cool junk. I didn't know what else he had back at the house. We had always used Jimmy's inventions to play at being secret agents or super heroes, and until the Professor came along, we never had to really use any of it. They had all been for play, to me anyway.

For the longest time Jimmy had been working on a whole bunch of other neat stuff, but for now he had the usual standby gadgets. In the schoolbag he put the exploding darts, which most of the time did not work. He had brought enough stuff to explode. If blowing up the Gravity Boxes was going to be faked, I guess it had to look real good. There was some other stuff that Jimmy had shoved into the schoolbag just incase, but I'll tell you about that later.

Tuesday was the mission, but the Professor wanted us to get there early. That was 'cause he needed time to teach us how to use the time skipping devices, skip three days into the past, not destroy the Gravity Boxes, but make Flynn and his agents think that we did. Then make sure we had enough time to save the world. Me, all I wanted to do was make sure I loaded up on some peanut butter and jelly sandwiches just in case. If I slipped out of that time belt, and was gonna be bouncing from one time to another for the rest of eternity, I wanted to go on a full stomach.

Chapter 4: The Three Day Journey Into The Middle Ages

Somebody had set the dials wrong, or the machine was messed up, but whatever the problem, me and Jimmy had landed somewhere around the time of King Arthur. We didn't actually see King Arthur, but the guys running around in Armor, and chasing us with swords gave us our first clue that something had gone wrong. As we were just leaving you might remember that the whole world was about to be destroyed, by a giant comet smashing into the Earth. Actually it was due to hit on downtown Main Street.

Let me get back to how the whole mess began. It was right before the whole sky fell in. Yeah that's right the sky fell in. We waited 'til noon just like the Professor said. After school Jimmy had picked up some of his secret agent junk back at his place. He had thrown it all into his schoolbag, and we headed back to the woods, and to the Professor's place. Sometime Jimmy ate over at my house, and sometimes I ate at his. Both of us told our parents we were eating at the other's house. Okay it was lying, but we had a planet to save here. We figured that even if we were running late, at least this time we'd be able to skip through that inter-dimensional corridor, or whatever the Professor had called that thing, and make it home in plenty of time for supper even if we were running three weeks late.

When we got back to the lab, the Professor had already cut down the time tearing belts to our sizes, made all of the necessary settings, and they fit pretty good. I didn't really mind that they were a little tight on us. I just wanted to make sure that they didn't fall off while we were coasting through that inter-dimensional thing.

"I will select the settings for the exact moment of departure, and return. You," and he looked at Jimmy, 'cause he trusted him the most with following directions and stuff, "you will have to control the device while you are away."

"What do we do Professor," Jimmy asked.

"As I have said that time is divided like a series of chambers, which one must enter into to reach the desired destination. Although the belts draw their power from the mother station which is generating power from the garage, the controls are actually on the front of the belt, that little dial that you see."

We both looked down to check out the dial at the front of the belt. It had several lines going around, but nowhere was there any sign of a clock, or anything to tell us what day or time we were actually headed to.

"Professor," Jimmy said, "this isn't a dial, and it doesn't tell you anything... There's no settings or..."

"Of course there are settings, do you think I was planning to just go from time to time without knowing how or where I was going, do you take me for an idiot?"

"No... no Professor," Jimmy tried defending what he had said, "it's just..." he tried to get out.

He seemed upset with Jimmy, and then quickly brought himself under control.

"I'm sorry boys, this whole comet smashing into the planet mess has my nerves up in arms." He then reached down to the round

51

metal part that was situated on Jimmy's belt. With his finger the Professor lifted the lid, which for the first time I noticed had little screws on the side that acted as a hinge. Underneath was a set of buttons with what looked to be a digital calendar just above them. It looked something like the clock radio in my bedroom only a heck of a lot smaller.

"The settings are hidden," said Jimmy.

"Not so much hidden, but designed to protect against accidental changing of the settings."

"Professor," I said, and I raised my hand like I was back in school, 'cause that's what he made me feel like when he was irritated, and snapping at everything. In fact I was almost afraid to ask. He always seemed to be annoyed with me like he was expecting a stupid question, but I really thought that I had a good question cooking this time. "Professor, what happens if the main mother…"

"The what," said the Professor.

"He's talking about the mother station Professor."

"And what about it?"

"What," I said, "will happen if that mother station goes down, and we're in a different time."

He stopped, and looked down for a moment, and by the look on his face, it didn't look like he had a good answer, so I was thinking, okay, give me a good lie, so that I could go off with a little bit of hope.

"I have an emergency generator hooked up to the central power source, if it goes down for any reason, the back up generator kicks in."

"And it works real good right," I asked.

"It's been running steadily for the last six months, I wanted to be sure that if I ever visited another time that I wouldn't be trapped there."

That's all I wanted to hear, and since I knew that the man never really lied, I was really happy with his answer.

He knelt down, and adjusted the dials on my time belt and on Jimmy's. Then he showed us the button on the side. It was sitting right on top of the thing that looked like a battery.

"This is like a starter button. Once the dials are set in, and the button is pressed then you will open a gap that will create conduit into, let us say, a time chamber…"

"A time chamber," Jimmy said like he was really excited. Again I'm thinking maybe I was the smart one; at least I had the good sense to be a little scared.

The Professor stopped, and thought about it for a minute. "Well, you see the way it works is, that what I called chambers are actually tiny pockets of time that are all around us, and interconnected."

"Wow," Jimmy's face lit up again.

"Because we have passed into another chamber, we no longer have contact with the previous ones. The inter-dimensional time manager on the belt allows one to clear up all that clutter, and find the desired destination, it is all very simple as long as we don't think of it in terms of travel."

"Time skipping," I said. And again he looked annoyed at me. I had said the right thing, but he still looked annoyed. So I figured that I just couldn't win with this guy.

"What are the limits of the time belt," Jimmy asked, and the Professor smiled at him. Why is it that every time Jimmy asked something he got the smiles, and I got the annoyed looks?

"The limits are the beginning of time till the end of time, and you are free to travel anyplace in between. But not for the moment, for the moment we must concern ourselves with a dark and stormy night, three days ago. Are you boys ready," he asked.

"Ready," Jimmy snapped to attention like a soldier on command.

"I guess so," I still wasn't so sure. Remember I had never traveled; I mean skipped my way through time before.

"Now all you must do is press the button on the right side of the belt and…"

"Wait… wait," Jimmy stopped him. "How do we get back," and I was glad that he had thought of that. The three-day wait wouldn't have been so bad, but I didn't know we were about to take a terrible turn through that time corridor thing, and end up nine hundred years off course.

"Like I told you boys, the settings have already been made, and all you have to… oh" he said kind of upset, "I forgot to tell you about the return button."

"That would be a really good idea," I know I was just being cocky with the Professor, but that seemed like an important thing to know about.

"Shut up Shawn," Jimmy said.

"Well I just didn't want to get there, and have to count on nothing else but clicking my heels together to get back home."

"Shut up,' Jimmy said again.

"No, no" said the Professor, "that control is not in the heels, it is actually located on the left side of the belt, above the atomic power supply."

"This has an atomic power supply," Jimmy for the first time looked a little scared."

"Of course boy, you can't go tracing across time and space with a nine volt battery. It has a half life of fifty thousand years, so that should give you enough time…"

"Half life," that was me interrupting this time.

"Half life," Jimmy explained, "is the time it will take the power source in the belt to be reduced to half its power."

"And since the belts don't really use up that much power," the Professor went on, "you should be able to go a good seventy-five thousand years without a hitch."

"By then we'll be as old as you Professor," I tried to joke, and now was getting that annoyed look from both Jimmy and the Professor.

Professor Burkhardt got right back to business. "Now to the business of three days ago," the Professor said looking down at the belts. "I have set the time of your arrival to eleven o'clock at night. That is exactly two hours before you ran into the agents, and were forced to destroy the levitation machines," and then he asked the dreaded question once again. "Are you boy's ready?"

Jimmy snapped to attention once again, and shouted, "Ready sir!" And I just nodded my head. Like I said this was gonna be our first big step into another time, so I wasn't as thrilled as Jimmy about the whole trip.

"I will check the destination setting one more time," said the Professor, "just to make sure…"

And as he was talking something strange began to happen. Above us the entire sky began to turn black. Before I looked up, I thought that it might be a dark cloud passing over or a plane, but when I looked up I couldn't see nothing. I walked out of the garage to see what was up, and Jimmy and the Professor followed. The look on the Professor's face told me that it was something really terrible about to happen.

"What wrong," Jimmy tried to get the Professor's attention, but for that minute it looked like he was just hypnotized by what he was looking at. Again all I saw was a dark sky, and then I could feel the wind begin to blow harder. Yeah the wind had come up fast, and out of nowhere. Then suddenly the birds began to fly from the trees, thousands at a time screeching across the sky like they knew something that we didn't. Well maybe something that I didn't, but the look on the Professor's face told me that he knew real good what was going on.

"You must go now boys," he all at once looked away from the sky, and back to us.

"What is it Professor," Jimmy said, looking more scared than ever.

"Yeah Professor, what's going on…" 'cause now the sky was getting even darker, almost black.

That's all I got out, when he kneeled down, and began to check the controls on the time belts once again. As he fixed the dials he spoke to us, and he spoke to us with a shaky voice that seemed to be jumping along with his shaky hands as he worked the controls.

"My calculations were wrong, we do not have as much time as I thought," he said.

"What," I wanted to make sure that I had heard him right.

"Professor, what do we do," Jimmy said.

"You must get yourself to safety first."

"You have to come with us Professor," Jimmy said.

"No, there is no time, and the belts will only carry you two to safety, but there can be no further delays."

"Professor, the planet," Jimmy was trying to find out as much as he could, but it didn't seem like there was much time left.

"We only have minutes, maybe seconds…"

And then everything around us began to tremble, and rock back and forth. We all wanted to grab onto something to keep from falling, but the Professor grabbed the both of us by our arms, and looked us straight in the eyes.

"Boys, this is the end, if there is any hope for the world it is in your hands, but you must leave here, you must leave here at once."

Jimmy rushed, and picked up his schoolbag with all of the spy equipment in it. He looked back at the Professor, "but the mother station will be destroyed too."

"No more talk" and this time he yelled at the both of us. He knelt down quickly again, and hit the buttons on the sides of the time belts. The Professor's face had turned white as a sheet, and had this look of total terror written all over it. The last thing that I remember was looking up, and seeing what looked like the sky about to fall in, and then we were gone.

Chapter 5: How We Were Mistaken for Witches and How That's Not a Good Thing

If the Professor was right, then that giant comet had already crushed everyone that I knew and cared about. I was feeling terrible, and I wasn't sure that being one of the only ones to walk away from that disaster was such a good thing. The truth is that we somehow ended up in the twelfth century about nine hundred years away from the dinner table, and everyone that we knew. And the way things turned out, it didn't look like me and Jimmy were gonna be in much better shape than all the people we were suppose to have helped. Remember we were now a long way from the mother station, the Gravity Boxes, and any hope of getting back to that time. But let me tell you what happened when we got to the twelfth century, 'cause that's when things really got crazy.

It was a field we found ourselves in, that's right, with big tall grass, and a couple of old cows grazing nearby. And the first thing I remember was how it didn't look like home, or any place near to it. First of all it was the middle of the day, and the Professor had set our time belts to eleven o'clock at night. I kept thinking that if the future had already been destroyed, than what was the point of even trying. Still I couldn't get my mind off the fact that everything looked different, more different than it should've looked back at home.

The trip was the strangest feeling I had ever had. The Professor had been right about one thing; it was definitely like stepping into another world. When he first pressed the button on the side of the time belt I could feel my whole body shake. It was like I was standing on top of a giant blender that my Mom used to mix stuff, or one of those machines they use to shake the paint at the hardware store. Everything looked like it was going crazy around us, and then I saw sky up over me, that same sky that had been turned black by the arrival of giant comet overhead had begun to rip apart. Yeah, that's right, it was like the time belts were tearing a hole in the middle of world, and we were about to be sucked into that hole. I only got a second to look over to Jimmy, but I could see that he was now just as scared as me. In front of us was the Professor, and he was just looking pale, and as if all the life had already started to run out of him, that was until he started to fade. In fact everything started to disappear right before my eyes, but through the tear in the time space thing, what I saw looked like several different worlds moving back and forth, and jumbled around like a giant kaleidoscope. And that fast it pulled us in and we were falling, or flying. The truth is that I didn't know which way was up, and which way was down, I just grabbed hold of my stomach, 'cause it felt like it was gonna jump right out of me. And I didn't know if the time belts were having trouble deciding where to dump me and Jimmy; 'cause one minute they seemed to take us into one of the chambers of time, and then just that quick it would change its mind, and pull us out. Right then and there I was sorry that I had stuffed down those peanut butter and jelly sandwiches. It really didn't seem like they wanted to stay down. I think the Professor had some bugs with this invention that needed to be worked out, and it didn't seem like we were ever gonna see those problems fixed. Then there were flashes of things, visions of the past that just seemed to hit me in the face like a bad music video. There were Roman armies marching, bombs falling from the skies, and exploding, but before we could be hurt the time belt would zap us out of that place, and toss us into another. It's like the time belts didn't know where they wanted to take us. A minute later we were in the field with the cows.

Both me and Jimmy couldn't talk for the longest time. We just looked about, and tried to figure what the heck had actually happened. The cows weren't that far away, but they didn't seem to notice or care that we were there.

I think it was me who spoke first. "Jimmy, I don't remember anything of this place. Do we live around here?"

It took a minute before he could come back with an answer. "Shawn, I don't think we're home."

And then that fast I remembered what had happened.

"Like it matters anyway," I said, and I could feel myself about to cry.

"Shawn, if there's any hope for the world..."

"What hope," I yelled at him, "they're all gone."

He looked down sad like, 'cause I think he knew it too.

"But we still have the belts," he said.

"And what good are they, the mother station was probably being destroyed when we left, and..."

"But if it is three days before..."

"Do you think," I jumped with the little hope that I had left stirring inside of me.

"In that time the mother station is still working."

"I hope! I hope!"

"We just have to find out where we are and what time it is."

We just both continued to look around, and wonder where we were, and then we heard the voices. The first seemed to be that of a young kid, maybe younger than us guys.

"Over there," the voice called out, and that got our attention quick enough. When we looked behind us we saw him running towards us. Now if it had only been some little kid that wouldn't have been such a bad thing. But it was who was with him that really got my attention. Riding next to the little kid, who by the way seemed to be dressed in rags, and pointing the finger at us, was a large knight, covered in black armor. In a second he had raced past the little kid, and was charging right at me and Jimmy.

"I think we're definitely not home," I called to Jimmy.

We just started running, and the guy on horseback he just started riding faster. Behind us I could hear the sound of the horses hooves pounding into the dirt, and they were getting louder and quicker all the time. I guess it was kind of stupid trying to outrun a horse, but we didn't know what plans this guy had for us, and if we had known, we would've tried to run a whole lot faster.

"Let's get to another time," Jimmy called to me as we raced across the field.

We both started to reach for the buttons on the left of the time belts. I mean it really didn't seem to matter what time we landed in; it all looked better than what was riding our tails right then and there.

"But the mother station, its gone," I called back to him.

"Maybe not, I told you," he screamed back at me.

It hadn't mattered anyway, we had moved too slow. In no time the guy in the black armor was on top of us. From his horse he had drawn his sword, and kicked me down in to the dirt with his foot. That stopped me quick enough, and when he put the tip of the sword to my throat I just froze. Truth is, I was too afraid to move.

"Oh foulest demon," he screamed at me, "thou shalt spread your evil no further vile dog."

Jimmy still could have reached for his time belt. Even if he could have slipped into another time, I don't think he would've done it. I was sure glad that I wasn't gonna be left alone.

"But Mister," I tried to speak, and then the black knight pushed me back into to dirt with his boot again as he leaped down off of his horse.

"Silence dog from hell, or your tongue shall pay the forfeit."

"But Mister," Jimmy tried to get a word in.

"Any incantation on your part as well shall bring death to this abhorrent creature."

I think what this all meant was that we were in big trouble. Both of us were afraid to move, Jimmy for me, and me for myself. The knight circled, keeping his thick and heavy sword all too close to my scrawny, little neck.

"I have been assured by the Priest that your demon powers may manifest themselves only in the dark of night, you are all too easy to hold capture in the light of day. And so easy to detect with your witches garb"

I guess anybody with jeans and high top sneakers would've been considered a witch in those days. Actually I was wearing shorts, but I think even that would've made me an easy target for a witch-hunt.

And then in a loud booming voice the knight in black called to other knights already riding our way. "Over here," he yelled, "the dastardly vermin hath been subdued."

In no time the other knights were racing in our direction. In the nearby field was the little kid. At first I couldn't tell if it was a boy or a girl, he was so filthy, but then he came closer, and I could see that wearing those torn rags was a boy. He was a dirty, little boy with a big mouth, who had seen us appear in the field, and had steered the nearby knights our way.

"That be them master," the boy said. "They just appeared like devils in the middle of the crops."

"Even now the stench of this fetid behemoth poisons my lungs with its pungent odor," said the black knight. Now I don't know what any of that meant, only I was sure that it wasn't good.

"I think that's the cow sir," Jimmy said. The knight looked confused. "Making the smell I mean."

In my head I was thinking he wants us to keep our traps shut Jimmy, so just keep your big mouth closed, please.

Then the knight in black turned with rage that Jimmy had dared to talk again.

"Fortunately we arrived before you were able to bend the field animals to your will…"the black knight said, still keeping the tip of his sword pressed against my neck. "Or perhaps you merely intended to inhabit the bodies of these poor soulless creatures for your hideous delight."

"They did that to our Betsy sire," said the little boy, "the milk was soured, and she came down with the pox."

"Demons," screamed the black knight, he was doing a lot of screaming. "Tainting the milk of these harmless creatures, and spreading pestilence for the pleasure of your master in hell."

The others were now off of their horses, and surrounded Jimmy.

"But we're not demons…" Jimmy tried to get out.

He was cut off with another, "silence foul beast," from the black knight. "Bind them, and take them to the keep," he ordered the others. The way everyone was jumping to his commands, I was guessing that he was the boss knight. It wasn't until one of the other knights had taken hold of me, and tied my wrist with straps from his saddle that the guy in black took the blade away from my neck.

"Sir," Jimmy tried to get through to him once again, "we're not demons, we just…"

"The castle inquisitor will bring forth the truth from your lying tongues you disgusting ogre," he said.

"Inquisitor," Jimmy was really scared now.

"The law of the land requires trial by water before execution."

"Execution," I almost cried again, okay, I was actually crying this time.

"No doubt you shall receive a hardy welcome from Beelzebub upon your return to hell."

And just when you thought things couldn't get worse, the crazy knight in black looked down at the belts. He took the blade of his sword, and sliced my belt right off of me.

"No," I cried out, 'cause if there was any hope left for us, it was gone now, and we were definitely trapped in another time.

"Without their magical charms," he told the others, "any incantation they make will have little power." He then sliced Jimmy's time belt off of him while another knight grabbed hold of his schoolbag with all the secret agent stuff that Jimmy had brought along for this trip. The black knight then looked at us both and said, "You see, I know a little of science myself, I know the power of a witch lies in his amulets and charms." He turned to the others, "these two will give us no trouble on the way the stake."

"The stake," Jimmy said, like he couldn't believe what he had heard.

"The flames shall consume your evil," the knight in black screamed in our faces.

All that was because they thought we were messing around with a cow, and making her milk go bad, it was nuts. Still we were standing in a field with a bunch of crazy knights ready to cut our throats, so I guess it all shouldn't of been that hard to believe.

Then all of the knights climbed back onto their horses, and began to prod us along ahead of them like we were the cattle. Before we left the field the little kid, picked up a rock, and hit me in the back with it. "Ow," I cried out. He yelled at me and Jimmy as we were being taken away: "The two of you won't be tainting the milk no more of our Betsy."

I just wish I could've gotten my hands on that kid, heck they were gonna burn me at the stake for sour milk, what did I have to lose.

As we were being marched off to the keep, I found out later that that's just another word for dungeon, me and Jimmy just looked at each other. I don't think we had ever been in any trouble this deep before, and believe me we had gotten ourselves into some pretty big messes. I mean the world, and time we had come from had been destroyed; and we were being held by knights, who thought we were witches or demons. They had taken the time belts off of us, which probably wouldn't work anyway, with the mother station trashed by that comet. On top of that we were about to be burned at the stake. Yeah, I guess this was about the worse trouble that either of us had ever gotten into, and it was still early in the day.

Chapter 6: The Bringers of Evil, Death, and Destruction, I Think They Were Talking About Us

We must've walked for hours. I wanted to talk to Jimmy about what was going on, 'cause if anybody could've figured a way out of this mess, it would've been him. It was cold, so cold, and remember all that I was wearing were a tee shirt and some shorts. Guess that's what these crazy knights thought demons wore. When I looked over I could see Jimmy, the steam was coming off of his breath, and he was trembling just like me, 'cause he wasn't wearing much more than I was. He might've been shaking for other reasons too, but the freezing weather was a big part of it I'm sure. On top of everything my feet were killing me, and I was feeling a bit thirsty. Yet as much as I wanted a glass of water, I just didn't feel like asking for it. I was too sad and scared about what had happened, about my whole world being gone, and what was going to happen. So I wanted it, but at the same time I just didn't care if I ever drank anything again. And to tell the truth, I don't think I even cared that I was chilled to the bone. It hurt, but somehow it just didn't seem to matter. Yeah, that might have been the saddest I've ever been.

After they made us march for a long time, I saw the castle appear a little bit away. It was this big, stone fortress, not nice at all like the castles in the movies or in the storybooks that my Mom use to read to me. It looked like it was just a bunch of huge stones piled on top of one another, with a giant wooden drawbridge right in the center. I was guess'n that bridge was how they got in and out.

Around the ugly fortress was a large moat filled with dirty brown water that surrounded the entire thing. It also looked like a place that once you got into that you weren't gonna come out of unless you had the key.

"Ahead of you lies your destiny," said the black knight. "The castle is equipped with excellent torture devices, that can loosen the tongue of even the most powerful of enchanters."

"But sir," Jimmy tried again to get through to him.

"Save you're pleading for the dungeon master you odious scum."

In my head the trial had already begun, and I guessed the torture, and trial by water was just the only entertainment they had back in those days. So I figured, what the heck, they were gonna do all that stuff to me anyway, I might as well tell them the whole story. And I don't know where it came from, but all at once I got so angry at how unfair they were being I just turned to the guys on the horses and started yelling.

"You creeps already got it all worked out in your stupid heads, so what's the point of the trial and all..."

Jimmy didn't believe that I had turned on these guys, and I guess if I had thought about it I wouldn't have believed it either.

"Shawn," Jimmy said, and I think he was trying to shut me up.

"Silence," screamed the black knight.

"What are you gonna do, kill me," I said.

"Shawn, that's probably what he's gonna do," Jimmy was trying to calm me down.

"He's gonna do it anyway, so what do I care?"

"The young demon, may have stolen the spirit of the horses," cried out the black knight. "He is at once ill tempered, and ready to do battle."

"You don't know nothing," I kept yelling at them all, "the world's gonna get destroyed if we don't get back to…"

"Now threats of world destruction issue forth from his lips."

"He is perhaps a very powerful witch," said one of the other knights, backing away on his horse."

"I'm just a boy, but if you hold us here, then a giant flaming comet will crash into the Earth…"

"Shawn," Jimmy was still busy trying to stop me from getting myself killed.

That fast the black knight leaped down from his horse and raised his sword, and I thought that it was all over. I mean I really thought that he was gonna chop my head off, and kick the rest of me down the hill.

"Don't," Jimmy tried to stop him now.

Real fast like the black knight knocked me to the ground, and began to scream in my face. "So you are the keeper of the gate."

"He is the one," shouted one of the other knights. Then they all started backing up their horses a little.

"The evil one prophesized to bring forth the Apocalypse with him on this dark day."

"Not really," I said, 'cause all at once I got the brains to be scared again.

"Mister," Jimmy was still trying to stop him, but with our arms tied there wasn't much that either of us could do. Who am I kidding; with our arms untied there wasn't much we could do against these guys.

"I had hoped to live long enough to come face to face with the keeper, and fate has delivered you into my hands. I feared that my time would pass before this great darkness would be visited upon the world." Suddenly the black knight stood tall, and looked down at me. Slowly he pulled one of the time belts from off of his horse's saddle. "But I have stolen your power you wicked beast, stolen it before you could open the gates of Hades, and unleash this plague upon the world."

"Well not exactly," I said, not really knowing what he was talking about.

That's when the black knight looked real hard at the time belt. "But if I destroy your amulet…"

"Then his power will be destroyed with it," said one of the other knights.

"No, " I screamed again, still not sure if the time belt could work or not.

"Yes," Jimmy said real fast, and I still didn't know what he was getting at.

"And what, evil sprite, do you forecast with your fiendish tongue."

"Destroy the amulet, and you destroy our power, the legions of the Apocalypse will have no way to leave their resting place in Hades. Destroy it, I tell you."

Whatever Jimmy had said had stopped the black knight in his tracks. He now turned his attention away from me and onto Jimmy.

"So it is true, these trinkets hold the power to open the gates of the Underworld."

For a minute Jimmy seemed stumped, like he didn't know how to answer that one, and then he turned to me and said, "why don't you ask him, he's the gate keeper."

All of the men including the black knight suddenly began to tremble as the sword was once more brought to my throat.

"Thanks Jim," I said.

"And what hast thou to say about these magical charms, gate keeper?"

It took me a minute to think, 'cause I just kept looking at Jimmy wondering what was going on in his head. In my mind we were just getting in deeper and deeper. Then I caught Jimmy nodding his head up and down, but not too much, just enough to be noticed by me. And then I said, "Sure, tear them up."

"And your power shall be destroyed," the black knight stared down at me as he said the words.

"The gate will be closed forever," Jimmy yelled, "and our power destroyed."

Without waiting a second two other knights jumped down off of their horses, and came to the side of the boss knight.

"Beware the tongues of demons Sire," one knight said. "He plots a fiendish trap."

"Seduce with your words to bend the will, so that only evil can come forth," said one of the others.

The black knight now stood still in his tracks, and for the first time he looked almost as scared as me and Jimmy.

"Then the beast must think me a fool, but I know all too well consort of Satan that only lies will issue forth from your forked tongue. I know of your tricks servant of the Dark Prince, I know of them all too well."

"They want you to destroy the amulets…" came the first knight.

"And perhaps that is the key that will open the door to the Underworld," said the other.

"Yes," said the black knight, "it all makes sense now. When we arrived at the field you were just about to destroy the charms, had we not stopped you before you completed your heinous task…"

"No, you have to destroy them," Jimmy screamed out. Now all of the knights backed up a few feet. Jimmy was really acting good.

"I tremble at the thought," the one knight actually trembled as he said it.

"I will not fall prey to your villainous lie you hellish fiend."

"Sire," said the other knight, "you have saved the world from untold calamity, you are indeed a hero."

"Tis true," said the black knight, "But what to do with these two foul fiends".

"We must slay them instantly," said the knight closest to them.

"Yes," said the other knight, "their evil presence fills the air."

The two other knights then drew out their own swords, and looked like they were ready to take off our heads.

I turned to Jimmy, "Good plan, genius."

He just shrugged his shoulders as if to say he was sorry. And then the swords were raised above our heads. I just closed my eyes, 'cause that was all I could think to do. That's when I heard Jimmy's voice, and I really didn't think I was ever gonna hear it again.

"The magical charms have great power," he shouted quick like. And I guess he was trying to get that out before our heads came off. "Destroy them, destroy us you will never know of that power."

"Halt," shouted the black knight, and everyone stopped in their tracks then. "The keys to the kingdom," said the black knight.

"Perhaps more trickery Sire," said one of the other knights, "you would make bargains with the devil?"

"I believe not an utterance from this foul creature's wretched tongue, but I'll need them alive for my triumphant entrance into the castle. When the rabble see these hideous demons they will cheer, when the court hears of my bravery, and courage in delivering these servants of the Underworld I shall be exalted above all other men."

"Except the king," said one of the knights.

"Except the king," said the black knight. "Go and give rumor of my arrival, tell all that I have triumphed over evil, and hath made safe the kingdom for our beloved King."

"Yes Sire," came the knight back at him. In no time he had jumped back on his horse, and headed for the castle.

And then the black knight looked down at the both of us, and smiled. It wasn't a friendly smile, it was that kind of smile that told you that whatever was cooking in his head was gonna be good for him, but not so good for us.

"Your journey to the stake will bear great fruit for me spawn of hell. I will gain favor with the King, and your ashes will pave the way."

None of it was sounding good. And then he lifted up the charm, I mean time belt, and looked at it even more closely than before. Carefully he used his sword to check it over as if he were afraid to open it himself. And then the blade of his sword touched the dial cover, and it flicked up, so that he could see the controls underneath. They were all lit up and the time was flashing on and off. That quick he dropped the belt, and jumped back from it. Both me and Jimmy looked at each other, 'cause we didn't know what he was gonna do next. And then the black knight used the tip of his sword to touch the controls, and we could see the time setting change. Another thing that couldn't be so good for us. I mean if there was any chance of getting back to our time, we had to have the right time set into the controls. From the corner of my eye I could see Jimmy shaking his head sadly, as our last hope for rescue lay in the mud at the feet of the black knight.

Concept Art In Finding The Perfect Knight.

Chapter 7: Basil the Laughing Dungeon Master and Will the Whipping Boy

On the way to the main gate of the castle, we could hear the crowds cheering the arrival of the black knight. By the way my feet were even more tired, and the cold was really starting to kill me. I think that my fingers were starting to turn blue, but none of that mattered, 'cause my brain was back home thinking about my Mom, and Dad, and all of the people I cared about, and even my little sister who could sometimes be a big pain. Besides that we were about to be given a nice comfortable dungeon to catch up on our rest.

Up close the castle looked a lot bigger and scarier. From the top of the high stonewalls there were soldiers with helmets looking down, and cheering the black knight who had captured us. The giant wooden bridge swung down, so that the horses and us could cross over the moat.

Inside was more of the same thing. More cheering, only this time it wasn't from the soldiers, it was from all the people lining the dirt street that led all the way up to the castle in the middle of the small town inside the giant walls. While they cheered the black knight, they tossed rotten tomatoes, and dark soggy potatoes at me and Jimmy. It hurt, and I just tried to keep my head down, so that I wouldn't get hit in the eyes with a flying cabbage or something.

Then they started calling out the name of the black knight, and that was the first time I had heard it. "Hail Sagamore, the Mighty."

So his name was Sagamore, but I don't know why they thought he was so Mighty? If they had looked real close they might have seen that what Sir Sagamore and his gang of knights had captured was a couple of twelve-year-old boys. And even as dangerous as we must've looked in our sneakers and tee shirts, I didn't think that we deserved such a mean welcome. Heck, they hadn't even said hello when they started hitting us in the face with stinky garbage. Must've caught most of it in my ears, and by the time I got past the crowd I could hardly hear them screaming anymore.

Like the boy in the field they were all dressed pretty much in rags, or what looked like rags. They all looked dirty, and there was a real bad smell that hit you in the face when you first came through those gates. Maybe it was because they had saved their smelly fruit and vegetables for fun times like that one.

Along the way to the castle we passed some wooden stands that looked like they sold stuff off of. Behind the stands were some old stone buildings that might've been houses, or stores. From the top of the not too tall buildings, and from the holes in the walls that I was guess'n was their idea of windows, there were other people hurling slop and stuff down at us too. I was thinking that it couldn't get any worse when we finally got to the castle, boy was I wrong.

As we got nearer to the castle several large guards came over to us. Sir Sagamore jumped down from his horse to meet with them.

"Sir Sagamore," one of the guards from the castle went right up to him. "Word of your triumphant return from the Valley of Death has reached our ears."

I was guessing that the Valley of Death was that field right next to the crappy barn on that run down old farm.

"It is the devil's own ear that these two demons have."

The guard looked nervous like as he backed away from me and Jimmy.

"The story of your life and death battle in the Field of Despair against the keepers of the gate of the Underworld has reached the King. Already there is talk of a festival in your honor."

"My duty to my King and country needs not reward," said Sagamore. And I kept wondering if that was the truth, then why did he send that other knight back to spread the word of his great deed. And that deadly battle must've come and gone while I was trying to climb myself out of the mud, 'cause I didn't remember any of it.

That's when Sagamore pulled out the time belts, and held them in front of the guard. The guard's eyes lit up like he had just seen a genie fly out of a bottle. He backed up a few feet looking even more scared.

"This is the magical charm that was created in the devil's own workshop, and was transported from the fiery depths with these two unwashed vipers to destroy humanity," said Sagamore. The guard just kept looking as if the time belts had hypnotized him. That's when Sagamore lifted the dial on the front, and showed him the digital numbers flashing underneath.

"What manner of evil is this," cried the guard.

"Only in the fires of Hades could such a contrivance be created. This vile scum have undeniably been sent to proclaim the end of the world," said Sagamore.

"The kingdom will forever be in your debt Sire," said the guard as he bowed in head in respect. I kept thinking can't anybody see we're only twelve.

"The safety of the kingdom," said Lord Sagamore, "is all the thanks that this humble servant requires."

Jimmy was now looking at me again. It was my guess that his ears were filled with junk like mine, so maybe he couldn't hear too well either, but Sagamore and the guard were right next to us, so I knew he had heard the part about the great battle of good and evil in the "Field of Despair".

Then the guard looked over at us and said, "Let them sit in the dungeon while they await judgment, so that their heads will adorn the castle entrance for the King's delight."

"No," Sagamore stopped him in his tracks, "to stop this evil they must be consumed by the flames." And the guard nodded as if he understood. Whether they were gonna toast us on the stake, or put our heads up on a stick for decoration, none of it sounded good. Whatever they decided to do, I didn't want them making up their minds too quick.

"But first some brandy, to wash away the pain of the battle," said Sagamore, "and proclaim my arrival to the King with all due hast." However we were gonna die it was going to have to wait until after Sagamore had been proclaimed, and he had taken his brandy break.

Jimmy was still thinking, that much I could tell, but what he was thinking about I had no way of telling. I could only see his eyes going back and forth to the time belts, but I knew that there was no way of getting to them, not now anyway.

The next place we found ourselves was in the dungeon. The floor was wet, mostly mud. It was still cold as heck. And we could hear the sound of rats screeching as we entered. It was damp and it was dark. We could only see because of the dim lanterns that lit the way to the cell. Along the way we saw one guy hanging from the wall by heavy chains. He begged for water, and Basil, the dungeon master laughed. I could only guess that the guy on the wall was a demon too.

Getting back to Basil… Yep, we were tossed into a cell by the laughing dungeon keeper named Basil. He was a creepy, old dude, who smelled as bad as everyone else at the castle did. I guess in the Middle Ages nobody ever took a bath. It seemed pretty empty down in that cold dark stone basement of the castle. So I was guessing that business was slow for Basil. It wasn't so much that he was friendly, but he just seemed to laugh at everything, and it didn't matter how dumb or unfunny it was. When Jimmy stumbled coming down the steps, and almost landed on his head, Basil laughed. When Sagamore told of the plans to torture and kill us, Basil laughed. In fact Basil seemed to enjoy his job very much, too much if you ask me.

They had tried to hook us up to the walls in chains, but our wrists were too small. Of course Basil laughed at that, and Sagamore told him he was gonna have to make some new shackles to hold us, because of how dangerous we were. Basil didn't really laugh at that, he was actually stopped in his tracks thinking that maybe it was true. Remember, me and Jimmy were the keepers of the gate to the Underworld, so we had to be pretty dangerous dudes, and that was probably a better job than old Basil had. Truth of the matter is that I didn't even know what that meant, keeper of the gate. Just knew the more dangerous we looked the better Sagamore looked.

There weren't any chairs or cots in the cell, and the only place to sit was on the soggy muddy floor. My feet were so tired that I didn't really care where I was sitting as long as the rats kept themselves hidden, and out of sight.

"Cover yourselves, and be decent you loathsome creatures," said Basil, and he tossed into our cells what looked like old dusty sacks with holes cut in them, so we could stick our heads and arms through. The dirt just flew off of them as the hit us. We didn't know if it was just some old bag that had been used to carry potatoes, or if they had been somebody's clothes. They were grungy, and covered with crud. We used the cloth to wrap ourselves in, and huddled together to try and stay warm.

When Basil went off to make some smaller cuffs to hold me and Jimmy, that was the first time we had to talk since getting to this century.

"They're gonna kill us," I said, and I know he could tell how scared I was by how shaky my voice was.

"Not if we can get to those time belts," he said.

"And what are the chances of that, and even if we did get them, the mother station is down."

"We were suppose to end up three days before the comet hit the planet, maybe in that time the mother stations still up and running."

"But why didn't it work this time? Look around you, we're a little off base here."

"I've been thinking about that," he said. "Suppose the comet hit down right when we were beginning to skip through the time chambers."

"And," because I really didn't know where he was going with this.

"And the impact knocked the Earth out of its loop right then and there."

"I still don't get it."

"Well Shawn, in science, time and space are considered pretty much the same thing. If the Earth was moved to another space, then maybe so was the Earth's time, and all the space that time is kept in."

"Do you really think that there's a chance that we can get back?"

That's when he stopped, and looked around at the stonewalls and the heavy iron cell that had us locked in.

"We've gotten out of tight places before."

"But they've got everything, the time belts, your schoolbag with the spy junk in it…"

"I didn't say it was gonna be easy." That's when he looked sadly at the walls that had us jailed in. "Not easy at all."

And I could tell from that look on his face that Jimmy didn't seem to have much hope either. Usually he would try and think his way out of any situation, but this really had him scared. That's when we both slid down the wall, and sat on the cold muddy floor. For what seemed like the longest time we just stared at the bars that had us locked in. And then out of nowhere, we heard it. At first I wasn't sure that I had really heard what I had heard. It was a laugh, and for a minute I thought Basil had seen somebody fall and break their neck, or something else that might have given him a good laugh. But the laugh seemed like it was coming from somebody a lot younger. And like I said, I thought that I was imagining it until I saw Jimmy look up too. The sound seemed to be echoing from just outside of the cell that we were in. Both of us got up at the same time, and walked slowly to the bars, and looked out. That's when we heard it again, and that time I was sure that I wasn't imagining it, somebody was outside of the cell laughing at us.

"Whose out there," I said.

But all that got was more giggles, and we both jumped when a shadow seemed to run right past us.

"That's not that idiot Basil," I said to Jimmy.

"No," he said, and then he tried to squeeze his head out of the bars, and look around the corner. "It sounds like a kid, like us." And then he tried to call to whoever was out in the darkness. "Who is it, who's out there?"

Again there was only quiet, and for the longest time that was all there was. I was headed back to the wall to sit down, when the giggle echoed through the dungeon again. I moved back quickly to be near Jimmy, who still had his head stuck inside of the bars trying to look out.

"Do you think Basil has an idiot son," I said.

"Shhh, " Jimmy came back at me quick like, "let's just listen."

We stood there with those dusty sacks hanging off our shoulders, tugging them tight around us trying to stay warm.

"Please," Jimmy said, "let us see you."

"No," a voice suddenly cut through the darkness. And the voice coming out of the shadows sounded a little scared. It definitely belonged to a kid like us.

"Who is it," I said.

"If you promise not to place your demon's gaze on me, I'll come out in to the light."

"We don't have any demon's gaze you dumb…" and that's all I got out, before Jimmy shushed me. He was always trying to keep me from putting my foot in my mouth, so out of habit, I just shut my trap.

"We promise," Jimmy said.

"Look away, look away," came the voice belonging to the hidden stranger.

I saw Jimmy turn his head to the side, and so I did the same thing. From the corner of my eye I could see the shadow come across the floor, and move towards the cell.

"We won't hurt you," said Jimmy.

"I've heard tales," said the young boy, who had just come out of the darkness, and was now moving towards me and Jimmy. "I've heard tales how the likes of you can snatch up a young lad's spirit, and put it into a frog."

Without looking at him Jimmy kept talking. "We're just young lad's too," he said.

And I could still see him out of the corner of my eye as the boy came closer, but not too close. He seemed really scared, and at the same time curious about us.

"My Master says that you are demons inhabiting the bodies of young boys, bodies that you stole from them."

"No, no," said Jimmy, "we are just boys like yourself. We mean you know harm."

"Word of your magical spells and of the evil charms you bring is known throughout the land."

"We just got here," I said. "How have they heard of us?" That's all I got out when Jimmy shushed me again, with an added shove on the shoulder to make sure I kept my big trap shut.

"It's all a mistake…" Jimmy tried to get that out when the sound of running feet and a girl's laughter hit our ears.

The boy turned quickly, and then we turned to look at him. A second later the girl came running from behind a giant stone pillar in the middle of the dark corridor. When she saw us she stopped dead in her tracks. It was at that point that the boy panicked. He held out his hands in front of his face, and turned away begging.

"Don't turn us to frogs, please don't use your evil incantations upon us."

He fell to the floor in terror, and the young girl ran to his side.

"Don't harm us please, we're good children, we are," said the girl.

"We promise, we promise, not to hurt you," said Jimmy.

"But the word of a witch…" the girl tried to get out.

"We're not witches," I said, "It's all some stupid mistake."

"It's true, it's true," Jimmy said. His voice seemed real excited now, 'cause I know he wanted them to believe it as much as me.

The young girl helped the boy to his feet, and he slowly pulled his hand down from his face. For the first time we were able to get a good look at the both of them. He was dressed quite well, and looked like he might have taken a bath sometime that year. The girl, well she was a different story. She seemed to be wearing the same kind of rags that most of the people outside were wearing. And that just looked like a bunch of old cloth sewn together.

"What's your names," Jimmy asked.

And for the longest time they were still quiet, and looking like they were really afraid of us.

"You don't have to be afraid," I told them. "We haven't done anything to you, and we won't."

"I'm Jimmy and this is Shawn," Jimmy told them, and I think they actually took a step closer.

"It has been foretold that you bring the plague with you," said the girl.

"Look at us," Jimmy said. "We're the same as you, and we're even more scared then you are right now."

"Yes a mirage," said the boy, "a trick of the mind to confound we mortals."

The boy and the girl looked at each other not knowing what to believe.

"But your powers are great," the girl said.

"If we had all that power, do you think we'd let them lock us away in this dungeon," Jimmy said.

"You're power was weakened when Sagamore, the Mighty, the great warrior, and the hero of the great battle of the Field of

Despair, snatched it away from you," that was the girl speaking, and she seemed to be trying to figure us out. And in that time they had not taken one more step forward. They seemed frozen on that same spot, so I couldn't tell if they were believing us or not.

"And wouldn't a real witch or demon," Jimmy kept trying to get through to them, "wouldn't he simply vanquish Sir Sagamore, or turn him into a frog?"

"And you'd better believe that if I were a real demon, I would've turned that bag of wind into a toad, or some kind of swamp creature," I told her.

"But your clothes, surely it is a witches wardrobe that you be wearing," she said pointing her finger as if she were trying to point out how evil my shorts sticking out the bottom of the dirty sack looked to her.

"We just come from a different..."

That's all I got out before Jimmy cut me off again, "A different land," he said.

I guess if I had said different time that would've seemed just as creepy to these two as us being witches.

"What strange garb," the boy now took another step towards us. And I was guessing that was a good sign.

"And what is your name," asked Jimmy.

And it looked like he was gathering all of his nerve just to say it, but after a moment he did. "I be Will, the whipping boy."

"The what," I said.

"For the Prince," answered the girl. "When the Prince be mischievous Will gets to take his licks for him."

"Its a great honor," said Will. "And in return I get to eat fine food, and get educated along side the Prince."

"Well that stinks," I said, "Why don't the Prince just take his own licks?"

And they both looked horrified that I had said what I said. Then Jimmy jumped in, and started explaining.

"No Shawn, the law of the land makes it wrong for anyone to lay a hand upon the Prince."

"Well that still stinks," I said again.

So I guess the Prince got to get away with all kinds of crazy stuff knowing that Will the whipping boy would be there to take the punishment for him. But old Will, he didn't seem to mind at all, in fact he seemed quite proud of it. I mean he looked better dressed than most of the other people that we had seen since we landed in this century. And I guess he ate pretty well, but still I think I would get a little mad if every time the Prince messed up, and I ended up getting hit for it.

"Will takes a good beating, he does," said the girl, almost proud of the fact.

"I take the finest birching in all the land," the boy almost smiled.

"And who are you," Jimmy asked the girl.

"She'd be Kate," said Will. "She's my sister. When I come to the castle, the King let me bring her along to work in the royal kitchen."

"I get to clean up after the King," she seemed to be happy about it too. So what could I say, seeing the way the other people were living in that time, and I guess in the kitchen of the King wasn't such a bad place to be.

Will and Kate started to get a little more talkative.

"Is Sagamore the boss around here," asked Jimmy.

"Sir Sagamore in all of his greatness," said Will, "is not the King."

"And who is the King," said Jimmy.

Jimmy told me later, if we could figure out who the King was, than we might be able to start getting a fix on the time we were stuck in.

"That'd be King Henry the second, Lord protector of England, Ireland, Normandy…" Will had started to tell us all that King Henry was the boss of when out of nowhere another set of footsteps came running into the dungeon. Will and Kate looked terrified, and turned to see another boy standing there behind them.

"I found you out," said the new boy to arrive. And this one was dressed even better than Will. He, like them stopped, and looked at us trapped behind the thick bars of the cell. Both of the other kids turned, and bowed as he came closer.

"Your Highness," said Will.

"Your Highness," said Kate.

So it wasn't too hard guessing who this other kid was. He had to be the Prince. And even him, safely out of reach, seemed afraid of me and Jimmy.

"So these be the witches that my father is to burn," said the Prince.

"Your Highness," Jimmy tried to talk to him.

90

"Do not gaze upon me dog," said the Prince. And I don't know if he had called me a dog or Jimmy a dog, but I didn't think we were making a good first impression on him.

"We best be out of here, before we are transformed into pigs," said the Prince.

"But your Highness," said Will, "they are boys just like us."

"Like us," the Prince now seemed more annoyed than scared.

"Like me," Will corrected himself. The Prince obviously thought he was better than everybody else, and I guess he wasn't scared enough to give up being better than us.

It was the kinda nutty insane laughter of Basil that we heard next. Both Will and Kate turned quickly as if scared of still one more thing. There was sure a lot of stuff to be scared about back then. The Prince he just turned slowly, and waited for Basil to bow to him, which he did.

"You're Highness," said Basil. "I see you be playing one of your games of hide and seek down here again. These are dangerous times you're Highness, and these two weave a powerful spell. I don't think your father, the King…"

"Then I don't think you should tell him," the Prince shut him up, and what he said came out sounding almost like an order.

"Your Highness," Jimmy called to him, "we're not witches, I swear."

Basil laughed, "they be looking for mercy, your Highness." And then even the Prince laughed at us. I was really starting to dislike this kid now. The Prince turned back to us, and smiled.

"I know of your tricks demon, Sagamore has warned me of your evil ways. My father has promised me that I shall be there to witness you cast into the flames, it will be all part of my birthday celebration."

"And a happy day that will be your Highness," Basil laughed. "But it won't be much of a celebration, if these two steal your soul fore the festivities, now will it?"

The Prince did not answer; he just turned, and walked from the dungeon. Right behind them were Kate and Will. Will looked back at us sadly, and shrugged his shoulders. And it looked like our only hope was going out the door with them.

Basil shook his head, and laughed some more. It really didn't take much to get him started. Basil then turned to us. "Come the celebration for the young Prince, you two shall be the center of it all. A good burnings the perfect way to spark off a new year."

Me and Jimmy, well we just slumped back against the cold stone wall. We watched Basil laugh hysterically as he walked off to do more dungeon business. Will and Kate had left us now, and it seemed like the time belts might as well be a million miles away for all the good they would do us in that dungeon.

Chapter 8: Lord Hoxley, and How He Got Us Killed

"I hope Sagamore hasn't messed with the time belt settings," said Jimmy.

"That Sagamore guy was acting like he had never seen a digital clock before," I said to Jimmy.

"Shawn, they won't invent clocks for another two hundred years, so I'm guessing that he never did see a digital clock before. And that poses another problem."

"We're trapped in the Twilight Zone here, don't tell me something else can go wrong."

"Even if we get our hands on the time belts, if the settings have been changed…"

"And you're saying that there's no way we can reset them?"

"First we've got to know what time it is and the day, that has to be fed into the main controls…"

"No big deal, we ask somebody the date…"

"Shawn, very few people have calendars, and all over the world, the first of the year comes at different times."

"Well who's the Bozo who worked that out?"

"If we can get a calendar for the date, we still won't be able to get an accurate time unless… unless we can find a sundial…"

"And if there's no sun that day?"

"Another problem…"

I got really annoyed all of the sudden. It's something I did when I was lost without hope, which by the way I was. "You're telling me something else can go wrong," I yelled at Jimmy.

"Look Shawn, if we don't know what the problems are, we can't try and fix them." I guess he was right, I just kept wondering how we were gonna fix the problem of the iron bars that had us locked in.

"What about those hour glasses, I'm sure they got one of them lying around the castle some place."

"Extremely inaccurate," Jimmy came back at me.

"Darn, is there anything in this century that works, I mean besides the torture chamber? How we gonna get our hands on a calendar, or a Sundial even if we could get our hands on the time belts?"

That's all I got out when a new voice came into the cell.

"Perhaps I can help you," said the voice.

When we looked to see, in front of us was an older guy. He also seemed to be dressed a lot better than most of the people we had run into. But he had a crusty old beard, and seemed to be squinting from the darkness of the dungeon. He also seemed to be better fed then most of the people we had seen 'cause he had belly on him, and reminded me a little of Santa Claus in strange clothes. Most of the people that we had come across looked pale, and like they could use a good meal. Maybe everybody cooked like Basil, so eating was something you only did when you were starving to death. But you couldn't say that about this new visitor. At first we thought it might be that Royal Torture guy that everybody had been talking about since we landed in this crazy place. We really didn't want to run into him. Torture must've been very popular back then, 'cause they talked about that guy like an all star. He was gonna "loosen our wicked tongues," or "bring forth the truth," or "make us curse the day," which by the way, I was already doing. So I'm thinking that this new guy is the Royal Torturer, and his job was to make us confess to being witches. And with that kinda help we'd end up toasting like marshmallows over an open barbecue pit. Yeah, that kinda help we could definitely live without. But still I wasn't sure that was who was in standing in front of us right then. He seemed kinda nice for somebody who was gonna do such mean things to us. So it wasn't easy, but I finally got myself to open my mouth.

"Mister," I said, "can you help us?" And I really wanted to know. I was so scared, and it didn't seem like anybody cared about how scared I was, or whether we were gonna live or die, or anything. When Jimmy told me that there was a chance that we might be able to get back to our century, and save my parents, I started thinking about our whole situation from a different direction. Before I knew that saving the world was still possible I just didn't care about anything. I mean what was the point of trying to survive; there was nothing to go back for. But with that slim hope that Jimmy had dangled in front of me I got real scared, 'cause now I really wanted to live, and thought there might actually be a chance of that happening. Got real scared and real hungry. Since we had been locked away in that cold, damp cell all we had gotten to fill our bellies was a bowl of muddy water that smelled like it had been dipped into the swamp. For food there was some moldy, brown bread, with worms crawling around in it.

We were both so hungry that we actually ended up eating it, after picking out the worms of course. Wasn't sure I had even gotten out all of them, but I had been starving, so I just looked the other way through most of what I guess was suppose to be a meal. I mean maybe Will and Kate would've helped if they could, but they were just kids like us, so what were they gonna do? So when this old guy showed up, whoever he was, I wanted to hear what he had to say, and wanted it to be good news.

"We're not witches," Jimmy said, and I guess he was sounding pretty desperate himself right about then.

The man then walked closer to us. He wasn't looking at us like the others, he wasn't scared, and he looked more curious, like he was looking at us through a microscope.

"I know you're not witches," he said.

"You do," I said. I felt so excited that somebody believed me, and I felt a tear come to my eye. I hate to tell you that, it's just that I had never been so happy that I actually felt like crying.

"There are no such thing as witches," he said.

"Will you tell that to the others," Jimmy said.

"Oh that shall not do any good," said the man. "They're primitive people, but of course that you already know. And if I were to tell them that I don't believe in witches, they might burn me right along side the two of you."

It didn't sound like this guy was gonna be so much help after all.

"But you said you could help," Jimmy came back at him. We both really wanted to hear something good.

"Oh I can get you a calendar," said the man, "but the only way for you two boys to get out of this dungeon is to die."

Yeah, this was definitely not the kinda help we were looking for. Or at least that's what I thought in the beginning, but how was I to know that getting killed was exactly what we had to do to get out of that place.

"You got any better ideas Mister," I said.

"I am Lord Hoxley, and I have seen the charms that you boys have brought with you."

"They're not charms," Jimmy told him.

"Of course they are not, and you two are not from around here, are you? Pardon me for eavesdropping on the tale end of your conversation."

"No," I said, "we're not from around here."

Lord Hoxley then smiled at us. "The world... does it get any better?"

"Better," said Jimmy.

"I am a man of science, I teach the Prince and his whipping boy Will. I look at the stars, and wonder what is out there, and what lies beyond our times. All questions that I thought that I would never know the answers to, but now maybe some answers do exist."

"So you don't believe Sir Sagamore," Jimmy said.

"Sagamore is an idiot," said Lord Hoxley. "Last year he blamed the gambling of the guards on High Holy Days for the drought and subsequent famine."

"And what happened to them?" I wasn't sure I really wanted to know.

"They were drawn and quartered for the King's pleasure," said Lord Hoxley. "There remains scattered in the woods to ensure an early spring thaw, and to appease the forest trolls."

"Doesn't this Sagamore know about causal effect," said Jimmy. And that got a big smile out of Lord Hoxley, and he repeated what Jimmy had said.

"Causal effect, as described by Aristotle."

"What," I said, 'cause I was lost all over.

"What causes something to happen," said Jimmy. "Everything happens for a reason, and that reason should make sense."

Lord Hoxley now came even closer. No he wasn't afraid of us at all. "Yes," he said, "the reason it happens would be cause and..."

"Effect," Jimmy finished it for him."

"And this would be the way that everything in the Universe works," Hoxley seemed to be very excited by all of this. "So it is proven in centuries to come?"

"I didn't come up with it," Jimmy said, not wanting to take credit for it.

"Do we remain a small minded, superstitious people," Hoxley then asked sadly.

"It gets a little better," Jimmy answered.

I didn't know what any of it was about, but as long as this Hoxley character was interested in helping us, I just kept my mouth shut and listened.

"We live in darkness here boys," said Lord Hoxley. "And it is not just by the hand of the dim witted Sagamore that you suffer these indignities."

"It's not the indignity that we mind so much Lord Hoxley," said Jimmy, "it's the torture and burning that we're not happy about."

"If you are to escape from this place," Lord Hoxley looked sadly around the dungeon, "then we must use that darkness, that superstition to help you escape."

"But how," said Jimmy.

"Like I have told you…" Lord Hoxley started to say.

"Isn't there a better way than letting them kill us," Jimmy cut him off.

"Unfortunately that is the only way that I can think of," Hoxley said. And I kept thinking that I could've come up with something as good as that.

Then Jimmy looked real close at him, and said, "but we wouldn't really be dying, would we Lord Hoxley?"

"It is trial by water that you shall be judged," said Hoxley.

"What is that," I said, and I was real scared like, 'cause it seemed like no matter what happened it wasn't gonna be a happy ending for us.

"They shall bind you, weigh you down with rocks, and toss you into the moat," Lord Hoxley, went on. Yeah, this was like the worst escape plan I had ever heard. "If you sink, that proves your innocence…"

"Then they dive in and save you right," I kept waiting for some good part.

"They rarely react in time, but your good name is saved, and Sagamore comes off looking rather foolish, I must say."

"And how is that a trial," I found myself yelling at Lord Hoxley as if it were all his idea.

"Sometimes people don't go under," said Jimmy.

"And so they let you go," I said, trying to calm my voice, 'cause I could here it echoing in the dungeon, and I kept waiting for Basil to come back, and spoil the party. But I guess that they were so use to screaming in that place they probably just thought that it was that Royal Torturer guy doing a good job.

"Then they burn you at the stake as a witch, because the water would not accept your evil into its depths," Hoxley said. "It's a lose lose situation."

I looked around and lowered my voice, making sure that only Jimmy and Lord Hoxley could hear what I was gonna say. "Couldn't you just sneak the key off of Basil? I'm sure he wouldn't be that hard to get over on, then we make a run for it."

Lord Hoxley shook his head sadly. "Basil is a cousin to the King, that is the only reason he has this job, or any job, I mean look at him. The man is an imbecile".

Jimmy looked around at the dingy dungeon, "cousin to the King and this is the best job that Basil could land?"

"He's actually Lord Basil, but the King was embarrassed having him attend court, so Lord Basil became keeper of the… the keep."

"Guess around here it doesn't help having friends in high places," I said.

"Had Basil not been the cousin to the King, Sagamore would have surely had him tried as a troll. It was only the generosity of the King that sent him to the dungeons to end his days out of sight of the royal court. Here Basil is free to imprison and torture to his heart's delight, and the rats don't seem to mind."

"Then Basil is the Royal Torturer," Jimmy asked.

"No, no, no" said Lord Hoxley, "that is a highly skilled profession. Basil merely tortures as a hobby. It must get terribly boring for the poor chap, but I guess he has to keep his hands occupied somehow."

"But you don't think we could get by him," I asked.

"It doesn't take much intelligence to lurk around the dungeon, and play hide and go seek with the vermin. But once by Basil, you would have to contend with the dungeon guards. They would cut you down liked dogs before you got into the first corridor."

"So you're saying that the best we can hope for is to drown in the moat." I really didn't like this idea.

"I think Lord Hoxley has an idea, Shawn," Jimmy said.

"Are you boys good swimmers," asked Hoxley.

"Not with my hands tied and weighed down with rocks," I told him.

"The moat is muddy and murky, once below the surface no one can see you."

"And that's why they are rarely able to rescue people," Jimmy said.

"Most are reluctant to enter into the foul, fetid waters of the moat to save even kin. And why the drowned bodies are left on the bottom until the bondage breaks away and they float to the surface. In more merciful times the soldiers plunge their spears into the murky depths to catch a hold of what flesh they can, but even that charity generally results in death."

"What about a trial," I yelled at him. I know none of this was Lord Hoxley's fault, but I just felt that I had to yell at somebody.

"That is the trial," Jimmy said.

"And all we got to do is hold our breath till sometime in the spring when we become undone." I know I was being cocky with this guy, but I knew a long time ago that two minutes was about the longest time I could hold my breath.

"No," Hoxley went on, "two minutes time should be sufficient to affect a rescue."

"Rescue," I said, now I was interested.

"Unless," Lord Hoxley was thinking on it.

"Unless," I hated hearing that unless.

"The wintry breeze from the North has chilled the moat," this was sounding scarier all of the time.

"You're thinking hypothermia," said Jimmy.

"Hypo…" I tried to get out.

"Hypothermia," Lord Hoxley smiled just happy to be learning something new.

"When the body temperature gets dangerously low," Jimmy explained to him.

"And the body dies," Lord Hoxley said real quick like still carrying that smile on his face.

"Oh goody," I guess I was still being sarcastic.

"And death from the wintry elements is caused by this thing, called hypothermia," asked Lord Hoxley. "The workings of the human body they come under great study?"

"In later centuries they start dissecting human bodies to learn how they work," Jimmy told him.

"Dissecting…" Lord Hoxley was trying to figure that one out.

"Cutting them open, and checking out the junk inside," I had that one covered.

"What a marvelous thing," Lord Hoxley with his eyes wide open like little kid seeing his first Christmas tree.

"Yeah really great! That is how we know a whole other way we can die," I was really hating this plan.

"What do you have in mind Lord Hoxley," Jimmy jumped with a little excitement himself.

"I'm a bit of an inventor myself," he said. "Not on the same level as the two of you, of course."

"Sir," Jimmy stopped him, "we didn't' invent the time belts. We merely traveled here with them."

"I am still humbled by your magnificent deed, but there is little time to discuss any of this. Basil will awaken from his slumber soon."

"You knocked him out," I asked.

Lord Hoxley looked at me strangely, as if he were trying to figure out what I was talking about.

"Made him unconscious," Jimmy cleared things up.

"Not at all," Lord Hoxley told us. "Basil sleeps most of the day. It's actually quite a disgrace. Nepotism places him of such high

regard as the dungeon master, and he callously ignores his duties."
That was probably good for us I thought.

"But how can he sleep down here with the bugs and the rats…" I asked him. I had spent half the day just swatting the creepy-crawly things that were climbing all over me.

"The pest and Basil seem to share a mutual respect, even the fleas seem to look the other way where Basil's concerned." Lord Hoxley told us. And I was thinking that maybe it was just the smell coming off of Basil that kept the bugs away. But I guess it was better to have Basil sleeping through the job, disgrace that he was than to have him up and torturing people, especially me and Jimmy.

"Before he comes back," Jimmy wanted to move on with the plan, "how are we gonna escape from the moat?"

"As I said before, I'm a bit of an inventor myself. But we shall require the assistance of others."

"Others," Jimmy said.

Since we didn't know a heck of a lot of people in the twelfth century I couldn't run to the phone and call a friend. Actually none of the people we met here could we call friends. Will, the whipping boy and Kate, his sister, I guess came the closest, and I was hoping this Lord Hoxley was really gonna to be able to save us. Doing that I guess would make him our best friend.

Lord Hoxley's plan did sound of crazy, and it all depended on whether we could hold our breaths under water for about two minutes. I was thinking that I might be able to make it, but I wasn't sure about Jimmy. I was the better swimmer, and Jimmy knew it. I know he was a little nervous about the whole thing, and we both got a lot more nervous when Lord Hoxley told us his crazy plan.

Chapter 9: The Bones at the Bottom of the Moat, and How They Were Gonna Be Ours

We didn't really have much time to get all the details from Lord Hoxley, before Basil, the laughing dungeon master returned to give us our daily rations of muddy water and buggy bread. After hours of nothing to drink or eat, it kinda tasted good just to have something wet going down your throat, and filling your belly. When you got hungry enough, everything tasted like the best meal you'd ever had. And as long as it didn't wiggle or squirm on the way down, I just tried to pretend that it was all good stuff. Still a fresh cool glass of lemonade and a slice of pizza would've hit the spot a lot better.

Lord Hoxley didn't give us the whole plan, but here's what we knew: Trials where people actually sat around and talked about whether a person was guilty or not weren't gonna to happen for a real long time. And we weren't gonna get a lawyer, 'cause, well they didn't do that either. Sometimes they would torture a confession out of you, and nobody seemed to see the problem with that. Of course if the King didn't like you, you were really done for. Now me and Jimmy we had been accused of what they called magical crimes. I think they were trying to pin that whole thing with the cows or sheep getting sick on us. And you didn't want to mess with the cows back then, 'cause that was a really big deal. We were going to be taken out to the moat, tied with long ropes and rocks and tossed into the water. If by some miracle we were thrown out of the water by a tidal wave, we would be burnt at the stake for those magical crimes. Now, Lord Hoxley told us that getting tossed into the moat was gonna happen, and there was no way that he could stop it. It was all part of a big festival being planned for the Prince's birthday, and me and Jimmy being tossed into the moat was the main entertainment that day. And the worst part, yeah, it could actually get worse, that if we didn't drown then we were in really big trouble, and would be burnt to death for everybody's enjoyment. You think with all the money the King had they could've just hired clowns or jugglers, something to keep everybody happy, but that wasn't the way it worked either.

Well anyway, Lord Hoxley had invented a way to breathe under water using a bellows and a twine duct that sounded an awful lot like a hose. He could blow air from the bellows into the twine duct and into us, but he said there was one major problem. And naturally there always had to be a problem. What was the point of making anything easy? Although covered with thick coatings of sap from the trees near to the castle, the water would quickly seep through, and into the duct that was delivering the air supply. Within three to five minutes the water would begin to replace the air in the duct, and we would then be sucking down the muddy water of the moat.

Both Kate and Will were suppose to be good swimmers, and Will had helped Lord Hoxley experiment secretly with the underwater device before. Of course that was in the summer, and the water was a whole lot friendlier in the summer. At the time we were talking Will and Kate hadn't agreed to do any of this, and we were just hoping that they would be good sports.

Lord Hoxley seemed to be something like our Professor Burkhardt, only nine centuries too soon. He had at first developed the underwater breathing device, so that it might be possible to rescue people who had been accepted by the water, and could not possibly be witches. The problem was, Lord Hoxley said, "that science is frowned upon as dangerous." And if he had told the King that it was possible for a man to breathe underwater, he might possibly be in the same cell with us awaiting the same dip in the moat. So after a lot of thought Lord Hoxley had decided to keep his yap shut about the breathing tube.

Once under the water, me and Jimmy would have to hold our breaths until Will and Kate were able to swim to us, and cut the ropes that we had been tied up with, and that was only if they had signed on to help us. They would have to carry the hoses with them, and pass them off to us, so that we could breath too. Lord Hoxley would then pump the air to us from the land, and be hidden behind some trees or something, and out of sight. After Will and Kate had cut our ropes, we would all have to swim underwater to the far end of the moat. Mostly that would be unwatched 'cause everybody would be fixed on where we had gone under, trying to see if we were witches or not. It could all work as long as the sap from the trees held the water from the moat out of the pipeline. There was another problem that the two of us didn't know about, but we were about to find out.

Later that night Will the whipping boy came by to see us. I kept thinking that it was so easy to get into this place, but getting out seemed impossible.

"Playing more hide and go seek with the Prince," Jimmy asked Will.

"No," said Will, "the Prince just threw horse dung onto the Captain of the royal guards. That always gets a beating… so I came down here to hide. Sometimes he forgets that he is angry with the Prince, and I'm spared a strapping."

"That must be terrible, taking the punishment for that guy," said Jimmy.

"Not at all," said Will. "It is a great honor to be thrashed for the Prince. It's just that sometimes the honor makes it hard to sit in class the next day. And my studies are important to me, that's why I try and avoid the honor whenever possible. Have the two of you found comfort?"

"Once you get use to sitting in the cold mud, it's kinda comfy," I said, "and when the rats take a rest and stop running through, it's just like home."

"It must be a grand and wonderful land that the two of you hail from," said Will.

"Oh I was just joking…"

"We're fine, and how are you," said Jimmy.

"A wee bit nervous about tomorrow…"

"Is tomorrow the day?"

"Tomorrow is the day that we celebrate the Prince's birthday."

Jimmy went closer to the bars of the cell, and spoke quietly to Will. "We really appreciate you doing this for us," he said.

"Lord Hoxley," Will told us, "said it is a terrible injustice that Lord Sagamore is committing upon the two of you. You two being great visitors from another time and all, and not being witches at all."

His eyes dropped like he was afraid of us once more. "You truly not be witches?"

"I promise you," said Jimmy, "we're not witches." But still Will looked nervous, and not wanting to look up at us, so Jimmy went on. "But you're afraid anyway, aren't you Will?" Still Will would not answer him. That's when I came closer.

"Is there something else scaring you," I said.

"He's taking a really big chance in helping us," Jimmy told me. "Aren't you Will?"

And for the first time he looked up, and we could see right into his eyes.

"Not for me so much," said Will, "But Kate... If we get caught, we'll be looked upon as witches like the two of you. We will be known as they who gave aid to the demons."

"But we're not demons..." I started to yell, "And we're not witches, I wish they'd make up their minds," and then Jimmy jumped in and stopped me.

"Harboring an agent of the devil receives the same punishment as being an agent yourself." You could see that this kid was still having serious doubts with our story, and who could blame him.

"What Shawn told you is true," Jimmy said, "you and your sister are taking a real big chance here. And I'm not sure we even have a right to ask you, but the truth is, that if we don't get back to our time, then a whole lot of people are gonna die. People we love, and all the people of the world in fact."

Will was now looking curiously at us again. "You have such power," he said.

"Not us," Jimmy told him, "but we may have a way to make this terrible thing not happen, but without your help, the world will end. So you see you're as important here as we are. We have to all work together, or it will be the end of all mankind."

Will nodded his head as if understanding, but did not say anything.

"Are you all right," I asked.

It took another minute for him to talk to us again. It was like he was trying to get his thoughts together, so that he could understand just how important what we were about to do really was.

"The moat is dark and deep," Will started. "That was done to keep the castle safe from enemies of the King. When first Kate and me see you thrown into the water we will set out to bring you the breather devices of Lord Hoxley. The breathers are weighed down with tiny stones, so as not to rise to the surface. On the bottom you must stay still, so that we can cut the ropes, and get the air to you. We shall have to take turns. Kate and I shall tap you on the shoulder when we need to partake of the air from the breathers. We must stay hidden at the far end of the castle with Lord Hoxley, so that we will not be seen entering the water. Lord Hoxley has assured us that all eyes will be on you, so we will not be witnessed. It is very important that once we cut you free of the ropes that you take caution not to break the waters surface. If you are seen above you will be taken prisoner once more, and sentenced to death. There will be no other opportunity for rescue. And we dare not dally. If we are caught, then we shall all burn together."

"If we feel we're about to float up, then we'd better grab onto one of the rocks and carry it as we walk the bottom of the moat," Jimmy came up with that idea.

"Kate and I will guide you to a place of safe keeping," said Will. And then he lifted a bowl off of the floor that he had kept hidden behind one of the pillars of the dungeon. It was filled with some black, sticky, and smelly stuff. "Lord Hoxley wishes the two of you to have this."

"What is it," asked Jimmy.

"He says to cover your bodies with it where it will not show. It will help to shield you from the water, and to keep warm."

Jimmy stuck his finger in and sniffed at it. "It smells like grease or something."

"Lord Hoxley extracts it from the roots of certain plants in the forest."

"So it is tar," said Jimmy.

Will looked confused and then just continued. "Be careful to spread the mixture over your body, being sure to place it over your heart. Over that cloth must be worn to keep the mixture from being detected by the guards and Sir Sagamore." Lord Hoxley had given Will all the instructions to feed to us.

"Coating the skin to keep the cold away from our major organs just might help," Jimmy said.

Will was still standing looking like a frightened puppy, and for the first time I realized just what a sacrifice he was making for two kids who had a crazy story about saving the world.

"Thanks Will," I said.

He looked at us sadly. "It is my sincerest wish that I have not entered into a pact with the devil," he said.

"Can't you tell by looking at us that we're just kids like you," I asked him.

He did not answer my question. "Lord Hoxley has said that there are no demons, and I want to believe him, but what is a lad to do if you have cast your spell over him…"

"No spells, no magic…" Jimmy said to Will

"Kate and I will forfeit our lives if I'm wrong with this undertaking. Be ready and waiting for us at the bottom of the moat," Will said with an unhappy voice, and slipped back into the darkness of the dungeon shadows.

The next day was Prince John's birthday, and me and Jimmy were just a couple of party favors sent back from the twenty-first century. We had nothing to do now but wait, wait for the next day when we would be taken outside and tried as witches. Lord Sagamore and his men would take us to the moat, tie us up with rocks, and toss us into the deep, muddy water. If we could hold our breath, and if Will and Kate could get to us before our lungs gave out, we had a good chance of getting out alive. So we started right then and there practicing, taking in deep gulps of air. We had no watches, so we couldn't tell how long we could hold onto a gulp of air, but was just holding it as long as we could. Jimmy thought that it would be good practice just he same. Yeah, I guess we were both scared. The fate of the whole world was now riding on four kids and an old teacher, who would be pumping air to us through a makeshift hose. I kept thinking had we ever been in a more dangerous situation, and I couldn't seem to remember one. Just then I thought to let go of the breath that I had been holding onto for what seemed to be forever. I had been practicing all night, and time had slipped away so fast that I didn't realize that it was almost morning. I didn't know that until I heard the sound of footsteps that seemed to be marching into the dungeon, and headed right in our direction. Both Me and Jimmy stood up, and looked through the bars that had us trapped inside. In a moment the entrance door swung open, and I could see just a bit of light from the outside creep in through the darkness. Lord Sagamore and his men had arrived, and we knew it was Prince John's birthday.

Concept Art For First Gravity Box Book.

Chapter 10: The Serpent From the Underworld Comes to the Rescue

Sir Sagamore and his soldiers didn't seem to waste much time. They drew their swords when they first came in. They were all standing like they were ready for battle against me and Jimmy, like we were fire-breathing dragons that had threatened to destroy the kingdom.

"Dare not gaze them directly in the eye," Sagamore warned his men. "They have the ear of Lucifer himself, and hold his trust. They were about to inhabit the body of the sheep, when I captured them, and stole away their most powerful charm."

Boy, did Sagamore have a wild imagination. By charm, I was guessing that he meant the time belts. And I still kept trying to figure out what demons would do once they took over the body of the sheep? It wasn't like taking over the body of a tiger or a lion, or some other dangerous animal, and I didn't think they had killer sheep, even back in the twelfth century. So what exactly was the point of hiding inside of the sheep? There wasn't really time to think of that right there and then, 'cause we were being taken outside to stand trial as witches. We didn't even have time to say goodbye to Basil who was laughing like an idiot as we were taken out. At least his day had gotten off to a good start.

Luckily we never got to meet with that Royal Torturer guy. He had been off on vacation or whatever Royal Torturers do with their time off from making people miserable. The Prince's party was coming up fast, and there wasn't enough time to make us "agonize in the pit of unbearable sorrow" before the celebration. Basil had wanted to try his hand at torturing us himself, but Sagamore was afraid that he might botch the job, and kill us before the big bash. Sagamore being the twelfth-century party hound that he was did not want to see the celebration ruined.

"It be the right of all royal subjects to be placed on the rack, have their fingernails plucked, and to have hot coals pressed to the flesh," Basil whined, "if only to prove their innocents."

"But these are not royal subjects," Sagamore disagreed.

"Do not even demons and servants of sin deserve the same justice," Basil really wanted to put those hot coals onto us, and somehow I didn't think I wanted him arguing our case. Believe me this guy would've made a terrible lawyer.

"Out of my way fool," Sagamore got real annoyed, and just shoved Basil out of the way as he brushed on by him.

Jimmy guessed that Sagamore just didn't want us confessing up too fast. They would've skipped the whole trial by water, and ruined Prince John's favorite party game.

The Sun was already up, and its brightness hurt my eyes after being stuck in the dark and dirty dungeon for so long. To my surprise everybody seemed to be already up, and screaming at us as we came out of the cold stone building. The rotten fruit smashed against the outside walls told me that they were already warming up their pitching arms. Jimmy had told me later that since they didn't have any electricity back then, and that most people were early risers. They had to get all their work done before the Sun went down, and couldn't stay up watching late night television and stuff.

117

In no time the throwing soggy fruit and vegetables had gotten started. You'd think people that were so hungry wouldn't be throwing potatoes around like they were old baseballs, but they did. It was all smelly and rotten, so maybe that's why they didn't mind getting rid of some of it.

It was cold that day, especially for me and Jimmy. The smelly stuff that Lord Hoxley had cooked up to keep us warmer in the water seemed kinda cold when it was put onto the skin. But Jimmy seemed to think that it would help. We were still wrapped in the dirty sacks that Basil had been so kind to throw at us, and underneath that was our witches jeans, shorts, and tee shirts. And the both of us were trembling, not only from the cold, but also from the terror of what was about to happen to us.

"Stand back, stand back, let the vile scum pass" Sagamore warned as his guards pushed us through the angry crowd.

Me and Jimmy looked at each other. We knew the plan, and we knew how likely it was to work, especially with all these people watching. As we moved along we could see in front of us Prince John standing next to a tall man, who was dressed in robes too, and wearing a crown, so I guessed that had to be King Henry. That's when all of the sudden another hard potato hit me right in the ear. Boy did it hurt. Even when they were soft and rotten it really hurt. For a minute I forgot all about being drowned, and I turned and yelled at whoever had thrown it.

"Watch it creep," I screamed into the crowd, and they all backed up like I was an angry giant or something.

"Beware," Sagamore called into the crowd, "the demon has teeth."

While King Henry watched quietly, Prince John walked over to us, and looked at us closely.

"They don't look so dangerous to me," said Prince John.

"Approach with caution my Lord," said Sagamore, "evil can come in many shapes and sizes."

For a moment Prince John just looked at us. He walked around like he was looking at insects about to be stomped on, and then he turned back to Sagamore. "Sagamore, did you not say that you have taken hold of their powers?"

It was now Sagamore who became nervous. "The magical amulets may be the seat of their power your Highness, but we cannot know what reserve of might these hideous beings may have kept hidden for mind bending and soul stealing."

"We're not witches," Jimmy said to Prince John.

Prince John did not answer Jimmy, he just looked at us all the harder, and once more turned to Sagamore. "If they had any mind bending powers would they not have used them on Uncle Basil, the dungeon master."

"Perhaps there was no mind to bend there Johnny," came the first words we had heard from King Henry. The crowd roared with laughter at the King's joke.

"Quite amusing, Sire," Sagamore forced a laugh to please the King.

"No Father," said Prince John. "All their power has been left where the sheep graze, and in the magical amulets that Sagamore has wrestled away from them in his already legendary battle in the Field of Death, or else they would have flown from here on the wings of vultures."

Field of Death, was he kidding, I guess not, because already murmurs of agreement raced through the people who had come to see me and Jimmy tossed into the moat.

Through the crowds came the roar: "Hail Sagamore, the Mighty."

King Henry didn't seem to be happy about this. He smiled, kinda a mean smile over to Sagamore.

"Perhaps the people think you more powerful than the King himself, Sagamore," said King Henry.

Now Sagamore really looked upset. His head twisted back and forth as he forced a smile through his clenched teeth, "you Sire indeed are the greatest power on God's green earth. This humble servant is merely a speck in the eye of that storm."

King Henry didn't even look back at Sagamore as he answered him. "It is good to keep remembrance of that Sagamore. A speck that gets blown into the wrong eye can sometimes lose its head."

Sagamore just bobbed his head nervously, "yes Sire, my sword is devoted to you and you alone. My feeble efforts in the field bare only the fruits of that devotion. All Hail Henry, long live the King," Sagamore screamed at the top of his lungs, and then there were some others in the crowd who echoed the same back. Somehow it was no surprise that Sagamore who had been so brave in "the Field of Death," had been such a punk with the King. Was it the Field of

Death or the Field of Despair I was getting confused about where this heroic battle took place.

It was then that Prince John signaled to one of the guards who pulled the time belts out of a large wooden box, near to the King, and raised it into the air. As he lifted it up to show everybody the noise from the crowd got even louder. The flashing numbers on the time set was a big selling point, the crowd seemed almost hypnotized by the sight of the time belt. You could see that they were buying into it as magic, and without Hoxley's help, drowning might be the best thing that could happen to us that day.

"If that idiot breaks the containment around the atomic battery…" Jimmy was wide eyed as he saw the time belt being waved in the air.

"What could happen," I asked.

"Not only would we never get back home, but it could create a chain reaction that might cause an nuclear explosion."

"What," I said, not believing what I had heard. We had been skipping though time with an atomic bomb strapped to our sides.

"Probably need a lot of energy to skip through time. It would be a small explosion," Jimmy said, but enough to put a nice big hole in the time space continuum, not to mention wherever we happened to be."

Before I could ask anymore about that whole time space thing, Sagamore shoved me, and ordered me to be quiet.

"Silence vile dog," he said, "and prepare to meet your fate."

It was then that I saw one of the most disturbing sights that I had ever seen. Across from us, standing on the other side of the moat stood Will. He just stood there silently watching. I nudged Jimmy, who looked to see, and I could tell that he wasn't happy about that either. How was Will going to save me and Jimmy if he was in plain sight of everybody? Had he gotten so scared that he had changed his mind? It was then that Prince John smiled cruelly at the both of us and said, "Let my birthday festivities begin."

All at once the crowds cheered the birthday boy, and Sagamore's guards grabbed hold of us, and began to tie us with some thick and slimy rope that looked like it had been used before at just such celebrations. I tried to put up a fight, but what could I do against all those soldiers grabbing me, and tying me with that rope? It cut deep into my wrist and ankles as I tried to pull away. That made me cry out from the pain, and the crowd laughed at my being hurt. One guard was about to tie a sack with rocks to our legs, but Sagamore motioned for him not to. It was then that I realized that it would make Sagamore look a heck of a lot mightier if we did float to the top of the water. That would make us look more like witches. I mean it didn't take a real tough guy to take on two young boys in the Field Despair, but demons that could actually float on water… well that was something else. And besides a witch burning seemed like it would be the perfect ending for the Prince's birthday celebration, and maybe the only way to get warm in this place.

"But we're not witches or demons…" Jimmy cried out, and you could hear it in his voice just how scared he was. I guess seeing Will standing across from us made him lose faith in Lord Hoxley's plan.

"Depraved beast, the waters will judge your innocence or guilt," said Sagamore.

"But… but," Jimmy yelled to him and to the crowd, "don't people who aren't witches drown… don't people who are just like you…"

"Silence," Sagamore shouted right into Jimmy's face, and then turned to the King and to the others in the crowd. "The young demon is trying to befuddle and perplex with logic and reasoning, all tricks of the Prince of Darkness himself."

These words started more screams from all the people who had come to see the trial.

"Demons!" "Unholy creatures!" "We shall not be fooled by reason!" "Use logic on us, will you!" And that was just some of the things that they were calling to us. I was hoping that Jimmy wasn't going to try anymore of that logic and reasoning, that seemed to get them all riled up and even angrier.

Before we knew it we were being pushed to the edge of the moat, and to the cold and muddy waters that were to be the testing ground for our innocence. There was a heavy smell in the air, and as I got a closer look at the moat, I could see where the odor was coming from. Floating along the surface of the filthy water was all kinds of garbage. I guessed that the people had used the moat for a sewer, 'cause the sludge was thick, and reeked like a breeze coming off a dump. Yeah, swimming in all of that junk was gonna make the dip a lot more fun.

"Jimmy… Jimmy," I tried to say to him, but he was too busy pushing back with his feet. It was useless, but he kept trying to keep himself out of the water. True for the plan to work we had to get into the water, but when I looked down I saw my feet pushing away the ground too.

The good news was that I could no longer see Will, the whipping boy standing on the other side of the moat. So maybe the rescue plan was still going ahead.

A laughing Prince John, ran up behind Jimmy, and the King shouted to him: "Give him the boot Johnny," and with those words. Prince John kicked Jimmy into the dirty waters of the moat. I heard Jimmy let go with a scream as he went in, and I was hoping that he had remembered to take in a deep breath before hitting the water.

"This is the best birthday ever," shouted Prince John.

The crowd of people cheered as Jimmy splashed into the moat, and then got sucked under. Then I was next. As I was pushed even closer to the edge, I tried to think of nothing else, but holding my breath. All of the screaming from the mob, and all of the rotten vegetables being tossed at me, they were something that I couldn't think about right then and there. If the rescue plan was still going to happen, it all depended on whether or not me and Jimmy could hold our breaths for around two minutes.

All at once I got slammed in the gut with a rock or something hard. It knocked the wind out of me, and I gasped for air and fell to the ground. Yeah, gasping for air, and trying to fight off the pain as the guards kept dragging me along. But still I couldn't catch my breath, and I was only feet away from the water's edge. I didn't know what to do. There was no way I was gonna hold my breath if I couldn't stop choking. Still they kept dragging me closer and closer.

I had to stall them somehow, but all I could do was to try and suck down air. I was desperate, so right then I stomped as hard as I could down on the nearest guard's foot. That's all I could think of. Didn't see any reason to worry about getting them mad at me, they were already trying to kill me. How bad could it get after that?

He was a big, gnarly dude, and when the pain shot through to his brain he yelled out and shoved me hard and forward. Not exactly the direction that I had wanted to go. It was good to see that crowd could enjoy anybodies pain, and that it wasn't just me that they wanted to see get hurt. They let go with more laughter as the soldier grabbed hold of his foot. But he only held it for a second before he pushed the other men aside, and grabbed hold of me by the ropes, and lifted me over his head and high into the air.

"Cursed fiend, I shall impose the test myself." And that fast he was moving towards the water ready to toss me in headfirst. But I still hadn't gotten my breath. My eyes were tearing from the pain of getting hit, but I could still see the dip into the moat coming up fast. Now raised up high into the air, I could see more of the mean faces that were cheering as I was being taken to my death. In only seconds I was right over the water. I had started to get back some of my wind, but I still was choking, and needed a few more seconds so I could do what I had to do. Strange enough it was King Henry who gave to me the time I needed. The soldier who had hold of me was very strong, and swung me back over his head, so that he could hurl me into the middle of the moat.

"Into the drink with you unearthly beast..." he had started to say, when King Henry stopped him.

"Halt in thy step knave," and those words seemed to have stopped everybody all at once, even the crowd. The soldier turned back to the King with me still right over his head.

"Yes your Majesty," the soldier looked terrified.

"It's my Johnny's birthday, let the pleasure be his."

The soldier was still frozen at the words of the King. It was Sagamore who told him what to do.

"Put the witch down you dolt," Sagamore ordered, and so he did.

By that time on the ground I had finally gotten my wind back, and it was just in time. I grabbed hold of all the air I could get in one giant gulp.

Suddenly the King's voice rang in my ears once more: "Give this one the boot Johnny." It was then that I felt the foot of Prince John kick me right in my butt. It hurt only for a second, and then I started to fall into the waters below. When I hit the chilly waters of the ice-cold moat, I almost gasped for air, and swallow in some of the water. Didn't want to do that. Before falling in I had taken in as much air as I could. So I didn't want to open my mouth, and let anymore in or out. But the water was so cold that I felt my body just shake violently as it seemed to bite right through my skin. And I couldn't tell if Lord Hoxley's mixture was helping to keep me any warmer or not. It really didn't feel like it as I sunk below. I tried to open my eyes to see if I could spot Jimmy, but the only thing that I could see was the brown, dingy water right in front of my face, and feeling like it was burning my eyes. It seemed like forever that I was down there, and then suddenly I felt myself floating to the surface. I

126

knew that that wasn't such a good thing either. In just a second my head cut through the surface of the water, and I could hear the people on land still shouting at me, and calling me a witch and a demon. Like they just couldn't make up their minds. Quickly I took another deep breath when all at once I got pulled under again. There was a tap on my shoulder, and I opened my eyes, and right in front of me was Will. Quickly he shoved the breather hose into my mouth, and grabbed hold of my nose, and to my surprise it worked. The hose was not what I expected. It was a big fat round thing, not like a garden hose at all. At the end there was a small opening with a pipe stuck in that we could suck the air out of. Will was holding my nose while I breathed. He tapped once more and then took the hose from me, so that he could take a breath of the air being pumped from somewhere else. While he did that he began to cut through the ropes that were tied around my wrist. I could feel his hands shake as he cut and hacked through to get me free. It was the coldest that I had ever been, and Will and Kate had come into the freezing cold waters for us. He shook my arm, and shoved the breather back into my mouth. I knew if I ever got out of this alive I would owe the both of them big time.

My guess was that Kate was doing the same thing for Jimmy. At least I hoped so. When my arms got free, Will grabbed the hose back off of me, and began to pull me along under the icy cold waters. Then all of the sudden I began to float upwards. I tried to hold myself down, but the air in my lungs must've been making me shoot to the surface. Will kept trying to pull me down, and then finally pulled the hose from my mouth, so I let go of most of my air, and swam down once more to the bottom of the moat. There Will handed me a heavy rock, and we began to walk along the bottom of the water.

Down deep I could only hear a rumble coming from the crowd, and could not really tell what they were screaming about, I could only guess. Still the icy chill ate through my skin, and most of me was beginning to feel numb. My legs and arms started to stiffen, and I was having trouble making them move. Somehow Will was doing it all better, and he started pulling me along. Even with the air being pumped into my lungs I didn't know how long I could stand being at the bottom of that moat. Aside from not being able to feel my body, Lord Hoxley's plan seemed to be working just fine, at least for me. I still didn't know if Jimmy was all right or not, and that kept me worried. Still Will pulled me along like he had made this trip before. I was sure he knew the way better than me, so I just let myself get dragged like a dog on a leash.

Will and I were passing the breathing hose back and forth between the two of us. A tap on the shoulder was the signal we used when we needed air, but sometimes I would just get desperate and try and grab it from him. That could've been a really dangerous thing to do, but even with the air pouring in through the hose it started to feel like I was suffocating underneath the chilly water. I really didn't know how far we had to travel, but between the freezing cold that felt like sharpened teeth biting into my skin, and worrying about Jimmy it seemed like we had been down there forever. I kept thinking that any second the hose would burst like Lord Hoxley had warned, and he would be pumping moat water down our throats and into our lungs instead of air. But it was something else that happened that was totally unexpected that gave us even bigger trouble. The breather hose that had been weighed down along the way got loose from the sacks of rocks holding it under. Like a bullet it shot right up to the surface. The people standing at the edge of the moat could see it instantly. Will had raced to the top quickly trying to catch the escaped air hose, but he couldn't make it in time. Floating on top of the muddy waters the twine duct must've looked like a giant snake skimming along the surface. I went with Will, and ended up accidentally popping through the top of the water myself. There I could see Sagamore, and all of his guards racing along the side of the moat like they were trying to kill what they thought was a giant snake. Several of Sagamore's men were slashing with swords and stabbing at the thing with spears. When he saw me, Sagamore cried out: "The Serpent from the Underworld has come to the rescue of the demons."

I was only on top of the water for a second when Will jumped up and, grabbed me the neck and pulled me back under. It was so unexpected that I gulped in some more water when I went under, and was having trouble not choking. Will pushed the breather into my mouth as I desperately tried not to swallow in more water. Even though I was having a rough time, Will grabbing me like that probably saved my life, again. Some of the men armed with swords had begun swiping at the top of my head just before it went under. One sword must've just missed me 'cause I could swear the blade had brushed across the top of my head. Then they started throwing rocks into the water, and I even saw a spear shoot on by me. I didn't know what we could have done. Now even Will froze underneath the water

129

as the rocks came hurling down from all direction, and we were just trying not to get hit. A couple had smashed against my arms and hurt, but I guess got slowed down enough by the water not to do any real damage. We both stood still for the longest time when I felt something appear to be coming at us from the bottom of the moat. At first I thought that it might be soldiers coming into to capture us. The water was so dark that it was hard to tell until something was right on top of you. Then something happened that made me not only surprised, but gave me a bit of hope. What I saw swimming towards me and Will were Jimmy and Kate.

We stood there unmoving, trying to figure out what they were doing. Jimmy motioned for Will and me to give up the breather, and hand it to him. Kate then handed Will the second breather, and allowed him to get a bit of air. In the meantime Jimmy using a loose piece of twine tied the end of the breather that Will had brought to me. Right away he started to shove it to the top of the moat. Not being held down any longer and still being pumped full of air, the hose quickly went to the surface. The water was muddy and kinda burnt my eyes, but I could make out a little what was happening up there. Once on the surface the hose stood up almost straight in the air like a giant serpent coming out of the water.

Now you could hear loud screams echoing, and even under the water you could hear them. It must've scared the heck out of everyone up there. The shifting shadows that raced across the top of the water made me think that they must've been running for cover. Just above my head Jimmy kept pushing the imaginary snake up higher and higher. It had to be standing twenty feet out of the water by now, and must've looked like the Loch Ness Monster or something.

In a moment the hose got up too high, and began to sway back and forth and fall to the side. Jimmy acted quickly to balance it, and make it stand straight once more, but it just splashed down into the moat. I saw he needed help, so I grabbed a mouth full of air off of the other hose and went to help. We had to come up out of the water to make it stand straight again. Up there we saw Sagamore and his men standing back terrified at the twine duct that they thought was a giant serpent sent by Satan. And now the hose that had been blocked off at the end began to grow fat and blow up like a balloon making it look even meaner as it swelled. The sap that kept this thing glued together began to bubble, making the skin of the fake serpent look alive. That was all that we needed to finish up the illusion. The rest of the people were running in terror away from where we had popped up.

Me and Jimmy stuck our heads out of the water again just a little to control the snake and to get some air. All eyes were on what everyone thought was a giant snake. No one seemed to notice me and Jimmy pressed against the side of the moat.

"You're all right," I said trying to catch my breath when I could finally talk to Jimmy.

"Let's not come up too high," he said and grabbed higher up on the hose so that he could make it stand up once more.

At the edge of the water was Sagamore looking like he was ready to faint 'cause now he really believed that we might be working with the Devil. Many of the others were running away, and backed against the castle wall as if afraid that the serpent might come out of the water, and go after them.

"Abandon all hope," Sagamore screamed, and began to run away. Several of his men stayed, and attempted to take further swipes with their swords at the imaginary snake. They were getting pretty close too, 'cause now the swords were chopping just above where me and Jimmy were hiding. We had to go back under water where Jimmy continued to balance the snake until the sap finally gave way, and it exploded shooting the filthy water of the moat way into the air. It sounded like a giant balloon bursting, and under water it felt like it was going to burst our eardrums.

Real quick like Will and Kate pulled us along to the other side of the moat and away from danger. There Lord Hoxley was waiting.

Lord Hoxley looked frightened as we pulled ourselves out of the water. For the longest time the air still chilled my body, and my muscles still didn't want to move, but I was just glad to be able to breathe air. We all stunk from the sewer like water that we had just been swimming in. But there didn't seem to be any time to think about any of that.

"Hurry… hurry," Lord Hoxley warned us. "When they learn of the deception they will have the hounds out after us all."

That fast we were off and moving again. We were dragged by Will and Kate to the far end of the castle. Hoxley told us to stay close to the walls so that the guards that watched from the guard post above would have trouble spotting us. When we all got there Hoxley looked about nervously, and pressed hard against a large stone in the wall. For the longest time he just pushed and pushed. Suddenly Will moved beside him to help move the stone. Then all at once a secret entrance opened, and we were going inside the castle walls one more time.

Chapter 11: The Secret Behind the Castle Wall

It had been like a magical entrance that had just appeared in the side of the castle wall. Through a darkened passageway lit only by torches we were lead along quickly. I was still breathing heavy, and trying to cough up the rest of the muddy water that I had drunk while being chased in the moat.

In a few minutes we came to a place that seemed to be hidden from the rest of the castle. Lord Hoxley could see that we were all still freezing, and handed us heavy cloth blankets to throw over ourselves. He turned, and then looked at Will and Kate. He smiled and rubbed them both on their heads.

"You have done well children. You have saved our friends from another time, and I shall see that you are both rewarded." Lord Hoxley then looked to me and Jimmy. "We have saved you my two young friends, but saving your mission that may be another matter indeed."

"What do you mean Lord Hoxley," said Jimmy through his chattering teeth, and I could see that he still hadn't gotten over his dip in the moat.

"Will has explained your plight to me boys, and it chills my heart to think what awaits the world if you do not complete the task set for you by Burkhardt the Great." The Professor would've loved that one.

For the first time that day I remembered my parents and my little pain in the neck sister, and the whole reason that we had been sent back in time to begin with.

"All we have to do is get the time belts and…" Jimmy started right in.

"Not so easily accomplished my young friend," said Lord Hoxley. "Sagamore believes, and now the King that the belts have great power. Your illusion in the moat will only make them more certain of the dark powers of your Professor's invention. They will be very heavily guarded."

"There must be a way," I said.

"Is your mission a true one," Will asked again, still not sure of us, and part of him still believing that we were working with the Devil.

"Will," Jimmy said, "we are boys, just like you. And we don't come from the Underworld we come from another time. That world will be gone forever if we don't get back to it."

Will turned sadly, and seemed to stare at the wall. He then spoke without looking at us. "I just want to know that I have not given up my soul to Lucifer…" He then turned quickly to Lord Hoxley. "Would that not place me in his power forever."

"What is wrong young Will," Lord Hoxley said, seeing that Will was really upset, and we could all see that there were tears in Will's eyes.

"What is it Will," Kate raced to his side and held him tightly. Will spoke as he fought back the tears.

"He saw me…"

"He," asked Lord Hoxley. His voice trembling as he spoke the words.

"Sir Sagamore, when my head went to the surface for just a bit. His eyes came fixed upon me, and now he believes me to be in league with the two of you, in league with Satan. For that deed it will be more than a whipping I'll be getting."

We were all quiet for the longest time, 'cause we all knew what that meant. Will if captured by Sagamore and his men would be sentenced to death. Will then crumbled weakly to the floor, and just sat there looking down to the ground.

"Oh my, this is terrible," said Lord Hoxley, and he was right. Even if me and Jimmy were able to escape back into the future, Will would be left here to be sentenced to the stake.

"Even if Sagamore realizes the deception," Lord Hoxley said, "Will shall be branded as a traitor, an enemy of the state."

"We have to think of something," said Jimmy.

"What can we do," I said.

Jimmy looked to Lord Hoxley, "where is this place that we're at right now?"

"A hidden chamber that I happened onto when I came upon the designs for the castle. Rather than share it, I decided to use it for my experiments. You see young one, science must always be hidden from the ignorant. It challenges reality, and makes them fear. And all creatures when frightened can be reduced to violence."

"Can Will hide here for a while," Jimmy asked.

"He could remain hidden forever," Lord Hoxley said.

"The rest of my days in this dark place," said Will. "It would be like living in the castle keep."

"My poor brother kept prisoner forever," Kate cried out.

"No," I have an idea," Jimmy said, and he always did. "But first we have to get our hands on the time belts."

"My world is ending," said Will, "and so..."

"Maybe not," Jimmy stopped him, "maybe not..."

"When you come to the end of a road," Will went on...

"Perhaps not," Lord Hoxley spoke quietly, "Young James thinks he has a plan."

"Plan or not," said Will. "If what you say is true, then it's the entire world that is in dire need of my assistance. What is one life..."

Kate cried more, and hugged him tighter, "No Will, no..." she said.

"Kate's right," said Jimmy, "the trick is to come out of this alive and kicking, and I do have an idea, but first we've got to get our hands on those time belts and on the schoolbag that Sir Sagamore stole from us."

"Schoolbag," Will looked confused.

"And what is your plan young Master James," said Lord Hoxley.

Jimmy smiled, and that cued me that this was going to be a good idea. "What is the weakest part in Sagamore's armor?"

Even Lord Hoxley looked strangely at Jimmy, not understanding where Jimmy was headed with all of this. I didn't either, but I pretended to understand exactly what was going on in Jimmy's head. That way I could at least look smart, and maybe take credit for some of it somewhere down the line. Then if it was a lousy idea, I could pretend to had nothing to do with it.

"It is his mind," said Jimmy. "His ignorance can be dangerous Lord Hoxley, that is quite true, but it can also be used to our advantage."

Now Lord Hoxley, in fact all of us were hanging on with each word. Jimmy knew how to capture an audience, I'll give him that. Then he went on: "I knew that if people thought that there could be a giant demon snake, then it wouldn't even have to look that real, their minds were filling in all the details. So a large piece of tubing became a giant serpent rising out of the moat. I say we use that same power to bring more demons to the castle. When we're done with Sagamore, he'll be begging us to take back the time belts. First we make us a ghost."

Everyone was up for the plan. Will looked upset for a long time, but soon got with the spirit of the thing.

"A ghost, you have such power," asked Kate.

"In a world where innocent people can be tried and burned as witches, in such a world a ghost seems a possibility," said Lord Hoxley.

"Exactly," said Jimmy. "They believed us to be witches, they believe the time belts to be magical charms, why not let them have their magic, why not give them all that they expect and more."

"And how shall we accomplish this great feat James," said Will.

"It's Jimmy," said Jimmy, "and we accomplish it by taking what they already believe in, and making it come true."

"Very exciting," said Lord Hoxley. "Sagamore is a fool, that can work greatly to our advantage."

"That will make this a whole lot easier," Jimmy told him, and then he stopped and thought for a minute. "Lord Hoxley, are there any other secret chambers in the castle?"

"No," Hoxley said sadly, "but there is a passage way…"

"That's where we play Hide and Seek," Will shouted excitedly.

"It's not a secret if everybody knows about it," I said.

"The secret passage is the only place that we can hide from the Prince," said Kate, "he is still perplexed by our sudden disappearances."

"That he is," said Will.

"And he doesn't ask where you go to," I said.

"The Prince, should know more than his servants," Kate answered.

"So he won't ask," Jimmy smiled, "because that would mean…"

"That we know something that he does not," Kate smiled back.

"And Will knows the passageway best," added Lord Hoxley.

"'Tis true," said Will, "I've escaped many a strapping by hiding in that passage until the anger at Prince John had passed.

"And where," said Jimmy, "would they take such a magical and wondrous thing as the time belts?"

"My guess," said Lord Hoxley, "is they would be taken to the tower."

"The tower," I said.

"The tower," is where the King keeps his most precious possessions. His gold, his jewels…"

"And the Queen," Will jumped in.

"He keeps his wife up there," said Jimmy.

"The Queen," said Lord Hoxley, "she's a bit of a troublemaker, if he didn't keep her locked away, he would have to lop off her head."

"Sounds like a nice guy," I said.

"When the Queen is let to roam free she invariably raises an Army to do battle with the King. Can hardly blame the poor fellow for locking her away," and Lord Hoxley almost sounded sad for King Henry.

"How easy is it to get into the tower," asked Jimmy.

"The tower is guarded quite heavily," said Lord Hoxley.

"It is death even to approach the tower," said Kate.

"Even for the Prince," said Jimmy.

"He hardly goes up to visit his Mom," said Will. "The only time he goes is when… is when…"

"When Prince John is playing Hide and Seek," Kate joined in excitedly.

"And when you're playing," asked Jimmy, "can you venture close to the tower."

"If we are chasing after the Prince," Will said.

"That could work," I jumped in.

"No… no," said Will, "Sagamore now believes me to be in league with Satan."

"The boy is quite right," said Lord Hoxley. "Will would now be the last one permitted to go into the tower."

Jimmy stopped for a long minute, and looked around at the darkened chamber. I could tell that his brain was racing a mile a minute. The plan was half way there, and he was just trying to add the final pieces to the puzzle. After a couple of seconds his eyes fell upon me, and I wasn't sure that I liked that too much.

"Then we'll just have to get Prince John to help us get to the tower."

"Are you daft," said Will.

"Prince John," said Hoxley, "is the cruelest child that the world has ever breathed life into."

"I seemed to remember him kicking the two of us into the moat," I said, 'cause now I really didn't know where Jimmy was headed with this plan. And Lord Hoxley had been right about the Prince being mean. Even the worst bullies back at my school would have untied your hands before kicking you into the water.

"Remember," Jimmy went on, "it's all about illusion. The ghost and demons are not going to be real, so why should Prince John."

We all just stopped for a long minute and just stared at Jimmy.

He turned quickly to Will. "When you're playing with the Prince, do the guards pay much attention to you?"

"They don't like to see him coming," said Will, "the Prince can be a bit of a thorn in their sides. This I know because the guards see that I'm punished good and proper for his transgressions."

141

Jimmy turned back to Lord Hoxley, "and how hard would it be to get hold of some of Prince John's clothes?"

"The Prince is perhaps the most bathless boy in the kingdom. He changes little, and smells like the compost heap. Yet aside from when he dresses for court, he dresses quite the same as young Will here."

Jimmy looked to me, and I knew right away what was going on in his head.

"Are you crazy," I said. I didn't really even have to ask, 'cause I already knew the answer.

"It's the only way to get to the time belts," he came right back at me.

"Why don't you do it," I yelled at him.

"What is this strange code, and how does one communicate with it," said Lord Hoxley curiously.

"He's reading his mind, he's reading his mind," Will shook nervously.

"No, no," Jimmy told him. "He's just being a baby".

"Then why don't you do it," I said again.

"Then how do you know what he's thinking," Will didn't want to leave it go.

"Tis puzzling," said Lord Hoxley.

"Cause this is how he thinks, and I know…" I tried to get out.

"No," Jimmy cut me off. "It's because you look more like Prince John," said Jimmy.

"Well you smell more like him…" It wasn't a great come back, but it was all that I could come up at that moment.

"You want young Shawn here to play act as the Prince," asked Lord Hoxley, "daring, quite daring." Lord Hoxley I guess was beginning to pick up on the strange code that Jimmy and I were speaking in. Actually we had known each other for so long that one guy didn't usually have to finish a sentence for the other to know what was going on inside his head.

True my hair was the same color as Prince Johns, or at least closer to it than Jimmy's, but... and that was a big but, I wasn't so sure that I was willing to be that "daring." How was I going to get all the way up to the tower, past guards, past the Queen, and fool them all?

"How am I going to get away with it," I said to Jimmy, "they'll take one look..."

"No they won't," he said. "They won't see you, because they don't want to see him."

"What", what the heck did that mean?

"Tis true," said Lord Hoxley. "That boy is one of the strongest irritants in the kingdom. He is tolerated only because he is the son of the King."

"Else wise, he would have been tied in a sack, and tossed into the moat years ago," said Kate.

"Smudge his face with dirt to enhance the illusion," Lord Hoxley said. "Prince John is a filthy, filthy boy."

"We could toss him in the pig droppings," Kate, was now adding to the game plan.

"Wait a second, I haven't agreed to any of this…" I was still trying to get my two cents in before they had me rolling around with the pigs to smell right for the part.

"If we have to die…" Will started to say.

"Let's try not to do that," Jimmy stopped him in his tracks.

"But it is for the future of mankind," Will came back at him. "We must take the risk." That fast Will had stopped asking if we were demons, and was going along with this crazy plan.

All that bravery from Will was making me look really bad. Okay, now they were trying to shame me into it. It was usually Jimmy by himself using that tactic, but now he was double-teaming me with Will. I knew what they were all saying was true. Somewhere in the future the whole planet was about to be destroyed by a giant comet crashing into the Earth, and somewhere in the future it had already been destroyed. So I knew what had to be done. I guess I had just wanted a few minutes to get over being dunked in the moat before going off on another crazy mission that there was little chance of coming back from alive. So I took a deep breath, and looked over to Will. Our showing up in merry old England had definitely put a big dent into his life, but he was willing to go on and try and save the world, a world that he had never known. But most importantly he was around the same size as me.

"How'd you like to wear some real witches clothes," I said to Will.

"I'd be honored," he said.

We went into the corner, and started to change our clothes. Today I was going to become the Prince of the Kingdom, and I had to hope that the real Prince would not show up, and what Lord Hoxley had said was true. I had to hope that Prince John was so irritating that people just tried to stay out of his way when they smelled him coming.

Chapter 12: Hide and Seek in the Tower of Death

After we had changed clothes, both me and Will looked at each other. He looked so strange in my clothes, and I guess I looked just as strange in his. Staring down at himself in his "witches garb" he started to laugh, and I was glad that he could laugh about it. Earlier that day he had been worried about keeping his soul out of Satan's hands, and now he was wearing stuff that everybody back then thought had been hand sewn by the Devil himself.

"It is a tight fit," he said about the shorts. I guess everything that they wore back in those days was baggy and loose, except for the knights who walked around in tin suits all day. I bet being stuck in a metal suit was real comfortable on a hot summer day. Both me and Will still reeked from the stench of the moat, so I guess there wouldn't be any need for me to go rolling around in pig droppings to smell more like the Prince.

Kate rubbed her hands in some dirt that made up the floor of this dark and smelly chamber in the castle. Real quick like she ran over, and began rubbing it on my face.

"What are you doing," I yelled at her.

She looked at me angrily, "if you're going to be play acting the part of the Prince, then you best be looking like him." And that fast she slapped more dirt onto my cheeks.

"Ow," I yelled as she pressed the dirt that felt like it was mixed with tiny rocks into my face. "Like I'm not dirty enough."

"Don't be acting like a baby," Kate said as pushed more of that junk onto my face.

"She's right," said Jimmy.

"You're really enjoying this," I looked at him while Kate kept pushing more dirt in to my face and hair. I could tell that Jimmy wanted to laugh, but for the sake of the mission, he wasn't gonna bust on me until it was over. There was still a chance that I might back out, and that was one chance that he didn't want to take. Think I was getting more respect as a witch.

"The girl is right," said Lord Hoxley, "his Highness is a filthy, filthy boy."

"And think of it," Jimmy added, "the less people see of you, the more easy it will be to fool them."

"He is a brazen lad too, remember that" said Lord Hoxley. "He acts as if he owns the castle, and of course he will some day, but not yet."

"He treats everyone like they be dogs," said Kate. "And not like dogs that he be fond of…"

"And if a guard has his back to you," said Will, "give him the boot."

"What," I wasn't sure I had heard him right.

"Give him the boot right on the backside," Will told me again.

"The Prince is the only one that can get away with it," said Kate.

"And so he does," Will went on. "And move quickly, the Prince always be running…"

"Runs everywhere," said Lord Hoxley," he acts as if the world was his playground, for indeed it is. It is a sad thing the way the King spoils that boy."

The part of Prince John seemed like a pretty easy part to play. All I had to do was to get dirty, smell bad, and act like a jerk. Got to thinking that it might actually be kinda fun.

"And as for the Queen," Lord Hoxley went on, "she's the most dangerous of the lot. She will slice you to the quick if she gets wind of the goings on. And the Queen is not all too fond of the young Prince. So she may not take your side, even if momentarily fooled by your guise. She's got a lot of rage in her, that one." He turned to Jimmy, "being locked in the tower for years on end can do that to a disposition."

Things just kept sounding better and better. Not only were Sir Sagamore and his guards out to kill me, I had to watch out for the Prince's psycho mom, who was locked in the tower along with the time belts.

"Now how do we get Shawn to the tower," Jimmy asked.

"He can take the secret passageway almost to the top of the castle, but once there he shall run into the guards," said Lord Hoxley.

Jimmy turned to me, and said real serious like, "when you get in there, you must get not only the time belts, but the schoolbag."

"I know, I know," I said.

"The bag has the explosives," he said.

"The what," Lord Hoxley looked at him real curious like. For an older guy he was like a little kid when it came to science and stuff.

"We're in the twelfth century, right," said Jimmy.

"Of that I am quite certain," said Lord Hoxley.

"Then you won't have come across black powder, for at least another century," Jimmy told him.

"Black powder," Lord Hoxley was still looking at Jimmy with wide eyes, and dying to know what he was talking about.

"Black powder," Will all the sudden got upset, "you are in league with the Devil," he began to cry, and tear at my shorts as if he were trying to rip them off.

"Woo dude," I yelled at him, "those are my good pants, my Mom will kill me if..."

"They want to get the black powder so they can perform their evil on..." Will was yelling. That fast he had gone back to thinking we were buddies with the Devil.

"No, that's not true..." Jimmy started to say.

"Casting their black powder first to enchant the sheep..." Will was going nuts. Again with the sheep, what was it with these people and sheep?

"Silence Will," Lord Hoxley demanded. "The only witches that live, live inside of your head, we must stop existing in fear, so that we can go on. If not then you shall be trapped in that same world of darkness and ignorance that plagues the rest of humanity."

Will still didn't look like he was buying it, so Jimmy came face to face with him. He put his hand on Will's shoulder. "Will," he said, "I know from the history books that black powder was invented in China..."

"China," Lord Hoxley looked curious like at Jimmy.

149

"It's a country you guys probably haven't heard about yet," Jimmy told him.

"Fascinating," said Lord Hoxley.

"Well anyway long before this part of the world ever gets to see black powder, the people of China have it. It's not magic, it's not made by the Devil, its a mixture of chemicals that can make things blow up."

"Blow up," Will looked at Jimmy, not quite understanding, and backing himself tighter to the wall.

"This is intriguing," said Lord Hoxley.

"Black powder can be a powerful weapon, or it can be a way to make people who don't know about it believe that we do have magical powers, which we don't." He looked right at Will when he said that. "Now without you, none of this will be possible, without you, your sister, and Lord Hoxley, Shawn and me would probably be dead right now, and the world will be destroyed in around nine hundred years. See, I know that all this is strange to you, and you have every right to be skeptical…"

"Skeptical," Will looked nervously at Jimmy.

"Unsure of us," said Jimmy. "I know I would be, but I am asking you… No, I am begging you to trust us. Everything in the world that we know and love will be gone forever if you don't."

Will looked down at the shorts he was wearing, and then he looked back at us. "But if I give aid to the Master of the Underworld, then my soul will be lost forever, and perhaps I will be doomed to wear this strange garb for all eternity."

I couldn't help it, I started laughing. I mean think about it, the whole world was falling in on this kid, and he's worried about fashion, and being trapped in my shorts forever and ever. Will looked at me, and then he started in to laughing too. Soon they were all caught up in the moment, and for one minute we were able to forget about the end of the world, and the deadly mission ahead of us.

"Will," laughed Lord Hoxley, "you are a loon lad, truly a loon."

Kate came close to Will, she held him tightly, "I believe them Will. I think this tale too incredible to be a falsehood."

"Then I guess I believe so too," he said, but he still didn't sound too sure.

"Then we should move quickly," Lord Hoxley announced out loudly, like the idea had just popped into his head. We all turned kinda startled. "Whilst the Prince is still occupied with the festivities of the day."

"That's right," Jimmy said, "we can't have two Prince John's running around the tower."

"Won't the guards know that he's supposed to be somewhere else," I said, "because that's what I would think."

"The guards in the tower are soldiers, all they know are orders, when the young Prince runs through they will jump to command. The Prince is the King's favorite son, it puzzles me to know for what reason; so they will want to keep in the boy's favor. It is my guess that they will not stop to question."

"I hope your guessing right Lord Hoxley, if not..." I started to say.

"If not," Jimmy finished my sentence, "we can't think that way, just run through like they're not even there, because that's what Prince John would do."

"But once in the tower, I won't know where I'm going, or what..."

"I'll be going with him," Kate jumped in.

"No," Will shouted.

"And why not Will," she came back at him. "I know the tower as well as any of you, am I not the one who aids the chamber maids in their duties to the Queen."

"Kate," Will looked her right in the eye, "there's no need for this to fall on your head. Sagamore and his men, they know not of your entanglement with this affair."

"Then I should be safe..."

"But..."

"You listen to me Will," she was coming back at him with fire in her eyes. I didn't think he had much of a chance of winning this battle. "Just because you go off saving the world, doesn't mean that you can be bossing me around like you be the Prince."

"It's just that I want to keep you safe..."

"The worlds going to be destroyed Will, if we don't do this thing, the world is going to be gone, forever. I for one can't be running around with that over my head, now can I?" It didn't look like Will had any come back for her, and then all at once the strangest thing happened, Kate began to take control of the whole mission. "Now here's what we'll be doing. I'll run to the tower first. We often play hide and go seek near to that end of the castle. There is a dark corridor that comes right before it. When the guards see me they won't be surprised when his Royal Highness comes running after like a hound to the chase."

Yeah, Kate was taking over, and no one was trying to stop her. Usually Jimmy would've gotten upset, 'cause he likes to be the one running things, but her ideas seemed good, so he just went along for the ride.

"It's only when you reach the hallway leading to the Queen's nest," said Lord Hoxley, "that the guards will be a problem. Their job is to keep intruders out, and more importantly keep the Queen locked in, a terrible, terrible woman."

"Then what," I said.

"Then," said Jimmy, "we bring out the big guns. That's when the ghost of the castle comes out to play."

"The ghost of the castle," Will looked terrified once more.

"Not a real ghost," Jimmy tried to calm him down.

"Stop being such a twit Will, the boy already explained..." Kate yelled at him. At that moment I was so glad she wasn't my sister.

"Exactly," Jimmy went on, "it would be a ghost made by us. I mean everyone here seems so determined to see magic, all we've got to do is give it to them."

So that's how it was set up. Me and Kate were going to go playing hide and seek near to the tower, and Jimmy had come up with the rest.

The passageway that leads to the tower was dark and dusty just like mostly everything else that we had seen in the twelfth century. And I could believe that it hadn't had a good cleaning in years. This was where the King lived, you think they could've hired a housekeeper to vacuum or sweep up. We were all being very quiet as we tiptoed along behind the stonewalls of the old castle. We had only a single torch to guide the way. Will and Lord Hoxley had come along just to help with Jimmy's plan. It was all going to be a group effort. In fact it had to be.

From behind those walls we could hear other things going on in the castle. The sound seemed to echo right through the stone, and bounce around inside the passageway, so we knew to keep our voices low, and to whisper as we moved quietly along.

Before leaving the hidden chamber, Lord Hoxley had given Jimmy a large wool blanket that was going to be the body of our ghost.

"But it doesn't look like a ghost," said Will.

"And what does a ghost look like Will, you mutton-head," said Kate. She was tough.

"Well I suspect…" Will tried to get out.

Jimmy cut them off, "they'll be too busy running to stop and take a second look." Then Jimmy threw the dirty old blanket over himself, and raised his arms into the air. Maybe it was because I knew it was Jimmy, but it just wasn't scary.

"Sorry dude," I said, "but that sucks."

He started to get angry, and then he stopped himself. "Maybe you're right Shawn, we've got to plant a few seeds first."

We had reached the end of the secret passageway, and it was time to go out and face the guards who stood watch over the tower.

I was so scared, and Kate looked scared. She was trying to act like she was tough, but I could tell that she was just as afraid as me. It was Lord Hoxley who edged out of the hidden entrance, and dared to look around first. As he pressed against a stone in the wall, the rest of it started to push out letting a dim and flickering light from outside in. It was that single torch hanging off of the wall that let us see to the outside. There was nobody standing nearby, so then me and Kate slipped out of the opening. Jimmy had planned it all out, and all we had to do was go through the actions.

Both me and Kate edged along the corridor until we came to the stairway leading up to the tower. At the top of the steps were two guards leaning against the wall. They looked pretty tired from just standing there all day. It was kinda dark in there, and there was just the light from a dying torch to show us the way. Me and Kate looked at each other, 'cause we didn't want to make any sounds, not just yet anyway. With a nod of our heads we knew that it was time to go into action. Still we waited. Neither of us really wanted to go running up those steps, but what else could we do?

All at once Kate let loose with a loud scream. I knew it was coming, and it still scared the heck out of me. Then she shot up those stairs. The guards, they too were caught by surprise. They jumped and drew their swords. I was watching from behind the wall, and could see that they relaxed when they saw that it was only Kate running towards them.

"Are you daft girl," the guard called to Kate.

She stopped at the top of the steps, and hid behind one of the guards. "He's after me, he's after me," she said.

The guard looked with squinted eyes down into the long, dark corridor at the bottom of the steps.

"Who is it girl, who would it be chasing after you," he said.

I took another deep breath, and began my own rush up the stairs.

"You best not be playing your games in the tower..." the one guard had started to say, and was cut off by my sudden arrival.

At the top of the steps I could see that the guards were still blocking the way, so I did what I thought Prince John would've done, I yelled at them: "Out of my way dogs," I called to them, and my voice sounded kinda cool as it bounced off the castle walls. In fact it didn't really seem to sound like me.

"Your Highness," one of them said, as he seemed to stumble backwards.

That made an opening for Kate to skate on by them, and so she ran further towards the door to the tower.

By the time I had gotten to the top of the stairs the guards had backed up all the way to the wall like they were now standing at attention. I didn't want to say too much. I thought that they might realize that I really didn't sound like the Prince. So I just turned and pointed. They both looked to the bottom of the steps.

"Your Highness," one of the men said.

I didn't want to say another word, but I had to plant the seed like Jimmy had told me to. "Stop him," I screamed, "stop the ghost."

"Ghost," the guard seemed startled. And right then they were too busy looking for a ghost to even notice that I didn't really sound too much like Prince John. And I guess my voice bouncing off the walls made it hard to tell. It was then that Kate remembered that she was supposed to work with me. She ran back to my side.

"The witches from the field they have brought spirits with them, spirits from the Underworld, spirits of the dead," she cried out. She was acting really good.

"Even Sagamore the Mighty is powerless to stop these hideous apparitions," cried out one of the guards.

At that moment, Jimmy appeared at the bottom of the stairs covered with the blanket, and howled like a wolf. Don't ask me where that came from, but that's right, he howled like a wolf. The guards backed away from the sight of the dirty blanket sending clouds of dust into the air as Jimmy shook it from the inside. For a moment they seemed frozen by what they saw, which was actually a boy wrapped in a dirty blanket. Then Jimmy ducked behind the wall, and seemed to disappear.

"Seize the spirit," I ordered the guards, remembering that I was suppose to be mean and kinda pushy, but they didn't take their eyes off of the place where our fake ghost had stood only a few seconds before.

"Did you not hear the Prince," Kate joined in.

"But what can we do against a spirit reaching out of the grave your Highness," the one guard came back.

All of the sudden one of the guards grabbed a spear that had been lying against the wall, and prepared to throw it at Jimmy when he reappeared again. All I could think he's gonna kill Jimmy.

"He disappears at will, we should stay here and… and protect you, your Highness," said the others. "Yes, that is what the King

157

would want." And all this meant to me was that they were too chicken to go down those stairs. Jimmy was right; they had seen only what their imaginations had created for them.

Guessing Jimmy didn't know about the spear, so he didn't wait much longer before he jumped out from behind the wall again, and began to howl like a wolf all over. I wasn't sure that a wolf call was exactly the kinda noise a ghost would be making, but it didn't seem to stop these guys from being really scared. The guard got ready to throw the spear again. I was so scared he was gonna kill Jimmy with that thing, that as he was throwing it I kicked him in the butt 'cause I figured that's what Prince John would do. The spear hit the wall but still almost hit Jimmy as it flew by his head.

"Get down there you cowardly dog," and at this point they were both too afraid to care that I didn't sound too much like the Prince. The guards drew their swords, and Jimmy began to climb up the steps. He was howling all the way, flapping his arms, and sending more dust from the blanket into the air. In that shadowy stairway, it looked like there was smoke coming off of him.

"With him he brings the fires of Hades", cried one of the guards. Guess he was talking about all the dust. We shall be consumed by the flames," cried out the other guard as they both began to retreat towards the large heavy door that was the entrance to the Queens chamber in the tower.

"We must protect the Queen," one of the guards said as he raced to get to the other side of that door almost knocking Kate down the stairs. Me and Kate ran with them as Jimmy wrapped in the blanket continued walking our way. At the top of the steps, the lights

158

coming from the torch hit on Jimmy's shadow, and made it seem like it was growing bigger and bigger. It was actually pretty creepy to see, and I knew that it was only a shadow. Quickly the one guard pulled out a set of large keys, and began to unlock the door. I could tell that he was scared, 'cause he fumbled several times before getting the key into the keyhole. Suddenly the door swung open, and we were going inside. Kate and I were now in the tower with the time belts, the guards, and the psycho Queen that had been locked in there for starting wars against the King. Yes, we were in terrible danger, and that's how I knew that everything was going exactly on schedule.

Art Design For The King's Knights.

Chapter 13: How the Psycho Queen Met the Demon from the Underworld, and How Much Fun That Was

Yes we were finally inside, inside the tower. And Jimmy had been right, no one had bothered to take a second look at me while they thought a ghost was chasing them, but now we were inside the actual chamber where they kept the Queen locked up. It was my guess that the Queen might take a better look at the boy who was supposed to be her son, so we had to move fast. First of all the lighting in that chamber was much brighter than in the hallway outside. There were more torches, lots of candles, and even an opening in the wall. I guess that was their idea of a window. And it worked 'cause all the daylight was just pouring in, and making me feel really uncomfortable. The Queen didn't seem to mind the cold that was blowing in through that hole in the wall. The burning logs in the fireplace must've given her enough heat, so that she didn't mind the wintry wind that was blasting through the tower. Guess'n that hole in the wall was the only way she could see the world outside.

The Queen and one of her servants came rushing to the door to see what all the noise was about. As for the two guards, they hadn't taken their eyes off of the door, fearing that any second that howling ghost might come walking right on through it.

"Who dares to disturb the tranquility of the Queen," the Queen screamed as she came closer, and she had that psycho glare in her eyes that let you know right away that she was definitely the one that was always going to war with her husband the King. And those guards must've felt it too 'cause they backed themselves to the wall like puppy dogs as she got closer to them.

"The tower has been invaded by an abominable ghost your Majesty," said one of the guards, and you could hear his voice shake like he was just as afraid of her as he was the ghost.

"A ghost," said the Queen, who sounded like she wasn't actually buying that story.

"A monstrous specter unleashed from the fiery pits of the Underworld by the demons from the Field of Death," said the other, "and it stood the size of giant oak."

"The size of a giant oak," said the Queen, "and it stands within the castle walls?" Yeah, she really wasn't buying a word of that story.

It was then that Jimmy's wolf call came echoing through the door that led to the corridor outside. She stopped for a minute frozen in her tracks. In all of the commotion she still hadn't stopped to look at me, which was a good thing. With everything going on around me I started looking for the time belts. The tower was quite large, and there was even a second chamber that I couldn't see into. I nodded to Kate to see if she could slip off and check it out.

The Queen started to move towards the door. "Ghost brought by the demons," she said.

"Yes your Majesty," said one of the guards.

"They are in alliance with Lucifer himself," the other almost cried.

"And what hideous creatures they be," the first guard came back.

Then there was a loud banging on the door. The sound of the knocking echoed all over the tower. She turned real angry like back to the guards, "and you have brought this specter of doom to my doorstep," she screamed.

"But we were only trying to protect the young Prince," the guard defended himself. Trying to protect, right, they almost trampled over me and Kate running for safety.

That's when the Queen turned and looked at me, and there was nothing I could do, but stand there. The truth is that this was really the first time any of them had stopped to look at me.

The Queen stared in disbelief, and seemed to be looking right through me.

"It is the demon from the field," cried one of the guards, and you could tell that he was terrified by the sight of me standing right in front of him.

"I see this is all part of a plot," said the Queen. "Has this revolting creature promised you the Kingdom for your betrayal?"

"No, your Majesty," one guard begged, "a moment ago he looked to be the Prince."

"He weaves his magic to trick the eyes of we mortals," the other one almost cried.

I still didn't know what to do, I was still scanning the place for the time belts and the schoolbag, but still I couldn't see any of it. Then all of the sudden Kate joined in with the guards, and I wasn't sure what she was trying to do.

"'Tis true your Majesty," said Kate, "he transfigured into this ghastly beast as we entered into your lair."

Beast, I thought. I wasn't exactly the best looking kid in school or nothing, but my Mom never had to take me out with a sack over my head. I mean my ears might have been a little big, but a beast.

"The beast has the power to take many forms your Majesty," cried the chambermaid. Now even she was an expert.

With everybody calling me an ugly beast I might have gotten a hang up over my looks, but there was no time to think about that now. I thought that all this might've scared the Queen too, but no, suddenly she pulled out a dagger from underneath her robes, and moved towards me. The psycho Queen had come ready to rumble.

"What have you done with the Royal Prince," she screamed. This woman did a lot of screaming. "Johnny's a venomous bag of stench, but he is of my blood, royal blood! Kill the beast," she ordered. And that's when the guards turned their swords on to me. The guards were scared, but they were still coming.

I began backing away as fast as I could as they moved closer with their weapons drawn. Jimmy's plan had worked real good up until just a minute before, but now I was in serious trouble. Still I didn't see any sign of the time belts or Jimmy's schoolbag. At first the guards were slow to come chasing after, still believing that I was a demon with magical powers, but the psycho Queen kept ordering them to cut me down like a dog, and chop me to bits. None of this was part of Jimmy's strategy, I'm sure. I raced to the far end of the chamber looking for the time belts and the schoolbag. Mostly I was just trying to get out of the way of the swords that were now hacking and cutting through the air all around me. Lucky for me the guards still didn't want to get too close. Still I couldn't find any of what I was looking for. In the meantime Kate had just seemed to disappear. Some help she was turning out to be.

With the Queen not slowing down in her attack, the guards felt that they should try and get a little closer. Guess it wouldn't look good if the Queen was the only one going after this demon. There was some stuff on a nearby table, and so I just started pitching it at the guards. They backed up a little, but only for a second. I guess they figured if that was my best magic, they didn't have to be too scared. In no time they were right on top of me with their swords raised. With his blade high over my head, the one guard called out; "may providence guide my hand as I cut down this accursed creature from the bottomless pit." And just then, just before he could bring the sword crashing down on my head, there was another loud thumping at the door, and Jimmy's wolf call came howling into the room.

"Waste not of time," yelled the Queen, "take the jackal's head."

The guard turned quickly back to me at the same exact second Kate came running out of the other chamber. In her hands were the schoolbag and the time belts.

"Take what you need demon," Kate cried out, "and leave this place in peace". It looked like she tossed the schoolbag to me, but it hit the guard on the shoulder knocking his arm as he came slashing down with the sword just missing my head. I kinda think she had hit him on purpose. But before he could swing again, I dived to the floor, and grabbed the schoolbag.

"What are you doing you foolish girl," cried out the Queen.

"His magic is great," Kate cried out, "His power could destroy us all, destroy the empire." Kate was laying it on a bit thick, but I liked it, and it made me sound kinda cool.

"The beast power lies in those trinkets that he brings from the nether world, my Queen," said one of the guards.

"You foolish girl," cried out the Queen as she threw the dagger, just missing me. I was doing a lot of dodging and rolling that day. It was like playing football; only I was going to lose more than just a game if I got hit.

"Out of my way you cowardly dogs, I shall smite this monstrous ogre myself," the Queen cried out as she reached down and scooped up the dagger before charging towards me. When he saw the psycho Queen coming in my direction even the guard moved out of the way.

"Be cautious my Queen," yelled one of the guards as he dodged out of this crazy ladies way.

I wasn't taking my time right then, I had reached into the bag, and was searching for some of the stuff that Jimmy had told me should be in there. It was secret weapon kinda stuff that Jimmy had cooked up in his lab, well actually his basement back home. I was only hoping that Sagamore and his gang hadn't taken any of those things away with them. In only seconds the Queen was standing over me, and went to kick me. Quick as I could I rolled out of the way, and she almost slipped to the floor, and dropped the dagger, but that didn't stop her, she just kept coming, and trying to stomp on me like I was a bug under her foot.

"Die you hideous creature, die," she screeched as she continued to chase after me.

As quick as I would move out of the way she'd run right after me and attack again. It was really hard searching through that old schoolbag, and dodging the psycho Queen all at same time. After a minute of some non-stop attacking, she stooped down real quick like, and picked her dagger up off of the floor. She was such a mad lady, that the guards were just trying to keep out of her way. Now with the dagger back in her hand she began trying to stick me with it on the floor. Where were those exploding darts, and all the other junk that Jimmy had packed away just for this trip? They were his own invention, and had come in handy before, that is when they worked, 'cause to be honest they didn't always work. And all of the sudden I had found one. In fact it had stuck me in my hand as I was groping around inside of the bag. I cried out, "darn," 'cause it had really hurt. While I was doing all that moving around and searching Kate had ran to the chamber door and started opening it.

"Help you fools," the Queen screamed at the guards who were just trying to not get too close to the action. All at once they seemed to get their courage back, but were still staying a little behind the Queen.

"What are you doing foolish girl," cried out the chambermaid.

"She'll let in the ghost," one of the guards shouted out terrified. Then he turned away from me, and began to run after Kate. He now had his sword raised up high ready to slice her to bits. She reached the door, and was trying to fiddle with the lock, but it was old and rusty just like everything else in this place, and just didn't want to turn.

"She must be in league with the demons," cried out the Queen.

Kate quick like moved out of the way as the guard's sword swung down almost taking her head off. Wow she was quick. Now I had the exploding dart in my hand, rolling out of the way I was able to jump to my feet, and faced off with the Queen. She seemed to slow down in her tracks at the sight of that dart raised into the air.

"What manner of weaponry is this you vile fiend," her voice screeched out loudly.

My brain was racing a mile a minute looking for the right answer, the right words that would stop her murderous attack. Still she and one of the guards circled, and all the while they were moving around me, the guard at the other end of the chamber was chasing after Kate. Now we were both dodging death, and trying just to stay alive.

I knew if Jimmy had been there he could've come up with something good to say, and so I tried to think like he would. I knew that I had seen enough horror and monster movies to make up something, but they all seemed to be out of my brain right then and there. Still my mind kept racing in circles looking for the right thing, and then it hit me. I stopped and looked the Queen right in the eye, 'cause I said to myself that's what a demon would do. At least that's what they always did in the movies. I remembered how the whole crowd had stopped and backed away when I shouted at them by the moat. So I made my voice loud, and screamed right at the Queen. What was really neat was that my voice came booming out and bounced off of those old stonewalls making it sound kinda eerie in there too.

"It is by the might of Lucifer that I have come to seal your fate." Now to tell the truth, I didn't know where that all come from, I guess I must've seen it on television or something, and it sounded corny enough that they all just seemed to buy it. Anyway I was probably watching too many bad movies. Even the guard that was chasing Kate around the chamber stopped in his tracks. And Jimmy too, he had stopped his howling outside of the door, wondering what was going on, I guess. It was then that I threw the dart to the floor, but nothing. And the fact that it didn't explode didn't seem to make any difference to these people; they all still seemed scared of me.

"What strange powers do you possess," said the Queen staring back right into my eyes.

"It is true your Majesty, the stories have already reached our ears of the giant serpent that has risen out of the moat to rescue this young monster," said the guard near to Kate.

"The powers of darkness are at his beck and call my Queen," said the other.

Still she looked as if she didn't really believe any of it. "Then," she said coldly, "we must stop this evil here, before it spreads to the rest of the kingdom, for the kingdom," she shouted out loud, and with these words she took another step forward with the dagger.

"No," screamed Kate.

The Queen had turned for just a second to look at Kate when she turned back she accidentally stepped on the dart. It was then that it exploded. It wasn't a big explosion, kinda like a firecracker going

169

off, but it was just big enough to make them all jump back away from this big, bad demon who had just came onto their turf.

"My Queen," said the guard nearest to us, "his powers are far beyond that of we mere mortals."

"Attack you cowards," cried out the Queen, "attack before he transforms back into his demon form."

Real scared like the guards and the Queen began to surround me. Now I really had to find another one of Jimmy's exploding darts, and one that worked right off the bat.

While they were all watching me, the chambermaid was crying in the corner, and Kate took another shot at opening the door. I ran as fast as I could to make some distance between the Queen, the guards, and myself. All the time my hand was digging into the schoolbag looking for another dart. Problem was that Jimmy had packed so much junk, and I was finding everything but what I was looking for.

Everyone was distracted for a second when the crying chambermaid called out, and told them that Kate was trying to open the door again.

"The ghost," the chambermaid cried out, "she's going to let in the specter of death."

Only the Queens head turned, and she announced to the guard closest to the door, "slay the traitorous witch."

That was one off of me, but now he was headed to the door to carve up Kate. I had to think of something, and all I could think of was: "Whoop-de-do." Yeah, that's what I came up with, and it seemed to slow them down once more, so I said it again real loud:

"Whoop-de-do." And I only remembered that because it was something my Father would say when he was making fun of something me or my Mother was telling him

"What strange incantation is this," ordered the Queen, like she even had the power to boss us demons around.

And that's when I felt another sting in my hand, and knew that I had come across a second dart. I raised it quickly out of the bag, and held it as high as I could into the air.

"It is the chant of the demon," said one of the guards.

"This one holds sway with his master in Hell, my Queen," the chambermaid guessed.

"Or perhaps a call to his demon brother," cried out one of the guards.

With this distraction, Kate tugged as hard as she could on the door and opened it. Jimmy came through the door, still covered in his dusty blanket and howling. They all seemed plenty scared, so maybe ghosts did sound like wolves.

"Retreat," screamed one of the guards, "it is the spirit of "Whoop-de-do!"

It was now the guards who backed against the wall, and huddled next to the chambermaid.

The Queen turned angrily on them, "if we fail to stop this Whoop-de-do here, then all hope is lost." So I could tell right away that she wasn't backing off. I dodged around her, and scooped up the time belts along the way. She turned right after me, and was coming on quick. Jimmy flapped his arms in the air and howled again. Some of the dust flying off of that old cloth must've gotten into his throat, 'cause he started coughing like a madman. I think that's what gave us away.

"This demon has the consumption," said the Queen, and she was real angry like as she ran over, and pulled the blanket off of Jimmy. He was still choking on dust, and couldn't move too fast. That's when she grabbed him around the neck, and put the blade of the dagger to his throat. Now that wasn't good.

"This, Whoop-de-do is no demon at all," said the Queen.

"But we have seen his power my Queen," said one of the guards still pressed against the wall.

"But now he has taken his mortal form, and that is when we must strike at this evil. Against a demon we are powerless, but in his corporeal form…" the Queen said.

"Their power can be vanquished only by the flames," one of the guards finished her sentence.

I could tell that Jimmy was having a tough time catching his breath. The Queen seemed to have the knife pressed pretty tight against his neck, and I even saw a trickle of blood drip down onto his shirt.

"We shall leave the kingdom in peace," Jimmy tried to talk to her.

Now the guards were moving closer while the psycho Queen kept her grip on Jimmy.

"They are all conspirators against the kingdom," she looked at Kate, "the girl too."

The guard closest to Kate ran over, and grabbed hold of her. Now the only one not being held was me, but I still had the dart in my

172

hand and didn't know what to do. If I threw it and it went off, the Queen might cut Jimmy, and if I didn't use it, they would probably take us all prisoners again. I remembered the words of Lord Hoxley, I remembered him telling us that if the first escape plan didn't work, that there wouldn't be another chance. So I guess that left it all up to me. I looked into Jimmy's eyes that seemed to be tearing up as he was being held by the Queen. I could tell that she was really hurting him.

Not having any idea in my own head what to do, I decided to borrow from old movies again. I turned to the guard holding Kate. Once again I let my voice boom, and it was easy in that room, everything sounded like it was from another world. "Abracadabra, hocus, pocus, whose soul shall I steal for my Master," I thought that any good demon should be able to steal a soul; at least I was hoping that they would believe it. I knew better than to try and trick the Queen. She was good and ready to go to battle with the Devil himself if he showed his face in that tower.

"My Queen, he is going to steal my soul," cried out the guard.

"You have sworn your life for the King," she screamed back at him, "and your life should pay the forfeit..."

"But my soul your Majesty, my soul..."

"It shall be the main course for my Master's dinner," I growled like an angry monster, and I really didn't know where that all came from, but it sounded kinda cool, and Jimmy joined in trying to squeeze off a few words past the Queens grip on him.

"The fresh souls are baked over an open fire, and served up with pinto beans and rice," Jimmy said.

"Silence demon," the Queen ordered him, she sure was bossy. All of these royal people seemed to be so rude.

"My soul… my soul," cried the guard. "If I arrive at eternity's gates without a soul…"

"And you too fool, silence" she said, and then looked down at the trickle of blood on Jimmy's shirt. "This demon bleeds, I dare say so should the other one." Darn, she was tough.

"Bleed, hence it can die! Destroy the beasts before they turn back…" screamed out the one guard.

The plan really wasn't going good at all. The Queen had a knife to Jimmy's throat, one of the guards had grabbed hold of Kate, and the other was now coming after me. It was starting to look like going to the tower of death wasn't such a good idea after all.

Chapter 14: Just When Things Couldn't Get Any Worst, How They Did

I had my hands on the time belts, and was still the only one who wasn't being held. Jimmy looked right at me, and I could tell that he was dead serious.

"Whatever you do Shawn, you have to get back to three days before…"

"Silence," the Queen pressed the knife tighter to his throat, but Jimmy would not shut up. I could tell that he was still scared, but he thought me getting out of there with the time belts was even more important than his life.

"It doesn't matter what they do to me," Jimmy went on, "you know what's really important."

"But…" I tried get out.

"No buts," he yelled at me, "I'd leave you."

"You would," and I was kinda surprised that he had said that.

"In a nanosecond," he said. "Now get the heck out of here!"

"Silence you vile creature," the Queen screamed out again.

He was talking about me getting back to the time we came from, to our town, and stopping the comet from smashing into the Earth. But I wasn't sure I could do it without him, I knew I really didn't want to try. The truth is that I wasn't sure even Jimmy could figure out how to get the belts working good. But Jimmy was right, the time belts were the only chance of getting to the Gravity Box, and the world had of surviving the comet, and I guess that was more important than either of us.

"Get out of here," Jimmy yelled at me.

"I said silence," the Queen screamed at him again. She was not changing her tune. She held the knife even tighter to Jimmy's neck, and he cried out with pain.

The guard was closing in on me, and I knew what I had to do. I looked Jimmy right in the eye, and to be honest I thought that that was going to be the last time I ever saw him. Right away I threw the dart at the floor in front of the guard coming after me. I threw it really hard and this time it exploded when it was supposed to. The shock of the explosion bought me just enough time to dodge around him and head towards the door.

"Do not let him escape with the amulets you fool," darn the Queen was loud.

The guard holding Kate released her, and was now trying to block me from getting out of the tower. As he moved away from her, she tripped him with her foot, and he fell to the floor. As he hit the floor he reached out for my leg.

"This foul beast must be cut down," the Queen ordered.

As the guard grabbed hold of my ankle, I swung down with the schoolbag smacking him right on the top of his helmet. I could hear the clang of metal hitting against the floor. He cried out in pain. I was almost at the door when another surprise hit me right in the face. Prince John came racing into the chamber.

"Mommy, you missed my birthday celebration, there were demons and a giant serpent..." he called out as he came running in bumping right into me. "Out of my way pig," he said before even getting a good look at me. I mean this kid was really rude, with what my Dad would call social issues.

I didn't have time to waste, what with the world going to be destroyed, and the guard about to cut off my head. So I spun Prince John out of the way, and tossed him right over the fallen guard, and into the Queen who was still holding tight to Jimmy. With the Queen distracted Jimmy grabbed hold of her knife hand, and dropped down under her arm. This all happened just as the Prince came bouncing into her, almost getting stuck with the dagger himself. Jimmy crawled out of the way, and now he was free.

"You little cretin," the Queen screamed at the Prince as she pushed him away and kicked him in the butt.

Jimmy was quick to pick up the dirty blanket off of the floor, swung it, and smacked the Queen right in the face with it. It made its own little dust storm, and now it was the Queen and the Prince coughing their brains out.

"Let's get out here," Jimmy yelled to me and Kate.

We were all now racing for the door.

"If they escape," the Queen was trying to speak while trying not to cough, "your heads shall pay the forfeit," she threatened the guards who were quick to get to their feet and chase after us.

At last we were back in the corridor again. Even with the torches lighting the way it was really dark out there, so we had to go real slow like, right at the beginning. In no time the footsteps of the guards were coming up fast behind us. Kate was leading us along now, 'cause she knew the place a whole lot better than we did. I was right behind her, and she was dragging me along, and I was dragging

Jimmy. Going down the stairs was kinda scary 'cause I could hardly see the steps under my feet, and I was still carrying the schoolbag and the time belts. I had turned real quick like to see those guys chasing us. It was a good thing too, 'cause one of them had tossed a torch down at us, and almost hit Jimmy in the back. I pulled him out of the way just in the nick of time.

"Give me the bag," Jimmy called out while we were running.

"We don't have time..."I said.

"Give it to me," he called again to me. So I swung it back over my shoulder and he grabbed it. In that time we still hadn't stopped running, and neither did the guards who were coming up quick behind us.

"There's no time for your chattering," Kate warned us as she continued to drag us along.

I guess Jimmy knew where things were in the bag better than I did, 'cause he pulled out something real quick, and told us to stop. That was something me and Kate really didn't want to do. All at once Jimmy jumped up, and pulled one of the torches that were overhead down from the wall.

"What are you gonna do," I asked trying to catch my breath.

"We fight fire with fire," he said, and then touched the torch to whatever he had just pulled out of the bag. Suddenly a big burst of black smoke exploded into the air behind us. We all stood still for a minute wanting to see if the smoke bomb from Jimmy's schoolbag had stopped the guards. For a minute we didn't see anything coming through the dark mist. Slowly we had started to back away when we heard footsteps clanging along from the other direction. It sounded like more knights coming our way. I was thinking that it must've been the explosions coming from the tower that had gotten their attention.

Kate looked at the smoke coming from the smoke bomb and then to Jimmy. "You must truly be a wizard to make such magic," she said.

"No, this is a whole different kind of magic," he said to her. "Now get us out of here."

Just as he spoke those words, the image of the Queen came cutting through smoke that was already beginning to die down.

"Out of my way you pusillanimous daisies who deem yourself servants of the King." Had no idea what any of that meant.

"But my Queen…" one of the guards tried to get out.

"Silence," she was still bossing everyone around even as she and her raised dagger came cutting through what was left of the smoke.

Kate had been right on the ball, and started dragging us again in the other direction. But the trouble with that was that there were still more knights coming from that way.

"Make haste," Kate ordered, and I was really glad she was taking charge right then and there, 'cause I didn't know where I was, and I'm sure neither did Jimmy. The whole place was like a maze to me as we made our way along. As we turned a corner there were more torches coming right at us.

"This isn't good," I said.

"Kate," Jimmy seemed to plead as he asked the next question, "Where do you go when you play hide and seek" Good idea, good idea, I thought.

Kate did not say a word; she just started moving us along down a smaller corridor that hopefully led away from the danger.

"Where are we…" I tried to get out.

"Stay quiet," Kate warned, as we saw a bunch of torches at the end of the corridor move quickly by. They were all over the place looking for us, but the only one who knew exactly where we were was Kate. For a minute it seemed like the knights and the Queen were going off to look somewhere else. Our luck lasted about ten-seconds before a whole bunch of soldiers began to storm down the dark pathway where Kate had taken us.

We heard them calling out war cries as their swords sliced through the air at the dark patches along the way. They seemed really mad and scared as they slashed wildly hoping to hit something, anything that was in their way. We seemed to be standing still for too long as they came closer.

I looked back to Jimmy, after all he was the smart one, and right now we needed smarts to get us out of here.

"What about the time belts," I whispered to him, and I could feel the trembling in my voice as death got closer and closer.

"I can't set them in here, we don't know the time and day, besides there's only two." he whispered back. Jimmy was trying to catch his breath when he turned to Kate, "what do we do now?"

"Do you have any more magic in your bag wizard," she said.

And now the clanging of footsteps, and the shouting of the Queen was tightening in on us.

"Slaughter them, hack them to pieces, and feed them to the dogs," she ordered the knights. She was really not a nice lady.

It was getting easier to make out the shapes as they got closer, so I knew that they'd be able to see us easy too, and in only seconds.

"Do you," I said to Jimmy.

"Do I," he answered.

"Have anymore magic in that bag?"

"A little more smoke but..." and that's all I heard him get out as I was grabbed, and pulled through the secret entrance in the wall by a hand that had seemed to come out of nowhere.

It was only when we had a moment to get ourselves together on the other side of the wall that we realized what had happened. While Will had pulled me to safety, Lord Hoxley had grabbed hold of Jimmy and Kate. It was real dark in there, and all I could feel was Will's hand across my mouth, and him whispering to me to be quiet, which wasn't an easy thing to do with a scream just ready to shoot out of my mouth.

On the other side of the wall I could hear the voices of the knights and of the Queen as they echoed through the thick stone that was between us.

"The devils have disappeared before our very eyes," said the Queen. They must've made us out right before we had been taken through the wall.

"Such power exist, my Queen," came a voice that I recognized right away. It was Lord Sagamore. He was hot on our trail again, and I thought this guy had called it quits when he saw the giant hose coming out of the water. "My investigation into the manifestation of the great serpent, a particularly nasty abomination spawned in hell, and found it to be none other than a familiar of Lucifer himself…" That's all that Sagamore got out when the rumblings of terror ran through the guards. 'Cause they had heard about magical things their whole lives, but none of them had actually ever seen a real witch or monster. Not until me and Jimmy had popped in from the twenty-first century anyway. Once again it was the good old Queen who shut them up.

"Silence, pretenders to knighthood," her voice bounced off of the walls. "Continue Sagamore with your horrific uncovering." For some reason she seemed interested in what Sagamore the Mighty had to say.

"As keepers of the gate these demons hold great favor with the Prince of Darkness. The life and death battle in The Moat of Insurmountable Anguish has proven conclusively my earlier findings to be true. Giving credence to my theory that these two monsters that roam freely the castle are indeed the head of Satan's legions. The demons have invaded this sanctuary for the sole purpose of destroying the kingdom, perhaps to bring doom to mankind itself."

More murmurs of fear came from the other side of the wall from the guards who were soaking up every word of it. And as they continued to look for us, Lord Hoxley and Will led us quietly away from that place. In a few minutes we were back at the hidden chamber where Lord Hoxley had first taken us for safety after escaping from the moat. We really didn't mind the dark and the rats right about then, we were just glad to be alive, and out of the reach of Eleanor, the psycho Queen.

"Why is Sagamore saying all those things," Jimmy asked.

"His words add credence to his account of the Field of Death 'tis true," said Lord Hoxley. "Sagamore weaves a dark tale that intrigues, but loses the truth along the way. An investigation of the moat has been made, and this much of what Sagamore imparts to the Queen be not falsehood. Yet to perpetuate the myth of Sagamore he cannot find the giant snake from the moat false. He would look a fool. To keep his fable sound, and his legend steadfast he must keep you two boys the purveyors of all that is unholy."

"That's a heck of a calling card," Jimmy said.

"So he's lying to…" I started to say.

"So that he can look like a big shot in front of the King and his friends," said Jimmy. "But now we've got to get back to our time, remember there's a planet that needs to be saved."

"And me," said Will, "you said that there was a plan…"

Jimmy turned to Will; he took a deep breath and spoke. I could tell that Jimmy was uncomfortable with what he was about to say. "Will, none of what we are about to do would be possible without you. You said you would give up your life to save the world…"

"No," Kate cried out."

"I'm only talking about his life here," said Jimmy, "in this time".

Will looked back to Lord Hoxley. I could tell that he was scared. It seemed like the idea of living in another time terrified this kid more than dying in his own.

"You won't be taking my Will," said Kate.

Jimmy turned real quick to her, "they think you're part of this all too," he said. "So we can't think of leaving you behind."

Now they were both looking to Lord Hoxley for answers that I didn't think anybody had.

"It would be a great adventure," Lord Hoxley said and smiled. I could tell that he was a little nervous too, and maybe just a little bit jealous.

"I have a question," I said to Jimmy. "We only have two time belts, how are they…"

He didn't let me finish, he hardly ever let me finish. "We expand the size of the time belts to fit two…"

"But what if…"

"If we fall out…" darn he did it again. "If we fall out we are in big trouble. So we've got to make sure that we're all in tight before we take off."

"A new-world, a new time," Will said to Lord Hoxley. In Will's voice you could tell that he was still not sure.

"Providence has left you no choice lad, neither you nor your sister will be safe here. Lord Sagamore must appear powerful, even if it is by burning children on the stake."

Lord Hoxley reached down and hugged Will. He then reached out and grabbed hold of Kate. "I am envious of your journey," he said, "The future is a world that I have longed for since I was your age, and I shall never see."

"And we shall have to wear this witches garb in that time," Will looked down at my clothes that he was now wearing.

"For all time," Lord Hoxley smiled again.

"Mom, is gone, and Dad took to thrashing you more than you ever got from this place," said Kate. "We have little enough to keep us here." Kate seemed like she was up for the trip. But Will stayed quiet, still he was afraid to say yes or no, so Kate said what had to be said, "and if you stay here the best that you can hope for is a swift death, so we'll be going away from this place."

Will looked at Kate, and back to me and Jimmy, "I guess I'll be joining you in this new world," he said, and he laughed. And it wasn't a happy laugh, it was a laugh like he was really scared, but was just covering that up with a laugh.

"So," said Jimmy, "I guess it's off to the twenty-first century, and all we have to do is know the time and date we're stuck in right now."

"It's Prince John's day of birth, so that part of the puzzle we have," said Lord Hoxley, "it is 24th of December."

"December," I jumped, no wonder it was so darn cold in that water."

"Born 1167 this day," Lord Hoxley went on, "the young rascal being twelve years old, that makes this…"

"Making this 1179," Jimmy jumped in. He was always quick with the math. "Now we must calculate the time in with the Earth's speed…"

"The Earth's speed, it is moving," said Lord Hoxley with amazement.

"Oh sure," Jimmy went on, and I could tell that he was kinda excited, and proud being able to showoff to Lord Hoxley with all this knowledge he had in his head. "The Earth spins…"

"Spins," Lord Hoxley looked at him in disbelief, "perhaps like a top that the children play with?"

"Not exactly, it's more like a ball, it's round," said Jimmy.

"Is not the Earth flat," Lord Hoxley now sounded like he was having trouble believing in that part of Jimmy's story. Strange how out of all the crazy stuff he was hearing from us, the Earth not being flat, he was having trouble buying.

"In the next century that will all be cleared up," Jimmy told him.

"It spins," Lord Hoxley repeated curiously.

"At approximately a thousand miles an hour."

"It rotates that quickly," Lord Hoxley's jaw had just dropped, 'cause the stuff that Jimmy was telling him was stranger than all the witchcraft stories that Sagamore was trying to sell everybody on.

"When the Earth suddenly stopped all time was shifted, but we still don't know how much."

"And how is it…" Lord Hoxley seemed almost afraid to say what he wanted to say.

"How is what," Jimmy looked at him.

"How is it we don't fall off of the planet," Lord Hoxley finally found the words. Now his eyes were fixed on Jimmy, and he was hanging on every word he was saying.

"We don't fall off because of a little thing called gravity, that keeps us stuck to the earth."

"Gravity," Lord Hoxley stopped and thought about it for a minute. "This thing called gravity, might one compare it to pitch?"

That's when Jimmy took a firecracker out of the schoolbag. He held it up and let it drop to the ground.

"Oh my," Lord Hoxley seemed to understand right away.

"Not exactly like pitch", Jimmy went on, "and it's a couple of centuries before it's discovered by Sir Isaac Newton. An apple falls on his head and…"

"I do hope this Newton fellow is not injured."

"I think he survives, at least long enough to figure out that gravity is what keeps us from flying off into space."

"Very fortunate," Lord Hoxley seemed relieved that Newton had survived the whole apple incident.

"There's just one thing I got to tell you Shawn," and I could tell that it wasn't gonna be something that I wanted to hear, 'cause all of the energy that he had just built up suddenly dropped out of his voice.

"This is gonna be bad, ain't it," I said.

"Real bad," he said, "but we got this far, didn't we."

I just closed my eyes, 'cause I thought we had just come through the worst times of all, but just when you thought things couldn't get worse, they somehow always did.

Chapter 15: Altering the Time Space Continuum, or Playing Dodge Ball With the Comet

My eyes were closed tight, and I still couldn't believe what Jimmy was telling me.

"The thing is," Jimmy said and then he gritted his teeth, 'cause he really didn't want to tell me.

"This is gonna be bad, " I said again, "ain't it."

"The thing is that I won't be able to get us back to the exact place we left…"

"How come?"

"What you got to remember Shawn," is that the time belts travel through time and space…"

"And…"

"And," Jimmy went on; "the comet must have altered the time-space continuum when it hit."

"And…" I still wasn't getting it.

"And," he said, "if it was only time that was effected by the collision, then we should have been sent to the twelfth-century in our own country, in our own town. And the only way to get back there is to jump into the time when the Earth is about to be destroyed."

"Again!"

"Actually it will be just destroyed once, we'll just be going through it again."

"Oh, now I feel a whole lot better," I told Jimmy, and he knew I didn't mean a word of it.

"Now if we calculate the distance of where we are to where we came from," I could see the wheels turning in Jimmy's head, "I think I can get us within a hundred miles of our hometown."

"A hundred miles," I yelled.

"My geographies not so good," Jimmy looked down almost embarrassed.

"That's just swell, you're geography sucks, so we could land in the ocean or something."

"Lord Hoxley has given us a good idea of where this castle is situated, I think I can get us pretty close," he came back, but he really didn't sound so sure of himself.

"You really don't know for sure," I tried to look Jimmy straight in the eye, 'cause that was the best way to tell when he was being honest. He wasn't a very good liar when you were looking him right in the eye.

In a moment Jimmy looked straight back at me, he was looking a little surer of himself now.

"We can do this," he said. He still didn't come off as being too confident, but as he kept talking, he started to sound more and more like he believed what he was saying. And Jimmy could do that, he wasn't much of a liar, but the guy could talk himself into anything. "So here's what we do," he went on, "we put all the elements together, right now all I need is the exact time…"

"If the sundial in the courtyard is not hindered in its duties by the clouds on high a fairly accurate reading of the time may be had," Lord Hoxley went on.

"A sun dial…" I tried to get out, but Jimmy wasn't listening, he was too busy getting himself psyched for the next part of our adventure, while I was still beat up from the last adventure.

"This is crazy," I screamed.

"What is the matter lad," Lord Hoxley looked upset too.

"There's a little problem Lord Hoxley," Jimmy went on.

"Demons, witches, Sagamore thinking we be traitors," Will cried out, "and now you're saying things can get worst."

"Quiet down Will we still don't know what…" Kate tried to calm him.

"It's just a little thing that if we're lucky," Jimmy cut Kate off while he was trying to calm us all down.

"A little," I still couldn't believe what I was hearing. "Jimmy I think we've used up pretty much all of our luck on this trip."

"The thing is," Jimmy went on trying to explain everything, "is that basically we'll be reversing time, but we won't be in the same place we arrived, and since everything will be running backwards…"

"We could land anywhere," I yelled again.

"No, no, "said Jimmy. "I can't say exactly where we'll land. It was a long walk to the castle, but we weren't that far from the field. I think I can get us within fifteen, twenty miles."

"We could land in a river or…"

"Good thing we all can swim," Jimmy tried to smile.

"It ain't funny," I told him.

Then Jimmy took a deep breath, and let me have the rest of the good news. "There's one other thing."

"You gotta be kidding me," I really couldn't believe that there was a glitch in this already perfect day.

Will got hysterical again, he turned terrified to Kate, "Sagamore thinking we be demons, traitors, and keeping the Devil's giant serpent as a pet, and now he be telling us…"

Kate grabbed him this time, and looked him right into the eye. "You got to be keeping your wits about you Will," she told him.

"Lad, get yourself under control," Lord Hoxley told Will, but Will wasn't hearing any of it.

"And yesterday my only concern was a good whipping…"

Kate had heard enough, she smacked Will in the head as she kept yelling at him. "Will enough of your whining," she shouted right into his face. And again I was really glad she wasn't my sister. That at least took Will's mind off of our new problem for a second.

"You like conking me on the nob, admit it, you like it?"

"You'll be getting another conk…" that's all Kate got out when Jimmy yelled to all of us.

"Please everyone," Jimmy tried to calm us all down. "First of all we won't be too far from where we left, and once we get our bearings we should be all right, but since we don't know exactly where we'll be landing, I think we should arrive as close to the time of the comet hitting as possible."

"Why," because I really didn't understand.

"If we get anything like the reception we got when we arrived here…"

"There not gonna think we're witches," I said, "not in our own time."

Will all at once went back into panic mode, "they be thinking we are witches in the future too…"

That was all that Kate let him get out before delivering another swat to Will. Will let loose with a loud "Ow," but then knew enough not to say anymore.

"My, my," said Lord Hoxley, "I thought people were more civilized in your time."

"For the most part " Jimmy went on, "but my concern is that at that moment the comet is crashing down we have to be completely focused. If people see us, if there's a crowd…"

"What can we do," 'cause I really didn't know.

"Get there early, but not too early, so we only have one thing to focus on, the time belts."

"Oh this is great," I was really upset. I took a quick look over to Kate to make sure there wasn't a smack to the head coming my way.

"It's the only way! Works best if we get there just as the Earth's about to destroyed."

"Yeah we don't want to be late for that" I still didn't believe any of this.

"It's the best way… Now I have to make some calculations…"

"I don't want to hear about calculations!" That's what I said, but Jimmy wasn't hearing any of it.

"We have to calculate the exact time the comet is going to crash, and set our controls to get us out of there just as the Earth shifts in its orbit."

"That sounds easy," I said. I was being sarcastic, I know, but what else did I have?

"Actually if Lord Hoxley can give us the correct time."

"He's got a sundial," I yelled.

"Noon is usually pretty accurate on those things."

"Pretty accurate," I was still screaming.

"They can be off about two minutes…"

"I do hope it is not cloudy," Lord Hoxley spoke real soft like he was afraid to say it at all.

"Cloudy," I threw my hands up in the air. I guess I was getting Will and Kate upset too, but after all we had gone through to find out that now we had to go back to the twenty-first century, and play dodge ball with a giant comet. It just wasn't something I was very happy about.

"Now all you've got to do is change the settings just like I tell you…"

"Why is no one listening to me? You're saying we change the settings after the comet has already hit the Earth…"

"No, that's not what I'm saying," Jimmy came back at me. "But we got to be able to change it fast in case we don't get a lot of time. If there are other people around, if we are in water, he looked at me real fast. "I don't think that's gonna happen," Jimmy came right back at me, we've got to be able to move quick. It'll be our moment of maximum risk."

"Darn Jimmy, they've all been our moment of maximum risk. Tell me one minute of this whole trip back in time that hasn't been one big moment of maximum risk?"

"If we're a minute late, if we show up after the world has been destroyed."

"Yeah I get it, we're toast."

"I know we've been through a lot…"

"And why are you just telling me this?"

"Is that why you're upset," Jimmy looked at me like he knew that was a big part of it. He had kept me in the dark like I would've backed out if I had known all of the danger. But I didn't get a chance to even answer him, because suddenly Kate jumped in, and started to take control again. She pushed me against the wall, like she was a schoolyard bully or something.

"Hey, what are you doing," I said to her. I didn't want to push her back 'cause she was a girl, besides she seemed pretty tough, not that that would've stopped me, well probably not.

"And aren't you a dainty little flower, all worried about landing in the wrong time and such. Open your eyes canker blossom," and I really got mad about what she had called me, and I didn't even know what that meant. "You're already in the muck of it and deep," she went on. "Me and my Will we got ourselves one bit of a problem, now don't we, what with Lord Sagamore wanting to stoke us good and proper on the flames."

"Listen, " I tried to get out.

"And don't be telling me of your woes, because I've been stuck in this fine castle carrying the chamber pots, and cleaning after the horses long since I was six years old, with sometimes only the fleas to keep me company. And poor Will here, not a day goes by that his backside does not burn red from a good thrashing. And all for what? I'll tell you what, all because jolly Prince John has been a mischievous lad."

"The sting is something frightful," said Will.

"Sorry, but…"

"And it's sorry you should be. Because if you don't die in this dark and dirty place, then you'll be doomed to living here, which is a worst fate?"

"Children, children," Lord Hoxley said, "this mission is too important for all this quibbling. For you to be successful you must work as one."

It was then that Kate let go of me and backed away. For the longest time nobody said anything. They were all just looking at me, and again I knew that she and Jimmy were right. I think I just wanted to take a breather from the danger, just long enough to catch my second wind.

I looked back at Jimmy, "so how do I set the dial on this thing." He smiled at me, he knew all along that I was going to give in. Besides I think he just liked seeing me get pushed around by Kate. I looked at her, and gave her one of those I don't care looks that said she wasn't the reason that I was giving in. "I was gonna do it anyway, I just wanted…"

"It's true," said Jimmy, "Shawn just likes to be coaxed into everything."

"That's right," I told Kate, just so that she would know that she really wasn't the boss. Even when I was giving Jimmy a hard time over all of this stuff I knew there really wasn't any choice, not if

I ever wanted to see my Mom, Dad, and little sister again, not if I ever wanted to see the world that I lived in again.

"Look Shawn," Jimmy stared me right in the eye, "I'll try and get us there a few minutes early, but since we really don't know where we'll land, or who we'll run into, I don't want to get there too early." That sounded a little better to me.

After that we spent a good twenty minutes, me learning how to change the settings on the time belts, and to do it quickly. It took a little math, which I really wasn't good at, but once I had it down it seemed easy enough. In all that time Lord Hoxley just looked on like a little kid watching the Saturday morning cartoons. Everybody else was being pretty much quiet, even Kate who seemed to have the biggest mouth out of the bunch of us.

Next Jimmy went looking for string. What he did was he took some rope that Lord Hoxley was able to dig up for him, and began untwisting the rope until he had pieces of string that were thin enough to fit in the notches on the time belts. I guess when it was time we were gonna get tied in there with Will and Kate. While Jimmy was preparing all of this stuff, I kept remembering Professor Burkhardt's words about what would happen if something went wrong with the time belts. "You will be lost forever in the ever expanding inter-dimensional time warp." He had thrown in some words about endless blackness, but what else could you expect in an inter-dimensional time warp, whatever that was. None of us were very big, so Jimmy really didn't have to use too much of the rope to make it a tight fit.

"So this principle is called the warping of time," Lord Hoxley looked to Jimmy.

"Actually the Professor called it time skipping," Jimmy said back to him.

"Then it is possible to change destiny," Lord Hoxley said to Jimmy with his eyes looking like they were gonna pop out of his head.

Jimmy looked sadly at him, "I'm afraid Lord Hoxley we don't know that yet. I guess before now no one's ever had a preview of the future, so maybe it is. There's only one way we're gonna to know for sure."

"Then perhaps we've always been victim's of fate, because we could never see it coming," Lord Hoxley said.

"That's what we're hoping," said Jimmy. "If not then the world we know is gone forever." He then looked at Will, Kate, and me. "It's time."

And those words just sent chills up my back, "cause I knew what happened next. It was time for me and Jimmy to once more become the two most powerful kids in the Universe, 'cause it seemed like nobody else was gonna be out saving the world. But, and here was the big but, we only became super heroes if we could get our hands on the Gravity Boxes again, and the Gravity Boxes were half a world and centuries away from us.

It was hard to believe that it wasn't noon yet. We had been up for hours, and from getting dunked in the moat, and fighting off the psycho Queen I figured it had to be almost night time. But I had forgotten that we had been dragged from the dungeon real early that morning 'cause it seemed that everybody was a morning person back then. Imagine it, we had already been nearly killed a bunch of times,

197

and we hadn't even had lunch yet. Which reminded me that I was kinda hungry. That slop that they had fed me last night in the dungeon wasn't too filling. It was something called porridge, and it tasted kinda like wet plaster, or at least what I imagined wet plaster would taste like if it had been served with a nice refreshing glass of muddy water. And there were no forks. These people couldn't even get that right. I had to eat with my fingers. Me and Jimmy mostly ended up slurping it from the bowel.

Before I could mention my empty stomach, Jimmy turned to Lord Hoxley, "Lord Hoxley, we really have to be getting to that sundial now. It's got to be nearing noon."

"I would suspect so," said the old teacher.

Jimmy turned back to me, "here's the plan," he said, "we set the time belts for twelve noon on the dot. Then all we gotta do when we get to the sundial is hit the switch when it reads twelve."

"There's gonna be a whole mess of people in that courtyard," I told him.

"May I offer a possible solution to your dilemma," Lord Hoxley seemed so happy to be able to help us out.

"Please do," Jimmy said.

"There is only one thing that the people loathe to set their eyes upon more than witches and demons."

"There is," I said, 'cause we had gotten called so many nasty names that I really didn't know what that could be.

"And that would be," he went on, "the poor."

"The poor," Jimmy looked at him.

"Where as witches and demons may steal an occasional soul, the poor are always looking to partake of your foodstuff, or inflict even greater pain by seeking to empty ones purse."

"So when they see the poor coming…" I started to say.

"The poor become invisible," Jimmy finished my sentence, and he really didn't have to do that, 'cause I had figured that much out myself.

"And when the children of the poor come to do their begging," Lord Hoxley went on, "it is better to look the other way. You see a hungry child can employ guilt much more effectively than a hungry adult."

"But everybody here looks poor," I said.

"There are degrees of poverty," Lord Hoxley said. "The poorest of us are looked down on by those who have slightly more in their purse."

"Can we all get disguises," Jimmy was definitely up for this plan.

"That can be accomplished easily," Lord Hoxley looked over to Will and Kate. "When the wintry breeze came, and chilled these old bones of mine, it was Will who thought to protect this drafty retreat." Will grinned proudly as Lord Hoxley spoke of his good deed. "Will," he said, "we have numerous rags that have been stuffed into the cracks and crevices of this old forgotten place. In effect keeping the cold out, and the stiffness from this tired old body."

"It is not quite as cold is it my Lord," asked Will.

"You're fine boy, Will," Lord Hoxley smiled at Will. "Now collect our spoils of dirty rags with all due haste."

"Yes indeed," Will jumped, and went to feeling his way around the cracks in the wall."

"Rags," I said.

"The peasants wear little more than rags," said Lord Hoxley, "did you not see that boys with your very own eyes? And they are happy enough to have them. 'Tis only the rich that come to wear fine things and eat everyday, and believe me that they do not want to spoil the good feeling that comes with being a swell, by gazing upon the poor and downtrodden."

"But rags," I said again

"It's the dress of the day," Kate said, and she said it almost like she was making a joke, or maybe just making fun of me.

"Tattered rags, tied on with rope, you'll make a fine peasant," smiled Lord Hoxley.

"Thanks," I said. Once again I was trying to be sarcastic, but this was the twelfth-century, and nobody was picking up on just how funny I was being.

Will was still rubbing his hand along the walls, and feeling around the floor. It was kinda dark in that hidden room with only a single torch lighting the place; so I guess he had to just drag his hand along until he came across the spots where he had stuffed the rags that were gonna be our new clothes.

When Will finally gathered them, the rags were dirty and smelly like almost everything else that seemed to be around in that time. We used them to cover our regular clothes. Remember Will was still wearing my clothes, and I was wearing his. But with those filthy rags heaped onto us it didn't really seem to matter. I never wanted to take a bath so much in my whole life, and I wouldn't need my Mom yelling at me, "get into the tub or else." I would've jumped in and stayed for hours. It would've taken that long just to get the grime off of me from my swim in the moat.

When we finally got dressed in our peasant disguises, I looked at Jimmy, and he looked at me. We had to laugh 'cause we looked like we had really entered the twelfth century, and had been living there for years. Think my hair was a little short, but we were so dirty that I didn't think anybody would notice. And since we were supposed to be poor, and maybe asking for money, they'd be trying not to even look at us. Aside from that we looked and smelled just like mostly everyone else we had seen since we arrived here.

"It must be getting near to the time," Lord Hoxley warned.

"Let's get moving," Jimmy jumped. He moved quickly to the time belts, and began to fiddle with the controls. "If the sundial is in the middle of the courtyard…"

"People here view it as a decoration and little more," said Lord Hoxley, "in regards to time it is only the arrival and departure of the sun that has any meaning to these people."

"So there shouldn't be too many people hanging around it," said Jimmy.

"I dare say not," Lord Hoxley told him.

Jimmy loosened the string, and handed me one of the time belts. "Shawn," you know what button to hit when the time arrives?

"I think I do," I said.

"Shawn," you've got to know," he yelled at me.

"All right, all right, I know."

"You're sure," he came very close, and looked me right in the eye.

"Yeah, yeah, I know."

"Now the second that that sundial hits noon…"

"You've already gone over that…" I said.

"Well, I'm saying it again," Jimmy kept telling us the same stuff over and over, but I guess he had to make sure we had it down right. "We've all got to move real fast. In the courtyard will be our moment of. Maximum..."

"Risk. Yeah I know, I know!"

"Shawn! Stop whining, we don't have a lot of time."

There again was another moment of maximum risk, we had been running into them all day. And just so you know I wasn't whining.

"Will and Kate…" they were both paying close attention to Jimmy. "We'll only have a couple of seconds at most to get the two of you tied in to the time belts with us before people start getting curious about what we're doing. Do you understand?"

Both of them just bobbed their heads up and down. It was like they didn't want to speak, or couldn't speak. I knew the feeling real good. Like when the knots in your stomach got all tied up, and you just wanted something to be over with.

"Okay," Jimmy showed us again, "we've got to be tied real snug inside these things, so I've made a slip knot, and all you've got to do is get inside, and tug on the end, and hold it tight. And whatever you do, do not let go of the end."

"Okay," I said, and I grabbed hold of Will, "Will and me can ride in this one."

Kate looked at me with a bit of fire in her eyes. She could tell right off that I didn't want to take this trip with her. I didn't like the way she was always being so pushy. She gave me a cold stare, and Jimmy could tell that she wasn't happy with me, so he just kept talking, 'cause he knew that we all had to work together on this thing, or it just wasn't going to work. Being his best friend, I knew how his head worked, so I was counting on him to take the heat off of me.

"Now once we get to the twenty-first century we might not have much time to change the settings, and skip into another time. Which will be three days back."

Sounded simple enough, just as the Earth was being knocked out of orbit by the giant comet all we had to do was duck out of the way. I think if Jimmy called that our moment of maximum risk I would've socked him, but he didn't.

"What if we end up where the comet's crashing down," I asked. Now Jimmy looked at me, and didn't say a word. The look I got made me sorry that I had asked the question. Then he said, "on the first skip we are going to end up right about here, and we know that the comet is gonna hit around where we live. It's the force of the comet hitting down that knocks the planet out of whack, and sends us closer to home." I was sure glad Jimmy was handling all the planning.

Lord Hoxley looked at us all sadly. I almost thought he was gonna cry. "I envy you all this great journey in which you are about to partake," he said. "My two friends from the future," he looked at me and Jimmy, "you have quenched an old man's thirst for knowledge far beyond his hopes and greatest expectations." I was feeling a bit sad myself as he said those things. I think I was gonna miss the old guy. He had done so much for us. "And Kate, I will miss your sweet cherub face, and your kindness in tending my needs." Kate bowed her head, and then smiled at him. Then Lord Hoxley turned to Will. "Will, you have been my greatest student. In this time when a thirst for truth can lead one on a dangerous and treacherous path, and where that yearning to reach out, and to touch the unknown is suffocated by the oppression of mediocre spirits born of superstitious minds, you have been a steadfast and learned scholar. You have assisted me in my exploration of that dark and forbidden land called science. Even though fearful, yes always fearful..." he smiled at Will, and Will bowed his head shyly. "You have overcome your fear, and dared to climb those slippery slopes, and walk those rocky roads that lead oft times to that evasive thing called enlightenment. I salute you boy, indeed I salute all you courageous explorers of this new world where wisdom and knowledge may finally find space to breathe."

Will stood quiet, and just looked back at Lord Hoxley. There were tears running down his cheek, and you could tell the kid really loved the old guy. In a moment Lord Hoxley walked over, and hugged Will tightly. He then reached over and pulled Kate into the hugging session. "The magnificent future that I predict for the two of you will make you forget many things. But I pray you do not forget Hoxley. Carry my memory into that new time, so that my essence shall live on."

Will suddenly broke down; he hugged Lord Hoxley even tighter as more tears rolled down his face. "I'll never forget you my Lord, never!"

They all continued to hold tight to each other for a little longer when Lord Hoxley pulled away. He looked over to me and Jimmy, and we knew that it was time to leave.

We moved out right away to get back to the courtyard. Every eye inside those walls had been glued on us the last time we were out there. This time we couldn't afford to have anybody notice us. We were dressed in rags, covered in dirt, and we smelled like old garbage, we should've fit in perfectly, or at least that's what we thought.

Lord Hoxley had peeked out of a small hole in the wall to see if the coast was clear, before opening the secret passageway to the outside. He kept a close lookout for any sign of danger as we slipped out to the side of the castle. We had no trouble getting out into the open. The little bit of sun shinning down actually made it seem warmer than it had been inside the dark, gray walls of the hidden chamber. The mud along the way made it hard to walk as we got sucked into it with every step. Our footstep made a kinda slurping sound as we were pulling our feet out. It felt like our sneaks might come off with every step we took. Our sneakers were mostly covered up by the mud and dirty old rags hanging down off of us. Just had to hope that nobody would notice them. My toes were getting frosty as we moved across the mushy edge of the castle. We knew if we had to make a run for it we would all be in big trouble.

Overhead there were some guards patrolling the top of the castle. We stuck tight to the wall so that we couldn't be seen unless they looked straight down. That was kinda' tough, 'cause the ground sloped down into the moat that was all around us. The guards seemed to be looking out into the distance, 'cause if there was trouble coming, it would be coming from out there first. So we just took our steps slow, and hoped that the guards wouldn't pick up on the slurping of mud that seemed so loud to us down below.

Not far away we could hear the sound of people making noise. It was getting louder as we got closer to the front of the castle. Once there we would have to hide in the crowd. It seemed the best place with everybody just walking in and out of the gate. I could feel my stomach churning, 'cause I knew what had happened the last time I had been with this mob.

At the edge of the castle wall we saw all the people coming and going, and it was Kate who just moved quickly into the crowd, and seemed to become part of it. Jimmy did the same, and then Will and me joined in. As soon as we could we got close to each other. Lord Hoxley was trailing behind knowing that if he was seen with us it might draw attention, and that was the one thing we didn't need right then.

I was more nervous walking by the guards, and in my head it felt like they were watching me all the time I was going past. I think Will was just as bad as me, maybe worst. Yeah, he was definitely worst. He just kept looking down at the ground, and then taking quick looks around to see if they were looking back. He also stood out a little bit more because his clothes were nicer. There weren't enough rags to cover us all. So we muddied up what he was wearing, and covered his face with dirt, but still he was dressed a lot better than the rest of us. I got so scared by the way he was acting that I rushed over and grabbed him by the arm. Then I pulled him along like we were playing. Will began to talk real fast, like he had been spotted.

"The Captain of the Guards, his eyes fell upon me," he said.

"We're peasant kids right now," I told him, "they don't pay attention to us unless we give them a good reason to."

"He knows me all too well, and he gives the fiercest thrashing in the land…" he stopped and thought about it, "no that would be Sir Sagamore."

"Just don't look at him," I said as I pulled him quicker away from the guards at the gate.

I should've taken my own advice, 'cause I had looked back for just a second to make sure Will hadn't gotten any attention. The Captain of the guards had left the gate, and was headed in our direction. Up ahead of us Jimmy and Kate were moving towards the center of the courtyard where the sundial was. So I started pulling Will along faster.

"What is it," he said.

"Just don't look back again," I told him. Which made Will right away start to look back, so I jerked his arm, and pulled him harder. In just a second we were both moving fast away from the Captain of the guards.

Maybe the Captain of the guards wasn't following us, maybe he was gonna leave the gate anyway, but I knew that looking back was a bad idea right about then. He had actually gotten a really good look at us all earlier that day. Standing right next to King Henry and

Prince John as we were tied and thrown into the moat, he could hardly miss us.

Up ahead Jimmy and Kate had disappeared in to the crowd.

"Will…" I said.

"Does the Captain of the guards follow us," he spit the words out as if he was terrified, and I could tell you that he was, and he wasn't the only one.

"Get me to the sundial," I didn't want to look back, 'cause I was pretty scared myself.

"I can feel his icy breath down my neck," he said.

"Just get us to the sundial," I shoved him along. And now I was thinking that maybe I should've picked Kate for a traveling partner. By the time we could see them again Jimmy and Kate were already near to the sundial. I was so worried that I couldn't help it, so I looked back. My worst fear had become true. The Captain seemed to be catching up and quick. He saw me look at him, which I promised myself I wouldn't do, and I saw him seeing me. On no, I thought, he was only steps behind. And then out of nowhere, Lord Hoxley's voice cut through the crowd.

"Oh Captain," I heard him call.

Another dumb and quick look back let me see the Captain stopping for Lord Hoxley, who had rushed quickly through the mob of people to catch up with him.

"Yes my Lord," said the Captain.

"The festivities seemed to have died down Captain," I could hear Lord Hoxley past the other people that were moving around us.

"Yes my Lord," said the Captain, "the escape of the two witches seems to have dampened the spirit of the young Prince."

After that their voices trailed off as we moved away from them. Lord Hoxley had come to the rescue just in the nick of time. From the way it sounded, I was supposed to feel bad that my not drowning had ruined the Prince's birthday celebration. I decided to cry about that later, and meet up with Jimmy and Kate as fast as possible.

When we got to the sundial, there weren't too many people standing around, enough to make us nervous, but still not too many. It might have been better if there were more people, we wouldn't have been standing out so much. Overhead was the biggest, meanest, and grayest cloud just getting in the way. I could see the gears inside Jimmy's head turning. That stupid cloud was blocking the sun from hitting the sundial. And without that we had no idea when twelve o'clock was. Jimmy was deep in thought, as if he could think of something to get that cloud out of the way. But that old cloud just didn't seem to care about our situation, it was just floating there like it had nothing better to do all day.

I was still looking around, 'cause I really wasn't comfortable standing out in the middle of that courtyard. Not far away was the Captain of the guards with Lord Hoxley still beating his ear about whatever. About anything but us was my guess, but how long could he keep that going? Sooner or later the Captain was gonna turn, and start looking for Will and me again. In a minute the cloud started to drift off, and a thin beam of sunlight touched down on the courtyard. But it wasn't enough to show us the time, and taking a guess wasn't such a good idea. In fact it was an especially bad idea if the wrong guess could land us in never ending time warp, or worst yet after the world had been totally destroyed. All we could do was to hope that the cloud would keep going on its merry way, so that more sun could get through.

Now from out of one of the doors to the castle came more trouble, Prince John escorted by Sagamore and some more of the guards. At first they seemed to be walking past us, and not really paying much attention. Remember we were supposed to be peasants, so no one was paying us much mind. That was until Will started to get nervous again, and began looking around. His breathing became real heavy, and he started shaking.

"What are you doing," I said to him, real low and under my breath.

"It's the Prince and Sagamore," he said to me like I wouldn't recognize the guy who had tried to drown me in the moat, and wanted to toast me like a marshmallow just that day.

"Just watch the sundial," Jimmy warned, but Will was the worst. He would've been a terrible spy, 'cause he just kept looking around like he had done something wrong. And if you looked that way long enough, everybody was gonna think that you actually did do something wrong.

"What if he cast his gaze in our direction," and I could hear Will's teeth chatter as he said those words.

"You're suppose to be a peasant," I kept whispering to him, "can't you at least try and be ignored."

"Calm down Will," said Kate, "before I give ya' a cuff on the ear."

Yes I had definitely picked the wrong traveling partner, and just as that thought was racing through my head things got worst, a whole lot worst. Will twisting and turning to see if he was being watched caught the eye of Prince John. I was sure that all of the trembling and gasping for air didn't help. Will had turned away quickly as the Prince looked over in our direction, but that came too late, and the Prince was already curious and on his way.

"This way Sagamore," I could hear Prince John order him. And as for Sagamore being such a tough guy he followed the Prince like a scared puppy.

"Yes my Prince," Sagamore said back.

I wasn't looking at them as the Prince came closer with Sagamore, but I could tell from the way Jimmy and Kate were looking down that trouble was definitely headed in our direction.

But still that darn sun just didn't seem bright enough, and still I could tell that trouble was getting closer.

"We've got to get out of here," I said to Jimmy.

Jimmy looked around for a way out, but the problem was that we had to be near the sundial to know what time it was.

Behind us I could hear Sagamore's voice calling to the Prince, "but they're just peasants your highness."

"Will, you have done us in," said Kate.

A breeze moving across the sky must've pushed that old cloud along, 'cause now we could see the time on the sundial.

"Now," I said to Jimmy, "we've got to go now!"

211

Jimmy looked up at me; there was a lot of fear on his face. "We've got about three minutes before twelve."

"Does that matter," I almost screamed out the words.

"Can't change the settings now. We could land in the middle of the earth's destruction," he said, "we'd be toast before we had a chance to use the belts again."

"They are going to burn us at the stake," Will almost cried out.

"Keep a tight lip on it Will," said Kate, and this time I was on her side.

Will's outburst had gotten the attention of people nearby who looked at us. And now that they were looking, they started to remember. That morning, the two witches being tossed into the moat. Some of them began to back away, and I could hear nervous muttering coming from the crowd.

A little boy pointed at my sneakers that we had kept mostly covered in mud, and hidden by the rags hanging down over our ankles. "It's the devil's own footwear with which they tread," the kid cried out.

"Like demon's hooves they be," his mother shrieked as she dragged the child away from where we stood.

And I wondered if our "witches footwear" was how Prince John had spotted us in the first place? No, he would have had to have eyes like an eagle to spot our sneakers from across the courtyard.

One little girl who had been at ringside earlier, called to her father, "Da," she said, "it be the masters of the serpent."

Great we had graduated from witches, to masters of the serpent, and all in one day. I guess Sagamore still was letting people believe that me and Jimmy had rode the giant snake all the way back to the Underworld. Once there we had just enough time to stop for a quick snack with Satan, before heading back to the surface to do more evil. Like Lord Hoxley had said, us looking bad only made Sagamore look good, and he was gonna keep us looking bad until we were charbroiled on the stake, and he got to play hero all over.

Then suddenly I heard the voice of Lord Hoxley calling to the Prince and Sagamore once more. He was being quite loud, and I guess he had to be to cut through the noise of all the people in the courtyard. "Your Highness, Sir Sagamore," he said. "I had no chance to convey to you my fondest wishes on this the occasion of your birthday." But this time Lord Hoxley's attempt to take the attention off of us came too late.

"Out of my way you old fool," said Prince John. Boy was he rude. The Prince was still focused on Will. With everybody backing away, and people starting to point and whispers of fear spreading through the crowd Will couldn't help himself, he turned to see the Prince looking directly at him.

"Oh my," cried out Will, yeah we were once again the focus of all that unwanted attention.

Real loud like Prince John shouted to the guards, "seize them."

That fast he had recognized all of us, and the guards were after us. Like lightening they had pulled out their swords, and began to run through the gang of people who were busy stampeding the other way.

"Now," I screamed to Jimmy.

He looked down at the sundial, the time was not yet quite right.

"Run," he said to us all, and that's just what we did.

We could hear the armor clanging, as the guards were right on our tail. All around us we could see people running for safety, screaming and terrified trying to get out of our way as we were racing on by them. Guess they were still terrified by the "Masters of the Serpent."

"Stop in the name of the King," someone screamed, but now just didn't seem like a good time to stop running.

We got to the corner of the castle wall, and I turned real fast to see that the guards, Sagamore, and the Prince were right behind us, and coming on quick. It looked like we were trapped, when Kate grabbed hold of Jimmy, and pulled him towards a ladder that was hanging from the top of the wall. With nowhere to go but up, we began to climb. Up and up we went, even Will, who had been the last one on to the ladder.

On the way up the rickety legs of the ladder began to wobble back and forth, and I thought it was gonna collapse and fall. Then we'd all go crashing to the ground. If that happened I just wanted to make sure that I landed on the birthday boy, Prince John. At the far end of the wall were the other soldiers who had been keeping watch; they started to move towards the place where the ladder was anchored against the edge. As we got near to the top, we had to keep moving just to stay out of the way of Sagamore and the guards that were now following us up. I was sure that the ladder was gonna give way with all that weight on it. Even Prince John had joined in on the climb. I guess he was thinking that it was all part of his big birthday bash. Finally we had been trapped between the guards from above and the ones down below.

"Now," I yelled to Jimmy again.

"I think we've got about another minute," he said.

"How will we know when…"

He looked down to see Lord Hoxley still standing near the sundial and looking up. He didn't seem to look too happy, but we were sure that he was staying there just to give us some kinda signal when the sundial hit twelve.

The guards, Sagamore, and Prince John were closing in fast.

"Tie in Will," Jimmy told me, and I grabbed hold of Will who just seemed to be frozen as the guards got closer. Jimmy then started to do the same thing to Kate. Believe me it was tough to do standing on that wobbly ladder that swaying all over the place.

"Come here," I pulled Will closer, and slipped the time belt around him. I looked down to take another quick look at Lord Hoxley, who still hadn't given the signal. The guys after us had slowed down as they got closer. I think they were still a little scared of us, but it was Prince John who stopped them in their tracks.

We were all standing on the ladder now, and it was swaying and wobbling like crazy.

"Halt," he said, and the men stopped on the dime. Prince John looked at Will sadly, "Will, you've joined in league with the devil," he said.

"No, your Highness," Will came back, "it's science that they bring with them not witchcraft."

"These are the words inspired by the Devil," Sagamore yelled out.

"Silence", ordered Prince John as he now used the body of Sagamore to climb up onto the higher step of the ladder. Everything shook even more.

"But your Majesty," Sagamore tried to get out.

"I said silence," Prince John was practically standing on Sagamore's head when he got closer to us, and he kept his eyes stuck right on Will.

"They are enemies of the kingdom," said Prince John, and you have given them comfort."

"No my Prince," Will tried to get out.

"We are not your enemy," said Jimmy.

"They wish to deceive you with their childlike forms your Highness, do not be fooled by their cleaver guise," said Sagamore as he was trying to get the Prince's foot out of his face. Boy this guy was giving us a lot of trouble. Even while he kept talking I could tell that Jimmy was still looking down at Lord Hoxley far below. Looking down and waiting for a sign.

"No," said Jimmy, "we are just like you, kids, but from another time…"

That's all that Jimmy could get out before being cut off by Sagamore.

"We have all seen their enchantment over the serpent… No mortal could possess such power your Highness."

"It was a trick," cried out Jimmy, still waiting for the sign, anything from Lord Hoxley. A quick look let me know that Hoxley was still looking down at the sundial. What was only supposed to be three minutes now seemed like hours… days.

"It's all been tricks your Highness," Sagamore went on, "but tricks to deceive and confuse conjured by the blackest spirit of the Underworld himself. We have all seen their evil with our own eyes."

"No, Master," said Will, "they are good boys… They just want to go home…and."

And then Sagamore cut him off again. This guy was as rude as the Prince. "And you, you young disciple of evil, it is more than a good thrashing that you'll be getting for this transgression."

And for the longest time the Prince was just being quiet, and looking really sad and disappointed with Will. It kinda felt like Prince John might of really liked Will.

"If your Majesty will permit, we can get the real truth in the torture chamber with the help of your Uncle Basil", Sagamore kept pushing.

The Prince looked sadder as he spoke, "I need to know the truth Will." Once again he ordered Sagamore to get hold of Will and us. "Seize them Sagamore." With these words Prince John moved out of the way of Sagamore by swinging to the outside of the ladder. The ladder shook even more fiercely.

"A pleasure your Majesty." Sagamore continued his climb. With him below, and more guards up above we were really running out of places to run.

"But I swear…" Will tried to get out.

"These devils have your mind in their power," Prince John yelled to Will.

"No," Will cried out, but that didn't stop Sagamore from climbing closer towards me and Will. Will started to pull away pulling me with him. Didn't know where he thought he was going.

We both began to climb higher. It was really hard with me and Will now tied to each other, but like I said with Jimmy and Kate just overhead we were really running out of space. All that was left was that and the ground far below. If we jumped I felt for sure we'd be killed. But still Sagamore kept coming, so either way it looked like we were gonna be killed. I didn't know what to do. We were kinda stuck with no place to go but down.

Then suddenly out of nowhere Lord Hoxley called out from the ground, "commit them to the flames," he cried out.

And we all knew what his words meant, that was the signal, it had to be twelve noon on the sundial.

"NOW," Jimmy screamed out just as Sagamore and a few of the guards climbed closer. There was no time to waste, I pressed the button on the time belt, and at that exact moment Sagamore reached out at us knocking me and Will off of the ladder. We began to fall to the ground, but we were taking Sir Sagamore with us.

The screams of both me and Will seemed to mix with those of Sagamore as down, down we went. And as we fell to what looked to be sure death waiting below I could feel my stomach just hanging in the air while the rest of me just dropped like a rock. I knew that there wouldn't be any green beam blasting at me to break my fall. It would only be seconds before we all crashed onto the muddy and rocky slope that surrounded the castle wall. So I closed my eyes, and screamed out, and waited for the end of the ride.

Early Concept Art For The Gravity Box II.

Part 2: Back For the End of the World and Just in Time

Chapter 1: In the Belly of the Beast

I couldn't tell you who was screaming the loudest Sagamore or us kids as the fall off of the castle wall seemed to go on forever. When it felt like we had been falling a little bit too long I opened my eyes again, finding that the time belt had kicked in, and we were now skipping through time. I guess it was the time belt pulling us into a different time that had saved us all from a head on collision with muddy ground below. Like before it seemed that we were being bounced around from time to time, but I guess that was how the time belts worked, it kept trying until it landed you in the right time slot. All we had to do was hope that Jimmy had figured the whole thing out right.

I think we screamed for a long, long time, and when I looked over at him I could see that Sir Sagamore was still hanging on for dear life. So much that it felt like he was crushing my ribs, but I was too busy being terrified to worry about that right then. Somehow his holding on had let him get brought along with us into that time space thing. The sky seemed to open up, and we were being bounced back and forth like we were on the bumping car ride. Then suddenly as we had been flung into all that craziness everything seemed to come to a dead halt. We were once again falling, and then we landed in a field. Right near by was the castle, and for a minute I was afraid that we were still in the twelfth century. But looking up at the castle it now looked older with weeds all around the edges, and climbing up the side.

Flat on his butt Sir Sagamore looked up at me and Will. He was staring at us as if he was terrified, and I could tell you that he was. Will wasn't doing any better; he just wobbled next to me not saying a word. He looked around in disbelief at the field, and the now abandoned castle. But still there was no sign of Jimmy and Kate. Then all at once there was a crackle in the sky, it flashed white like it had been charged with lightening, and then Jimmy and Kate just seemed to fall from out of mid air. They didn't fall too far though; just enough to land on Sagamore, and knock him flat on his back again. Quickly Jimmy and Kate jumped to their feet. For a minute Jimmy didn't speak, he just looked around scared like. Then he started talking.

"We don't know how much time we have, so let's get set up and ready," Jimmy looked around really scared that we might not have enough time to set the time belts right.

But we're still at the castle, " I yelled at him.

"That's where we're supposed to be," he yelled back at me.

He just started looking around. He knew that whatever was happening we weren't going to have a lot of time for talk. It was funny that no one seemed to have anything to say but Kate.

"And this be your magical world," she said kinda disappointed.

"It's not magical, it's just not..." Jimmy was explaining while he worked on the time belts.

"Devils," cried out Sagamore still groggy from the ground.

222

Will and I jumped back away from him. He was in the wrong century, but he was still crazy, so we just wanted to stay clear.

"We really don't have time for this right now," Jimmy told him.

Sagamore got to his feet real fast, and started to pull out his sword.

"What have you done with the Prince," Sagamore shouted at the top of his lungs. "Sweet boy… sweet boy…" I had been in the twelfth century just long enough to know that Sagamore was lying his head off, because nobody liked Prince John. I was just beginning to see just how big a chicken Sagamore really was.

We all backed away, but Jimmy didn't seem to be paying attention, his eyes were fixed on something in the distance.

"We made it," he yelled, and that even stopped Sagamore as we all turned to see what he was talking about. Then Jimmy didn't sound so sure, " I think." Jimmy kept looking around nervous like, "but why is everything so still?"

And there it was across the field, a great big silo next to a giant barn, next to a farmhouse. Sure that had been built long ago, but way after the time of Prince John, the psycho Queen, and all that other crazy stuff.

They all stopped, even Sagamore to take in the old silo.

"Behold the citadel of Satan," Sagamore cried out. I was guessing that Sagamore wasn't all that up on his farming.

"Give it a rest," Jimmy told him.

"Are you sure we made it," I said.

"My timing should have gotten us here a short time before the Earth was being destroyed. Like I said I didn't want to get here too early, because I thought there might be complications." When he said that he looked over at Sagamore.

"You really thought Sagamore…"

"Why do you fiends speak the name of Sagamore," Sagamore cried out. Yeah he cried out.

"Put a lid on it," Jimmy yelled at Sagamore.

"You dare to speak to me Sagamore the Mighty" Sagamore started to say when Jimmy looked him right in the eye and shut him up quick.

"The world is about to be destroyed," Jimmy yelled at him. And at this point Sagamore really believed in our magic, because he had now stepped into another world. He truly believed that we were good buddies with the Devil. "If we are gonna make it out of here alive, I need you to shut your trap."

Sagamore crumbled back to the ground, "I'm doomed, I'm doomed," he cried out.

"Yep," Jimmy said.

Kate and Will were still looking around in complete disbelief. Then Jimmy turned back to me, "I just didn't want a hundred people standing around while we were having to change the time belts. People knowing that they were about to be crushed by a giant comet."

"What now," I said because I really wanted to know what the heck was happening.

"There should be some sign something…"

"What do you mean?"

Even that big mouth Sagamore was too shook to say anything. All of them including Will and Kate just looked around like they were in another world, which they kind of were.

"The Earth should be being destroyed just about…" Jimmy looked confused and scared, "just didn't want to get here too early…" and that's all Jimmy got out when the sky turned black around us.

"Earth destroyed…" Sagamore cried out in terror.

We all looked up to see what was making everything get dark all at once, and there it was. A giant cloud of dusts was forming overhead. "No actually, this is perfect timing," Jimmy said.

"This is what we want," I tried to yell above the loud rumbling the Earth was making. Looking at the sky about to fall in didn't look like perfect timing to me. Then all of the sudden the ground started to rumble, and breakup underneath our feet. Mile long cracks in the earth spreading out in all directions, and coming very close to where we were standing.

"I'm sure," Jimmy yelled, "now quick, get ready."

Kate and Will were still just looking around scared to death. Sagamore froze as he looked at the world collapsing around him. He looked like he was ready to cry. Then Sagamore looked at Jimmy as he clutched tightly to his sword. "Son of Lucifer," he called out to Jimmy with all the courage that he had left. "I command you to stop this evil now!" Jimmy could see just how scared Sagamore was, and put his hand on the time belt and commanded Sagamore to move away.

"One more step," Jimmy ordered Sagamore, "and I'll turn you into a frog."

Sagamore moved back quick like totally buying that Jimmy could do what he said.

Jimmy then looked back at me, "Shawn we don't have much time get ready!"

"I'm doing it! I'm doing it." I yelled back at him.

I started to do what we had practiced doing back in Lord Hoxley's hidden chamber, and I knew I only had seconds to get it ready. Jimmy's timing had been perfect. The comet must've just hit down as we arrived, and coming at us was a giant shock wave of black dust. It was just sweeping across the landscape, and headed right at us. In a moment it hit the farmhouse, and tossed it high into the air. The silo fell on its side, and was headed at us like a giant bullet shot from a giant gun. The cloud of dust was thick and heavy, and was knocking down everything in sight. Trees, the large hill that was not that far away, they were all flattened out, and being crushed as it raced over to the spot to where we had landed. And still the never ending cracks in the earth kept moving across the ground. They were like the long arms of a monstrous octopus that kept reaching out and wanting to grab hold of us. Suddenly Will jumped out of the way just before being sucked under by one of those gigantic tentacles. He knocked me off balance 'cause we were still tied together in the time belts. I tried not to fall over as all around us the earth was chewing up, smashing, and mashing everything that got in its way. Death was only seconds away, and we were next in line.

The sight of the surf of rocks and sand crushing everything in its path froze Sagamore again. I think I would've frozen too, but I had no time to be scared right then.

Will began crying out. "It's the hand of the great spirit punishing us for our evil ways."

"Pipe down Will," Kate yelled at him, and then she reached past Jimmy, and kicked him in the butt. No wonder Will had been made whipping boy, he was so good at it.

Because she was tied to Jimmy he was jerked backwards. "Stop it we got to focus," he yelled.

Me and Jimmy, we didn't have time to stop and explain again to them what was happening, we had only a second or two before being squashed under that enormous cloud of dirt that was now racing towards us. The earth beneath our feet was shaking so much right then that we almost fell over.

"What the…" I tried to get out.

"It's the wake from the comet," Jimmy yelled out, "ready."

"Almost," I said.

"Shawn," Jimmy yelled again.

And then I had it set. At least I hoped so. I grabbed tight to Will, and Jimmy pulled Kate closer as we both got ready for the return trip home with the time belt. At least we were hoping for a return trip.

The giant dust storm was ripping through the air, and just about to reach out for us. I think Will was crying. I might've cried myself, but like I said we just didn't have the time.

"We go in three, two…" Jimmy started the countdown.

And all at once with the world about to collapse in on us, I saw Sagamore standing right in front of me, unable to move at the sight of death flying right in to his face like a monstrous fly swatter about to flatten him.

"One," I heard Jimmy scream out the signal, to hit the button on the time belt.

Sure Sagamore was a creep, but he was about to be crushed like a bug, so I grabbed him by his arm, and tried to pull him along for the ride. It had worked before I thought maybe it would work again.

Then suddenly the ground opened up right beneath our feet. Will, Sagamore, and me had been dropped into the center of a hole that seemed only a few feet deep. In just a second the dirt was collapsing in all around us. We were all stunned, but still I knew that there was no time to freeze up, or we would all be ground into mush by the shifting earth. No time to cry or to waste, Jimmy had already said the magical word "ONE", and I pressed the button on the time belt.

It was like being thrown in to that blender all over again. We were skipping through time that fast, and we had just missed being eaten alive by the earth closing in all around us. There was dust and dirt flying in all directions from the fallen comet that we had just escaped being gobbled up by. The tidal wave of dust created by the comet crashing into the Earth was followed quickly by an incredible flash. It was like super bright lightning or a giant bomb going off. And then somehow that flash of light and the loud bang of the explosion was chasing us through time. Thinking the skipping through time must have made a crack in the Universe or something. Somehow the light and noise from the explosion had followed us in through that opening. As if caught in the time warp the light seemed to be drawn to us, and was hot on our trail. But there was nothing that we could do. The time belt was just taking us along for the ride. I thought if the explosive lightning caught up to us it would fry us good and crispy.

As time was knocking us all over the place, suddenly a gap in space just seemed to open up before us. Like a great, giant doorway it unlocked, and tossed us onto an open road. We landed flat on our butts again. I jumped up as quickly as I could, and tried to pull Will and Sagamore along knowing that the sizzling blaze of light was only seconds behind. And then it happened. As quickly as it had opened up, the doorway slammed shut blocking out the dangerous lightning that had been chasing after us. There was a loud crashing sound, and then a rumble as the lightning seemed to be trying to bust through that now closed door.

We were shaking so much that I didn't know which direction I was standing, or even whether I was up or down. I could hear Will screaming in my ear, and there right in front of me I could feel Sagamore stuck to me like I was flypaper. Right then and there I think I was his favorite witch. Still I didn't suppose he was liking his arrival into the twenty-first century too much. I fell back to the ground and wanted to cry.

Like a small child Sagamore began walking on his knees towards me. He was holding his arms out as if pleading. It was creeping me out.

"Oh kind, benevolent witch," he said as the tears streamed down his face, "your magic is too powerful for this tired and humble warrior, your mercy I beseech…" That's all Sagamore got out when another spark of light blasted through the sky, and Jimmy and Kate fell out of it and landed right on Sagamore's head. It seemed like he was always getting in the way. He fell to the ground once more, and dropped back into the dirt and continued crying. "Ow," Kate shouted as her butt bounced off of the hard black helmet that was somehow still sitting on Sagamore's head.

"Does not my purity not mean anything, that providence should deliver me to this world of bitter darkness," Sagamore went on.

"I guess not Saggy," I said as I untied myself from Will and rushed to see if Jimmy and Kate needed any help. Yeah, I had called the black knight Saggy. It just came out, but it seemed to me that this character should have a nickname. By the way I knew that Saggy was gonna hate his new nickname, but ain't that half the fun of giving someone a nickname? "You all right," I asked them?

Jimmy did not answer he just untied himself from Kate and jumped up, and began looking around to figure out just where we had landed. Kate stood up and began brushing herself off. She started looking around at the dirt road and the surroundings.

"This be the world you were so anxious to return to," she said as if not believing that we would want to come back there. She didn't seem happy with anyplace we landed. I wasn't freezing for the first time in forever, so it felt like at least we were closer to home. Jimmy cut himself free of Kate, and I did the same with Will.

"No time, no time for chit chat," said Jimmy. "We've got to get our bearings." He started looking to see what was around us.

"We're still here, so I guess we've missed getting squashed by the comet."

Right then Sagamore came crawling towards us, gently he grabbed hold of Jimmy's foot, and began to beg once more: "Dear, sweet demon, I crawl on these tired knees to beg…"

"There's no time for any of this," Jimmy said, and pulled his foot away from Sagamore, who fell back into the dirt.

A second later a car came speeding down the road. It could've been a dragon the way Kate, Will, and Sagamore looked as it came closer. It was coming pretty fast, and kicking up a lot of dust as it whizzed along. Jimmy went and stood out to the middle of the road, and begun waving his hands in the air.

"What are you doing," I called to him.

"He is confronting the creature unarmed," cried Sagamore.

"I don't know how accurate we were in our settings, or where the second shock wave from the comet has sent us," Jimmy called to me from the middle of the road. "I'm only sure we don't have that much time to get to the Gravity Boxes, and do all we've got to do before the comet hits down again," Jimmy stood his ground as the car raced towards him. And whoever was driving that car didn't seem to notice or didn't seem to care that there was a kid standing in the middle of the road right in front of them, 'cause they showed no signs of slowing down.

"Jim… Jimmy," I yelled to him, "it's not gonna stop."

"It's got to," he called back. "We've got to find out where we are."

"The creature will devour him," Will called out.

"And the heinous beast is made armor, and spewing fire and smoke," cried Sagamore. And he sounded kinda concerned about the cars bad muffler, and I couldn't tell if that concern was for Jimmy, or out of fear that he would be eaten alive after the "creature" had eaten Jimmy. To tell the truth the creature… car had me scared for Jimmy too. Still it came closer… closer, and Jimmy wouldn't move, and the car showed no signs of slowing down.

"Jimmy," I called to him again, "we'll wait for the next car…"

"How long we gonna wait Shawn," he now yelled back. His voice was high and shaky, and I could tell by the sound of it that he wasn't so sure the car was gonna stop either.

True the comet was going to hit the Earth, and probably soon, but without knowing where we were, and the exact time we were in we had no way of getting to the Gravity Boxes. And they were the only hope the world had of not being destroyed.

The sweat was rolling down Jimmy's face. I could see it, and it seemed so strange, with all that was going on that my eyes were fixed on drops of sweat pouring off of Jimmy's face. He was the one playing chicken with the car, but I could feel my heart pumping faster and faster. And my heart hadn't slowed down from the last near death call. What were those people thinking as they continued to speed head on at the boy standing in the middle of the road, 'cause they still showed no sign of hitting the brakes. Then, suddenly, I heard it, I heard the sound that explained why the car was not stopping for Jimmy, and the reason a car might be ready to run down a kid who had stepped into its path. Coming up fast behind the speeding car was the sound of sirens and flashing lights. The police

232

were hot on the trail of the car about to have a head on collision with my best friend. It was the most scared I had been in minutes, to realize that Jimmy was standing right in front of a high-speed chase.

"They're not gonna stop," I screamed to Jimmy, "they're getting chased by the cops." And I wasn't sure he had heard me. That car was steering directly at him, and he seemed to be staring it down, daring it not to stop. Or just maybe it was that he was too scared to move out of the way?

Right about then the car being chased started blasting its horn. Now I knew that they saw Jimmy, but that still didn't mean that they were gonna stop for him. That car was roaring down the road at about a hundred miles an hour. The blast of the horn shrieked through the air once more. Sagamore grabbed on tightly to his sword, and seemed so scared that I thought he was gonna faint. Will ran to be beside Kate. Well actually he was crouching down behind her.

"The roar of the behemoth signifies that I have truly entered the land of lost souls," Sagamore cried out, and his knees started to buckle as he crumbled to the ground once more. He was doing a lot of buckling and crumbling that day.

I swear it looked like the end for Jimmy. Still I couldn't tell if he was just being brave, stupid, or just too scared to move at this point. We had been through a lot of dangerous times together, so it was a pretty good guess that he wasn't frozen to the spot. The smart money was riding on brave or stupid. When the car was only a few yards away from him, I couldn't take it anymore, I ran towards Jimmy, and tackled him out of the way. We both landed hard on the side of the road. The landing was a little softer on me 'cause I had fallen on top of him. His scream of pain hit my ears at the same time the car screeched, and ran off of the road. In a minute the police car would be there.

Two young guys jumped out of the car, they were both looking at us like we were crazy. One was hollering out calling us names as they raced off into the surrounding woods that lined the road.

"You crazy #@%*<", he shouted, words that I can't really repeat right here. They didn't really have much time for name-calling 'cause the police car pulled up only seconds later. Two policemen jumped out of the car and looked at us, and then to Sagamore, Will, and Kate who were standing across the road. They didn't know what to think. They could stop to see what we were about, or continue after the guys they were chasing. Good thing they decided to keep after the guys that they were chasing.

"You almost killed me," Jimmy yelled at me as he picked himself off of the ground.

"Those guys were two feet from squashing you like a bug," I yelled back at him.

He looked at me again, and I could tell that he was still angry, but I think he was more angry about the scratches he got when I knocked him to the ground. That fast he cleared his head, and got back to what was important.

"Okay, okay, no time for this now, we've got a planet to save."

A moment later Sagamore, Will, and Kate came running to our sides. And I got the feeling that Sagamore was rushing to be by us 'cause he was scared being by himself on the other side of the road.

"You stared down the beast," said Sagamore.

"And saved the lives of those it had swallowed up," Will joined in.

"Yeah, yeah, yeah," Jimmy kept looking around trying to figure where exactly we were.

But it was only Kate who had dared to go near to the cars that were by the edge of the road. Still she kept some distance. She wasn't brave enough to actually go up, and touch the monsters that had eaten up the cops and the guys they were chasing, and then spit them out on to the road. So I could tell that she was curious, but still scared.

"Their bodies are made of armor, what bravery to have stared the creatures down," she called back to Jimmy not taking her eyes off of the cars.

"Only the eye of a demon could have vanquished these horrid creatures," said Sagamore sadly and still scared out of his head.

"You are demons," cried Will as he once more backed away terrified. All at once this crazy kid was siding with Sagamore.

"I don't think he'll ever get it right," I said to Jimmy.

But Jimmy wasn't listening to any of it. He had gone off to look at the car that was lying in the ditch.

"I don't think it will start," Jimmy said.

"We can't drive anyway," I said back.

"It shouldn't be too hard to figure out," he went to look at the police car. That's when I ran to his side.

"You've got to be kidding," I couldn't believe what he was planning.

"If we don't get to the Gravity Boxes there won't be any jails left to throw us into."

"But we can't drive, we're kids, we're…"

"We can figure it out, and besides we've got an adult with us." I looked back to see that he was talking about Sagamore.

"Now I know you're kidding, Saggy?

"You named him Saggy," and I actually saw a quick smile cross Jimmy's face.

"It seemed to fit."

But it was back to business fast enough for Jimmy. "We're gonna need all the help we can get along the way." And he turned to the others. "Guys we've got to get out of here now, Sir Sagamore…"

"Has Heaven closed its doors completely on this poor knight," he said.

"I think so," Jimmy told him. He was more quiet when he turned back to me, "and I think Saggy will make a perfect distraction. If we get stopped we'll just say that this old loony kidnapped us, and forced us to dress like medieval peasants. If we save the world we can always come back and rescue him later."

"Or not," I said.

"Or not," Jimmy laughed. "Everybody in," Jimmy said as he opened the doors to the police car.

"Into the belly of the beast," Sagamore looked alarmed. Then he looked sadly back to me and Jimmy, "and my soul…"

"Gone," said Jimmy and shrugged his shoulders, "the gates of Heaven closed, and you are now our servant. Do you have any problems with that?"

"So it was a pack of lies you fed to Lord Hoxley, my Will and me," cried Kate.

"And we are all doomed," cried Will.

Jimmy wasted no time in pulling them off and away from Sagamore.

"If we want Sagamore's cooperation, than we must have him thinking that all hope is lost. We did not lie to you, and lying is not a good thing, but with a guy like Sagamore, I'm willing to make exceptions. Besides I'm trying to save a planet here."

Kate seemed to understand, but Will was a little shaky as they walked back to the car.

"If I be in Hades…" Will tried to get out.

"You're not," Jimmy cut him off, and put his finger quickly up to Will's lips.

Kate quickly gave Will a boot to the butt. He turned scared, but didn't say a word. He just continued to walk kinda spooked to the car.

"Now," said Jimmy as he sat in the front seat driver's side of the police car. And I could tell that they were all trembling as they slowly entered the car. They weren't the only ones who were frightened. Me too, 'cause coming out of the woods were the two policemen bringing the guys from the first car along with them, and there was us trapped in the "belly of the beast."

Chapter 2: Sir Sagamore to the Rescue

At first I don't think that the policemen saw us. They were too busy keeping guard on the guys who had tried to escape from them.

"Let's do something," I yelled to Jimmy, "here comes..."

And I didn't have to finish the sentence 'cause Jimmy had seen them too.

"I've seen my Dad do this a thousand times, so..." he started to say.

"So let's get going," I heard my voice getting louder and higher as the cops finally saw us sitting in their car.

"First I turn the key," Jimmy seemed to be trying to guide himself through it.

"Press the gas," I yelled at him.

"The brazen fools have come back to challenge the beast," shouted Sagamore.

"Shut up Saggy," I told him.

"Saggy," Sagamore stopped to think about his new nickname for the first time.

"You kids..." one of the Policeman called out from across the road. He had hardly spit out the words when he began rushing towards the car.

"This can't be good," I told Jimmy.

"The gentlemen seems to be trying to gain your attention," said Will.

"Perhaps they want to reward you for slaying this hideous creature," Sagamore put another two cents in. And I realized that it didn't matter what century this guy was in he just didn't have a clue.

Jimmy had turned the key, and the engine started to grind, and then stop.

"Hit the gas," I said again.

"My foot won't reach it," Jimmy yelled as he slid down off of the seat and tried to reach the pedal. Now at the same time his neck was stretched up and over the dashboard trying to look out of the windshield. It seemed like he could do one or the other, but not both at the same time.

"Hold it right there," the cop yelled even louder as he got closer. At that time the other Policeman was keeping guard over his two prisoners.

The key turned again, and Jimmy pushed his foot to the floor. This time the engine kept running, but the cop was almost on top of us.

"You've got to press down that stick thing on the steering wheel," I said, but Jimmy had already remembered from watching his Dad do it so many times. Pushing the lever down onto the letter D made the car jolt forward. It was a hard jerk 'cause Jimmy was pressing real heavy onto the gas pedal when he did it. There was a screech of the tires as we started to roll. The big problem now was that Jimmy could hardly see where we were going.

"I said hold it," the Policeman ordered real loud as we began to move forward and jerk, forward and jerk. By now he was at the side of the car, and I thought that he was gonna take out his gun.

Suddenly he grabbed hold of Jimmy's arm, and tried to pull him up and out of the seat.

"I beg you sir, do not trifle, they are powerful wizards indeed." Sagamore was finally giving us some respect.

"What the," the Policeman tried to get out as he got a good look at Sagamore.

"He saved your miserable hide you ungrateful wretch," Kate cried out as she lunged towards the window, and bit hard into the Policeman's arm. He cried out in pain, and pulled away from the car.

"I'll shoot," the Policeman warned, and this time he really seemed to be going for his gun. And I wasn't exactly sure that he would have shot us kids or not. He was definitely looking at Sagamore as if he was a dangerous character. And I guess back in the twelfth-century that was true, but here in this time Sagamore was like a scared puppy that just didn't want to get smacked with the newspaper.

"Jimmy," I think I wanted him to stop.

"It's the world depending on us Shawn, the whole world," Jimmy said. And at that moment he stood up away from the seat, pressed his foot to the floor, and was now able to see over the dashboard. The car screeched once more as we began to zoom down the road.

We were all tossed back by the sudden motion and then forward.

"We've evoked the rage in this one," cried out Will.

"Ungrateful rabble," said Sagamore, "you should have not wasted your magic releasing them from this..." it was then that he

240

remembered that he was the one now inside the car. "Oh precious spirit from the great beyond!"

Behind I could see the one Policeman running still up the road after us. Jimmy was doing his best to keep an even pressure on the gas pedal, but it was rough for him just barely being able to see over the dashboard.

"Where we going," I yelled to him. The others were all being quiet. I guess the first time being swallowed by a beast made it easy to keep their mouths shut.

"We're almost home," Jimmy called to me.

"We are," I felt kinda excited.

"This police car belongs to the town right next to ours, I guess I was only off by a few miles." That's what he said, and then we heard another siren. This was also not a good thing. The flashing lights of the second police car were not far behind. The sound of the siren growing louder told me that they were coming after us now. The sound of the siren wasn't the only clue. There were the voices coming over the radio in the car.

"We have a stolen police vehicle traveling along route…"

That's all that they could get out when our guests in the back seat became even more scared about the voices coming over the radio.

"Even this hideous beast is inhabited by evil spirits…" Sagamore may not have been in the lower world, but I think he would have been just as happy to be there right about then.

"We'll have to dump this car and soon," Jimmy said.

"Then why'd we take it," I yelled at him.

"I didn't know how much time we'd have to get back home before…"

"I thought we were suppose to arrive three days before…"

"We were off on the location, I was afraid that we might be off on the time."

"Another beast is in pursuit," cried out Kate as she was looking out of the back window. The second police car was coming up fast behind us.

"And quite ferocious I dare say," Will now on his knees with his face pressed to the rear window.

"Is there no end to this nightmare," cried Sagamore.

"We'd better ditch it," Jimmy yelled back to me. Yeah, that's what kids do when they're scared, they yelled, and it didn't matter if they were only inches away from each other.

"How 'bout ditching it right now," I shouted.

"Good idea," Jimmy came back at me, "they've called ahead." He looked at me like a little kid, and said, "this other pedal, that'll stop us right."

"It usually does," I said, "but not too hard…"

Jimmy didn't let me finish my sentence as he stomped down onto the pedal. All at once everything in that car was flung forward. I had had my hands pressed against the dashboard, but that didn't stop me from smacking my head into it. Jimmy was holding tight to the steering wheel, and Kate and Will both flew into the back of the front seat. It was Sagamore who got the worst of it I think. The weight of his heavy metal helmet just didn't want to stop. The force of the car suddenly braking had turned him into a human torpedo that went crashing through the windshield, and landed him on the hood of the car. Luckily he had flown over the heads of both me and Jimmy, and went right through the glass. Lying out on the top of the car Sagamore looked like a big, cheesy hood ornament.

Like I said, Sagamore was creep, but we really thought that he had gotten hurt, so both me and Jimmy jumped out of the car to see if he was okay. Real weak like, he had fallen off the side of the hood and onto the ground. He was already getting up when we reached him.

"Sir Sagamore," Jimmy called out as we ran to his side.

"Is my punishment over," Sagamore said as he tried to stand up and staggered around like he was drunk.

"Are you all right," Jimmy tried to find out.

"No, no," he went on, still dizzy, and not listening to Jimmy. "In the Underworld the punishment goes on forever, yes, yes, now I remember. I must be suffering forever…" It was then that he looked sadly at Jimmy. "A moment of quiet Master, I beg thee, so that I may prepare for this eternity of hellacious torment, just one moment I plead thee…" That's about all he got out when he collapsed against the car, and almost fell to the ground again.

"No time for this Sagamore," Jimmy said as the sirens got even louder. The flashing lights were almost on top of us, and so we had to get away from there and into the woods that surrounded the road. Moving Sagamore was the problem. He was dizzy and stumbling all over the road.

"One more task," said Jimmy, "then you shall rest."

"Oh please great one," Sagamore begged as Jimmy began to pull him away from the police car and into the woods.

"Get Kate and Will out of the car," Jimmy told me. And as I looked back I could hear the blasting sirens, and see the flashing lights charging right at us.

"Hurry," I screamed at Will and Kate trying to get them moving. They were having trouble getting the door open. They'd never seen car handles before, so I ran over, and pulled the handle for them from the outside.

"The beast had us captured," Will said jumping from the car like he was afraid the door would close again trapping him inside.

"Yeah, yeah, yeah," I dragged him along, not having time to explain. Kate just ran after us.

Sagamore wasn't being any help. He still staggered, and I guess he figured if he was gonna be battling these beasts forever it really didn't make any sense to rush. Jimmy knew he couldn't waste any time with Sagamore, so he pushed him against a tree and began to scream through his helmet.

"Sir Sagamore, you have slain this beast," I guess Jimmy was talking about the police car we had borrowed and trashed. "Now its evil twin is coming to seek vengeance upon you."

Almost instantly Sagamore seemed to become alert. He looked in horror at the second police car about to arrive.

"But it is the duty of a knight to… to do battle with the forces of evil…" Sagamore said weakly, and sounding like he was gonna cry.

244

"It's a beast he won't understand," Jimmy continued to yell at him. "We must escape!"

"Yes, yes, retreat!" It was now Sagamore yelling back to us. "Retreat with honor," he called as he began to rush into the woods. You see Saggy wasn't just taking on two twelve year olds with an army behind him, this situation might actually be dangerous.

Me, Kate, and Will, were already moving in that direction, but Sagamore who was moving full speed ahead passed us, and that was with wearing a ton of armor. To retreat with anymore honor Sagamore would have to have super speed. Jimmy right away caught up with us. In no time the second police car screeched to a halt, and other cops jumped out and started chasing after us. This time I was really scared that they were gonna start shooting.

Once inside those woods I knew right away where we were. I should've, I played there often enough. On the other side of all those trees was my hometown, and in the middle of it all was Professor Burkhardt's house and his laboratory.

"I was only about a half mile off," Jimmy called to me. He seemed happy even though the police were catching up and quick. There were more "hold its," and "stops in the name of the laws," called to us, but we were home now, and that was were we had played our own games of hide and seek. We had played in those woods long enough to throw anybody off of our tracks. I was sure that Will and Kate could play along easy enough, but I wasn't so sure about Sagamore. The clanking of his armor was echoing throughout the forest, and acted like a signal to lead anyone right to us.

Suddenly Jimmy stopped, and told Sagamore to do the same. For a long minute it all seemed quiet except for the pounding inside my chest again. I was sure that that could be heard as easy as Sagamore's clanking armor. Right then we had all stopped, and were trying to catch our breaths.

"Do you think…" Will tried to get out, and then Kate booted him in the butt, and held her finger up to her lips to remind him that this was no time to be opening his big mouth. She was turning out to be cooler than I first thought she was. I still wouldn't want her for my sister.

"Over here," I heard the voice of one of the policeman call to the others. But I couldn't tell if they were coming our way or not. In fact with all the trees around us it was hard to tell where they were coming from.

Jimmy had had the right idea. Just standing still was our best bet with Sagamore along for the ride. Besides the woods was so big that someone could search for weeks, and still not cover the same ground twice. After awhile we thought that it might be all right to move on. All the sounds that the police had been making had died down, and I thought that they might have gone back to their car. That hope lasted only about a minute longer when we heard it. More sirens, lots of sirens headed our way. The police must've called for more backup and plenty of it. I guess you steal one police car the cops lose it. The screeching sounds of several other police cars hit our ears, and we knew we were in it and deep. But wait it gets scarier, there were now dog's barking. Yeah, that's right, dogs yelping as they were released into the woods.

To my side were Will and Kate frozen with fear. It was a sight that I was getting use to seeing. Sagamore pressed himself against the nearby tree. He hadn't taken a step, but his body shaking kinda hard inside of the armor was sending a rattle into the air.

"The hounds of hell have been unleashed," Sagamore cried out.

"Quiet," Jimmy warned him.

"My evil ways, my evil ways," Sagamore just went on, his body trembling and teeth chattering. "I would abandon them all for one chance, one opportunity to make amends for my transgressions."

The sounds of the dogs racing through those woods got louder. I really didn't think that all of our experience playing hide and seek could save us from the noses of those police dogs now hunting us down. None of us were talking right there and then. There were just eyes darting back and forth to each other waiting for answers. Answers that I wasn't sure were there. Then Jimmy came through. If anybody could figure a way out of this, I knew that it would be him. The problem with the plan he came up with was that it all depended on Sagamore. Jimmy went right up to Sagamore, and looked directly into his eyes. That was easy to do because once again Sagamore had crumbled to the ground, and was lying weakly against the tree.

"Did you mean what you just said," Jimmy asked Sagamore. Sagamore looked at him wide eyed and terrified. "About wanting a second chance, what price would you pay for that?" And at first Sagamore didn't answer him. It was like he was thinking if he really wanted that second chance to do good things, or he was just saying that, because he thought that that's what we wanted to hear. Remember he still thought he was in the Underworld, and he wasn't sure who was in charge, and who he should try and please. "Did you mean it," Jimmy pushed for an answer.

"I was hoping that perhaps a sincere apology and my heartfelt promise…"

"That won't be enough Sir Sagamore," Jimmy was being rough, and holding him to what he had said, and he had to, 'cause we didn't have much time before the police and the dogs got there.

Sagamore took a deep breath and then answered. "Yes my Lord," he said as he sunk even further to the ground.

"Then you must face the beast head on," Jimmy said.

"But Master," Sagamore tried to get out.

"It's out there waiting for you," and as Jimmy spoke those words the yelping of the dogs got louder and echoed through the trees. Now it really sounded like some kind of beast was hunting us down, in fact it sounded like a bunch of wild beasts were chasing after us.

"Out there," Sagamore looked around even more terrified.

"Out there," Jimmy went on, but you must call the creature to you, and you must plead our case."

"Plead our case?" Sagamore was really confused now. "Master is this a test… to see…"

Jimmy didn't let him finish "Only a man of your culture and articulation could possibly hold sway over the creatures enormous appetites."

"So it devours its victims…" Sagamore was really creeped out by that.

"I'm talking about his lust for power," Jimmy made a good save as he changed the story around.

"But I am only a man your Greatness, and a pitiful challenge for any such task." He then looked over to Will and Kate. "Perhaps it would be best to send the children to stave off the creatures voracious appetites. A small sacrifice could appease the beasts until we are better positioned to do battle." Will and Kate looked at Sagamore with total horror and disbelief. Sagamore really wanted to get out of this, and was willing to feed Kate and Will to the beasts to do it.

"The sacrifice must be yours Sir Sagamore," Jimmy told him. "If you are to find salvation."

"Ah yes, it would have to be," Sagamore answered him sadly.

"Why do you think you have been brought here? Word of your charm, your magnificent persuasive powers have swept the lands and the seven seas…"

"Seven, there are seven…" I could tell he didn't really care, but wanted to talk about anything, but the sacrifice that Jimmy was asking him to make.

"I think so!" Jimmy drove the point home, "and those stories of your incredible might have reached our ears…"

"I'm that good," Sagamore was now really confused, and I think that that's what Jimmy was going for. "But Master, I fear rumor of my abilities may have been slightly exaggerated."

But Jimmy wasn't letting him off the hook that easy. He grabbed hold of his helmet, and looked him straight in the eye.

Which Jimmy could do now 'cause Saggy had slid further down and was now slumped weakly against the tree. "Lord Sagamore, the beasts are ready to consume the world, and there is only one man who can save it."

"Oh please say that that man is not me, your wonderfulness."

"You've hurt a lot of people Sir Sagamore, innocent people," Jimmy said to him, his voice sounding very serious as he forced Sagamore to look directly into his eyes. Jimmy had stopped playing on Sagamore's ego, and was now pleading to his conscience. "There is only one way to wash the bloodshed from your hands, and to cleanse your spirit of its blackness."

Sagamore looked away from him, embarrassed, and afraid at the same time 'cause he knew that what Jimmy was saying was all true.

"And you don't think the children…" Sagamore tried to offer up Will and Kate again for the sacrifice.

Jimmy stopped him in his tracks. "No," he yelled, "you are the hope of the world Sir Sagamore, and maybe, just maybe you can take your soul cleansed from this place."

"So my soul," said Sagamore, "it can be regained by me?"

"And that's the only way out of this place of torment?"

For the first time since arriving in this century Sagamore looked like he had some hope in his eyes.

"If you really want to make amends for your past deeds, then this is what you've got to do." Sagamore nodded his head nervously as if understanding. Jimmy had not really answered his question, but to be honest there was no way that he could.

We still weren't sure of the exact time and even the day, and just how close that comet was to hitting the Earth. A lot of what we had going on was all guess work. What we had to think about now was getting to the Gravity Boxes. That was the only chance we had if we were gonna save the planet.

It was now the voices of the police mixed with the yelping of the dogs letting us know that danger was getting closer and closer.

"Well," Jimmy said to him.

Sadly, slowly Sagamore lifted his sword as if grabbing onto that little bit of hope that Jimmy was handing him, and was getting ready to run with it.

"No," Jimmy said, "you must not take a weapon. Words will be your power. Besides it would be useless, the minions of Lucifer bare daggers that spit lightening." And that fast Jimmy had snatched the sword out of Sagamore's hand and any hope from his eyes. Sagamore trembled again and fell back against the tree. Jimmy looked at me, "if he walks out there with a sword he's going to get shot."

"No weapon," Sagamore whimpered, "daggers that shoot lightening?"

"You'll have your words... Use only your words."

"Yes my words," Sagamore looked with terror past the trees that seemed to hold all of the danger.

"It is your only chance for salvation," Jimmy told him, "and I will not abandon you if you do this thing for us, for the world."

"And they be the hounds that guard the gate to his kingdom?"

"There's no time to talk now," Jimmy went on, "if you shout with all your might at the devil's henchmen they will lose their power over you."

Suddenly the first policeman and his dog came into sight. We saw him, but I don't think that he saw us, not yet.

"Now," Jimmy pushed Sagamore to make him move.

Sagamore slowly moved away from the tree that was holding him up.

"You must raise your voice to tame the evil," Jimmy said.

Sagamore looked sadly back at the sword lying against the tree. "Perhaps the might of my sword could strike some fear into the hearts of these devils."

"No," Jimmy commanded him, yeah that's right commanded the Black Knight. "Your sword is useless against their lightening daggers," and then Jimmy motioned for us to all start moving in the opposite direction away from Sagamore.

As we did, the policeman spotted Sagamore. At first he didn't know what to make of the knight in black armor standing not far from him. Jimmy was right to make Sagamore leave his sword behind, and he knew that the dogs couldn't bite him through that tin suit that he was wearing. We kept looking back as we moved away from Sagamore and the police. Still Sagamore had not said a word. He just stood there like a statue, his knees trembling and clanging together. Aside from sounding like a rusty car's engine he was unable to move. Yes he was that scared.

We heard the policeman shout at him, "hold it right there!"

The other policeman and dogs were all around us, and we were still waiting for Sagamore to make a big enough stink to get everyone running over to him. We had stopped dead in our tracks, and just waited and hoped not to be spotted. It was Kate who came up with the next part of the plan. Out of nowhere she picked up a large stone, and hurled it at the back of Sagamore's armored suit. Hitting him in the head the trusty knight's helmet rang like a bell, and seemed to have jolted him into some kind of action.

"I fear not your evil ways oh deplorable servant of sin," he screamed to the policeman.

"Just stand right there Mister," the policeman said to him, and that's when it happened. Sagamore began to scream his head off calling all kinds of attention to himself. It was just what Jimmy had planned. Actually it was better than Jimmy had planned.

"I have come as a messenger of the great Wizards bidding all thee to abandon the evil of their ways. In the name of this glorious cause I beseech you to lay still your weapons, and to bare witness to my words. Find tranquility in my rhetoric, for it is by divine guidance that I have been sent before you..."

Sagamore was out there in the middle of the forest screaming like a maniac, and hopefully that would get the attention off of us kids who would just end up looking like victims of the mad man anyway. Yeah, he looked that crazy.

It worked like a charm. Suddenly all of the dogs and police began running towards Sagamore. We had hoped that leaving him defenseless without his sword would also keep him safe from being shot. Hearing all of the noise one cop just ran by us on the way to arresting Sagamore. He was making such a spectacle of himself that no one was paying attention to the rest of us.

Me and Jimmy began pulling the rags off of us that we had used to escape from the twelfth century, so we would look more normal. Before leaving I had gotten my clothes back from Will, but there wasn't too much that we could do about Will or for Kate right then. We were just trying to look like we belonged as much as possible.

Now it was back to the matter of saving the world, and we still didn't even know if we were in the right day, and what time it was. The only thing we knew for sure was that Professor Burkhardt's lab was not far away. I knew that Jimmy would keep his promise to save Sagamore if he could, but if the planet got destroyed that'd really be out of our hands.

As we sneaked deeper into the forest the yells coming from Sagamore began to fade out with the sounds of the barking dogs. We caught a glimpse of Sagamore being dragged to the ground by the police, and I was really glad that they didn't hurt him. Like I said he was a real creep, but when we got him here, to this time, he was kind of like a lost puppy, but not as tough.

Chapter 3: Home Sweet, Deadly Place

After all of the policemen had surrounded Sagamore getting away seemed kinda easy. The way Jimmy had figured it was that a guy in an armor screaming his head off was gonna draw more attention then four scared kids running for safety, four kids that were obviously victims of the nut job in the metal suit. That was the way we were gonna play it anyway, and in a way that was true, only not in this century.

It didn't seem right throwing Sagamore to the cops even after all the terrible things he had done to us and to others. But we were trying to save a whole planet, and leaving him behind seemed to be the only way that we could do that. Jimmy told me later that he thought it might do Sagamore some good to know what it felt like to be in the same situation that he had put so many others. Big difference being that that weren't gonna roast Saggy at the end of the day.

We headed as quick as we could over to the Professor's place. The sun was going down, and it was gonna be dark real soon. The woods always seemed like an unfriendly place after dark even if you did know it real good.

As soon as we were out of ear range of the police Will's tongue started wagging a mile a minute.

"So you're saying that the minions of Lucifer are going to devour Sir Sagamore?"

Jimmy just shook his head, and I was gonna explain to Will. I mean, I guess you could understand how he might be a little confused jumping from one century to another. But Will really didn't seem like he was trying. Before I could start to bring him up to date Kate jumped in.

"Will, you silly twit," she said, "it's already been explained in to your muddled head that we're not in Hades, and there are no demons."

And she was right. Actually the only real demon we had met along the way was Sagamore. And he was not nearly as scary as he had been in the beginning. I kept wondering how Lord Hoxley had gotten Will involved with so many experiments back in the twelfth-century. The kid seemed like he was afraid of everything, but then he did save our lives, so that was cool. Guess doing what he had to do even when he was scared, that was kinda brave if you think about it.

"But we've seen the beast made of iron with glaring eyes, and that shrill tongue that chilled the bones."

Will was obviously talking about the flashing lights and the sirens on the police cars, and nine hundred years ago that would've been the obvious conclusion to such a sight.

"It's an invention of our time," Jimmy finally jumped in. "I promise you what seems like magic are just things that you don't yet understand."

"But we shall understand," Kate added, trying to reassure Will and I think herself.

"Soon," Jimmy said, "I promise."

Will became silent. He looked at us as if trying to take it all in, but still not quite trusting us totally. I didn't know how much we had to do to get this kid to trust us, but the good thing is that Kate seemed to be on our side, even if she didn't quite understand the situation herself yet.

The walk through the woods let us know that we were at least in the right place, and we could only hope the right time as well. Suddenly Jimmy stopped leading the way and turned to us. He seemed to be very excited about something.

"I got it," he said.

"Got what," I asked.

"The way to destroy the Gravity Boxes, and still have them," he grabbed me by the shoulders, and shook me like a little kid.

"Don't we have to get to them first, and don't we have to make sure that the world will still be here in five minutes?"

"Oh yeah," he stopped, "I forgot!"

"What is all your merriment for," Kate asked curiously.

"We don't have time for merriment yet," I said, "we still don't know how much time we have until the world is destroyed." Had no time to even wonder what merriment was.

"All right, all right," Jimmy said. "First we've got to hide Will and Kate."

"Hide us," Will jumped in.

"What will you be hiding us from now," Kate said right after.

"You and your brother are our secret weapons…"

"But we've got to keep walking," I warned Jimmy.

"Yeah, you're right," he said, "I'll explain along the way."

We started rushing once again, and Jimmy's mouth was moving a mile a minute. He had come up with a good plan, but now it all depended on Kate and Will to help us carry it out. True, they had

257

jumped into the moat to save us, but now we were gonna ask them to do something really scary.

It would be better to get to the Professor's place too early than too late. If we got there too early the Professor might not even know about the comet headed towards our planet, and then we would have to explain it to him, but if we were running behind schedule then we were really in trouble.

We got there as fast as we could. Jimmy had made Will and Kate hide behind some trees while we went up to the Professor's lab. We would've gone to the house that was attached to the lab first, but we saw that the lights were on in the lab. That's where you could usually find the Professor anyway. Most of the time he just ate and slept in the house, and then went out to the lab so he could work on some of his crazy inventions. Yeah, the Professor seemed like he liked inventing stuff more than just about anything else.

When we reached the house Jimmy called to him. He had to yell a couple of times to get his attention. It had been warm that day, and the windows to the lab were open. In a little bit the Professor came out and onto the porch.

"Boys... Jimmy, Shawn..." he looked confused to see us.

"Professor," Jimmy said, "can we talk to you?"

"You're parents are very upset, where have you been?"

"Professor..." Jimmy tried to get out.

"They have called here several times..."

"We'll have to come up with something to tell them..." I said.

"Something to tell them," the Professor looked confused.

"And you boys smell like you've been swimming in the cesspool, you're filthy."

"Professor, we've got to talk," Jimmy finally shouted out to try and get him to listen.

The Professor stopped in his tracks, and stared at us, "as a matter of fact I've been trying to get a hold of you boys."

"I know," said Jimmy.

"You do," the Professor looked even more confused.

"Can we talk out here," Jimmy said.

Professor Burkhardt looked about nervously. "Do you know already why I was going to call you," he said. And slowly he then walked off of the porch and came closer to us.

That's when Jimmy lifted up his shirt, and revealed the time belt underneath.

The Professor looked at it stunned for like a whole minute. He then moved us a little further from the house. "The world he said…"

"We know," I came back.

"Then why are you wearing the time belts, and I can't believe I told you about them."

"Professor, I don't know what day it is, or just how much time we have," said Jimmy.

"You don't," said the Professor.

"The world," Jimmy had trouble saying the next words to come out of his mouth, "its already been destroyed by the comet."

"My goodness," the Professor almost fell over.

"You sent us back through time to keep us from destroying the Gravity Boxes..."

"You destroyed them," he sounded amazed, as if he had forgotten all about the conversation we had had. Then again I had to remind myself that that talk hadn't really happened yet. But that was a good thing, 'cause that meant that we had some time before the comet did crash into the Earth.

We kept the Professor outside of the lab while we explained the whole story to him. And even though we had been through some incredible adventures together he was having trouble swallowing our whole tale. I think we lost him when we got rescued by the giant serpent in the moat. Then it was time to let him meet Will and Kate. They were real nervous when they came out of the forest like they were meeting a great sorcerer, and in a way they kinda were. I know I had seen what seemed like magic coming out of the Professor's lab. At first he looked at them with pure amazement, and then he looked sadly at me and Jimmy.

"What is it Professor," Jimmy said.

"So many things," he came back, "but let me feed you children first, you have come through quite a harrowing experience." Professor Burkhardt still didn't want to discuss any of this stuff inside the lab or his house. He had set up a barbecue near to the garage. For a long time Will and Kate just sat and enjoyed their first burger on a bun. Will was at first afraid of the catsup fearing that it was goats blood in a bottle. But not having eaten in nine hundred years he decided to give it a try, and was soon lapping it down with the ice cold lemonade that the Professor had made from a can. Still they didn't say much. I guess that they were just happy to be alive after all we had gone through. I was just happy to be chomping down food that didn't have worms crawling through it. While the rest of us were busy chowing down, Jimmy seemed more interested in what was going on in the Professor's head. While I stuffed my mouth I moved closer to find out just what that was.

"We do have time to save the Earth now," said Jimmy, "so what's wrong Professor?"

"Complications that I did not foresee," the Professor looked back at him sadly.

"Complications," Jimmy was trying to figure out just what they were.

"The Universe," said the Professor, "it works along a line…"

"A line," Jimmy said."

"So many possibilities, I keep running them over in my head."

"You do?"

"These children what impact would they have had upon the world that you took them out of? And how will that effect today."

"They're a couple of kids," Jimmy said, "what could they…"

"But they will grow into adults."

"Not if Sagamore has anything to say about it," I said.

The Professor seemed to explode, "they will have an effect upon the world, their world, and that could effect today."

Jimmy looked around, "Professor, we're still here, so what impact could they have had? The world is still here, and for sure would not be here in a couple of days if they had not saved our lives."

"And then there's that terrible knight, Sir Sagamore. Perhaps his reign of evil eliminated certain people who…"

"We'll have to ship him back to the twelfth-century as soon as… and how will that effect today," Jimmy seemed stumped.

"People will learn of the time skipping device…"

"When they hear his story they'll just think he's crazy," Jimmy was sure of that.

"For today he's crazy, but tomorrow…"

"But there won't be any tomorrow if we don't do something to stop that comet," Jimmy came right back at the Professor.

"And what if the line that the Universe travels along is immutable…"

"Immutable, what does that mean…" I tried to get out, but they both just ignored me.

"I had this same conversation with Lord Hoxley… But you must've thought there was some hope or else why…"

"Of course you're right we've got to try… You must not let your optimism and your mission be thwarted by a terrified old man."

Jimmy walked over and placed his arm on the Professor. "And maybe being forewarned is the way to get around destiny," Jimmy said. "The only thing that we know for sure is that fate has not given us anyway out of this dilemma except to take it head on."

"There is a way for you boys to survive this…" the Professor tried to get out.

"I know what you're going to say Professor, and I don't want to hear it."

"You could escape into the past to a safer time…"

"No!" Jimmy was serious about this, and I think it was the first time that I had ever heard Jimmy yell at the Professor. "My parents, my friends, and you would all be gone, it wouldn't be much of a world without the rest of you. And wouldn't us going into the past still be changing things that shouldn't be changed?"

The Professor nodded his head, smiled, and seemed to agree with Jimmy.

"Of course you're right my young friend. We must take good care to secure the future, that is if there is going to be a future."

"How can we do that," Jimmy looked confused.

"But the past we cannot change the past."

"Sure we can," I finally pushed my way into this conversation, "we've already done it." That's when I got another of the Professor's irritated looks. "And that must mean we can change the future, I think." Both looked at me, but they didn't argue with what I was saying.

"If we send Will and Kate back in time they'll be burnt as witches," Jimmy told the Professor.

"And if they stay here…" the Professor came right back at him.

"Will's not good for much, oh that's right he did save my life a couple times today," I said.

"And Kate did her share in the saving our butts department," said Jimmy.

"Besides she was a great little housekeeper and probably would still be," I told the Professor."

"Yeah she kept the castle immaculate," Jimmy was scamming the Professor too, 'cause the castle was a dump.

"And if you ever need to kick someone's butt," I joked, "Will would be perfect."

"Yeah, getting his butt kicked was his job," Jimmy went right along with me.

"I cannot keep these children here," the Professor sounded annoyed, "this is not a nursery, and I am not their legal guardian."

"Well we can't let them be found by the authorities," Jimmy said. "Then it would really all come out, about the time belts and the Gravity Boxes." Jimmy knew that the Professor would be wanting to keep a lid on all that stuff.

"When I had sent you two skipping through time I didn't expect you to pick up passengers along the way," the Professor almost yelled. That's when Will and Kate stopped shoving food into their mouths, and looked over at us a bit curious and nervous like.

"It's okay Jimmy told them, just keep eating." They were so hungry from their trip through time that that's exactly what they did.

"It doesn't matter right now," Jimmy told him. "If we don't get to those Gravity Boxes the planet gets destroyed..."

"Again," I felt I should add.

"Yes again," Jimmy said. "And truly Professor we need Kate and Will to save the planet, if it can be saved." He looked directly in the Professor's eyes, "agreed?"

"Agreed," said the Professor, but he really didn't sound like he wanted to agree with Jimmy.

"Kate and Will is the only way this mission works."

"I don't know how much help Kate and Will are gonna be, they are still chomping down those burgers like they hadn't eaten in centuries." I had told that little joke to Jimmy and the Professor. Even in this century my humor wasn't being appreciated. I started getting lonely for Basil, the laughing Dungeon Master.

After we had all finished eating we set off to stop what the Professor had called a "global disaster" for a second time. We practically had to drag Will away from the potato chips and coleslaw. Suddenly living in the devil's lair didn't seem like such a bad thing, especially at dinnertime. Somehow Will had turned this whole saving the world thing into a picnic. For any of this to work we were going to have to get to the Gravity Boxes, and to do that we had to get over to Jimmy's place. The problem with that was we were gonna have to do a lot of sneaking around, and we wouldn't have time to answer any questions. By the way this was the repeat of the same night that we had first destroyed the Gravity Boxes only now we knew that our houses were being watched by government agents. Jimmy's plan called for creating an illusion that would fool Flynn and the other agents who might be watching. We had tricked these guys before, but this time they'd be expecting us to try something, and they weren't gonna buy into our trick so easy. So whatever we did had to be good 'cause we had to keep the Gravity Boxes safe. Keep them safe, and in our hands right up until that old comet was ready to crash into the Earth.

Concept Art For Sagamore's Henchmen.

Chapter 4: Fe Fi Fo Fum, Here Comes Bobby

So once more we were off and running, and the Professor was left biting his nails and pulling out the little bit of hair he had left on his head waiting for us to come back. All of us were tired as heck, but didn't have much time left for what had to be done to save the world. We had had to take Will and Kate with us like I said. They were an important part of Jimmy's "master plan" as he was now calling it.

We were all pretty beat, but there wasn't any time to rest right then. Remember it had turned cold out that night, and that cold was starting to get to us. Jimmy thought that the polar plunge we had taken nine hundred years before should've toughened us up for it, made us immune. But that didn't happen, and the cold just seemed to be biting into us.

On top of everything we still stunk from that swim in the moat, and Kate and Will were carrying with them the smell of the twelfth-century too. All we needed was a good wind to kick up behind us for everybody to know that we were coming. So we headed over to Jimmy's house to get some fresh clothes. We had to get clean stuff for more than just smelling good, we had to make Will and Kate look like they fit in with the rest of today's world. Yeah, fitting in was an important part of Jimmy's "master plan", and part of the magical illusion that he wanted to create. To make all that work Jimmy had made sure that he brought along the schoolbag with all of his secret inventions inside.

First we had to get down to old man Jenkins super market. It wasn't exactly all that super, but it was the only place at our end of town where we could load up on groceries. The store was kinda small, and old man Jenkins was kinda mean. He one time kicked me out of the store when I tried to get a job as a box boy. Seems like a little mud on the shoes could turn the guy into a real wild man. Jimmy seemed to think that I was under qualified for the job. But I thought I could've at least packed canned fruit into cardboard boxes. Sometimes Jimmy could be kinda mean himself. Anyway we found ourselves at the store on very same night that we first destroyed the Gravity Boxes. The reason we were there was to get our hands on a couple of milk crates that in the dark could double for the Gravity Boxes.

Will and Kate looked bugged eyed as we went into town. The sight of a six story building sent shivers down Will's back. In his mind part of him still believed he had somehow landed in the Underworld, and everything he saw made him believe that that was true. At the very edge of town they could see the flashing neon lights coming off of the building's signs. That scared them too. Kate not as much as Will. She had slowed her walk a little as we entered the town, and got closer to the buildings, but Will had almost come to a dead halt.

"We don't have time to waste," Jimmy warned them.

"I've never seen anything like it," Kate said with her mouth wide opened.

"Of course not," Jimmy said, "where you're coming from none of this has happened for hundred's of years."

There were a few people moving about, and I didn't think it was a good idea to run into anybody until Kate and Will had had a change of clothes, or at least had a bath. Me and Jimmy we needed to get cleaned up too, but the stench coming off of those two just hung in the air like the backfire off of a frightened skunk. I couldn't imagine anybody smelling worst except for me and Jimmy. Me, I was getting a little use to it, but still couldn't wait to take a dunk in a hot bathtub. Yeah we must've smelled like a moving pig farm to people who got down wind of us.

Into the shadows of the super market rear entrance we pulled Kate and Will with us. It was still early that night, and old man Jenkins was busy ordering around whatever help he had working the loading dock. The dock was being cleaned, and we could hear Jenkins barking orders like a nasty drill sergeant as we got closer.

"That's not how you clean up this mess," he yelled at one of his employees, a kid from our school, Tommy Stoddard. Then he grabbed the broom from his hands.

"He must be kin to Sagamore," whispered Will as the grumpy old Jenkins angrily swept dirt from the loading dock onto the ground.

"Now that's how you push a broom," Jenkins swung the broom at Tommy almost hitting him. "How do you expect to get anywhere in life if you can't even handle a broom boy," the old man yelled, and he seemed so proud of his ability to push dirt around. The single dim light hanging above the loading dock let us see the angry look on Tommy's face as he caught the broom just before getting hit in the head by it. Maybe not getting that job was a lucky thing for me.

Jimmy figured that we needed two milk crates to make two fake Gravity Boxes when we pretended to destroy them. In the dark the milk crates could be made to look just like the Gravity Boxes Jimmy thought. I didn't know how old man Jenkins was gonna feel about us taking his milk crates, but Jimmy made it seem all so clear.

"He would probably rather have us take the milk crates than having the whole world destroyed," he said.

"That would really kill off business," I said and right away realized how bad that joke was. "Sorry."

Jimmy shook his head. "Anyway afterwards we can always replace them. We just don't have time to go scavenging somewhere else for them tonight."

"Who's out there," I heard a voice echo off of the alley walls where we were hiding in the dark. It had been the voice of Tommy Stoddard who must've caught wind of us laying low in the shadows. If not by the sound of our voices than definitely from the odor blowing off of us.

"Are you daft boy," old man Jenkins squinted his eyes, and gave a hard look out into the darkness that was hiding us. "There ain't nobody out there, now start moving your lazy butt and get your work done. I'm paying you to push that broom, not to stand around idly twiddling your thumbs all night."

"But sir," Tommy tried to get out.

"But sir nothing, Get to work." He looked out into the darkness once more. "Although that is quite a stench coming off of the refinery." I think he was talking about the smell coming off all of us.

"Yes sir," Tommy said, and went back to work, but he kept looking up trying to get a another look out into the alley. He was sure he had heard something, and to a kid standing all by himself in the shadows of that that old loading dock that could be quite a scary thing. I knew my imagination could have invented some creepy monsters hiding out there.

Soon Mister Jenkins went back into the store, but not before warning Tommy to keep sweeping "or else."

Jimmy knew that it was important to keep our secret of the Gravity Boxes just that, a secret. And that went the same for the arrival of Will and Kate into our time. So now we had to get to the milk crates that were still sitting up on the loading dock, but to do that we had to get by Tommy Stoddard.

Now the problem with that was that Tommy was famous for being a big blabbermouth, so he was the last one we wanted to let get a look at us, or know the truth about what was going on. Still we had to get to the milk crates, and to do that we had to get Tommy off of that loading dock and back inside of the store. Once in there we knew we would only have a minute or less before old man Jenkins was yelling, and screaming for him to get back outside and finish the job that he had been hired for. Worst yet he could come out to check the situation on his own.

Jimmy pulled us all over to the side away from the back of the building. There he whispered his plan to us. "You know things really haven't changed all that much."

"Yeah, old man Jenkins is still a jerk," I said.

"That's not what I mean," Jimmy said.

"What are you talking about," I asked him.

"Keep it down," Jimmy warned me. "The thing is," he went on, "people are almost as superstitious now as they were when you guys lived," he said.

"We're still alive," Will reminded Jimmy nervously.

"Sorry," Jimmy apologized, and explained real fast, "I mean in yours and Kate's time."

"But we're still alive," Will wanted to know that for sure.

I wanted to swat at him myself, but once again Kate had beat me to the punch.

"Ow," Will cried out," and Kate quickly placed her hand over his mouth.

"Of course we're still alive you twit," she whispered kind of loud in his ear, "you felt that didn't ya'? Did it hurt good and proper," she whispered.

Will's head bobbed up and down happily; glad to know that he was still alive.

Slowly he peeled Kate's hand away from his face, and said quietly, "and that swat to my head, that was for my own good," he whispered back.

"Of course my darling brother, they're all for you own good."

Will looked at her unsure, but was still glad to be alive and kicking.

"Now we've established that you are still among the living," Jimmy said, "we've got to get that kid off of the loading dock."

"You have a plan," I said.

"Don't I always," Jimmy smiled.

And then once more we heard Tommy Stoddard call out into the darkness. "Is there somebody out there? Come on guys, don't mess around."

From the sound of his voice, I guessed that Tommy thought it might be a couple school buddies playing games with him. That's when Jimmy pulled us all back deeper into the shadows.

"What we need is a ghost," he said."

"How is it you summon the dead," Will was once again alarmed, and Kate was quick to add the comfort of another caring swat to the head for his own good.

"Ow," Will tried to get out, but before he could do that I had covered his mouth myself. I could see that swat coming a mile away, so I was ready for it. Funny Will couldn't see it.

Jimmy did not stop to explain what he meant, he just moved slowly through the dark to the dumpster at the edge of the alley. There he whispered his whole plan to us.

"I thought I saw some torn bags of flour that they must've tossed into the dumpster. They were right on top so…" And then he quietly moved towards the trash bin. There lying on top were two large, broken bags of flour.

"You think," I tried to get out, but Jimmy cut me off, which I really think was his favorite thing to do.

"Of course it will work," he said, "Tommy's already scared to death being on that dock all alone. We have the night, his fear, and a little make up…" he then placed a little of the flour on Will's face, "to make the illusion complete."

"What you planning to do with me all covered in flour like a fancy cake," Will whispered, now knowing to keep his voice low. "You not be baking me in the oven," his voice shook. This time Kate didn't swat him, but just shook her head in disbelief.

"You're going to be our ghost Will"

"What," Will jumped back hitting the side of the dumpster. Will letting go with a cry when he hit his elbow got another shout from Tommy, who had now stopped sweeping altogether. I was quick to shush Will and to cover his mouth while he was wanting to cry out more.

"Come on guys, it ain't funny no more," Tommy called out. He was really scared now. You could hear it in the shaking of his voice, which was just the sound that we were wanting to hear. I know that that sounds kinda mean, and maybe I kinda laughed to myself, but we really had to get to those milk crates.

Suddenly a flash of light came bursting from the inside of the store as old man Jenkins came through the door again. Tommy let go with a shriek.

"Aren't you finished yet boy," he yelled looking at the pile of dirt that Tommy had accidentally knocked out onto the loading dock when surprised by old man Jenkins.

"Sorry sir, I heard something," Tommy said nervously looking back and forth between his angry boss, and place where the noise was coming from.

"You'll be hearing the sound of yourself getting fired if you don't get this mess cleaned up and pronto, do ya' hear me boy?"

Tommy's head bobbed up and down, as he quickly began to sweep again.

"When I come out here again, this place better be spotless," old man Jenkins didn't even wait for Tommy to answer, he just grumbled something as he slammed the door behind him. Some of the dust that had been kicked up was still floating in the air, but Tommy didn't care, he just continued sweeping like a madman wanting to get back inside that store as fast as possible.

"How am I going to be…" Will tried to speak real soft, but his mouth was racing with the words as he tried to figure out what was going on.

"No time to explain," was Jimmy's answer, "we don't know how long we have before Flynn and his buddies go to my house." With these words Jimmy began covering Will with the flour. We were all trying to keep our voices down and whisper, but Will kept getting excited, and letting his voice get louder.

"Keep it down," Jimmy tried to shush him up almost getting loud himself.

"You guys ain't funny anymore," Tommy yelled out into the darkness.

Back behind the dumpster Jimmy kept trying to get Will ready.

"So it'll be like play acting," Kate said. I think she was trying to ease Will into the part he was going to be playing.

"But one of you could play the ghost as well," Will tried to explain.

"No," Jimmy came back, "you're already dressed for the part, its like you just stepped out of the past."

"But I did just come out of the past," Will said. And he said it like he didn't know we knew that. "And I'm still alive," he reminded us.

"Then it's perfect, first of all," Jimmy went on, "Tommy might recognize Shawn or me, so…"

"So I be your ghost."

"Exactly just go out there, and moan and slowly begin to walk towards that kid, he won't stay around for long. And…" Jimmy looked back at me, "when Tommy runs into the store, we're only going to have a minute, maybe less to get our hands on those crates."

"Got it," I said.

"What do I do," Kate said, and she seemed anxious to get in on the action.

"I've never played at being a ghost…" Will said.

"It's just a lot of whining and crying," Kate grabbed him by the lapels and looked him strait in the eye. "And that be something that you're already good at Will."

Will seemed to understand and almost kinda' pleased. "Tis true I do that well!"

"Keep it down, keep it down," Jimmy warned him again.

In that time Tommy Stoddard still hadn't taken his eyes off of the end of the alley all the while he was sweeping away at the small pile of dirt that had now started kicking up in the wind. This kid wasn't catching a break tonight.

"What if he loses his job," I stopped and asked Jimmy.

"If the world ends, where's he going to do his sweeping up then," Jimmy was once more annoyed with me.

"Now is everybody set," Jimmy asked us.

"Will could use a little more flour," I said. He just didn't look ghostly enough to me, so I began to toss what was left in the bag onto Will.

"No," Jimmy tried to warn me, but the warning had come too late, I had already flung what was left of the bag onto Will's head. Guess it was too much flour, 'cause Will started to cough on some that had gotten into his mouth and nose. In fact he started to choke like Jimmy in the tower.

"That's what happened to me in the past dummy," Jimmy was trying to keep his voice down, but he was mad with me so he got a little loud.

Now Tommy really knew that there was something out there. "I know you're out there man," he yelled out. Then Tommy moved the broom in his hand, and was holding it like big club. He called out again only this time even louder. "Don't mess with me man I know how to use this thing". Not really I thought, he'd been brushing at that small pile of dirt for about ten minutes. Guess if he got attacked he was planning on sweeping the guys coming after him to death.

"He knows we're out here," I said.

"But he's not going to do anything about it. Go," Jimmy was rushing Will, and then shoved him out into the center of the alley.

The flour stirring up with the wind blew into the air, and covered the arrival of Will as he coughed, and gagged, and moved into the alley.

"What do you want," Tommy screamed from the top of the loading dock.

And even if Will had wanted to, he couldn't answer him. Even with the choking and coughing that Will was doing he did look ghostly as he stepped through the flurry of flour that seemed to dance all around him looking something like a dust storm that had blown in out of nowhere.

But Tommy had surprised me; in fact he surprised us all. Instead of running inside he held the broom like a weapon, and was actually ready to defend that old loading dock and the pile of dirt that he had begun to collect there. He must've really loved that job.

"What's he doing," I turned to Jimmy.

Jimmy couldn't believe it himself when he turned to answer me, "Tommy Stoddard's protecting that mess he just cleaned up." Yeah, that seemed to be what he was doing, but no one could figure out why. In the meantime Will was still coughing his brains out, and making his way through the cloud of flour which had now gotten into his eyes, and had somewhat blinded him. He started staggering like he was drunk or something and trying to stay in a straight line.

"I mean it, I know how to use this thing," Tommy Stoddard yelled at Will as he was swinging the broom around like a big wooden sword.

"Well this isn't good," I said.

Jimmy didn't answer me, he just set his mind into overdrive trying to figure a way to pull this off, and not get Will killed. Will who was too busy trying to catch his breath to know that Tommy

Stoddard was ready to clobber him in the head with an unlicensed broom handle.

"What do you want," Tommy yelled at the top of his lungs at Will, who was busy trying to take in gulps of air, and rub the flour out of his eyes. Yeah, throwing that flour onto Will was kinda dumb.

There didn't seem to be anything that we could do. The dust storm of flour was dying around Will but he still couldn't see.

Tommy brought the broom back like he was about to swing a baseball bat. If we stepped out into the open it would give away what we were trying to do. More importantly we didn't want to give Tommy a story to tell all over town. Remember it was important that no one know about Kate and Will. They were our secret weapons and very important to Jimmy's "master plan."

"I'll clock you in the head with this thing, I swear…" Tommy looked like he meant it as Will stepped even closer into the danger zone.

Suddenly again the door to the rear of the store swung open. The light from within the store flooded the whole loading dock and out into the alley.

Mister Jenkins' voice barked like a mad dog as he stepped through onto the dock.

"What in Sam hill is going on out here," he screamed as he pushed through the door.

We were not the only ones surprised by the arrival of old man Jenkins. Tommy still terrified by the sight of Will turned out of fear swung wildly, and clobbered his boss right in the wrist with the broom handle. Old man Jenkins grabbed hold of his arm and cried out.

"Ow! What loony bin did they get you out of boy," the old man was now speaking from pain as well as just plain nastiness. Now I think that Tommy was more scared of that old man than he was of our pretend ghost. He rushed to his side, and began to try and give him help.

"Sorry Mister Jenkins," Tommy said as he tried to rub the old guy's arm.

"Get away from me you nut job," he pulled away. "Mad as a hatter, mad as a hatter," Mister Jenkins kept yelling at Tommy, and rubbing his arm.

"But," Tommy tried to explain as he was attempting to pull old man Jenkins to safety, and away from the spirit haunting the loading dock.

"Get your hands off of me," cried the old man, and shoved Tommy away. It was then that old man Jenkins saw Will for the first time. "What the devil…" he tried to get out, but he looked too scared to finish his words.

"We don't have time for this," Jimmy said, and that's when he pushed me into the center of the alley. "Now," he screamed. As he did that he grabbed the other bag of flour that had been sitting near the top of the dumpster. He turned to Kate, "get Will, and get him back here, NOW!"

With that we both began running towards the loading dock. I was a faster runner, so I made it there first. As I jumped up onto the dock I knew at once what Jimmy had grabbed the bag of flour for. To old man Jenkins we were just a couple of kids, but Tommy, he would recognize us. Me and Jimmy knew each other so well that we didn't have to say a word. I turned to him, and he threw the bag of flour up to me.

"What are you boys…" that's all that old man Jenkins got out before Tommy had turned back to see who was running towards him. I couldn't let him know who I was, so right then I pitched the bag with all my might, and smashed him in the face. The flour scattered everywhere. After he cried out with a loud "OW", the explosion of white powder all over the place stopped Tommy from seeing who I was. Just like Will he started to cough up a storm.

"This is private property," the old man called out. He too was having trouble seeing past the mini dust storm that was blowing all around them.

"Bobby! Bobby," old man Jenkins called out. Both me and Jimmy knew who he was calling to. Bobby was the security guard that worked at Jenkins Market. He was a big monster of a man, who walked the aisles of the store all day just to make sure that no one was stealing stuff or squeezing the tomatoes too hard.

As he came through the door Bobby was so big that his shadow blocked out most of the light that had tried to come out the door with him. So the dock got dark once more, but only for a minute.

"Mister Jenkins…" Bobby called out.

Me and Jimmy we were right near to the milk crates now so we grabbed hold of them and started to run.

"Hey you kids…" Bobby called out to us as we headed for the edge of the loading dock.

I was closest to Bobby, so he reached out to grab me. I could see the shadow his big sweaty paw just about to take hold when I ducked out of his grasp and moved to his side.

Tommy Stoddard was still rubbing the junk out of his eyes, and Kate was dragging poor Will away from all of the trouble. Both me and Jimmy jumped down off the loading dock and onto the ground. Bobby, as huge as he was, was right behind us, and catching up quick. For a big guy he was pretty darn fast, and you got to remember that we had the milk crates slowing us down.

Bobby even started yelling at us: "I'll kick your scrawny butts when I get my hands on ya'." And you could tell by the sound of his voice that he meant it.

We were almost to the end of the alley when I heard Jimmy let loose with a cry. I turned to see that Bobby had snagged him by the back of his shirt. The milk crate in Jimmy's hand had dropped to the ground, and the crashing sound from that echoed all over the alley.

"Bring him up hear," I heard old man Jenkins call out.

"My eyes…" cried Tommy.

"Oh shut up boy," the kindly old man Jenkins yelled at him. "It's flour, not acid, you little twit."

Like a small ball of cheese Bobby carried Jimmy, who was still dangling from his shirt.

"Let him go," I called to Bobby, who turned back to me.

"You're next punk," he said.

"But you don't understand…" Jimmy tried to tell him.

But old Bobby, he didn't want to listen. He was dragging Jimmy back to the loading dock where the old man was still rubbing his wound that Tommy had given him.

"Try and steal my milk crates will ya' boy," I could hear Jenkins growl, yeah that's right it sounded like he growled.

"We were going to bring them back," Jimmy was still trying to explain without saying that the end of the world was not far off, and we didn't have time to waste.

"Ya' want me to take him to the back room Mister Jenkins," Bobby laughed.

"That'll be a good place to keep him until the police arrive." I really didn't know what to do. I was really scared, I could say that I had been in worst situations, but the truth is with the end of the world just around the corner this one was moving to the top of the list. The only thing I knew for sure was that I had to get Jimmy loose from Bobby's grip.

"You don't understand…" Jimmy tried to get out, "PLEASE," he cried out.

"I understand that you tried to steal my milk crates sonny," the old man roared like an angry lion, and was sounding meaner every second.

"Let me take him in the back room," Bobby said again, and was beginning to sound a lot like Basil the laughing Dungeon Master. Suddenly, and I don't know why, but I flung the milk crate in my hands down and onto the ground. It didn't break, but the crashing sound got the attention of everyone, and even got Bobby to stop in his tracks.

"That's private property you little creep," Jenkins yelled at me.

"And you're a big bag of wind," I hollered real loud. And the way my voice boomed in that alleyway made me sound like a real bad dude, or maybe just a guy trying to get himself killed. Then with my foot I shoved the milk crate hard against the wall where it slammed, and made another crashing sound. Now both Jenkins and Bobby were startled. They didn't believe I was doing that. Most of the town was scared of Bobby, him being the "biggest land mammal in the whole county," as Jimmy had called him. And as for old man Jenkins, he was just plain nasty. No one ever messed with that guy, not if you didn't want to go clear across town for your produce and dairy products.

"And another thing you old goat your milk is sour, and you overcharge for the baked good." Remember I didn't know what I was saying, I was just trying to get Bobby mad enough to let go of Jimmy, and go after me. I was sure that I could out run him. Jimmy was the brains, but I was the one with the speed. "And you, you ugly gorilla," I was taking my big chance now by turning on Bobby, "the only thing scary about you is your breath. It smells like you've been chewing on an old sock."

"Carry that scrawny brat up here," Jenkins ordered Bobby, "then go get mister big mouth."

I couldn't believe Bobby hadn't gone after me. I had just called him those names, and he turned the other way with Jimmy still dangling in the air like puppet at the end of his arm.

"Please, you got to let me go... you don't know what..."
Jimmy tried to get out. But it sounded like he was having trouble
talking, like Bobby was squeezing the air out of him as he was
carrying him.

I didn't know what to do, but I knew that I had to keep trying.
Bobby was famous for his short fuse, so I guessed that I had to play
on that, "people around here say old Bobby's as strong as an ox, but I
bet you're twice as smart."

That was it. Bobby lost it. He looked real mean at me,
"You're dog meat," he yelled. Without a second thought, he tossed
Jimmy like an old basketball away from him. Jimmy landed kinda on
his feet, but then fell onto his butt. Bobby was now after me, and he
was charging ahead like an angry rhinoceros.

"You had your hands on the one little creep already," the old
man tried to warn, but it was too late. Bobby had changed course all
together.

I knew that I had to get my hands on that other milk crate, the
one that I had kicked away. So once more I took a chance. Running
at Bobby I zigzagged to the side, and dived under his arm to pick up
the milk crate that was now against the wall. Jimmy was taking full
advantage of his freedom to do the same and to get away.

As I snatched the milk crate from the ground I didn't have to
look to see what was happening behind me. The shadow looking like
that of a giant bear came up, and covered the whole wall. I swung
back with the milk crate, and I turned like I was gonna throw it, and
this made Bobby jump back from the fake toss. I then shot off to his

side, and was headed for the end of the alley with Bobby only steps behind me.

"Hurry, hurry," I could hear Jimmy calling me from up ahead. I didn't have to look back now. I could hear Bobby's big shoes slapping against the concrete and only a few feet away. My heart was racing, and my lungs were burning as I gasped for air. But he wouldn't stop. At one point I could feel his hand reach out and swat at the back of my neck. He was really mad now, and I wasn't sure he was gonna stop, or how long I could go on for. And then I felt it. Like a giant claw his hand came swooping out of the sky, and grabbed me up into the air. And now Bobby had me in his clutches.

"Put me down do you hear me," I ordered Bobby. Yes, you heard me right, I ordered him.

"You're going right into the back room he said, but the old man won't be calling the police right away, not for you we won't."

And right then I felt my entire stomach sink into the ground. I had a strange feeling if Bobby got me into that backroom that I wouldn't have to wait till Tuesday for the world to end. I felt so helpless being held up in the air by that giant of a man, his arms wrapped around my body and crushing my ribs. Now it was really tough catching my breath, because Bobby was squeezing me and hard. I was truly powerless, and figured the next move was up to Jimmy. But what could he do? It wasn't like we could gang up on Bobby. He was almost like a real giant.

"Bring him up here," old man Jenkins ordered from the top of the loading dock. "Steal my milk crates will ya' you little punk," he kept singing the same old song.

Tommy Stoddard still had his own problems. "Can I get some water to rinse out my eyes Mister Jenkins," he said.

"That's flour in your eyes, not acid I told you," the old man yelled.

"But it's really burning," Tommy kept rubbing his eyes.

"Go on, ya' make me sick you little milksop, you should try and tough it out like Bobby here."

Tommy kept pressing against his eyes, "As soon as I can see I'll be out to clean up the rest of the mess," he told the old man, and began to walk towards the light that he could see coming out of the rear entrance to the store.

"Alright, alright," Jimmy tried to reason with old man Jenkins, and Bobby the giant. "We were wrong, but we have a greater duty to a greater cause." Jimmy was being sure not to get too close to Bobby.

"Don't go too far buddy," said Bobby, "we'll discuss that greater cause as soon as I get my hands on your scrawny little neck."

"Mister Jenkins," Jimmy was still trying to get through to that nasty old man, "If you'll only listen to me, I'll try and make you understand the importance of what is going to happen if we don't get our hands on those milk crates."

"I think you're both crazy," said Jenkins, and turned to Bobby, "I think they're both crazy."

"Just let me get them in the backroom," Bobby almost seemed to be drooling as he said it. Actually he was drooling, it felt like some warm spit dripped down onto my arm. Ouuu, I thought.

Well I could see that talking wasn't working, and Jimmy had pretty much ran out of plans, so I decided to try one more thing on my own, but before I could take action I heard Kate's voice rise up from in the distance.

"Let him go," she said, "or the worlds gonna end you old fool."

"Well maybe for this little sucker," Bobby yelled back to her and laughed. I really didn't like that laugh.

Jimmy tried real quick like to shut her up, "Kate, don't say another…"

"This is no time to be wasting words with this twittering old goat and his behemoth lackey."

"Kate, don't…" Jimmy tried to get out only to be stopped in his tracks by the next words coming out of old man Jenkins.

"So it's a gang you brought with you to rob my store."

"I warned you about the gang activity, and these delinquents must be the ringleaders," Bobby told old man Jenkins. In that day we had gone from demons of the Underworld to gang leaders. Me and Jimmy must've really looked like tough guys.

Jenkins really didn't seem to be getting it at all. Like I said I had one more idea up my sleeve, and I just went for it. As Bobby carried me along his huge arm was wrapped around my chest almost crushing me. Without thinking anymore, 'cause thinking would've just gotten in the way. By that I mean that I would've been too chicken if I had thought about what I was gonna to do. I opened my mouth wide and took a big bite into Bobby's arm. His reaction was to squeeze harder as he screamed out from the pain, and then he dropped me. Like a rag doll I hit the ground trying to take in any air I could get into my lungs. I knew that the time was short. Bobby was fast, but so was I, and I had to move, run like I had never run before. I landed on my side, and my feet slid several times while I was trying to stand up.

"Run, run," I screamed as I raced towards Jimmy and the others. Bobby's shadow was right behind again, and I really didn't want to turn back to see just how close he was. If he caught me this time it was a good guess I probably wouldn't make it to the backroom.

"Move Shawn," Jimmy cried out as he moved away with the milk crate still in his hand. I knew that it would slow me down, but we really needed that other milk crate, so on the way to the end of the alley I swooped down and picked up the second one. As I did Bobby lunged, almost like he was trying to tackle me and shoved me. I fell. I really felt I was gonna die, and I wouldn't have to wait for the end of the world to do it. Bobby grabbed hold of my foot and slowly the giant of a man began to pull me back towards him, and scraped my knee and elbows along the ground as he did. I cried out, but Bobby wasn't interested in my pain or my tears. Now he was really mad and just wanted to punish me.

"We're not gonna wait for the backroom punk." He lifted me once more easily into the air and pressed me to the wall. His hand was tight against my throat, making me gasp to suck in more air. I really thought that that he was gonna kill me, I mean I really thought it. And then I heard it, his voice thundering and echoing into the alley.

"Unhand the master thou foul and unclean beast," it said. And it didn't take two seconds to figure out exactly who was saying those words. Angrily Bobby turned to see the shadowed figure of a twelfth-century Knight at the end of the alley. Yes, it was Saggy standing there, his sword raised and readied for battle.

Chapter 5: How Sagamore Destroyer of All Evil Helped Us Steal the Milk Crates

Yeah old Saggy really did look scary standing there, and for the first time since meeting this joker I was happy to see him. Although I didn't know why he had come, and how he had gotten there. You could barely make him out in the darkness with only his silhouette to give a clue to what was hidden in the shadows, and with his big booming voice bouncing off the walls. That docking area was great for that. And it was easy to forget that Saggy was not so brave himself here in the twenty-first century, if he had ever been.

Bobby's head had turned, but I could see him squinting trying to make out just what he was looking at. Saggy moved closer with the sword now over his head, and looked ready to do battle. Now to be honest Bobby the Security Guard was a giant of a man, but he wasn't really much of a match for a guy with a sword.

"What the heck is going on down there," old man Jenkins called out into the black of night. He was squinting too trying to see into dark shadows at the end of the alley. But he had seen just enough to start him backing away into the store. "Don't let them scare you Bobby," he cried out as he pressed his body against the wall.

Slowly I felt my back scrape against the brick building as Bobby let me slide down the wall.

"What do you want," Bobby called to Saggy as the sound of the clanging armor came even closer.

"Thou lowest of the low, thou canker blossom, desist in this unholy and heinous assault, or find yourself vanquished and earless by the sword of Sagamore the Mighty."

Yes, he was still calling himself "Sagamore the Mighty," and right now he was playing the part real good. But Bobby did not move, he stood there like he was actually going to do battle with an armored knight. This just didn't seem to be working out like it should've. Saggy was as much of a coward as any man could be, and without his army backing him up, I really doubted that he would continue his attack against the gigantic Bobby. On the other hand, I didn't want him to kill Bobby. That's the kinda' thing that would definitely go on somebody's permanent record somewhere. It was Jimmy that came to the rescue next. I guess everyone was taking turns that night saving butts. Before Saggy could back down, which by the way I later found out that we both thought he would, Jimmy began begging. Almost in tears he pleaded for Saggy to spare Bobby's life. Jimmy was using psychology to make Bobby think that Saggy was this incredible and dangerous warrior. If Bobby bought it he just might take a walk or run away from this fight.

"No Sir Sagamore, no don't kill this wretched creature, take his ears if you must, but spare this miserable dog of a man I beg of thee. He is the protector of all the fine treasures that are kept safe inside this great palace of fresh produce and fine dairy delights."

I thought Jimmy was laying it on a bit thick, but it was really a good acting job. And it was this crying out from Jimmy, and not the sword of Saggy that made the bullish Bobby think about the possibilities that might come out of a run in with Sagamore the Mighty.

"Don't back down Bobby, I think he's bluffing ya", Jenkins continued to give orders from the top of the dock, and far away from any possible danger.

Bobby let me drop to the ground. I was doing a lot of dropping out of the air that night. Saggy didn't stop; he seemed to be getting more courageous as if he too were buying into Jimmy's act.

"If the Master request it I shall spare your worthless and reprehensible hide," Saggy said.

"What", Bobby now looked really upset.

Then all at once there was another burst of light as Tommy Stoddard came out through the back door. The flash had lit up the entire alleyway, and now everybody got a good look at Saggy and his sword. Tommy missed it 'cause he was too busy trying to kiss up to old man Jenkins.

"I can finish sweeping now Mister Jenkins," Tommy said picking the worst time to get back to work.

"The heck with the sweeping," Jenkins told him, "I want you to get down there, and help Bobby with those punks and their hippy leader who's trying to steal my milk crates."

Tommy looked very confused for a real long minute, and then he made out the image of Saggy, sword raised, and looking ready to go to war.

"Sir," Tommy tried to explain to Jenkins, "I'm just here for restocking the shelves and sweeping up…"

"Why you little coward, I'm surrounded by cowards," Jenkins screamed at poor Tommy.

"But you don't even give me minimum wage," Tommy cried out.

Guess it was the thought of losing the milk crates that had turned Old Man Jenkins into Madman Jenkins. Out of nowhere he grabbed the broom out of Tommy's hand.

"Out of my way you little sissy," Jenkins shoved Tommy aside. Then he jumped down off of the dock, and charged towards Saggy. Yes he jumped down. It was crazy.

"I went through the war," he started yelling, "Did hand to hand combat with the enemy, so I'm not gonna let some punk, beatnik in fancy duds come to town and push me around."

It was unbelievable. Bobby had begun to back down; and Tommy was already trying to run back into the store.

"I'll be restocking the dairy aisle," Tommy yelled out as he ran through the door.

But the old man was ready to go into battle with an armored knight, a knight with a sword in his hands. We were all shocked, and Saggy especially. He had always been able to bully people, and threaten them with his size, and the fact that he rarely went anywhere without an army behind him. Now an old man with a broom was attacking him. Jenkins wasted no time when he got in front of Saggy. Right away he began pounding him in the head and body with the broom handle.

"Get off my property you #@%& Commie."

Saggy was too busy retreating to stop old man Jenkins. Me and Jimmy had to get in there, and try and rescue our knight in armor. I didn't know why or how Saggy had turned up, and the truth of the matter we didn't have time to ask. There was a giant comet gonna have a head on collision with Earth, and right then we were the only ones who had a chance of stopping it. Both of us went for the milk crates.

"Come on, come on," Jimmy yelled at Will and Kate. Right away they joined us in running away.

Our feet slapped against the cement, and our lungs kept burning as we began to run with them from the alley.

"Where do ya' think you're going with my milk crates you little punks," Jenkins called out. "Stop them Bobby."

"Thou hath left Sagamore with no recourse but to…" Saggy tried to get out, but he was too busy dodging the broom handle to finish that thought.

In the mean time Bobby seeing how brave old man Jenkins was decided to get brave himself, but not too brave, 'cause he moved to stop me and Jimmy. But we had a good head start and were moving fast.

Tommy Stoddard not knowing what to do stuck his head out the door. "Should I call the police Mister Jenkins?"

But the old man was too busy beating up on Saggy to get back to Tommy.

Suddenly we heard the screeching tires of a car, and I was sure that that was the police coming to throw us all into jail. That's when it happened, out of nowhere another figure, one that I didn't recognize right away stepped into the alley. Even in the shadows we could see that whoever it was had a gun in his hand. That stopped me and Jimmy right in our tracks. It was the sound of the gun going off that stopped everyone else though.

"You two," the man pointed at both me and Jimmy, "in the car."

At the end of the alley was a large black car. And the voice was one that we picked up on quick enough. It was the voice Flynn, the government agent.

"But," Jimmy tried to say.

"And take the milk crates with you," Flynn ordered.

"So it's a gang of hooligans that come to town to steal a man's milk crates," Jenkins smacked Saggy once more with the broom as our brave knight hobbled away from him.

"I flee to fight the forces of evil another day," Saggy cried out as he picked up speed and ran away. "Retreat with honor, retreat with honor," he cried out.

Inside the car Kate and Will were already seated, and looking terrified as we all piled into the back seat. Sagamore ran up to the car, and jumped into the front seat. He was suddenly all right with riding shotgun inside the belly of the beast.

Me and Jimmy, we had no idea what was going on. All we could see in the darkness of the alley now was Flynn backing away from old man Jenkins and Bobby. Tommy Stoddard was still watching through the half opened door. We could still hear some of what the old man and Bobby were saying. I mean heck the old man was still yelling at them as Flynn opened his door, and jumped into the driver's seat.

"But he had a gun Mister Jenkins," Bobby tried to defend himself.

"Aw shut up," the old man snarled, and went walking real mad like back into the store. "Cowards, I'm surrounded by cowards!"

"I'll get this mess up real good Mister Jenkins," Tommy called as Jenkins and Bobby walked towards the door.

"Your yellowed belly butt ain't worth minimum wage," old man Jenkins grumbled as he pushed Tommy out of the way and stormed back in the building.

That was the last thing we heard before the door slammed shut, and the car pulled away. There was only a second of strange silence before Flynn spoke.

"I only got part of the story from this guy," said Flynn talking about Saggy.

"We don't have a whole lot of time," Jimmy said.

"I know that," said Flynn, before turning real quick like onto a dark road.

"Do ya' have any potato chips," Will asked.

"Shut your mouth Will," Kate said to him.

"Aw the chips," said Saggy, "delightful, and the dungeon master at the keep served me a special treat called angels food cake."

"Keep," Jimmy asked.

"That's what this guy called the mental hospital where they had him locked away", Flynn told us.

"Where are you taking us," I asked.

"Right here," Flynn said, and pressed the brakes to the floor.

In a flash Flynn jumped out of the car and ordered me and Jimmy out onto the open road. We were a little scared, but did what he said.

"What are you going to do with us," Jimmy asked.

Flynn seemed to have trouble saying what he was gonna say.

"We've been watching the area for some time now," he said. "We were looking for anything strange, since we had reason to believe that you two were still in possession of the anti-gravity machines."

"The Professor doesn't want you to have them," Jimmy told him.

"I know that," Flynn barked back, "but what does this crazy knight and these kids have to do with any of it?"

Jimmy dug deep into his pockets, and handed Flynn his own business card back to him. It was kinda beat and messed up from being in the moat.

"Where did you get this," Flynn looked at him with disbelief.

"You gave it to us the night we destroyed the Gravity Boxes."

"You destroyed them," Flynn sounded mad, and looked at us and you could tell he didn't know what to think.

"That was the last time we met," Jimmy said to him, "on this very same night."

"What," Flynn's head shook.

"But," like you said, there's not a lot of time to explain. You know what's headed towards Earth."

Flynn looked down as if unable to answer, and then he raised his head and spoke to us; "That was a little bit of information that was being kept even from us. Since no one thought that there was anything that could be done. So we stayed at work on our little pet project, you guys. We were checking out all strange occurrences in this area. Then when I went to investigate your friend in armor, he spoke of a great disaster "about to befall God's green earth." He described two great wizards, somewhat about your ages and description…"

"You got curious," Jimmy said.

"I got curious, I investigated further, and then I heard some things I didn't think I wanted to know. A leak from the top told me that there wasn't really any reason for getting up early on Tuesday."

"They kept it even from you guys," I looked at Flynn.

"Everyone was so busy keeping everyone else in the shadows that's why the scientists never heard about the levitation machines from the big wigs."

"So only you've made the connection," Jimmy asked Flynn.

"As far as I know only I've made the connection, and then I came up with this crazy idea."

"To trust us," Jimmy asked

"How crazy is that," Flynn looked down at us both.

But Jimmy didn't answer his question he went right into telling us his plan.

"And it's going to hit a lot sooner than expected, that's why we have to get to the boxes…" Jimmy told him, and he wasn't being nice or polite about it, he was just getting to the point.

"But you destroyed them," Flynn yelled at Jimmy, like he was still upset.

"The last time, the last time, get with the program," I said to Flynn. I guess I sounded a little irritated, and why should he believe that we skipped through time, I hardly believed it myself.

"We don't have all night to fit the pieces together for you Mister Flynn," Jimmy said, "it's a long story."

"The crazy old Knight from the keep..." I said.

"What," said Flynn.

"The state hospital, Sagamore's crazy, but he is a real knight."

Flynn shook his head before answering, "it's just so hard to believe."

"Believe it, that armors nine hundred years old, and so is Sagamore." Jimmy told him.

"So you've traveled through time..." Flynn started to say.

"Like I said it's a long story," Jimmy cut him off. "Nobody can know about it, we shouldn't even be telling you."

"But you need me," Flynn looked Jimmy right in the eye.

"And you need us," Jimmy came right back at him.

"Nothing has changed," Flynn told us. "My men are still under the delusion that they are going to be here next week. They'll hunt you down, and do what they have to do in order to get their hands on those levitation devices."

"If we don't get a move on it there really won't be a next week," I said.

"The comet, it's massive, I guess that no one thought that it could be stopped." Jimmy just looked at Flynn without answering him. "Then you think that the levitation device can generate enough power to stop that thing," Flynn seemed to be hoping as much as we were.

"We got a shot," Jimmy told him, "but without them we don't even have that."

"If my men knew…" Flynn started to say.

"They wouldn't trust two kids to do the job," Jimmy said.

"No they would not," Flynn answered.

"Agent Flynn," he said, "Shawn and me, well we can handle the Gravity Boxes better than anybody. We've played with them for months."

"That's why I'm here," Flynn scratched his head. "I don't believe I'm doing this, but I also know that there isn't any time to train our people how to use them."

"Then you also know," I thought it was time for me to get a word or two in, "that the Professor doesn't want you to have them. He doesn't want anybody to have them."

"Once my people know that they still exist, they will take them from you."

"Not if they see them destroyed," Jimmy told him.

"Which is why you wanted the milk crates," Flynn said, "I figured it was something like that." There was a long moment of silence. "But no one can ever have them," Flynn at last seemed to understand.

"Agreed," said Jimmy. "So the plan is destroy the boxes right in front of everyone's eyes."

"Cause that's what we did the first time," I said.

"Only this time its milk crates that you'll see being destroyed," Jimmy told him.

"But how," Flynn was really curious.

"I hope we can trust you Agent Flynn," Jimmy didn't sound so sure.

"I have a wife and two kids," said Flynn. "I'd like to know that they're going to be alive and well next week."

"Let's get them to tomorrow first," Jimmy said.

As we stood there the clouds began to roll in and the wind began to blow strong. A dark cloud started covering the moon, and we knew that the storm would be coming soon.

Jimmy said, "It's almost time. Your men are positioning themselves around the house right now."

Flynn looked strangely down at his own business card that Jimmy had just handed back to him.

"Why didn't you bring them with you," Jimmy asked.

"Maybe I agree with you boys and the Professor," Flynn said. "Maybe I just didn't want to waste time on another hide and seek game with the fate of the world dangling over our heads."

"Then we should be going, the storm will be coming."

"Storm," Flynn asked, "there was no storm forecast for…" he then stopped himself. "Whatever you boy's think is best." And those were words I never thought I'd hear from this guy. Twice we had made a fool out of him, and he swore it would never happen again, so I had to wonder how much of what he was saying to us was the truth. Was Flynn just saying what he thought we wanted to hear to get his hands on the Gravity Boxes? Like Jimmy had said that comet wasn't giving us a heck of a lot of time to figure it out. It was headed for this planet, and was gonna drop right in the middle of town.

Seconds later we were in the backseat of the car again, and headed to Jimmy's house and the Gravity Boxes. All of the plans would have to be talked about on the way there.

We learned from Flynn the whole story, or at least what he was saying the whole story was. He told us that there had been rumors about unidentified flying objects or kids over the town, and that had sparked another investigation. They had set up surveillance on Professor Burkhardt and our families, and the plan was to seize the Gravity Boxes after we had put them to rest on this very night. They knew from the first time that they tangled with us that it would be best to wait until we had touched down before they tried to get their hands on the gravity machines. Once on the ground, and away from them we lost all control over the Gravity Boxes and their power.

When we had just dropped out of sight he, and in fact the whole government was a little concerned. There were rumors of enemy agents getting their hands on us and the Gravity Boxes. That put a scare into everyone who knew about us. Everything strange was being investigated. When the stories of Saggy had reached Flynn's ears, the police said that some kids were running away from this crazy old guy in knight's armor. Flynn learned Sagamore's version of the story, and was somehow from that able to put two and two together. Using his authority as a government agent he had Sagamore released into his custody.

Saggy, Will, and Kate were kinda quiet on the trip back to Jimmy's place. They were scared and with a lot of questions I'm sure. So they were just keeping their mouths shut hoping to hear some good news. Jimmy started to explain his plan. I know that he like me was still unsure about trusting Flynn, but what choice did we have?

"We have to get some kids clothes for Will and Kate, so they will look normal here," Jimmy explained. "If we can get some handlebars from the old bikes in my garage to hammer onto the milk crates, then we use the real Gravity Boxes to make these ones fly." He then turned slowly to Kate and Will. "We need your help," he said, "more than we've ever needed it." After all they had already done for us that was saying a lot.

"What do you need from us Jim," Kate looked him straight in the eye, and spoke for the first time since we got back into the car.

"For tonight you and Will are going to be Shawn and me."

"Like make believe," Will asked.

"This is the most important game of make believe ever played," Jimmy said.

Will just looked wide eyed, and Jimmy turned and spoke to Flynn. "Is there anyway of getting your men away from the house, so we can sneak them in, and get them some of our clothes?"

"Orders from the top are to keep surveillance until the levitation machines are confiscated. The men will stay posted until that objective is met or…"

"Or," I asked.

"If you didn't show up tonight we were going to enter the premises and conduct a search. If I were to change orders now…"

"It might look suspicious," I said.

"Then we've got to stop them before they do that," Jimmy told Flynn.

"Perhaps we need a distraction," Flynn looked back quickly to Sagamore. I saw Flynn make quick eye contact with Jimmy. They both understood at once that we had the greatest distraction in nine hundred years sitting right in that car with us.

Flynn pulled to a halt a few streets away from Jimmy's house. "I think it's best that my car isn't seen near your house," Flynn told us.

Flynn turned to Saggy, "give me your sword, Sir Sagamore," he said.

"It is the symbol of my knighthood, it keeps safe the King and his throne" Saggy grumbled. "And it would appear that I am the soul protector of our two young wizards."

Saggy sounded like he really meant all that, but I could tell that he was just looking for a way not to give up his sword.

Flynn looked Sagamore right in the eye. "You are going on a mission for our two wizards," Flynn told him.

"Another mission," Saggy whined sadly. "Another great honor," and you could tell he didn't really mean it.

"The men you will encounter will have weapons, fire sticks, if they think you are dangerous, they will use these weapons on you."

I knew at once that the fire sticks that Flynn talked about were really guns like the daggers that shoot lightening bunk that Jimmy had made up. It was the only way they could make Saggy understand how dangerous guns really were, and the only way to protect him like we did with the cops. If Sagamore appeared too dangerous then Flynn's

305

men would probably shoot him. Yeah, best to just have Saggy looking like a crazy old nutcase.

"Fire stick, daggers that shoot lightening, all heinous machinations of Lucifer himself I would imagine," Saggy began to tremble in his boots once more.

"That would be my guess," Flynn said to him.

"Mister Flynn's right Sir Sagamore," Jimmy said. "We must play into their hands, and let them think that you are helpless."

"Then this is a strategy oh great one?"

"Yes Sir Sagamore," Jimmy answered him.

"Be it the same strange strategy that landed me in the keep," Sagamore looked suspiciously at Jimmy.

"Where they served up fine helpings of potato chips and angels food cake," Flynn was selling the idea for us.

"That sounds to be a grand keep," said Will as if wanting to be locked away himself, "be there burgers and fries?" No one was surprised by the swat to the back of his head from Kate.

"Ow," Will cried out.

"It is quite delicious," Saggy said almost licking his lips at the thought of being tossed back into the mental hospital.

"Would we steer you wrong Saggy," I said.

Saggy looked confused, and a little insulted. "Saggy, you called me Saggy, again."

"Shawn," Jimmy tried to shut me up.

"Be this a title of honor afforded knights of exceptional valor in this curious place?"

"Yeah sure," I lied as I saw Jimmy shaking his head at me. I wasn't sure that Saggy was buying into the lie that I was feeding him, but then he sat up straight and announced: "Henceforth I shall be known as Sir Saggy Without Equal, protector of the great Wizards in the battle of…" and then he stopped and looked at Jimmy, "oh great and beneficent one, what shall we name this battle?"

"We'll name it later," Jimmy explained.

"We'll just go with Sir Saggy for right now," I told him.

That seemed to satisfy Sir Saggy, but Jimmy knew we had to get back to the business of saving of the planet.

"No one else could pull this off but the bravest of all knights," Jimmy told Saggy.

Somehow that gave Saggy more confidence. He straightened his body, and spoke boldly like when we first met, and all of his soldiers were standing behind him.

"Then I shall enter their camp like a lamb being led to the slaughter, and when they foolishly let down their defenses, then and only then will Sir Saggy the Mighty, slayer of demons, scourge of evil vanquish them with my trusty…" he stopped and thought for a minute. "Master," he looked at Jimmy, "how am I to vanquish these fiends without my sword?"

"Jimmy turned to him sincerely, "Sir Saggy, all the magic that you have seen before will seem like nothing compared to what you will witness tonight. Tonight," Jimmy went on, "you will serve only the noblest and most important part of your destiny. Tonight you will help to save the entire world."

"But without my sword…" Saggy tried to get the words out; he still wasn't buying all the way into our story.

"You're the only one Sir Saggy," Jimmy looked him right in the eye, "without your bravery the world will perish."

And it was like all true. It was like we were all pieces of a puzzle that had come together to save the world, each of us helping in some way. The Professor, Lord Hoxley, Will, Kate, Sagamore, and now even Flynn had come on board. We were all parts of the puzzle that were needed if this plan was to work.

For the longest time Saggy was quiet, and then he slowly handed his sword over to Flynn. "And if need be I will suffer the anguish of potato chips and angel food cake in the keep of dread once more," Saggy said bravely. Well almost bravely.

"We can come bring you comfort Sir Saggy," Will said excitedly dying to try that angel food cake.

"Good," that was all that Jimmy said to him. "And now we've got to get Will and Kate into the clouds, and we've got to make all of your men," he said to Flynn, "believe that it's Shawn and me up there."

"Up in the what," Will asked nervously.

"It's really great once you get use to it," I looked at him and to Kate. "Not at first, at first it's kinda scary, but then… but then it's the greatest feeing in the world."

Will looked out of the car window to the dark clouds that were starting to form overhead with the storm coming on.

"Up there," he said again with a shake in his throat."

"You've been at the bottom of the moat just today Will," Kate said to him. She seemed to be a little nervous herself, but she also seemed to understand the importance of what we were about to do. "And if you can come out of the moat alive and able to lick your wounds, a trip to the clouds should be like a child's game, yes, that's it, just like a child's game."

Will didn't look too sure he wanted to play that game, and I couldn't blame him. None of us really knew what the night had in store. It was then that we heard the first crack of thunder boom across the sky.

**Further Concept Art In Creating The Second Book
Cover.**

Chapter 6: The Shadow Creature in Jimmy's Room

The plan was easy, at least it had sounded easy when Jimmy told it. We would send Sir Saggy into their camp. By camp he meant Jimmy's yard where Flynn's men were staked out. And that's right, we were sending Sagamore the Mighty, slayer of demons, protector of the throne, and all that junk.

Jimmy and Flynn both thought that Saggy would be the best distraction while we got Will and Kate into his house, and dressed them in some modern day clothes. Will was still a little nervous about riding around on a milk crate a thousand feet up in the clouds. So was Kate, but she wasn't making as much noise about it.

"And what will be holding us up there in the sky," Will asked like for the tenth time.

"It's a green beam of light that will neutralize your gravity," Jimmy started to say.

But I could see the odd look coming off of Will as he tried to understand just what Jimmy was talking about. "It's a machine," I told him, "that will make you and Kate as light as a feather, so that you will just float in mid air."

Will's head shifted back and forth between me and Jimmy, and I think he ended up liking my explanation better.

"And this be not witch…" that's all that Will got out when Kate swatted him in the back of the head.

"Ow!" Will said. We were getting use to him crying out like that. "My noggin be getting a bump from all your thumping on it."

"It be not witchcraft you silly dolt," Kate cut him off. She just didn't seem to care about Will's injury. Like I said, I was liking her more all the time.

"For like the millionth time," I shook my head.

It was suddenly Saggy who got tired of hearing how brave everyone else was being who turned to Will. "You young wastrel it is Saggy the Fearless, this bravest of all knights that will be entering the camp of doom," yes he called Jimmy's yard the camp of doom. I kinda liked it. "Unarmed and ready to fight the monstrous barbarians in the battle of the… of the…" Saggy seemed stumped, and he turned towards Jimmy again. "Oh great one, what title shall we give this epic bloody skirmish?"

Before Jimmy could answer I jumped in, "I think you already named it Saggy, Sir Saggy's heroic battle in the Camp of Doom."

That's when Saggy nodded his head in agreement, "yes, yes, my heroic engagement in the Camp of Doom." It was then he turned to Flynn, "and if captured I will be forced once more to live in the pit of the keep of dread with only Angel's Food Cake and lemonade as my only sustenance."

"I want to go to the keep of dread," Will grumbled in a low, sad voice.

The way this was all suppose to work was that Sir Saggy was to play right into hands of the government agents. Make a lot of noise, get captured, and make enough commotion to take all eyes off of the house for just a little bit of time. Jimmy figured that we only needed about a thirty seconds to sneak Will and Kate into the garage.

It was getting late, and we really couldn't explain to Jimmy's parents, so we would have to hide Kate and Will in the garage until we were able to creep into the house, and get a change of clothes for the both of them.

Flynn was supposed to help by trying to draw his men into a pretend struggle with Sir Saggy. The G Men would have to keep him quiet, so that he didn't draw a lot of attention to the Camp of Doom, I mean Jimmy's yard. He figured with both of them working together they could have all eyes looking away from the house for the little time we needed to pull this off. I still couldn't believe that Flynn was helping us, and I knew that Jimmy still wasn't so sure about him yet.

It was getting cold and windy, just like the last time we went through this night. Jimmy's parents were usually in bed early, but there was still a single light shinning in the living room. They hadn't heard from us for the whole day, so I knew they were worried along with my parents. But what could we do? I knew that it was gonna be big trouble when I got home, and I really didn't want my parents to worry. But if I had called them then they'd want to know the whole story, and the government agents we knew would be listening in. In reality we had been gone nine hundred years, but only one day in our time. Yet that was enough to get them looking all over the place for us. The day we left we had told each of our parents that we would be staying at the others house. We did that a lot, but by now they knew that this time that was a lie. What they didn't know was that the whole time we had been in the twelfth-century was the only time that they didn't know that we were missing. Of course when we were back there the whole world had just been destroyed, so in my head

313

they were better off not knowing what had really gone on. Besides the part about me being with Jimmy, and him being with me was the truth. Okay most of it was a big lie, but I couldn't risk being called to come home right then. Everything had to be hush hush, there was still a lot of sneaking around that had to be done. Too much was happening, there was the "master plan," and Jimmy needed me there for that.

Right now there seemed only to be a single dim light shinning out of Jimmy's house. Sometimes Jimmy's Dad would read or watch television, and stay up a little later. But right then we thought that he just might be up waiting for Jimmy. Most of the time he fell asleep on the couch, but we didn't know if that was the case right then and there. We only knew that we didn't want to get caught by him or Jimmy's Mom. They had some idea about the Gravity Boxes and what they could do, so they would definitely understand, but we really didn't think that it was a good idea trying to explain to them. And if we started talking about going back in time, and stuff like that they might have just thought we were crazy, and put us into the "keep of dread," where I'd just grow fat scoffing down tons of Angel's Food cake and junk. We knew for sure now that people were listening, and that that might put them in danger. Besides they probably wouldn't be too happy about us saving the world on a school night.

Even if Jimmy's parents were both asleep we still had another big problem to deal with. That was Ricky, Jimmy's overgrown and over friendly, big, brown retriever. By over friendly I meant that Ricky would make the biggest fuss over you. Sometimes he was so happy to see you he could wake up the whole neighborhood.

We had to wait for our time. Me and Jimmy took Will and Kate up the block over from Jimmy's street. It was starting to get late, so there wasn't anybody out. My guess was that the storm would've had mostly everybody headed for cover soon enough anyway. I was sure that the last time we had lived through this night we had already gone sailing off into the clouds by this hour. So we had to move quick if we were gonna get the Gravity Boxes out of the house, and be air born before the agents broke into the house to take them off of us.

"When we hear Sagamore making a ruckus out front we run as fast as we can to the garage," Jimmy said to us all.

"Garage," Will looked confused.

"Will, you and Kate just follow Shawn and me." Jimmy then turned to me. "We got to hope they didn't bug the garage."

I was really hoping along with Jimmy.

But we seemed to be waiting for the longest time for something to happen. We were lying low and scared that we would be spotted by one of Flynn's men. Both me and Jimmy we still worried that Flynn might have double-crossed us. That he and his men were in the house already and stealing the Gravity Boxes. I mean he seemed sincere when he was talking to us, but we kept reminding ourselves that we had made him look like a fool two times already, and it just might be revenge time for him.

"I'm gonna go see what's going on," I said to Jimmy.

"If they see you," Jimmy tried to stop me.

"We've been waiting here a real long time," I came back at him. "If Flynn's double crossed us then we have to move, and move fast."

"What are we going to do if they got their hands on the Gravity Boxes," Jimmy said. And that was the really big question. This time they would be ready for whatever we were gonna throw at them. Maybe Flynn had used us to make sure the Gravity Boxes were in the house before he charged in there, and took them away from us. If we had had them hidden somewhere else it might eat up a lot of time trying to find them, or getting us to tell them where they were. But the world didn't have a lot of time, and Flynn knew that as much as we knew it.

"Even he knows that no one can handle the Gravity Boxes like we can," Jimmy said. He looked sad like he had real doubts about Flynn himself. He looked at me like he had lost all hope. I had never seen Jimmy look so miserable, and we had just spent time in a cold dungeon eating wormy bread. "Go slow, see if you can find out what's going on out there." And that's exactly what I did.

Real easy like I crouched down, got close to the ground, and started to make my way through the bushes. The thorns from the roses had cut into me a little, but I shoved my wanting to cry out way down deep inside. I would have to swallow the pain if I didn't want anybody to know that I was coming. If me and Jimmy were right Flynn and his men would already be inside of his house, and have the Gravity Boxes by now. I figured because we had made him look like a dummy more than once that he'd want us to see what he was doing. He'd want to see the look on our faces when we found out that we were tricked. Then I thought with the world about to be destroyed this was no time for stupid games. Hoping my imagination was just getting the best of me. Past the house that was right behind Jimmy's place, I could see the street all empty and quiet. All quiet except for the wind that was now kicking up, and blowing the branches of the trees and the leaves all over the place.

Near to the edge of that house, close to the back I could see something that looked like it could be an agent. I wasn't exactly sure what it was. It looked like a shadow against the wall, and I was guessing that that was close enough. They had all been staked out just like the first time we had lived through this night. Now on the ground with them we didn't have the Gravity Boxes to help us kick their butts. Right now we weren't the two most powerful kids in the universe. Right then and there we were just two kids who were probably gonna get squashed by a giant comet along with the rest of the world.

I was down on my belly now crawling through one of the neighbor's flowerbed. In all that time what looked like a shadow on the wall still hadn't moved, so I still wasn't sure what it was. He wasn't that close to Jimmy's house, so I figured they must be spread out around the neighborhood to cover the house from every angle. I looked around real easy like to see what could be making that shadow show up on the wall. The dark clouds were hiding the moon, so there was no light coming from that. In fact there was no light coming from anywhere. Most of the lights from the nearby houses were out, and the streetlights were at the corners. The way I figured it nothing could've been casting that shadow. Yeah, that was one of Flynn's

317

men all right. But was he waiting for us, or was he just part of the stake out that me and Jimmy had been told about. One thing for sure I couldn't go any further in that direction. Any closer and he was bound to hear me coming.

Real easy like I began to crawl back to where I had left Jimmy, Kate, and Will. Then something strange happened. The crickets stopped making their racket. It's like all at once everything became super quiet. The sound of all that silence really scared me. I started crawling back even quicker. I had only moved a couple of feet when I felt my foot hit against something, something that hadn't been there when I first crawled into that yard. I looked back real slow like to see what I had bumped into. What I saw did not make me happy, not happy at all. My foot had knocked against one of the shadow men. I froze for a long second. It seemed like forever that I was unable to move from that spot, and then the guy dressed in black knelt down like he was gonna grab me. I knew not to scream. I wanted to, but I knew that if there was any chance of this night working out, and if Flynn hadn't backstabbed us, I had to get away. What I did next I don't know why I did, or where I found the guts, but I flipped onto my back, and when this guy got down even closer I kicked out hitting him in the face. He didn't cry out or make any noise when I hit him. He just fell back on his butt. As fast as I could I started to get up, but my feet slipped a couple of times as they tried to dig into the dirt. That's when the guy in black grabbed hold of my ankle and tried to pull me back. With my free foot I stomped back like a mule and kicked him again. He landed back into the fence. Finally I was up and running. But when I kicked him again he hadn't yelled either. Remember we were both on a secret mission, so I was guessing that he was under orders to keep a lid on his noise no matter what. Don't know for sure if I could of done that.

In no time I was racing back to the street where Jimmy was waiting with the others. The only sound that I could hear was that of my own two feet hitting the ground and those of the shadow man that was coming up quick behind me. I was running as fast as I could, but this guy was really fast. I decided to go in a different direction from where I had left the others. If there was any hope for the world, or to save the Gravity Boxes then Jimmy and the others would have to be free to do it. Right then it looked like I was about to get nabbed by that guy in black, and I wasn't sure just how happy he would be about me kicking him in the face two times.

Even as I was changing direction I decided to make some noise to let the others know that there was trouble coming, and plenty of it. Running close to the side of the house I thumped it with the side of my fist. I really didn't want to make noise, but how else would they know to take cover. Out of nowhere dogs began yelping from inside the house that I had pounded on.

Suddenly a big hand reached out, and grabbed hold of my shirt. I was pulled back with a sudden jerk, and fell to the ground. At once the shadow man was on top of me pinning me by my shoulders. His hand clasped down onto my face, and for a minute I actually had trouble breathing. He didn't say anything, not for what seemed to be forever, and then I heard his voice whisper into my ear.

"What are you doing here," he whispered. And the voice seemed like one I knew. I had only heard it a couple of times, but when he pulled off the mask I found myself looking right up into Flynn's face.

I was so angry that I just started to yell at him, and then he put his hand back over my mouth. As I tried to suck air through his fingers he started to whisper again.

"We have to be quiet," he said. And the way he said it, it sounded almost like a threat.

So when he took his hand off of my face for the second time I spoke a lot softer. "You think you got over on us," I said. "We were trying to save the whole world," I told him. I started to get loud again, and then he put his finger to his lips to quiet me down. "I mean I thought we had a deal..."

"We did," he said.

"Then where the heck is Sagamore, why are your men still around the house and not chasing him down the street?"

Flynn took a deep breath. He tried to explain slow and easy to me, but I still wasn't sure that I could trust him. "Our agent in the back, he would not leave no matter what kind of commotion we had coming from the front of the house. He is a trained professional, and by now the tricks of you and your buddy are well known to us. No matter what happened, no matter what noise you made, this one would be waiting for you, so I have to get close to him, knock him unconscious, and get him out of your hair before I can unleash Sagamore the Unmerciful..."

"Sagamore the Mighty," I corrected him. "You know," I said to Flynn, "you can't have them."

"What," he said.

"The Gravity Boxes, when we're done doing what we have to do, you and your people still can't have them."

Flynn stopped, and took another deep breath, "I know, we've been over this," he said. "Now we don't have much time, in fact we don't have any time, Sagamore is getting ready as we speak to charge down the middle of the street, and I have to put my friend in the back to sleep, and get back out front to lead the charge, so that you kids can do what you have to do."

Made sense, I guess.

"Not a bad kick kid," Flynn shook his head, and left me and went towards the back of the house.

Slow like I got to my feet, and moved to get back to Jimmy and the others. When I got back out onto the street where I had left them I found it completely empty. I figured that it would be, since I had sent the signal ahead that there was trouble. I looked around for a long minute, but saw nobody. I tried to call for them, but more like a whisper hoping that them and only them would hear it.

"Jimmy, hey Jimmy, where are you guys?"

Still the street was quiet, and no sound of my friends, just the sound of the dogs barking still echoing in the air. I was guessing all of the agents were sitting still just waiting for us to be going back to the house. For the longest time I felt really alone out there. Suddenly Jimmy stood up from behind a car that was sitting a little way down the street. He didn't say anything. Then out or nowhere Will and Kate appeared close to him. They got a whole lot closer before any of us spoke.

"What the heck happened back there," Jimmy said. I could tell he was real nervous and who wasn't?

"Shadow men…" I told him. This right away got Will scared, and wishing he was back home getting his butt beat for whatever Prince John was doing wrong.

"Shadow men," Will said. His voice got real high, "the demons can take on the forms of shadows," he almost cried.

"You twit," Kate said to him. "There are no demons," she said. "Haven't you been listening with your thick skull? It's all science here, all science."

"Ah science," he said and then he nodded his head as if he knew what the heck she was talking about, but I could tell that he just didn't want to get swatted on his head again.

I told Jimmy just what had gone on behind his house. He like me still wasn't sure about buying into Flynn's story, but if he could get us all into the house, then we had a good chance of getting our hands on the Gravity Boxes.

There wasn't too long a wait after that. Out of nowhere we heard it start: "For England, King Henry, and Saint George," I heard Sir Saggy's voice booming as he came down the street. That was the only sound that we heard except for all the dogs in the neighborhood beginning to howl their heads off again. Now whoever was watching the house had to capture Sir Saggy, and try not giving themselves away. I figured that that wasn't gonna be too easy. He was really getting wild, and trampling into one of the neighbor's rose bushes. Come morning somebody was not going to be happy about that. We heard a little noise that sounded like people coming out to see just what was making all of the racket, but by then we were already on our way to the garage. Along the way we saw the first shadow agent who had been watching Jimmy's house from the rear lying unconscious in the dirt. Flynn seemed to have been honest about getting that guy out of our way. It looked like a clear shot to the garage as we all crept around to the side the wall to the house. The milk crates were light enough to handle as we moved along, and we just had to move fast.

In the middle of the street a couple of men in the black get ups were dragging Sir Saggy into a waiting car.

"Unhand me, unclean and vile spawn of Satan", Sagamore cried out as he was being pulled along.

This action was done so quickly, almost like it had been planned to pin down the old knight, and toss him into a car. In fact Sir Saggy was out of sight so fast that if you blinked you might've missed the whole thing altogether. In seconds the car would be on its way speeding down the street, and our chance would be gone. Sir Saggy as a distraction had not been very good at all this time.

The door to the garage was closed. Jimmy checked real fast to see if it was locked. It was usually left unlocked, and so it had been this time too. Easy like he lifted the door up just a little, and then we shoved the milk crates under.

"What is this strange," Will tried to get out, but Kate was right on top of things with her swat to the back of his head.

"Ow," Will started to get out, but Kate was quick to place her hand over his mouth. "What did I do," he tried to get out looking both annoyed and confused.

"Hold your tongue Will," she whispered.

Right after the crates were safe inside we were all able to roll under and in. Once inside Jimmy lowered the door behind us. There was a big sigh of relief that we had made it that far, and then we knew we had to get to work. Now there wasn't even a second to get our heads together before Ricky was scratching and yelping from behind the door that connected the garage to the house. We all stood still and silent, and even Jimmy was unsure what we should do. All of the dogs in the neighborhood were barking and howling their heads off at the noise that Sir Saggy had made as he charged into the Rose Garden of Incredible Torment, better known as the Mrs. Fenwick's front lawn. Somehow I knew if we lived through the night Sagamore would turn it into a great heroic tale. Sagamore the Mighty fights bare fisted to keep the minions of the devil from tearing out his throat, while the poisonous daggers from the witches evil rose bush cut through his flesh, or something like that. The fact that it was just poodles and cocker spaniels barking through screen doors would only get in the way of a really good story. But all the noise from the outside was beginning to die down. And if that hadn't awakened Jimmy's parents we now had Ricky to do that for us. On top of that we had to hope that that crazy dog wasn't getting everybody in the house checking out the garage. Jimmy knew that we had to do something, so he went over real quick like and opened the door. Ricky came in, and started making a bigger commotion. He was crying as if Jimmy had been gone for years, nine hundred of them, but Ricky really didn't know that. Ricky was always super happy to see me and Jimmy, and practically anybody who walked through the door.

324

"Will's eyes lit up. In fact I think that that was the first time since we had met that I had seen him not too scared, and to actually be happy, well that was really something.

"What a magnificent creature," Will almost shouted at the sight of Ricky.

"Shhh," Jimmy warned him, we had to quiet first Will then Ricky.

Ricky seemed to sense the love in Will's eyes instantly. He ran right over to him. Ricky started right in with a good face licking, and Will couldn't have been more happy. And all the while Ricky was licking Will, he was being only a little noisy. So that worked for us. Will would keep Ricky happy while we worked on getting the fake Gravity Boxes up and ready.

Jimmy at once began to scan the garage for parts needed to put the thing together.

"I spy a hammer," I said and went to get it off of the wall.

"No," Jimmy said, "we can't make that much noise. My parents will be in here in two seconds."

"But you said we'd hammer…"

"I know what I said," Jimmy came back at me, "but now I realize that that would make too much noise."

"Then how we gonna put these things together?"

Jimmy was still too busy looking around to give me an answer. Then after a minute he had that answer. "The handlebars don't really have to be practical, since it's night and starting to rain, and Will and Kate will be up so high that no one will be able to tell anyway."

"And…" I was waiting for the answer.

"And," he came back at me, "we need wire hangers to attach the handlebars to the milk crates."

"Can I do anything James," asked Kate.

"In just a few minutes you're going to be doing an awful lot," he said to her. "But for now," he turned back to me, "for now Shawn we have to get inside my room, and get a couple of coat hangers so we can put these things together."

"And clothes," I reminded Jimmy. When they were way up high they had to look something like us even if nobody was really able to get a good look at them.

"Right, right, right," Jimmy said nervously.

"Is this beautiful animal all yours Jim," Will was trying to speak while Ricky continued with the tongue bath.

"Ricky's all mine," Jimmy said, "now Will you just keep doing what you're doing, and that'll keep Ricky happy, and that should make all of us happy. Ready," Jimmy looked back at me. And I knew what that meant. We were both now going to go into the house and get those clothes hangers and the clothes for Will and Kate.

"What if your Dad…" I tried to ask.

"There's no turning back now," Jimmy said. "If Flynn is really on our side then he's given us the chance we need to make this work. We can't let anything stop us. The whole world is in danger. Right now the only thing standing between us and saving it is a couple of coat hangers." Then we started into the house.

Ricky turned away from Will for a minute when he heard the door to the inside opening. Both me and Jimmy froze on the spot.

326

Jimmy looked at Ricky, and placed his finger over his mouth. It was kind of a way to tell the dog to just be quiet, but Ricky wasn't too good at being quiet. He started to whine a real loud whine like he was happy to see Jimmy all over again. I'm telling you this dog was crazy.

We were still stopped at the door when Will broke in and told us; "I'll take care of him Jim, he likes me I think." Will reached out and began petting Ricky; and just as if he had known Will his whole life, Ricky went back to licking him and jumping all over him again. We both knew that Ricky had a good twenty minutes of face licking in him before he would tire of it, and went in search of another face to slobber all over.

Real easy like we moved into the recreation room that was attached to the garage. It was kinda quiet in there, but from the other room we could hear the sound of the television blasting. It was kinda loud, so maybe that's why Jimmy's Dad hadn't gotten wind of the noise coming in from the outside.

"Your Dad's still up," I whispered to Jimmy.

"Maybe not," he tiptoed to the entrance of the room. "Dad spends more time sleeping in front of the TV than watching it."

"But isn't he waiting for us?"

"My Dad may be waiting, but two minutes in front of the late news, and he crashes for the night. He'll fight it of course, but I'm counting on years of habit to carry him off to dreamland."

Just like Jimmy had thought his Dad was asleep on the couch, but he said his Dad was a light sleeper, so we had to go slow and easy trying to get past him.

"Why did you want me to come in with you," I finally thought to whisper before we stepped into the living room.

"I need some more stuff for my schoolbag if we're gonna make this mission work."

Every footstep made the floor creak. I was sure that it was only the loudness of the television blasting that kept Jimmy's Dad from waking up as we started to cross the room. A loud snort came out of his Dad, and we both thought that we had gotten nabbed. There was just that snort and a roll of his head and nothing else, but it was enough to keep me and Jimmy stuck in our tracks for a long minute. Slowly like we started to move again.

"You can wait for him just as good up here," I heard his Mom call down the steps just as we got between Jimmy's Dad and the television. Once again we both froze to the spot. Jimmy's Dad started to stir a little more, but didn't open his eyes.

"The show's almost over hon," he grumbled never opening his eyes as if he had been watching the television all along.

"This isn't the first time he's done this," his Mom yelled down the stairs. "You'd better have a good talk with him."

Jimmy gritted his teeth 'cause he knew he was in it and deep with is parents.

"I'll talk to him," his Dad whined still not opening his eyes.

"And don't go complaining to me that your back is sore in the morning," she called back down the steps, and then switched off the light at the top of the stairs.

"I love you too sweetheart," said Jimmy's Dad, and went right back to snoring.

Right away we started to move again across the floor. We knew we had to go slow 'cause his Mom had just closed the door to her bedroom, and was sure to hear anything above a whisper.

Took my next step and there was another squeak. Darn, I hated that. I was sure that it sounded a lot louder in my imagination than it did for real, but it still was scary. The loudness of the television had drowned out that noise, but once at the top of the stairs that noise wasn't gonna help with Jimmy's Mom.

Finally we got to the steps that led to the upstairs. It was mostly a hard wood and noisy stairway, and I was glad to be wearing my sneakers, or as they were called in the twelfth century, the devils footwear, as we started to climb them.

Creak, creak, creak, the sound just seemed to bounce off of the walls as we crept up the stairs. Every couple of steps we would stop, take a deep breath and get ready for the next step.

At the top of the stairs we could see under the door of his Mom's room that her light was still on. We stopped, and just waited for it to go out, but it seemed to stay on forever.

After a bit Jimmy decided that it was time to move on. He motioned to me with his finger, and we both started edging down the hall towards his room. Once again the floor just made so much noise. Even our sneakers screeched a couple of times against the hardwood floor. I really wish these people had bought some rugs.

Jimmy stopped at his bedroom door, "keep it low," he whispered.

"I know, I know," I whispered back at him.

"Thinking to bug up here they might have to get into the house, but I'm not sure."

A minute later we stood inside Jimmy's room. It was dark, but he knew it pretty well. He pulled me in and closed the door behind him. He still didn't feel it was safe to turn on the lights. So he spoke to me real soft like as he felt his way around the room searching for what we had come for. Lucky for us the clouds had blown away, and the moon was giving us a little light.

"We're gonna need the Ultra Diversionary Unit Nine," he said.

And I had almost forgotten about the Ultra Diversionary Unit Nine. It was another one of Jimmy's inventions that we had used to take on the spies when they had tried to steal the Gravity Boxes before. It wasn't much, mostly just a bigger smoke bomb that exploded. Jimmy was big into exploding stuff. He had put it together in case we had ever needed to fight off spies. Who would've thought that one day we would have really needed such a thing?

"We got to make it look like they really blew up." He then took the pillowcase off of his pillow, and started putting stuff into it. Junk like the Ultra Diversionary Unit Nine and more exploding darts were dumped into the pillowcase.

"Don't you think we got enough junk in the schoolbag to do the trick," I asked him real low.

Jimmy turned to me and was deadly serious. "Shawn, it's gotta be big, and they gotta believe it."

I bobbed my head up and down, because I knew exactly what he meant.

Anything that could explode and make smoke we were taking along. He also moved to his radio that was sitting on top of his desk. I only know this 'cause my eyes were starting to get used to the darkness, and I could see a little of what was going on.

There was still that bit of moonlight coming into through the window, and I could see Jimmy pulling the back off of his radio and pull out some of the wires.

"What you doing that for," I whispered, 'cause I really didn't know why he was destroying a perfectly good radio.

"The agents will have to find internal parts when the Gravity Boxes crash and burn he said.

"And what about the..." I started to say.

"Shhh, we'll talk about it down in the garage. First we've got to get Will and Kate up and flying.

We turned to start to leave and then I reminded him, "Don't forget, we need some clothes for those guys."

"That's right," Jimmy said, and then edged closer to his closet. "All I got is jeans and some tee shirts."

"From a thousand feet up that should be just fine," I told him, "besides it's dark and rainy."

So Jimmy tossed a few clothes into the pillowcase, and we started to head out of the room. Then something hit me that neither of us had thought about before.

"They're supposed to be us, right," I said.

"We've only been over it a hundred times..."

"Then how come we never noticed that Kate's got too much hair?"

"Huh," he said, and then stopped and thought for a minute. "Oh yeah, that's right."

We had been so busy dodging comets and saving our butts that no one thought about Kate's hair that was a lot longer than both my hair or Jimmy's. Jimmy went back to his bureau and grabbed a rubber band that was wrapped around one of his secret notebooks.

"We'll put it in a ponytail, and shove the rest of it down the back of her shirt." That seemed like it might work, and so we headed back to the garage.

In the terrible quiet of that room the door suddenly seemed to be opening all by itself. I felt myself grab hold of Jimmy's arm. I knew if we got caught Jimmy was gonna get grounded, and that was sure to mean the end of the world. Me and Jimmy, we pressed ourselves against the wall, and squatted down trying to hide behind his bureau.

I was so scared, and I really think my heart stopped. I know people say stuff like that, but I know mine at least skipped a beat or two. Jimmy put his finger up onto his lips warning me to be quiet, like that was something I had to be warned about. We tried to step back further into the darkness, but we had gone about as far as the wall would let us go. Then forever we waited for another sound, something to let us know what was going on. We just stood in the dark, quiet and scared. Only seconds later the door started to open more, and a low light from the hallway began to creep into the room. Both me and Jimmy we held our breath as what looked like a giant shadow entered into the room. We knew right away what it was. One of the men in black was standing there looking down on us. He was covered from head to toe in his dark costume, and we really didn't know what we were gonna do now. He stayed there just looking at us and creeping us out, but nobody was saying anything. It's like he was almost as surprised to see us as we were to see him. Slowly he stepped into the room, and closed the door behind him. But he hadn't made a sound. It was like he had been walking on air. Yeah, they could be that quiet.

"Time's running out boys," the voice said, and that was the first sound he had made since coming into the room.

"What," I barely could hear the word get past my mouth.

Before he answered he squatted down real close to us, and we came face to face. I was waiting for him to pull out a gun, or give us a karate chop, or something, but he just said those words again.

"Time's running out."

"I know," said Jimmy like he knew the guy, and he did. It was Flynn again. That's when he pulled the hood from off of his face, and we could see it was Flynn underneath there. This guy really got around.

Now I think I was more mad than scared. I wanted to yell at him, but I knew enough to keep my voice down.

"Are you crazy," I said to him. Yeah I was talking to a real spy like that, but I was really mad.

"Agent Flynn," Jimmy butted in right away, "what are you doing here? You said you wanted us to handle this..." Jimmy's voice sounded like he was demanding an answer.

Flynn didn't answer right away. Instead he walked over to the window beside Jimmy's bed and looked out. Then he turned back to

333

us, still keeping his voice real low. "I told you that I was in on this with you, but I have to know what direction to have my men looking when this all starts."

"We told you that all we had to do was get into the house," Jimmy told him. "The rest we would handle."

Flynn sat on the edge of Jimmy's bed, "you boy's know just how serious this whole situation is, so you have to know that I have my concerns."

"You said you would trust us to…" I tried to say.

"And I do, that's the reason I'm letting you get away with this. If my people get their hands on the gravity machines, then they will not let you two get near them. I on the other hand know that you two are the best qualified to pull this off. I will not let my people or my ego get in the way. But you have to know that time is running out. Even I can't hold them back much longer. Remember, my men are still counting on there being a future."

"Which there won't be,' Jimmy stopped him.

"Which there won't be if you boys don't pull this off. But all my people know is this mission, obtaining the gravity machines, and it has the highest priority for them. I hope I'm not wrong, but I happen to feel that you two are the best chance for that tomorrow."

"How much time we talking about," Jimmy said.

Flynn stood up. "Do what you have to do," he said, "but do it quickly. If I try to hold them back too long they'll get suspicious." He said those words, and then disappeared back out the door.

Me and Jimmy looked at each other. "Let's get a move on it," he said, and we did just that.

Jimmy had thrown everything we needed into that pillow sack. Now we had to get back down to the garage where Will and Kate were waiting.

On the way out of the house the floorboards creaked just as much, more even, 'cause we were rushing now. But we didn't really have the time to worry about that. Getting caught by Jimmy's Mom and Dad would put us in big trouble. If Flynn's men got their hands on us that would be the worst trouble we'd ever been in. And this is coming from a kid who was almost drowned in a moat just that morning. We climbed down the stairs to the sound of Jimmy's Dad still snoring loud, and the television blasting enough to cover the sound of our footsteps.

Any second we expected the government agents to come busting in on us, so we weren't wasting any time. We moved as quickly as we could still trying not to wake up anybody along the way.

Finally we were back in the garage. Ricky was as glad as ever to see us. With all that love came a lot of noise. Jimmy begged the dog to be quiet, but Ricky didn't seem to care about the end of the world, and just how much begging was going on.

Will helped out by coming over and hugging that nutty overgrown puppy again. And that seemed to quiet him down a little.

"We don't have a lot of time Jimmy said as he threw the clothes from the pillowcase on top of his Dad's car.

"What do you need from us James," Kate came over fast and stared down at the clothes lying on the hood of the car.

"I need you two to get dressed in these clothes," he told them.

335

Will was able to pull himself away from Ricky who started to cry as soon as he did. Ricky just wanted the attention, knowing that, I started petting him. It was easy enough 'cause Ricky was everybody's friend, and him and me had been buddies for years.

At the side of the car Will looked down in amazement at the clothes. It was almost like he had been hypnotized by the sight of them, and he had already seen and had actually worn my clothes.

"Just put them on please," Jimmy was being kind of bossy, but I knew why. It was the thought of those secret agents about to burst in on us that had him edgy and acting not so nice.

Will and Kate began throwing the clothes over the ones they were wearing.

"It looks like they got two pair of…" I was trying to tell Jimmy that I didn't think it was gonna work.

"We don't have the time," he said, "it's dark out, it'll be good enough." He then ran over to Kate, and started to put the rubber band around her hair. "Especially from a thousand feet in the air," Jimmy kept talking while he rushed about.

"What" said Will kind of nervous, but Kate didn't let him finish she was trying to figure out what Jimmy was up to.

"What the devil are you doing James," she cried out as her hair got caught in the rubber band. "Ow".

"Sorry," Jimmy tried to hush her up. "You've got to look like us," Jimmy told her. She seemed to understand right away, and stood quietly as Jimmy shoved the end of her hair down the back of the shirt she was now putting over her raggedy clothes from the past.

Will looked endlessly fascinated by the zipper on the pants that he just kept zipping up and down. He hadn't even put them on yet.

"Will," Jimmy stopped him, "we'll give you your own pants later, and you can play with them to your heart's content, but right now you've got to focus and get into those pants."

"It is a wonderment indeed," Will said, and then he stopped playing with it, and began to listen to Jimmy. Of all the things that he had seen along the way to the twenty-first century I think it was that zipper that had Will fascinated the most. I kept thinking of Will wearing my shorts back at the castle. If they had been kept up with anything more complicated than an elastic band we'd a never made it out of the hidden chamber.

After that the garage became like a madhouse. Jimmy took the wires that he had taken from his radio, and shoved them inside of the milk crates. He had me doing the same to the other one.

As Jimmy grabbed stuff, and began to put things together he explained it all. He said we were doing the only thing that we could do. That we had been given a chance not only to stop the comet in its tracks, but to keep the Gravity Boxes out of the hands of the government. He thought that was also important for the world. He said we had no time to figure out if Flynn's motives were good or not, but that we had to act as if they were.

In the middle of that he turned real angry like to Will. "No, no," he said. Jimmy then ran over to where Will was standing of the shirt. He had his arm and head coming out of the same opening. Kate seemed to be getting the hang of it pretty good, so we didn't have to tell her what to do. As he was shoving Will's arm into the right hole in the shirt Jimmy apologized, but never stopped dressing him. "I'm sorry Will, it's just that we don't have the time to explain everything. Right now you've just got to trust us. Can you do that?"

Will seemed a little scared at first like he always did, but then he bobbed his head up and down several times to let Jimmy know that he was gonna do whatever we asked him to do. Will had already saved our lives today, and was scared every step of the way; but maybe that's what a hero does, he's scared but he does stuff anyway.

A second later Jimmy was back at the milk crates. There he tossed me a wire coat hanger. "Wait, wait," he said, and then he looked around. There were two bicycles lying against the wall. His head was swinging back and forth. He was looking for something, but I couldn't tell what that was.

"What are you looking..." that all that I got out.

"A wrench, pliers..." he cut me off. "A wrench, pliers, anything to take those handlebars off."

Still he was moving around like a madman. Then I saw his Dad's toolbox.

"Over here," I called to him.

Jimmy rushed to the toolbox on the floor next to the car, and then he flung open the lid, and began to throw the tools on the ground. It was time to turn Ricky back over to Will to keep him quiet.

"Keep it down," I said. Jimmy was making an awful lot of noise.

"You're right," he came right back at me, but in all that time he hadn't slowed his pace. He found a wrench and a pair of pliers.

"See what you can do with this," he said as he tossed the wrench to me. I was good at catching stuff, so he knew that it wouldn't hit the ground.

In no time we were both really rushing, trying to take the bikes apart. In all that time Kate was just watching while Will kept Ricky happy. They were pretty much dressed by then and ready to play their parts. At least we hoped that they were ready.

"Darn," Jimmy called out as he tugged hard on the bolt that was holding the bike together.

"Keep it down," I warned him again. "What's a matter," I said back trying not to be too loud.

"It's stuck," he said, and then he pulled harder. The bike that he was working on looked kinda' rusty, so I guess that was what was slowing him down. I had almost gotten my handlebars off, but still had a little to go. Suddenly Kate said to Jimmy, "can I be of any assistance James?"

"Yeah, I need some help over here," he said. And he almost looked like he was gonna cry. I mean I could tell that he was scared that any minute that those guys in the black outfits were gonna come bursting into the garage, and then all our plans would be shot.

Will let go of Ricky and he and Kate rushed to Jimmy's side. As Jimmy continued to tug on the pliers, both Will and Kate grabbed hold of his arm, and started to pull with him. Ricky had gone over to sniff around.

"Please Ricky," Jimmy begged the dog, "just go sit down," and this time old Ricky seemed to understand and backed off, and just watched like he knew what was going on.

339

The three of them were now working together to get that one little bolt loose on the bike. Suddenly it was free, and Jimmy pushed Will and Kate away, and finished the job himself. "Thanks guys," he said, and then rushed the bars to the milk crates where the hangers had been lying on top.

I watched Jimmy while he attached the handlebars with the wire hanger and I did the same. As soon as that was done, he couldn't wait any longer. He ran to the garage door, and sneaked a peek out of the dirty window that was on the top of the door. What he saw must've scared the heck out of him.

"No," Jimmy almost shouted out. It was like he had just found the self-control not to scream.

"What is it," I said. Whatever it was didn't sound good.

"They're coming, now," he sounded like he wanted to cry.

"But we're not ready," I was sure that he knew that, but that's all that I could think to say.

"We've got to be ready," he said. With those words he looked at Will and Kate. "Now listen, and listen good." As he spoke he grabbed them and pulled them along. He knew that he had no time to explain it all in detail so he was trying to get them to do what had to be done in the little time that we had. First he put Will's hands on the handlebars. "No matter what happens," Jimmy was almost yelling at him, "don't let go of these bars." Kate did the same just by watching what her brother was doing.

Suddenly there was a rattling at the door.

"Jim..." I began to say.

"Get up in the loft," he ordered. Yes, that's right he ordered like a five star general he was taking total control. I really didn't mind I was too scared to take offense at being ordered around, and besides I was getting kinda use to it. We ran like crazy to get to the ladder that led to the top of the loft. On the way up there Jimmy grabbed hold of the white pillowcase, and the schoolbag that had all of our spy junk in it. There was another jiggle on the door, and I knew that any second it was gonna come rising up, and the government agents would swarm into the garage.

Up on top of the loft Jimmy ducked down, and rolled to get to the second Gravity Box. Quick like he poured all of the stuff from the schoolbag into the pillowcase.

"What..." I tried to get out.

"Makes all this junk easier to carry." Then he yelled at me again, "FOCUS!"

Right then the door to the garage swung open just as I was diving for the other Gravity Box. Jimmy looked at me, but didn't say a word. Whoever was down there couldn't know that there were two other kids in that garage.

It was only through the spaces between the junk piled onto the loft that we could see the action that was going on down on the ground. The guys in black had just opened the doors. Will and Kate were frozen onto the handlebars, and that was all that they had to do. Me and Jimmy had had it all planned out so we knew exactly what was going to happen next. He was gonna make Kate's phony box fly, and I was gonna make Will's. All they had to do was hold on for the ride of their lives. That's all they had to do.

The green beam from Jimmy's Gravity Box was the first one to flash across the garage. The light seemed to explode almost blinding the agent's who had just come through the door. Kate's milk crate with Kate hanging on went flying right at them. I got that look from Jimmy that said what was I waiting for. So right away I shot another green beam from my Gravity Box at Will. Like a giant green flare the beam lit up the entire garage, and had the agents below covering their eyes trying to stop what they were having a hard time seeing. But it was only a loud scream that they could catch hold of as Will shot past them like a bullet and straight into the air. We were pretty sure that they wouldn't shoot at them. Nobody wanted to take a chance on hurting the Gravity Boxes. I'm not so sure they were too worried about the kids hanging onto them, but they for sure didn't want to hurt those boxes.

One of the Agents pulled out a gun, and began to aim at Will when Flynn's voice yelled out.

"Put down that weapon you could destroy the levitation device. "They've escaped," I heard Flynn call out next, "let's get out there, and then he ordered all of the other agents outside.

We had to have our imaginations up and running to keep the bright green glow surrounding Will and Kate. We had done what the Professor called neutralize their gravity, but still the boxes had to be guided. Jimmy was sure that that would take all eyes away from us, or at least we hoped so. Like Fourth of July fireworks Will and Kate shot across the sky. And the goal was to keep them shinning a lot brighter than us, a whole lot brighter.

It was now only me and Jimmy left in the garage, but we were scared that there might be a few of Flynn's men still just outside of the door. We didn't know just how long to wait.

"What should we do," I said to him.

"First make sure you keep thinking of Will," he's probably scared to death. Second, let's get out of here."

"But what if they're out there still?"

"Right now we don't have any choice Shawn," we've got to get out of here. That's only place we can do any good."

Slowly we lifted into the air. Looking down to the outside it looked like no one was out there. And then through the loft window we flew, me, Jimmy, and the white pillowcase.

Chapter 7: Will and Kate Up in the Clouds And Not Happy About It

Zooming over the town Will and Kate looked like two gigantic sparklers lighting up the sky, or maybe even more like shooting stars streaking through the night, and that was pretty creepy. Any of the green beams from our Gravity Boxes showing looked just like a trail that they were leaving behind. Me and Jimmy had gained so much control over the Gravity Boxes that it seemed easy to make the beam grow smaller as it left the real boxes. All we had to do was see it in our minds.

The thunder had burst, and the lightening lit up the sky just above us as we took off out of Jimmy's loft window. We zoomed in to the air as fast as we could. We were hoping not to be seen by any of Flynn's men that had all raced around to the front of the house when the noise started. It was that flash of lightening that gave us a look at what was still out there, and there didn't seem to be anybody.

We flew fast to get up over the storm clouds. We thought we'd be safe there. In all that time me and Jimmy kept our thoughts on Will and Kate who were already up high, and probably having heart attacks as they shot across the sky.

Whizzing up to the clouds we could feel the strong winds blowing us all over the place. Just past the clouds we could hear both Kate and Will screaming at each other. Actually, I hate to say it, it sounded like Will was crying.

"We are going to die, we are going to die," I heard him scream out to Kate.

"We got to stay calm Will," I heard Kate's voice scream back and almost as terrified as Will. "James and Shawn are…"

"And where be they now," he shouted back at her, "they are demons, demons from the darkest pits of Hades I tell you."

"It be their science that is keeping us up here Will…"

And this time I heard Will go back at Kate. I think for the first time. "Keep it to yourself Kate, no one but demons with their black arts and wicked ways…"

It was actually me and Jimmy shooting through the clouds that shut Will up. He was still mad, but just scared enough not to want to get into a rumble with us demons.

"I told you Will that they'd be coming for us…"

"Sorry we had to get you up here so fast," Jimmy said.

"It needs some getting use to," I said.

"See Will…" Kate tried to get out, but now it was Will cutting everybody off.

"No, they be taunting us, that is what demons do."

Jimmy flew real close to Will who was clutching onto the box, and not the handlebars for his life.

"I'm you're friend Will, and right now I need you," Jimmy said to him. "Now I'm sorry that we've put you through a lot, and I haven't been too nice some of the time, but I have nothing to make you believe that I'm not going to hurt you except my word."

The wind seemed to be a little stiller up over the dark clouds, but still the cool breeze was making us bob around like a buoy in a stormy ocean. For the longest time Will just looked at Jim not answering. I knew that the reason that Will was acting so crazy was

345

that he was scared, terrified of being thousands of feet up in the sky with only a milk crate holding him up there. I knew the feeling 'cause I had been in the same position, so I knew exactly what Will was going through.

We were all waiting while Will just kept looking at Jimmy, drilling holes through him with his eyes. Finally he spoke. "And you are saying Jim that it be your science that hurled me and my Kate into the clouds."

Jimmy nodded his head, "it's not my science Will, but yes, that's what did that to you."

"Well," Will trembled as he called to Jimmy past the windy breeze that we all seemed to be trapped in, "your science, it be a terrible thing Jim, a terrible and frightening thing."

"It can be that," Jimmy didn't try to argue with him. "But right now we need it to make a magic trick."

"Magic," Will said.

"But just a trick like the snake in the moat."

That's when I moved closer and Jimmy drew Kate into the meeting taking place just above the thunder and lightening. Jimmy looked at us all, "this may not be the best magic trick ever, but I can promise all of you that it will be the most important trick ever."

"Me and Will, we'll be there for you," Kate told Jimmy.

"You have been up to now," Jimmy smiled back at her. Will still didn't seem sure, but at least now he was stopping to listen.

Then Jimmy explained the whole plan in detail, but real quick like. He had to make sure that they understood their part. We knew from the last time we lived out this night that helicopters would be arriving soon, real soon. So we had to get a move on it. We also knew that lightening was gonna strike the tree where we had first destroyed the Gravity Boxes. That would be real useful in selling the illusion Jimmy said.

Soon we heard that churning sound coming through the air, just like we had thought. The helicopters were almost on top of us, and we knew that we couldn't let them get a close look at Will and Kate.

I could tell that they were both still scared, and Will was really not happy about what was going to happen next. But he didn't argue or yell at us anymore, so we figured that he was once again up for helping us with the plan.

There was another flash of light from the clouds beneath. That was our signal. We sent Will and Kate dive-bombing towards the ground. Using all of our imaginations we made the beam powerful around them, so that all the attention would be going their way. The lightening had me and Jimmy both a little nervous. We had promised Will and Kate that we'd try and keep them as safe as possible, but with the lightening and the secret agents swarming all over the place we knew that that wouldn't be easy.

We could still hear the screams coming out of Will as he dropped to the ground below like a burning meteor falling from the sky. Still we were right behind them. The trick being to not get too close, so that only Will and Kate would be seen as they flew by the choppers. But still we had to keep them moving fast so no one could get a good look at them. We knew that this would get the choppers and everyone following them.

We were dropping down so fast that the chill from the wind was blasting right through our clothes, and felt like it was going straight to the bone. Close to the ground the trick then became to have Kate and Will fly past the spies just high enough for them to think that it was us, and to lead the agents on a chase. Once out of sight we had to arrange the destruction of the fake Gravity Boxes, and then take the place of our doubles. Yeah it was just like Jimmy had said, kinda like a magic trick.

All at once that churning sound got a whole lot louder, and the lights came cutting through the air. We knew then just how close the helicopters were, and that was too close for comfort. Now it was all the same as before, the agents down below, the lightening all around us, and the helicopters closing in. Still we had to make sure that the only ones that anybody saw were Will and Kate, but they couldn't be seeing them up too close. That would ruin Jimmy's "master plan," which if it worked would've been not too bad a plan at all.

Across the sky the choppers were coming at us real fast. Jimmy decided to distract those guys by having Will and Kate fly past them. Then we swooped around the choppers and behind them.

"Now we beat them to the ground, and get ready for the big switch," he said.

So that's what we did. We shot Will and Kate back up into the air, just high enough for the guys in the choppers to get a glimpse, just not too good a glimpse. The pounding rain was really helping us out with that.

Will cried out, "they be giant birds coming after us," but we didn't have time to explain what the helicopters really were. We

348

could still hear Will crying out as he zoomed across the sky. Kate might have been crying too, but if she was she was being drowned out by the storm, the choppers, and all of Will's noise. Yeah, that chopper sound was making it hard to hear anything including Will.

Jimmy flew closer to me. "Was I that scared my first time up," I asked him as we heard Will's scream dying out as he fell back to earth.

"You were pretty scared Shawn," he said. "Here's some grease I took from the garage. Rub it on yourself."

"Why would I…"

"We don't have time Shawn, just do it."

Keeping one hand on the Gravity Box I scooped a handful of the grease out of the pillowcase, and began rubbing in onto my face and arms.

"We've got a lot to do before…" and just as Jimmy was saying that a huge burst of lightening blasted out of the clouds, and lit up the whole sky. It was real easy to see Will and Kate now as they came closer to the ground again.

Jimmy took the pillowcase from my hand and started rubbing some grease on himself.

"I think it's time Shawn," he said.

"I think you're right," I said back to him.

There was nothing to think about anymore. Jimmy had explained his idea to all of us as we had traveled back to Jimmy's house in Flynn's car. Right then we started to soar down to the ground. We had to get there fast, and at the same time keep Will and Kate up in the air where the guys in black could see them.

In seconds we were close to the ground. Hovering just above the trees. The big fear was that there would be another flash of lightening and we could be seen. We stayed as far away from the house as we could so that the agents wouldn't see us. The lights from the choppers were flooding the whole area, so we were keeping Will and Kate a good distance away from them and us. Like in all good magic tricks, Will and Kate were only a distraction that would have all eyes looking the wrong way.

Once down on the grass we set the rest of Jimmy's "master plan" in motion. We knew that there wasn't much time with the agents closing in on what they thought was me and Jimmy.

For a little we stayed hidden in the shadows of the trees. From up there we could check out what was going on down below. With no one in sight we knew it was time to bring Will and Kate in for a landing. First we floated down to the ground ourselves, and then we guided our doubles to a place nearby. They had to get there before the agents and the helicopters could catch up with them, but not too much before.

Even if they hadn't seen the Gravity Boxes dropping down on that spot they could've probably followed the sound of Will's howling like a terrified baby. I really hoped I hadn't been that scared the first time I flew one of these things.

Once his feet hit the ground Will jumped away from the milk crate, and backed himself into a tree. He grabbed hold of it like he was hoping that the tree could keep him stuck on the ground.
"It be the devil's own torture," he almost screamed out as we came running out from the yard behind them.

"Quiet," Kate ordered him, yes, that's right ordered him. It seemed like everybody was handing out orders that night, and I was still so glad that she wasn't my sister.

"But we were up in the clouds with giant winged monsters chasing us…" Will tried to say again.

"No time for this," Jimmy said to him, but Will was still clutching on to the tree as if his life depended on it.

"What's he doing," I said.

"Will thinks that holding on to this tree will keep him from going back into the clouds," Kate shook her head.

"No more rides tonight, I promise," Jimmy said as he tried to pull Will's hand from the tree.

Kate was trying to get the other hand loose as Will struggled against them. While they were wrestling with Will to get him off of the tree the sound of the choppers were getting closer and closer. So we knew that the agents would be getting there real soon.

"No, no," Will begged as they pulled at his arms, "I don't want to… I don't want to."

Looking up we could see that the lights from the choppers cutting through the trees.

Then all at once one of the men in black had arrived on the spot. We all froze to the spot. He ran right over to us. Even Jimmy wasn't sure of what to do. I just began backing away trying to give myself a good head start back to my Gravity Box that was still hidden back in the yard, behind a tree.

The agent came right over to us, and kneeled down beside Will. He lifted his mask, and we could see that it was Flynn again. This guy really got around.

"There's no time for this son, the whole world needs you to get away from here now," he looked Will straight in the eye, and Will slowly left go of the tree.

"You guys hide over behind those trees," Jimmy told Kate. As Will and Kate ran off Jimmy looked up at Flynn. "Just like planned," Jimmy said, "you're going to be our witness."

"Just like planned," Flynn said, "now hurry!"

Jimmy dropped the pillowcase on the ground, he tossed the old radio parts inside of the milk crates, and then lit the fuses for the smoke bombs that he had brought along.

In all that time the choppers had moved in closer, and were almost overhead. Another flash of lightening lit the area and we could see, but only for a second the agents moving down the street.

"What are you waiting for," Flynn shouted.

"Get way back," Jimmy shouted to Flynn, "lightening is going to hit that tree."

"How do you know…" Flynn started to say, and then shut up and backed further away from the tree.

"But it won't be enough." Jimmy said to him.

"What! "

"Just stay away from that tree," Jimmy warned Flynn. Then Jimmy lit the fuse to the smoke bombs inside the fake Gravity Boxes. They would add to the illusion Jimmy said.

Just like before we were going to use the tree to smash the boxes. Only this time we were gonna be smashing two boxes, and this time they weren't gonna be real. The lightening hitting the tree would make the trick more convincing, and the damage enough to fool anybody.

Behind the tree where we had hidden the Gravity Boxes we saw Will and Kate. She was hugging him tight trying to comfort him, and I'm guess'n herself just a little.

"Stay here," we'll be back for you, but don't make a sound," Jimmy warned them.

Both of us now took the handles of the Gravity Boxes and pointed them at the tree. We wasted no time, there wasn't any to waste. Standing close to the fake Gravity Boxes that we had made, we heard Flynn shouting out, like he was yelling at us.

"Don't! Are you kids crazy," he called, and he yelled it just like we had been standing there. He was acting this all out for the other agents that were almost there. From hearing Flynn yell the other agents started to pick up their speed. They were getting closer.

The green beams from both boxes shot out and blasted the tree. With both beams hitting it the tree began to fall right away crashing onto the ground and smashing the fakes.

Without waiting me and Jimmy ran out to the sight where the tree had fallen. Flynn continued to yell at us.

Some of the others were just arriving, and were looking down at the crushed milk crates. The smoke bombs inside had gone off, and it looked like they had exploded when they got flattened.

One of the agents rushed in to try and salvage whatever might be left, but I knew that the lightening bolt was gonna hit the tree at any second.

"No," I screamed at him.

The agent just looked at me like he wanted to rip me apart, but what I had said had slowed him down just enough. Before he could take another step the lightening zapped the fallen tree and sent it up in flames. The agent jumped back, and then looked back to me. He didn't know what to think. He didn't say anything, but I thought that I at least should've gotten a thanks. By the looks on the faces of everyone else I really didn't think I was gonna get it. Most of those guys just stood frozen at what looked to be another failed mission lying in flames right at their feet. No one said a word; it was like they had lost all hope.

Flynn pulled out a walkie-talkie and called to the choppers, "X10 to Delta 9 return to base, Operation Fly Boys has been terminated. I repeat, Operation Fly Boys has been terminated. Over." I'm guess'n we were Operation Fly Boys. Up overhead the choppers like the men below just seemed to hover, and then slowly one by one they just drifted off. I guess they were all sad. After he had called to the helicopters, Flynn turned his attention back onto us.

"Do you know what you've done," Flynn pulled off his mask, and came closer like he was gonna hit us or something worst. And it didn't look like anybody was gonna try and stop him either. "You've destroyed a valuable tool that could have been used to help the world." He was a real good actor, and he stopped only a few steps from me and Jimmy. I was glad he stopped, I was worried he was

354

gonna really try and sell this thing by clocking one of us. Jimmy was the mastermind, so I thought if anybody was gonna get hit it should be him.

All of the commotion was bringing people out onto their porches and watching just like before. I was worried that any second my Dad would appear on the scene since history was repeating itself. So I kept looking around and waiting. I wanted to back away into the shadows, but the agents were all around us. I could see my house not far off, but still nobody came out. Something was different.

"Professor Burkhardt doesn't want you to have them, he doesn't want anybody to have them," Jimmy yelled back at him. It was like watching a real neat TV show or something. They actually yelled back and forth at each other a couple of things, and all through that act they were putting on Flynn looked like he was gonna hit Jimmy, so I just kept my mouth shut in case he really wanted to sell the double cross.

A couple of the guys were looking real close at the mess on the ground. I guess they were trying to see if there was anyway of putting it back together again. But just like with old Humpty Dumpty they didn't stand a chance. A couple of the others seemed like they wanted to come over and hit us too. One of them looked like he was ready to cry, and I kinda felt sorry for them knowing that these two kids had made jerks of them all over. Flynn too looked at the burning fakes real hard and good. It was like he was looking at the real thing. I mean he was really a good actor.

"Nothing to be done here," he said to the other men. And we knew that that was true. Even if it had been the real Gravity Boxes on

355

fire and smashed to bits under that fallen tree no one, not even the Professor could've put the pieces back together.

The others backed away slowly, only Flynn stayed behind. When they were out of hearing distance he looked at us both.

"There was a gas leak at your home tonight, your parents have gone to a neighbors house while it's being checked out," Flynn told me.

"Are they all right," I asked.

"I don't think Agent Flynn's talking about a real gas leak, are you?"

Flynn shook his head slowly and spoke, "they're fine. They'll be back in the house within the hour. I just couldn't have your parents throwing a monkey wrench into our mission." He looked at Jimmy. "I would have done that with your parents, but then my men would have just gone into the house without waiting."

So now we were on a real mission working with a real secret agent. All that playing at being spies and super heroes was finally paying off. All of the kid's games that might've seemed silly to adults had been just the training we needed if we were gonna pull this off and save the world.

"You know what you've got to do," Flynn said.

He didn't tell us not to mess up or anything, he just turned around and walked away. Yeah, having Flynn be an eyewitness really sold the destruction of the Gravity Boxes as something real.

All that was left to do now was to wait for that big comet that was headed our way to destroy the Earth. Aside from that there wasn't much else we could do.

Concept Art. I Think We Found Our Sagamore.

Chapter 8: The Last Tuesday On Earth

We got Will and Kate back to the Professor's house later that night. Jimmy had taken the Gravity Boxes, and made sure that they were hidden real good before we got there. We could've flown Kate and Will back, but I don't think that they were up for another ride in the sky, not just after their first trip to the clouds.

We headed back into the woods that lead to the Professor's house. The storm had already started to die down. Will, now glad to be on the ground was asking a lot of questions.

"Did you have to leave me up there so long Shawn," his voice was racing along as if we were still zooming around on the milk crates.

"We had no choice", I told him, "the men in black…"

"Those would be the shadow creatures you summoned?"

"No one summoned them," I told him.

"Will, would you be wanting another swat on your noggin," said Kate, "you seen for yourself that they be just rogues with mask over their heads."

"I'm beginning to believe that you enjoy hitting me on me noggin Kate," Will said ducking the question and maybe even another swat.

That's all he got out when Jimmy came running down the path. Not sure that it was Jimmy at first we all stopped and prepared for trouble.

"What are you trying to do," I yelled at him, "scare us to death?"

"If that didn't happen tonight then it isn't ever going to happen." Jimmy said. "We've got to get them to the Professor's fast. The commotion with the choppers got our parents out and searching for us again. One of the neighbors thought she saw us…"

"Nosy neighbors…"

"Shawn, this is serious…"

"I know, I know…"

"They've had the police out looking for us…"

"But we came back the same night that we…"

"We've been gone long enough and they haven't been able to get hold of us. They're worried."

"Between almost drowning in the moat and fighting the forces of evil…"

"Okay Superman…"

"Well I'm serious…"

"So am I Shawn, they called the Professor again wondering if he knew anything."

"He's a terrible liar…"

"I know, he hasn't had all the practice that you've had."

"Very funny."

"I'm serious."

"Like I don't know that we're in it and deep."

"When we first disappeared he didn't remember 'cause the Earth had been destroyed, and after that he was tossed back in time."

"Before he shipped us off to merry old England."

"That be when we met," Will said excitedly as if reliving the fun time we had back in the dungeon.

Me and Kate told him to "shut up." And we both said it at the exact same time, so we were at least on the same page where Will was concerned.

"The Professor had been telling the truth that time, so I guess it was easy to believe him."

"What did he tell them," I looked nervously at Jimmy.

"He didn't know what to tell them, so he told them that we had been by…"

"What did he do that for," I yelled at Jimmy, like it had been his fault."

"We knew we were going to have to go home sometime."

"We never stayed out this late before, we're gonna get killed."

"They've been really worried Shawn…"

"But it wasn't our fault…"

"It doesn't matter Shawn they've been out searching for us."

"If only we could just tell them…" I tried to say.

"We can't tell them, for one thing the agents may still have our houses wired. For another, do you really want to drop the bomb on your parents that the Earth might come to an end on Tuesday?"

"So what do we do?"

"We get Will and Kate to the Professor's house. He'll watch out for them while we get home and try not to get grounded."

"You seriously think that we're not gonna get grounded," I couldn't believe Jimmy was saying that, 'cause just getting grounded would be the best thing that could come out of this night.

"All we've got to do it get to school, I'm sure that they'll let us do that."

360

"My Dad's gonna be really mad about this…"

"That's fine," Jimmy seemed to think that that was okay.

"It is!"

"All we've got to do is be able to get to school Tuesday."

"So we can play hooky? That'll make him real happy."

Then Jimmy looked at me real serious like. "One way or the other we're in deep trouble. But only some of that trouble can we live with."

As usual Jimmy was right, so we started rushing as fast as we could to the Professor's house.

When we got there Professor Burkhardt was waiting outside near to the garage and looking nervously at us.

"Are you sure no one followed you," he said.

"They know where you live Professor," Jimmy said to him.

"All we have to do is keep everything down about what happened tonight in case they're still listening in on you."

"I have to talk to you all," he said sadly as he looked down at Will and Kate. "It is a grave subject that I must speak of."

"Grave," Will trembled.

"What is it Professor," Jimmy asked.

"If we can save the world…"

"We can do it Professor," I said, at least I hoped that we could. Why else had we gone through all the trouble?

"I have been researching England's history," he said, once more looking sadly down at Will and Kate. "The twelfth-century was a bloody period indeed," he went on.

"That's still true isn't it Professor," Jimmy asked him.

"The revised edition or what I must assume is the revised edition may have been affected by your actions...."

"But," Jimmy tried to get out.

"As I feared, as I feared," Professor Burkhardt came back at him.

"And don't I know that," I shook my head. Like the Professor was telling us something that we didn't know from actually being there. But I could tell just how serious the Professor was being when he didn't even bother to look annoyed with me.

"And," Jimmy wanted to know what the Professor was getting at. Curiosity was Jimmy's biggest weakness.

"And it appears the abduction of Sir Sagamore by witches..."

"See I told you," Will cried out. I wanted to hit him myself, and he moved out of the way as if expecting another smack from Kate.

"Keep a tight lip Will," Kate told him.

"But there were no witches, and he grabbed a ride along with us," I said.

"It is the appearance of black magic that caused all the trouble," the Professor told us.

"Trouble," Jimmy asked.

"After Sagamore disappeared there was a great witch hunt in England."

"But they went after us," I said.

"From what I remember, it was always bad, Professor, always bad," Jimmy said. "Hunting witches and stuff."

"You Jim, have been in both time lines, I have only recollection from this time line."

"But there were always inquisitions, witch hunts…"

"All I know is that the history books make special mention of the disappearance of the Black Knight."

"So send him back," and I yelled at the professor. Can't believe I yelled at him.

"Calm down Shawn," Jimmy yelled at me, all the time I could see Will and Kate getting upset by all of this.

"But they are part of the equation," the Professor came back at me.

"Then so are we," I was getting loud again, and not even knowing what equation meant. "Me and Jimmy were the witches," I said and then yelled over to Will, "Not real witches!"

"Thousands upon thousands of innocent people were tried as witches and executed," the Professor was trying to keep control of himself.

"What can we do," Jimmy asked him.

"They must go back," said the Professor.

Will and Kate looked terrified, and I can't say I blamed them.

"Aren't we rushing things," I said trying to calm the way I was saying things, "there's a good chance that after Tuesday we'll all be toast anyway." Probably not the smartest thing to say, but that's what came off the top of my head.

"But Will and Kate will be tried as witches if they're sent back," Jimmy told the Professor.

"Sometimes they roast them they think are witches on the stake," Will said with a shaky voice and his eyes wide. You could see a little tear starting to roll down his cheek, as he was terrified one more time on that scariest of all nights.

"Thousands, of lives will be lost," the Professor said, and I could tell that he was upset by the whole situation. The Professor was a good guy, and he kinda worried about everybody.

"But without these two helping us tonight, the whole world might end," I told him.

"And it still might," said the Professor. He sounded kinda gloomy when he said it, so that wasn't good. It was like he was having some doubts about the Gravity Boxes himself. "We must send them all back before the last day. If we fail we can still save all of those innocent people from being tortured and slaughtered…"

"Well," said Jimmy, "We're not going to go and get Sagamore until we've saved the world."

"I'm sorry children, but we cannot tamper with the time space continuum."

"But we've been doing it all week," I told him, 'cause we had been doing just that.

"We are not even sure what other disastrous consequences may have occurred or may occur," you could almost hear the Professor's voice about to break, that's how upset he was.

That's when Will and Kate turned to me and Jimmy. Kate just looked at us, but Will said what was in his head.

"They'll set fire to us good and proper James, Shawn." Will's head bounced back and forth between the two of us. I had been in their place, so there was no way I was gonna be sending them back. No the Professor was not getting my help for that one, but it was Jimmy that said it.

"Jim, you must listen to me," the Professor went on.

"No," said Jimmy, and it was the first time I had ever heard Jimmy go back at the Professor. He had forgotten all about his parents waiting for him back home. For the longest time the Professor and Jimmy just stood looking at each other. I kept waiting for one of them to say something else but they didn't.

After a moment the Professor looked back at Will and Kate. "They can stay here while you prepare for the comet. You had better be getting home, your parents are very worried."

He turned and went back into the house. Will and Kate just looked at us. Their faces were white as sheets, and their expressions were the saddest I had ever seen.

"Will you be sending us back James," asked Kate.

"To go to our death," Will jumped in scared as could be, and who could blame him.

"Everything's going to be all right," Jimmy said. "Wait here for us. We'll come and see you as soon as we can."

Slowly Will and Kate followed the Professor into his lab that was attached to the house. They kept looking back at us like they weren't sure that they should be going in there. There wasn't a lot of talking going on that night, especially after it seemed like the Professor had handed Will and Kate a death sentence. As they walked back into the house, we walked off towards home.

"That didn't sound like the Professor talking," I said to Jimmy.

"He's just taking in the whole picture," he said. And he answered me like he wasn't really even listening. It was like he didn't believe any of it himself.

"We're not gonna do it?"

"Do it," Jimmy looked back at me like he was still having trouble hearing anything that was going on outside of his own brain.

"Send them back."

"Send them…"

"Will and Kate," I yelled at him. He looked hypnotized, and I was trying to snap him out of whatever was going on inside of his head.

He looked at me sadly, "how could we do that," he said.

"I mean they saved us, we can't just make them go back and…"

"No, we can't," Jimmy said finally sounding like he was hearing me. "First we've got to get through tomorrow, then we've got to figure out what to do about Will and Kate."

"The Professor's worried about what could happen if those guys aren't sent back…"

"The big picture, he's worried about that, but after the comet, there may not be any big picture to worry about, so I say let's just get past Tuesday."

"First I've got to get past my Mom and Dad," I said. "It would be so easy if we just could tell them the truth."

"We can't, no one besides us can know. If we speak about it in the house, we may be being listened to."

"You think the houses are still bugged?"

"I don't know, but I can't take a chance, and do you really want to tell your Mom and Dad that Tuesday might be their last day on Earth."

"That would really bum them out," I said. I knew that for sure 'cause it was really bumming me out.

"And the more that they know the more danger they could be in if anyone comes looking for the Gravity Boxes later on."

"So nothing can be said."

"Nothing can be said."

"My Dad's not gonna be happy when I walk into the house this time of night."

"Neither are my parent's, they think we've been gone for..."

"You know my Dad hasn't taken a strap to me in a long time..."

"You can't tell him Shawn, no matter what you can't tell them."

"I know," I said, "I just wish I could find a way to get Will to take a licking for me. I mean he's so good at it."

"I don't think that's going to happen," and I could tell that Jimmy felt bad about the fix we were in. He was for sure in a load of trouble himself.

"I know, I know, I'm just saying that it's gonna be a rough night."

We didn't speak too much more as we walked out of the woods. The town looked like it had gone to sleep. Even the neon lights over old man Jenkins' store had been turned off. Slowly me and Jimmy walked through the town. It was so quiet and we didn't say it, but I know both of us were hoping that it would be just like this after Tuesday.

Chapter 9: How the End of the World Ruined Recess.

"You are in this house forever," my Dad yelled at me. He had been yelling for about an hour after I got back into the house. He still hadn't taken off his belt, so I was saying "I'm sorry," and "It'll never happen again," stuff like that. Sometimes you get enough "I'm sorrys" out there quick enough, parent's can get a little forgiving. And the truth is I really was sorry. I was sorry about a lot of things. I was sorry about spending all that time in the dungeon, and almost drowning in the moat, but I couldn't tell my Dad about that, so for just then and there I was just sorry. I really didn't want to make my parents worry, but if we didn't get the Gravity Boxes up and flying on Tuesday, then we were all gonna be sorry.

Like I said a whipping was something that hadn't happened in a long time, but still it was something that I could live without. My parents kept grilling me about where I had gone and what I had done. I came up with some lame excuse about forgetting about the time and playing in the woods. I knew they weren't buying it. It wasn't a very good story. The problem being that I had a perfectly good excuse for staying away for so long, and I was sure that it would've gotten me off of the hook, but like Jimmy said this was something so important that I might have to go through a lot and not say anything. Anyway, I was sure that Jimmy was getting the same ear beating over at his place that I was.

"And what is that smell," my Mom scrunched up her face with disgust as the stink that was left over from the moat finally reached her nose. "You're dirty, you're filthy…"

"Have you been playing in the sewer," my Dad screamed.

And I might as well have been playing down in the sewer as bad as I was stinking up the place.

Finally I was told to take a bath and go to bed, and I was relieved to hear that. I ran right up the stairs and hit the tub. Mom also gave me a plastic bag to dump my clothes in so that she could toss them into the trash. Hot water had never felt so good, and this was one bath that my parents didn't have to argue with me about. Right after that I hit the sheets. I was never so glad to be there. For the longest time I laid there staring at the ceiling thinking about Will and Kate, and how terrible it would be for them to be sent back to where they came from. Looking over at the clock I saw how late it was. I knew that I only had a few hours to sleep before it was time for school. Yeah, that's right I was going to school, and that was the only thing that would be getting me out of the house so that I could stop the comet from crashing into the middle of our town.

I closed my eyes and tried to sleep. At first I really didn't think I was gonna be able to do it. It's not like I wasn't beat from what had happened the last couple of days. It's just that all that had happened kept playing like a movie in my head, a real scary movie. First I saw Will and Kate looking at me through the bars in the dungeon. I remembered just how scared they were when they first tried to take a peek at me and Jimmy. And then there was Lord Hoxley, who had the same look on his face, just like a little kid when

370

he saw us for the first time. Mostly I remember Sir Saggy charging across the field on his horse and all of the soldiers that were with him. He was so brave hunting down two twelve year olds with only an army behind him. When I first saw them coming at us I really wasn't all that scared. It was almost like a dream, and something inside my head was telling me that it wasn't real. But in no time we could see that it wasn't a dream, and that's when I got scared. I think I had been scared from the time I got to the twelfth century until just then when I was laying in my bed trying to go to sleep. In fact for the longest time I had been scared, super scared, and Tuesday was going to be the scariest day of all. How brave would I be when I came face to face with that comet? And then when I was sure that I could never sleep that night it happened, I was in dreamland.

Drifting deeper and deeper, at first it felt almost like taking a ride on the Gravity Box. But then the cold, cold water of the moat splashing onto my face was the first thing I remember. It seemed for the longest time like I couldn't breathe. In the water with us were Sir Saggy and his soldiers. I tried to swim away, but I was tied with the ropes just like it had really happened, and those ropes were so tight that I couldn't move or get free of them. It was like my whole body was frozen, and all I could do was wait for them to come and get me. Their swords had been drawn out, and raised like they were gonna cut me to pieces. As Sir Saggy got closer I just closed my eyes, and waited for his sword to slice me in half. Suddenly I felt myself being pulled away from where he was. I opened my eyes under the water, and could see him trying to chase me, but now he was the one who was moving too slow. I turned around to see that it was Will and

Kate dragging me to safety. Suddenly I was able to breathe again, I jumped up, and was now back in my bedroom. I looked around nervously half asleep, and part of me still thinking that I was back in that moat. But I was alone, all alone. I knew the answer before the dream, but I knew for sure after, there was no way that I was letting anyone send Will and Kate back to the twelfth-century.

Next morning around the kitchen table there wasn't a lot of talking going on. Dad and Mom were still pretty mad at me, so we just all ate what was on our plates and didn't say much.

At school I found Jimmy first thing.

"Did you get it good last night," I asked him.

"The next time I'm allowed to watch TV I'll be as old as my parents. By the way they think you might be a bad influence on me."

"Me?"

"I never had to fight off enemy spies before I started hanging out with you," he laughed.

"Very funny. The next time I mess up it's gonna be real bad over at my place," I told him.

"That's going to be at exactly eleven o'clock tomorrow," Jimmy said.

"Recess," I asked.

"We've got to get to the Professor's early, the comet got to Earth a lot earlier than even the Professor expected."

"If I hooky school my Dad's gonna flip."

"Shawn!"

"I'm not gonna be able to sit down for a year," I must've sounded like whining puppy, but that's how I felt.

"Shawn!" That's all that Jimmy came back with 'cause he knew what was really important.

And Jimmy was right all the way. First we had to stop the comet, but then I really hated what might happen after that.

It was Monday and me and Jimmy were on our best behavior. We only had to stay good till that very next day. That big scary day, the day we were gonna go toe to toe with the comet. It was before school and I knew we were gonna be doing everything as usual until recess. We discussed our plan to hooky, and then I brought up something else that was really nagging me.

"Have you thought about Will and Kate, and what the Professor wants to do," I asked him.

"No way," he said, "they're not going back. We might just as well kill them."

I was glad to hear that Jimmy was on my side. Right after that the first bell rang for school.

As I walked through the school I saw a bunch of the guys hanging around Tommy Stoddard. He was telling them some wild tale about a Black Knight attacking old man Jenkins' food store and stealing milk crates. Naturally everyone just thought that he was acting crazy. I had stories to tell myself, but what could I say, I wasn't supposed to be there. I laughed to myself 'cause I knew that Tommy would probably go through his life telling that story, and no one would ever believe him even with old man Jenkins and Bobby the Security Guard backing him up. Heck, I was there and I found it hard to believe.

Tuesday came at us much too fast along with recess. The entire class was taken out to the schoolyard. Mr. Foster, the Principal was walking around keeping an eye on everyone, and I was hoping that me and Jimmy could sneak away without getting spotted by him or one of the teachers. Out of nowhere I saw my Dad's car pull up to the side gate of the school. I couldn't believe it. I knew that Jimmy's class would be coming out of the door any second, and he'd be wanting to ditch school, and get over to the Professor's.

Dad just looked at me as he walked across the schoolyard. He wasn't smiling, and I wasn't expecting a smile all that soon anyway. As he came towards me so did Mister Foster. It looked like the Principal had been waiting for my Dad.

"Mister Malloy," I heard Mister Foster call out as he came closer to me and my Father.

"Mister Foster," now my Dad smiled as he talked to him.

"Dad," I must've really looked surprised.

"You're father Shawn," Mister Foster said, "has come to see how we can help you do better with your grades."

"After the other night I thought that it might be good for you to focus more on your studies," Dad said, "and after you left for school today, I said to myself why wait? So I called Mister Foster."

This had to be the worst timing in the world. What kind of father comes to school in the middle of the day to talk about his kid's grades?

Out of the corner of my eye I saw Jimmy standing by the wall of the school. I didn't know what to do, so I just looked back at him and shrugged my shoulders.

"You're father feels that if you worked a little bit harder you might have a chance of fitting into an advanced class, how do you feel about that Shawn," Mister Foster asked.

And I really didn't know how to answer. I could see Jimmy motioning for me to get away from them, but I really didn't know how to do that, not with my Dad and the Principal standing right over me.

"We'll son, how do you feel about that," my Dad asked me.

"Ah... ah..." at first those were the only words to come out of my mouth, 'cause that's all I could think of.

"We could create an accelerated study program that is tailor made just for you Shawn," Mister Foster said.

"Go to town," I told him. And I know that it was a dumb thing to say, but it was the only thing that popped into my head at the time.

"Let's go!" Jimmy finally called from across the schoolyard, and I knew that was it, it was now or never.

"Whelp gotta go," I said, and I started moving off towards where Jimmy was waiting for me.

"Stand still Mister," my Dad ordered, and when he called me Mister I knew that I was in trouble, yes even more trouble, and I didn't think that was possible.

"This is for your own good Shawn," said Mister Foster.

"Set it up," I told him, "and I'll get right to it after recess," and I took another step back.

"Excuse me," Mister Foster looked at me with disbelief.

"Go to town, don't let me get in your way," I edged one step more away from my Dad and Mister Foster.

"Hold it," I heard my Dad's voice command, "you take one step more Shawn then you and I are going to have some serious issues."

I looked at my Dad and then I looked back at Jimmy standing across the yard. I knew then whether I saved the world or not, today was gonna be a bad day for Shawn Malloy.

Without thinking anymore about it I screamed to Jimmy, "RUN, RUN!"

And so we both did.

"Shawn," I heard my Dad's voice call to me again, but there was nothing that I could do. I had to keep running. As we ran across the schoolyard I could see all of the other students watching as we raced along. Watching and wondering what trouble I had gotten myself into this time.

At the opening in the gate Mister Fishman, another teacher stood there, and was blocking the entrance. Right behind me I could hear my Dad's footsteps coming up fast. I figured at the start he didn't believe that I was running away from him, so I had gotten a good head start by the time he realized that I was really doing it. I was a pretty fast runner, but I wasn't sure that I could outrun my Dad. I had never had to do that before. The footsteps were pounding behind me, and I didn't know what he'd do if he got his hands on me. I'm sure that he was about as angry as he'd ever been with me.

"All right, hold it right there boys," Mister Fishman held out his hand like a policeman stopping traffic as we got closer to him. I really wasn't sure what to do at first then I figured, what the heck, so I ran down a little ways from the gate, and began to climb over the fence. Jimmy had already thought of that, and had started over before I could get there.

Thump, thump, thump, my Dad's feet were slapping against the cement of the schoolyard hard and fast.

"Shawn, don't make me tell you again," he yelled at me, and I could tell that he was already losing his wind, but wasn't planning on stopping that soon. At the same time my Dad was riding up my back, Mister Fishman was racing over to where Jimmy had started to climb the fence.

Around the schoolyard all of the kids were still watching some laughing, some pointing, but none of them knowing what the heck was going on. Jimmy was closer to Mister Fishman who was just about to grab hold him as he went over the top. Through the fence the teacher tried to reach out and grab hold of Jimmy's arm.

"Stop right there, " Mister Fishman yelled at Jimmy

I was near to the top of the fence and almost over when my Dad grabbed hold of my sneaker and started to pull me back.

"Wait till I get you home," he shouted in front of everyone. To tell the truth I had a real good idea what he meant by that, but I had to keep going. I was scared like a rabbit caught in a trap, and I did something that I would feel sorry about for a long long time. And honest it wasn't on purpose, it's just that I was so crazy to get away that I kicked back and hit my Dad. I couldn't believe it either. As I fell over the other side of the fence I looked back to see him holding my sneaker in his hand, and holding his nose like he had been hurt. I felt so bad that I couldn't move. From behind me Jimmy kept calling.

"Shawn, we've got to go!"

But still I felt my legs not wanting to move from that spot. My Dad wasn't saying a word now. He just kept looking at me with that sneaker in his hand.

"Shawn," Jimmy yelled to me again.

"Dad," I said.

"NOW," Jimmy was right, but I still couldn't move from where I was standing.

At the same time Mister Fishman and Mister Foster were heading around the other side of the fence to grab hold of me and Jimmy.

"Dad, I'm sorry," I said. I really think I was ready to cry. Not because of being afraid, but because I had never thought that I could hurt my Dad, not ever.

"Shawn," Jimmy called once more, and I started to back away with only one sneaker on my foot.

And now there were other footsteps slapping the ground; that of the Teacher and the Principle coming after me fast, so I knew that I had to get away and quick.

All at once my Dad said, "you want to go so bad, go!" And then he tossed my sneaker to me. And I knew for sure that that was the most upset that he had ever been with me. It was like all at once he had just stopped being my Dad, and the look on his face that wasn't him being mad, that was disappointment, real bad disappointment in me.

"Shawn," Jimmy wouldn't stop calling to me, and I just didn't want to leave my Dad like that. All I wanted to do right then was to keep telling him how sorry I was, and I didn't care what he did to me as long as he didn't look at me like that anymore.

The footsteps coming up on me made me realize that I had to get out of there, or there wouldn't be a tomorrow to tell my Dad just how sorry I really was.

Only seconds before the Teacher was able to get hold of me, real quick like I dipped down and grabbed hold of that other sneaker off of the ground. Being good at football I just faked moving one way, and then sprinted off to get with Jimmy. The cement and junk in the street was hard on my foot. But I couldn't stop to put on my sneaker, not yet. They were still coming after us, but now outside of the schoolyard I was sure that we could get away from them.

There was one other problem that I had forgotten about. That was Mister Lang, the school truant officer. He was always hanging around the school, and in the center of town just waiting for kids to try and ditch classes.

"All right boys," he called to us from across the street, " that's far enough."

Darn, he was right in front of us and Mister Fishman and Mister Foster were coming up fast from behind.

"I got it from here," Mister Lang told the others as he just ran up and tried to grab hold of Jimmy. Jimmy tried to dodge him, but he wasn't as good at running and junk as I was, so Mister Lang got a hold of his shirt and pulled him backwards. Jimmy was struggling trying to tug himself away from the truant officer's grip. But Jimmy wasn't strong enough to pull away, and when Mister Lang tugged a little harder Jimmy fell back on his butt. The Teacher and the Principal were too close for comfort now, so I did the only thing that I could think of. While the truant officer was busy with Jimmy I threw a tackle at his legs. Being little my hitting Mister Lang didn't do much, but knock him off balance. He did stumble and stopped himself from falling by putting his hands on the ground. That was good enough to get Jimmy free, and then he rolled out of the way just as the Principle and the Teacher arrived.

The truant officer had turned all of his attention onto me now, and let me tell you that he was boiling mad. I seemed to be able to do that to people.

"You dirty little…" I knew he wanted to say more, but the Principal was getting close so he cut himself off. By that time Jimmy was on his feet and moving off the other way. We both knew where we had to meet, so it was all right to separate for right then.

Mister Lang was right on my tail, and I could tell that he couldn't wait to get his hands on me. That day everybody just wanted a piece of Shawn Malloy, and I was thinking that the world for me was gonna be a really sad place to live in, even if we were actually able to save it.

I was pushing my feet to the ground as fast as I could, but this Mister Lang was use to chasing kids. I'm guess'n 'cause it was part of his job. So he wasn't putting the brakes on, he just kept coming and coming. His feet were hitting the ground a lot faster than my Dad's had. I didn't dare to look back. I couldn't take a chance on slowing down. I didn't have to see, I could hear just how close he was, and just how much trouble I was in. At one point I could feel Mister Lang's hand reach out and try and grab hold of my shoulder. The tip of his fingers must've just touched me; so I knew I had to kick into high gear if I was gonna get away.

The air was burning my lungs as I pumped my legs faster and faster. "I'm going to get you… you little…" this time he did finish what he wanted to say, but I'm not allowed to use those kind of words. Just let me tell you it wasn't nice stuff that he was calling me. The muscles in my legs were about to give out, and the foot that didn't have a sneaker on it was killing me. Must've run over at least a dozen stones as I moved along. Each one of them hurting real bad.

I turned real quick to go down the opening to an alley. And just like I thought, Mister Lang was right on my tail. I didn't know just how long I could keep up the running. And Mister Lang, he wasn't like other adults, he was matching everything that I did, and I was beginning to think that he might be able to run even longer than me.

As I turned into the alley I got another scare coming at me. From the other direction, another guy came headed my way. It was somebody who lived around there I guess. That alley was a tight squeeze; so I really didn't know how I was gonna get by him.

"Stop that little creep," the truant officer called out, almost like he was a drill sergeant shouting out orders.

The guy I was running towards didn't know what the heck was going on. At first he just stood there, like he didn't know how to get out of the way.

I was gonna have to stop and soon. There wasn't enough room in that alleyway to squeeze through before Mister Lang got his hands on me. I didn't think I could've gotten much further anyway; this was one truant officer that was good at his job.

"What's going on," the other guy tried to say. His voice was high pitched, and he really sounded nervous as he yelled at us.

It was like a train wreck about to happen. I could just stop, but there was more than just having to face Mister Lang, and I had a comet to deal with. And that comet wasn't waiting for me to get out of detention, which I'd probably be in for a year.

"Hold it kid," the guy was saying one more time as I was about to crash into him. But I didn't even have that much time. In two seconds the truant officer would have his hands on me. And then it flashed into my head what to do. The only thing I had going for me right then and there was my size. Sure Mister Lang was a lot bigger than me, but I was a lot smaller. So I figured that I would use my size and I stopped. That's right, I stopped dead in my tracks. As I did that I ducked down, and just let Mister Lang sail over me. Like a torpedo he flew straight into that poor guy who had been coming the other way. A scream coming out of both of them was all I heard. I knew that I couldn't stop then, the truant officer was too quick, and I didn't want to go back in the opposite direction just in case Mister Fishman, or Mister Foster had been following. So what I did was I just ran across the two guys who were now on the ground. There was some ow-ing and ouuing as I did, and Mister Lang grabbed hold of my foot as I was trying to get over him.

"No ya' don't punk," he yelled at me as he tried to pull me back. I still had that one sneaker in my hand, so I used that to smack his hand away as hard as I could. There was another "ow," and then he let me go.

Now I was running as fast as I could to get back to the Professor's. I didn't know what had happened to Jimmy. Kept hoping that that he hadn't gotten caught, 'cause I really didn't know if only one of the Gravity Boxes would be enough to stop a giant comet the size of our whole town. Truthfully I didn't know if two would be enough.

The look on my Dad's face kept flashing in my head as I ran through the streets, but I knew that I couldn't let that stop me now. If I was ever gonna tell him how sorry I was I had to get to the Professor's, and get that Gravity Box up and flying.

I traveled between buildings trying to stay off of main streets, and out of sight as much as possible. I was sure that there were people out looking for me, and I had to make sure that no one was following me. Coming out of one alleyway I looked left and then I looked right. There was some traffic, but I didn't see my Dad's car, or anybody that I thought I knew, so I started to run across the street. Half way across I heard the sound of a loud horn blasting in my ear as a car screeched on its brakes. In the middle of the street I stopped dead in my tracks, and for a second I thought I was gonna get run down. Sitting in the driver's seat was Flynn. Next to him was Jimmy. Real quick like I ran around the side of the car, and jumped in the back seat. Jimmy just looked at me and didn't say a word at first. I was wondering what Flynn was doing there, and I was hoping that we were still on our way to the Professor's.

Chapter 10: The Shadow Over the Earth

"What are you guys doing," Flynn said to us, and he sounded like he was mad, I mean really mad.

"Doing," I tried to get out some words that Flynn didn't want to hear.

"You should be up in the sky already," Flynn yelled.

"We had to go to school first," I told him. "My Dad told me..."

"School," Flynn yelled at me again like he was our boss or something.

"Our parents they were really mad," I started to say, and I was wondering why Jimmy wasn't saying anything to this guy?

"I put my butt on the line for you kids, and..." it was now that Jimmy decided to come back at him.

"Because we were the best ones for the job, right?" I was glad that Jimmy had finally opened his mouth. Most of the time he couldn't keep it shut.

"You are the best ones for the job, I've seen the way you can handle the levitation machines. It would take my men a long time to learn that kind of control, but you don't do me or the world any good if you're not up in the sky when that comet is about to hit."

"We planned to get to the Professor's in plenty of time," Jimmy said. "We already know when it hits, we've lived through that before, don't you remember?"

"Okay," Flynn took a deep breath. "But I'm sure that you can understand why I'm a little edgy?"

"You're edgy," I came back at him, "if we do save the world from total destruction I'm in really big trouble."

Flynn didn't answer, he just shook his head and kept driving towards the Professor's place. I know he was scared. I was sure that anybody who knew about the comet was scared.

When we got to the lab the Professor seemed really uncomfortable having Flynn there. Who could blame him though, Flynn had already tried to steal the Professor's invention twice.

Outside Will and Kate were sitting at the lawn table at the back of the house. On the table in front of them was plenty of food. Fries and burgers, but they both seemed to just be looking down at the table like they had no appetite at all. And I guess I knew how they felt. I don't think I was feeling too hungry when I was about to go for that dip in the moat. And they might be thinking that this was their last meal.

The Professor looked coldly at Flynn before he spoke. "I appreciate what you've done for the boys," he said to Flynn, "but my inventions must not be given to any one government. The power is too great, and such power as you know can corrupt."

"We have a planet to save Professor," Flynn looked back at him. "And I've already been informed by your security," then he looked over to me, "that I will not be taking the levitation machines with me when this mission is completed."

The Professor looked at him unsure if he could believe Flynn or not. It was the same feeling that both me and Jimmy had. Sure Flynn knew that we were the best ones to handle the Gravity Boxes, but maybe once we had saved the planet Flynn would go back on his word. Maybe he would have his men come in and take the Gravity Boxes away from us. Once we were back on the ground that could be a real easy thing to do.

"Really Professor Burkhardt, this is no time to be debating the issue. At the present all we have is each other's word. Now we are working together for a good reason, an important purpose, to save the world. You have to trust me, just like I've got to trust that your boys can pull this off." Flynn really sounded like he was sincere, but remember I had seen him acting out that scene with Jimmy a couple nights before in front of his very own men, and Flynn was a real good actor.

"We'll go get the levitation machines now," Jimmy said.

"Will you need help," Flynn asked him.

"That's all right," Jimmy answered Flynn, "we can do this on our own."

"You still don't trust me do you kid," Flynn looked coldly at Jimmy.

"It may take a little time Mister Flynn, sorry," Jimmy told him.

"Just get the job done," Flynn said.

Before starting back into the woods Jimmy looked once more at Will and Kate and then to the Professor. I was having trouble looking at them, and I didn't know how they were feeling about me and Jimmy right then. Kept hoping they knew that we really were their friends.

"Professor Burkhardt," Jimmy said, "neither Shawn or I will assist in sending Will and Kate back to the twelfth-century."

The Professor nodded like he understood, but looked sad just the same. I was sure that he was sad for the thousands of people who he thought might have died in the past, but still was feeling real bad just for thinking of sending Will and Kate back to where they came from. Jimmy had to remind him that people were crazy in both time lines. So maybe Will and Kate didn't affect anything at all.

"Just stop the comet," the Professor said, "no one is safe until that is accomplished."

After the Professor said that both me and Jimmy turned and ran off into the woods.

What Jimmy had done was to hide the Gravity Boxes off in the woods somewhere, a place where no one could find them. He was still worried about Flynn's men getting their hands on the boxes. Jimmy being a smart boy came up with a plan to keep them hid away until we could figure out if Flynn was being honest with us or not.

In the woods I followed closely behind Jimmy, 'cause I didn't know where he had hidden the Gravity Boxes. I had had the job of getting Will and Kate back to the Professor's house, and those two had had all of the flying they ever wanted to do. But now it seemed like we were just walking around in circles.

"Where are we going, we've been here twice," I finally asked Jimmy.

"Just want to make sure..."

"Sure?"

"That we're not being followed."

"You still don't trust Flynn, do you?"

"It's too soon, he may be a good guy, but..."

"But we don't know that for sure."

"We don't know who we can trust Shawn except each other…"

"And the Professor…"

"Of course, the Professor…"

"And I think that Will and Kate can be trusted."

"All right, sure they can be trusted…" and Jimmy sounded like he was getting mad at me.

"And I think if Lord Hoxley was here…"

That's when Jimmy exploded. "He's nine hundred years from here. I know that they can be trusted, but for the here and now I know I can only count on you and me."

And I knew what he meant. Flynn pretending to be on our side would've been the perfect set up. He could make us think that he had knocked out his own man, that he helped us set up the big switch with the fake Gravity Boxes, and all to make us think that he was on our side. It was true that we were the best ones to handle the Gravity Boxes, but once he was done with us he might want to take them off of us again. Out there in those woods Flynn could have had some of his men staked out and following us, and we might not ever know. Remember being invisible and sneaky was part of their job.

I thought about what Jimmy had said, and I started looking behind every tree for someone who might be watching us. In my head every shadow or shaking branch became one of the guys in black. Now I knew why Jimmy was taking me around in circles.

"We'll go one more time around," he said. "Just to make sure that we're alone out here."

"Jimmy, we've been out here awhile."

And he stopped and thought for a long minute, "you're right," he said. "We'd better get to the Gravity Boxes right away."

That's when we heard it, it wasn't much, just the snapping of twig not far off, but we did hear it. For a moment I stopped, but Jimmy said in a real low voice, "just keep moving like you didn't hear a thing."

So we did just that, walking along, trying not to look back to where the sound had come from. It was hard, 'cause now we were pretty sure that we were being followed. Maybe it was an animal, or the wind that we had heard, or just maybe one of Flynn's men had finally made a mistake. I'm guessing being invisible and quiet forever was a tough job.

"What are we gonna do," I asked Jimmy.

"We've got to lose whoever is out there."

"But we're running out of time."

"We know these woods better than anyone."

"We should've brought a watch or something."

"I know you're right," Jimmy said, "I was just so afraid that we were being watched that…"

"They've got to let us get to them, that's the only reason that Flynn didn't take the Gravity Boxes off of us the other night. So they'll have to wait until after…"

"It's after that we'll have to worry, if there is an after."

"But we don't know who or how many men are out there. They could be all around us. They'll know the hiding place"

"My guess is that Flynn would only put a couple of his best guys on this. He wouldn't want to take a chance on them getting spotted."

"So are we gonna make a run for it?"

"We're going to make a run for it, right now!"

As Jimmy said the words we both started to race away from where we were. Running faster and faster from what, we really didn't know. From a snapping twig that only could've been somebody watching, that's what ran through our heads anyway. Like crazy we bolted, and ended up in a clearing that we knew was nearby.

Jimmy stopped first, and then called me back. Gasping for breath we began to look around to see if we could spy anybody else.

"What was that," I said trying to catch my wind.

"I don't know," Jimmy was slow to answer still being busy checking out the area. "Maybe just a deer, maybe just our imaginations…"

"But it had to be something," I said.

"I'm sure, but we don't have time to wonder anymore. Like you said we've been out here too long already, and Flynn's right, we should already be airborne."

"But if somebody's watching…"

"It doesn't matter Shawn, we don't have time to worry about that, not now. Let's get to…"

That was all that Jimmy got out when we felt the ground begin to rumble. At first it sounded like an earthquake coming right our way.

"What the heck is that," I said.

Jimmy looked around real nervous like, 'cause he didn't know either. The sound got louder and louder as the shaking on the ground got worse. It seemed to be coming from all around us, but from where we couldn't tell. Not far away we could see a cloud of dust rising up and headed right in our direction.

"Shawn," Jimmy yelled out, "get up in the tree!"

"What?"

"Just do it," he screamed, and he pushed me towards a nearby tree and started to climb up himself.

The storm of dust getting closer and closer told me that this wasn't really the time to ask questions. Jumping up, I caught hold of a low branch and pulled myself up onto it. Jimmy had shimmied up the side of the tree, and then crawled out onto the limb that I was pulling myself up onto. When he got there he helped me up.

It only took a few more seconds, but then we knew. The thundering sound was made by something that I had never seen in my life. Running all over the place were hundreds of deer stampeding through the woods. From up in that tree it didn't look like they would've stopped for us either. They just seemed to be running wildly and not ready to stop for anything.

"What's happening," I had to call to Jimmy even though he was right next to me.

"They know," he called back.

"How do they know?"

"Animals know these things, earthquakes, storms, they know, they seem to have sixth sense, and know enough to get out of wherever they are."

"But where are they going to?"

"They may not know that there's nowhere to run to."

It was right about then that the birds and other small animals seemed to go wild. From out of the trees the birds swarmed into the air. Thousands of them like a blinding storm screeched out of the trees and darting across the sky. And the squirrels and the small creatures had hit the dirt, and were going crazy all over the place.

"Maybe we have spent too much time out here Shawn," Jimmy said.

Just as Jimmy was saying that it happened. The whole sky began to get dark.

"What the heck's that," I yelled. It was still hard to hear, with the animals running wild, birds screeching, and making noise all around us.

We both looked up to see that everything above us was turning black. It was like a giant dark bird had spread its wings over our heads, and it had come on so fast.

"It's coming," Jimmy's voice got really shaky.

First, before we could do anything we had to get down from that tree.

Most of the deer had just about passed, so we climbed down slow, and tried to stay tight behind the tree where we wouldn't get trampled by the last of the stampede. Once down we started to run. I didn't bother asking where he was going, I already knew. Now we were both racing towards where Jimmy had hidden the Gravity Boxes.

We were running as fast as we could when all at once Jimmy's foot banged against a big rock that was sticking out of the ground. He fell and cried out. When I looked down at him he was clutching hold of his leg. It was covered in blood.

"Jimmy," I said. My voice was shaky as I saw the bloody mess pouring out of his leg. "You all right?"

"Get me up," he was screaming. I just started to move when he screamed out again, "NOW!"

I rushed over and started helping him get to his feet. He cried out with more pain as he pulled himself up.

"You alright," I yelled.

"Go, go," he screamed, and started hopping along as fast as he could. All I could do was follow.

By now the sky had turned even blacker. I took a quick look upwards and there it was. What looked like a giant glowing rock that was moving closer and soon would be covering the whole sky.

"It's gonna crash," I screamed out.

"It's still thousands of miles away," Jimmy yelled back as I was practically carrying him along.

Around us the birds in the trees were still screeching and flying off in all different directions. Their wings flapping so hard that it sounded more like thunder as they zoomed across the sky.

Jimmy was crying out in pain as I started to drag him so that he could keep up.

"This way, this way," he was screaming at me.

Luckily we really hadn't been too far from where the Gravity Boxes had been hidden. There was a big cave in the middle of woods where me and Jimmy use to play.

"In here," he cried out.

As we ran to the cave thousand of bats were flying out, on the ground there were rats, and they were all scrambling like a giant mountain cat was chasing them. I guess Jimmy was right about animals, somehow they knew what was going on, and they were just as scared as we were.

After dodging the rats and bats that weren't stopping to say hello we were inside the cave. It was really dark in there. The usual sunlight that lit the front part of the cave wasn't shining in because of the darkness filling the sky.

"You all right," I started to say again.

"Don't worry about me," Jimmy yelled, "behind the rock, move it out of the way."

I had to grope my way around 'cause like I said there wasn't much light in that cave. Finally I found my way to the big rock, but it wouldn't move.

"It's not budging," I yelled at him. Right then we were both just yelling and screaming at each other. Not that we were mad, it's just that we were scared out of our heads and it seemed like the right thing to do.

"Push harder," Jimmy yelled back.

And I did, but that rock still didn't want to move, not an inch. I was wondering how he had pushed it by himself in the first place.

I knew the pain was killing him, but with all of his strength Jimmy limped over to that big rock and leaned against it. Now we were both pushing that rock with all of our might.

"It must've settled, or," he started to say. "Push," he screamed again. We both knew that this was no time to explain things or even finish sentences, we just had to get to the Gravity Boxes.

At first my feet kept slipping and sliding in the dirt, but slowly the rock started to tip out of the way.

"Ahhh," I pushed with all the muscle I had.

Suddenly the rock tipped all the way over and behind it were the Gravity Boxes.

"Move," Jimmy ordered, but he really didn't have to order, 'cause I was already in that hole getting hold of the nearest Gravity Box. Real quick like I handed the first one over to Jimmy.

"Let's go," he said, and as I turned back to get hold of the second box, the whole cave began to glow bright green. When I turned Jimmy was already air born and had soared out of the cave. In a second I was right behind him headed towards the entrance to the cave.

Outside of the cave we flew quickly to get above the trees. The giant, glowing rock in the sky now looked a whole lot closer and meaner. A blazing red glare seemed to be burning all around with a tail that went on for miles shooting out of the back end. Not only could you feel the heat coming off of that thing, it was blinding. The whole sky had gone from night to the burning light of day in seconds as the comet had come a whole lot closer. The clouds just seemed to roll out of the way for that giant fireball headed our way. We squinted

396

to try and look up at it, but it was hard. The temperature off of that thing was incredible, and I thought that it might set the planet on fire even before it hit.

Around us the birds were still going nuts crashing into us and each other. They were getting in the way, and a couple of times almost knocked us off of the Gravity Boxes. When they hit it felt like darts being shot into your body. Some of them after hitting us fell to earth as if they had been knocked out by the collision.

Through the swarm of birds that had gone totally crazy, and flying in all different directions I screamed to Jimmy, "What do we do?"

"Aim at that thing," Jimmy screamed back at me, "and think light as a feather."

Up there the comet seemed to be affecting the weather too, not only the heat off of that thing, but the wind it was kicking up. The wind was powerful and blowing us around like mosquitoes in a storm. I tumbled and began to soar downward, but was able to get back my balance. A couple of times we almost smashed into each other. Getting knocked around like that made it hard to control the Gravity Boxes. So we had to get higher, above the birds above the clouds so we could get a good aim on the comet that actually did look big enough to crush the planet.

Up higher and higher we climbed. So high that the number of birds began to thin out as we got there.

The wind still was strong, and the heat coming off of that giant rock that was starting to bake us. We couldn't worry about that;

we had to just hang on tight for the whole ride. Time had run out. It was hit that comet with all we got or we say goodbye to the world.

Through my squinted eyes I saw the first blast of the green beam come out of Jimmy's box, and smash right against the comet. The burst of green light just seemed to bounce and not do anything.

"NOW SHAWN," Jimmy cried out.

To tell the truth for just a minute I couldn't think. It was like that giant comet had me hypnotized, and was keeping me from using my brain. Since it was my imagination that controlled the Gravity Box that was a big problem. Jimmy didn't wait for me. Right away he fired a second blast of the green beam right at the center of the comet. And for a second it actually seemed to slow down. But then something else happened, something that no one expected. I had learned later from Jimmy that comets are mostly made up of ice. And the comet coming into our atmosphere had started all of that ice to melting. So even though some of the comet had started to slow down the water off of it just continued to fall to earth. Like a large, boiling river it poured down at us. We both moved as fast as we could to get out of the way. I was real busy trying to save my own butt, but Jimmy was thinking a little faster. He knew that the falling water would boil anything below instantly. When the green beam hit the flood drenching down from the sky it instantly began to shoot back into the air. But in that time Jimmy had taken his mind off of the comet itself, and with his imagination some other place it had started falling all over.

"Shawn," Jimmy's voice cut through the trance, the fear, or whatever was keeping me from using my imagination.

398

In a second I was back. The next shot into the comet came from me. It was a giant blast of green light that had surrounded the entire fiery ball, and I thought "light as a feather, light as a feather," but it was so big, and nothing seemed to be happening.

Closer and closer the glowing ball of fire now looked like it was moving even faster towards us.

"What's wrong," I called to Jimmy.

"Do you believe we can do this," he called back.

"What?"

"Do you believe we can do this," he hollered back to me again.

"I don't know," I called out still so scared.

"But we've got to know, and we've both got to know now."

That had to be the answer. If the Gravity Box worked by our imaginations then we had to know that it was possible to stop the comet or the Gravity Boxes wouldn't know it either.

I screamed out and tried to shake all of the doubt right out of my head. I knew that Jimmy was trying to do the same thing.

"Light as a feather," I yelled out and then the green beam shot from the front of the Gravity Box. Like a bolt of lightening it smashed against the comet, and seemed to surround it with its green glow. The beam from Jimmy's box was doing the same thing. The whole sky was now turning bright green, but still the comet didn't seem like it wanted to get any lighter. It just kept coming, and it was so big and it seemed to be headed right in our direction.

"It's not stopping," I yelled to Jimmy.

"Keep trying, we've got nothing to lose."

And he was right. So I closed my eyes, and I imagined that that comet was a big baseball. Don't ask me where I came up with the idea of a big baseball. I'm a kid. In my head I turned the green beam from the Gravity Box into a giant bat, and smacked it against the side of the comet. When I opened my eyes the comet had shifted, and seemed to be moving away from us, and moving really fast.

"That was great Shawn," Jimmy called to me, but it wasn't good enough 'cause the comet seemed to go up a little, and then right away started falling again.

"You try and knock it away again," said Jimmy "and I'll try and make it lighter." For just a minute I was thinking about it and then Jimmy screamed real loud at me. "DO IT! KNOCK IT OUT OF THE PARK!"

As the beam from Jimmy's box was making the giant rock lighter, my beam was gonna to knock that comet back to outer space.

As the two beams shot out they met and exploded against the comet. And for a second, and just a second the comet stopped right over our heads.

"Harder, think harder," Jimmy called to me.

I gritted my teeth and closed my eyes again, and then took another giant swing at the comet. The gigantic green bat then clobbered the comet, and it started to fly back high into the sky.

I was so weak that I almost let go of the handles. Jimmy was still shooting his beam out, and was looking kind of beat himself.

Suddenly the beam stopped shooting out of his box, and we both looked up to see the comet sailing backwards through the sky, and disappearing as it moved back into space. Now it just seemed to be drifting away. We both screamed at the top of our lungs. I don't think I had ever been so excited before. And it wasn't just me, Jimmy was laughing. That's right just laughing, and it didn't look like he could stop. Then he reached his one arm out and squeezed me around the neck almost pulling my head off. He had never done that before, and it was actually hurting a little, but we were both so happy that I didn't really care about that. This was something that we wouldn't be able to talk to anyone about but the Professor, so I guess it was all right to be excited about what we had just done.

Soon the comet looked like a small pebble that had just been pitched into the air. In no time the Sun started to peak out through the clouds and the sky turned bright again. Not far below us we could see the birds flying back, not all crazy like before. They were chirping like nothing at all had happened, and it looked like the Earth had been saved.

Chapter 11: What To Do About Will and Kate

We were beat the both of us. Knocking a comet out of the sky can get you real tired. Just for safety sake in case it decided to head back to Earth me and Jimmy stayed up over the clouds, just for a while longer. Jimmy really didn't think that it would be coming back our way, but he also thought that we better not risk it. Once the Gravity Boxes were hidden away again we wouldn't have any chance of stopping the comet if it decided to take a second shot at hitting the planet.

When we felt for sure that the Earth was safe we headed back to the cave where Jimmy had hidden the Gravity Boxes. We went back real slow like to make sure that no one had seen us. Besides his leg was still hurting, but not bleeding now. I guess getting almost fried by the comet must've closed up the wound or something. So Jimmy was still walking slower, but seemed to moving a little better, and not hurting so much. Once the Gravity Boxes were hidden away behind the big rock in the cave we started back to the Professor's lab.

The woods seemed a lot more peaceful going back. The animals seemed to be back to normal, and since they seemed to know when things were gonna get bad that let me know that everything was gonna be just fine.

Back at the Professor's place Will and Kate were still sitting at the table in the yard. Resting on the bench with them was the Professor.

"I am so proud of you boys," he said, and he ran over and put his arms around us.

Will and Kate got up too, and came over to meet us.

"It was truly magnificent, Shawn, James," said Will.

"The whole sky turned a beautiful green..." Kate added in.

"The most beautiful sight I have ever seen," said the Professor.

"Well we've handled one problem," said Jimmy. "Now we've got to deal with another," he looked at Will and Kate.

"The Professor smiled at us, "I am a foolish old man," he said. "Of course you were right, Will and Kate are just children. To do what I suggested would be unconscionable."

"And Professor to ease your mind, like you said, I have been in both time lines," Jimmy told him. "In both people were irrational and violent. Will and Kate could do nothing for that not to be true."

"Agreed Jim," said the Professor.

"Un... what," I said.

"The Professor's not sending Will and Kate back," Jimmy explained.

Will and Kate looked so happy, and then we were all hugging. There was an awful lot of hugging going on that day.

"Professor," Jimmy asked, "what made you change your mind?"

"First," he pointed his finger like he was angry with us, but there was a little smile on his face as he said it, "you boys wouldn't let me do it. Secondly, I have checked numerous references, and can find no detail of Will or Kate's life any place in history. For all practical purposes they did not exist. In the history of the world they are insignificant."

"Did you hear that Kate," yelled Will kinda excited, "we're insig… something or other…"

True Will didn't know what it meant, but for right now he was happy to be just that.

"Ain't it grand," said Kate.

It was Jimmy who reminded everyone of the real truth, "Insignificant, except that they helped to save the world."

"Yes, yes, that is a good point," the Professor nodded his head. "Not to be forgotten, not to be forgotten," he said as he rubbed his hands through Will and Kate's hair.

Right then we heard a car come riding down the road. We all turned to see that it was Flynn's car coming towards us.

"That man frightens me," said the Professor.

"I think we're all a little frightened," Jimmy said.

When the car pulled up with its tinted windows we really couldn't see if anybody was with him, or if he was alone.

He stepped out of the car, and started to speak right away, "really great job boys," he said. For a moment Flynn was talking all kinds of excited like he was a kid himself. Sounded like he was really happy about not getting crushed to death by the comet. "The television and the radio are calling it a miracle. Somehow a comet just missed crashing into the planet by miles. The heat off of that thing singed the top of a few trees, but everything seems to have worked out fine. The scientists are still bewildered by the fact that Earth's gravity didn't pull that thing right into us."

"Perhaps the speed of the comet was great enough to allow it to pull out of our gravitational force, and continue on a course right on by us," said the Professor.

"I think we should run with that story," Flynn smiled at him. And as he was talking Flynn walked around and opened the passenger's door on the car. We still couldn't see who was sitting inside, so we were afraid that there might be some other agents. As the door swung opened we were all surprised when Sir Saggy stepped out. Outside of the car he stood up, and held his helmet under his arm.

"I think our guest has decided to not wear out his welcome," said Flynn.

"A very good idea," said the Professor.

"If I can ever be of service to you young masters," Sir Saggy said looking at me and Jimmy, "then I shall ride with all due haste to the rescue."

Jimmy slowly walked over to Sir Saggy. He looked at him real long and hard, and I could tell that this was making Sir Saggy a little nervous.

"Thanks for your help Sir Sagamore," Jimmy told him. "Remember to keep up your good deeds when you get home," and the way that Jimmy said that it sounded almost like a threat or something.

"As ever, I shall remain the defender of what is righteous and just," said Sir Saggy. Then he looked kinda sad at the ground, "though I will miss the angel food cake from the keep."

"And remember," Jimmy wasn't done yet, "that real witches have real power. They have more power than the sword."

Sir Saggy bobbed his head nervously. I guess that was Jimmy's way of telling him to lay off of the poor people that he had been torturing and slaughtering back in his day.

"I understand good master, in this magical land I have learned that and so much more," Saggy told him.

From out of the garage the Professor took out one of the time belts. He looked to Flynn, still not sure that he could trust him. Everybody was having trouble trusting this guy. "This is another secret that I would like to keep just that, a secret."

Flynn nodded like he understood.

"But Professor," said Jimmy "how will Sir Sagamore get back to England."

"I have calibrated the time belts to keep him suspended in the time space continuum until the proper moment that the earth can rotate to the exact spot where we must place Sir Sagamore."

"You can do that," said Jimmy.

"We'll see," the Professor smiled.

That's when the Professor snapped the belt around Sir Saggy. Our brave knight was scared out of his mind, and not able to move from the spot.

"Sir Sagamore," said the Professor, "if I hear of any evil deeds on your part, I shall send my two most powerful wizards to seek you out." The Professor then looked over to me and Jimmy and winked his eye.

"From henceforth, the name of Sagamore shall be one with the powers of good," Sir Saggy called out loudly.

"When you get back to your castle," said the Professor, release the belt immediately, because it will then be taking another trip. Anyone wearing the belt shall be taken along with it. Do you understand?"

"Indeed I do oh great one," shouted Sir Saggy like he was answering the King.

That's when the Professor set the dials on the time belt and hit the switch. Sir Saggy stood straight and tall like he was about to be shot and was trying not to look too scared.

Will ran over to him. "Sir Saggy," he said.

"Sir Saggy," he answered Will, "this is title of honor is it not," and he said it as if he still wasn't quite buying into it.

"Sure," I told him, and then he looked back down once again at Will.

"Yes boy," Sir Saggy said.

"Of all the beatings received back at the castle," Will told him, "your whippings were indeed some of the finest."

"I am only a humble soldier trying to do my best," he answered. "And someday if destiny decrees it boy, perhaps I will be able to thrash you again with even more vigor." Then Sir Saggy nodded his head and smiled back at Will like he had said something to be proud of. Seconds later he disappeared.

After he was gone, everyone just stayed quiet for the longest time. We were all waiting for someone else to say something. Jimmy was the one with the biggest mouth, so I was expecting him to say something first, and he did.

"So what happens now," Jimmy said to Flynn.

I knew we were all kinda curious, so someone had to say it.

"First we deal with Will and Kate," Flynn said.

"What will you be doing with us," Will looked back and forth at me and Jimmy.

"What I'm saying is that we have to help them assimilate into our society."

"That doesn't sound like a good thing," Will's body trembled as he spoke.

"Keep your mouth closed Will, or it's the boot you'll be getting," Kate told him.

Will's head bobbed a little 'cause he knew that she meant it. He had gotten out of the twelfth-century alive, dodged a comet, and now he had to try and survive his sister Kate. Darn I was glad she wasn't my sister.

"Assimilate," I said, 'cause I really wasn't sure what that meant either, or if it was a good thing or not.

"And how do you propose that we do that," asked the Professor.

"We have to keep them out of the public eye for awhile," said Flynn. "A place like this might work just fine…"

"I don't know if that's such a good idea… Children running all over the place…" the Professor started to say.

"And we have two perfect teachers for Will and Kate to model themselves after." Flynn looked over towards me and Jimmy.

We still didn't know what to make of this guy.

"I can get some paperwork done to validate their existence, give them a background..." that's when he looked over to Will and Kate. "Which they will have to learn."

I think Will and Kate and even me were still trying to figure out what assimilate meant.

"And why would you be doing all of this," the Professor asked.

"You just saved the world. There should be some reward for that. Also, I understand your concerns."

"You do," said the Professor.

"Yes, I do," Flynn said. "Maybe the world isn't ready for the levitation machines or time travel..."

"Time skipping," I cut Flynn off.

He just looked annoyed at me. It seemed adults were always getting annoyed with me, and then he went on. "But what I saw today makes me know for sure that they shouldn't be destroyed. No, that would be the greatest mistake."

"So what do you propose," asked the Professor.

"Look, I know you still don't trust me yet, and that's fine. But as you can see I can be of some value in keeping things like levitation machines and time belts a secret."

The Professor looked down at the ground, and I could tell that he was trying to think of how to answer Flynn.

"And you don't have to know where the Gravity Boxes are hidden, or anything," it was like Jimmy asked the questions for the Professor.

Flynn came closer and looked us right in the eye. "Keep them safe. Try not to use them often; we don't want you getting spotted by people like me. But I do think that you should definitely keep in practice. Someone has to know how to handle those things if the world should happen to need them again."

Wow, it seemed like Flynn was actually being a big help, but I knew that Jimmy and the Professor still wasn't sure about him. To tell the truth he already knew about everything, and we figured that as long as he didn't know the actual location of the Gravity Boxes they would be safe. Right then it all seemed good, but we would wait, wait to see if Flynn was really being honest with us.

"Professor," Jimmy finally asked 'cause I know he was dying to know. "Won't Sir Saggy be trapped in the time space continuum for quite a long time waiting for the earth to move into position enough."

"It should be quite an uncomfortable ride I'm sure, but he should get home safely," the Professor smiled. Jimmy smiled back at him, and it was this mischievous side of the Professor that I had never seen.

It was late in the day when we left for home, leaving Will and Kate behind with the Professor. We would try and get out there all the time so that Will wouldn't drive the Professor totally mad. So we finally knew what to do about Will and Kate, now what was I gonna do about my parents and me.

Flynn had offered to ride us back into town, but I wanted to take a little time getting home. Jimmy's leg was doing a lot better already, and I don't think he was too happy about facing his parents either. For a short time I had been able to forget the look on my Dad's face, and just how things were gonna probably be when I walked through the front door.

Jimmy said so long a block away from my house, and I started the long walk down my street. It kept thinking about walking around the block, and putting it off, but I knew that that would only make things worse, and that I would only worry more. I guessed the best thing to do was to just get it over with. Outside of my door I stopped and took a deep breath. It was time to go inside and face my parents. That was almost as scary as taking a dunk in the moat.

Chapter 12: My Talk With Dad, and Other Terrors

When I walked in Dad was sitting in front of the television. I could hear it playing as I came through the door. Mom was sitting next to him, and they had both seemed to be watching, but not watching. It was like they had both been just staring at the screen, and like it really didn't matter what show had been on. As I walked into the living room everything stopped. The set was switched off, and they both just looked at me. I tried to look back, but really all I could do was stare at the floor. I didn't want to see that look on my Dad's face again. I didn't think I could handle it. So I decided just say what I had to say, and try and see if I could get him to like me once more. After a minute when both of them hadn't said anything, I started.

"Look Dad, I know that you're really upset with me, and I don't blame you." You can't know how much I wanted to tell them the truth, but that wasn't possible. I thought that they might never be able to know. Jimmy was right, the more they knew the more danger they could be in. Even if Flynn could be trusted, there were others who might still be listening to everything we said. "I'm sorry about today," I kept fumbling for the right words, "and I just don't want you to hate me or anything. And Dad if you want to give me a licking I'm ready for it." That's all I said, that's all that I could think to say.

My Dad stood up and walked towards me. I looked up at him, but only for a second. And then I took a quick glance over to my

Mom, but couldn't keep my eyes on her either. It was just like I couldn't look at either of them. I didn't want to chance seeing the disappointment in their eyes.

Dad came and stood over me. He seemed so big standing there; and I thought that he always seemed like the biggest man in the world whenever I looked at him. I knew that he wasn't, but to me he had always been a giant. Then Dad put his hands on my shoulders and my body got all tight while I waited to get put across his knee for punishment. It had been a long time, but I could still remember that it wasn't gonna be fun.

"You've never spoke to me like that before," Dad said, and that was true.

"I know," I could hardly get the words out. My throat was all dry and my brain was just running all over the place looking for something to say, but the words just weren't there.

"When you didn't stop when I called..."

"Dad, I'm so sorry," I felt some tears trying to leak out, but I kept fighting to keep them inside.

"I thought that something was wrong, my boy Shawn, he wouldn't treat me like that unless..."

"It'll never happen again, I swear, I don't care what happens, I'll never treat you or Mom like that, not ever."

He pulled me close and held me tight to him.

"I came home, disappointed in you...'

"Please Dad, don't be, I'll never..." couldn't hold them back any more, the tears started rolling down my face. I didn't want to cry, but I felt so bad.

"Shawn, listen to me," he stopped me. "When I got home your Mom was sitting in front of the television. I had never seen her look so upset."

All the time he was speaking I was trying to sneak a peek at my Mom, and she just looked back at me. Still I was afraid to look into her eyes, so I only looked for a second. There I was her big disappointment blubbering like a baby. I couldn't have sunk any lower or felt any worst.

"The comet," Dad went on, "it almost killed everyone. When it was reported on the news that that thing was heading our way, I thought all that mattered was that I wanted to be with my family, to have them around me. When that dark shadow fell across the whole town I have never wanted so much to have my boy with me. And then a miracle, that's what everyone was calling it…"

I thought that I knew where he was going with this, and that was a place that we couldn't go. I was still afraid that someone might be listening in.

"Dad," I tried to stop him.

But Dad just went on, "missed us by only miles, the scientists say that they can't explain how that happened…"

"Dad," I just wanted him to not talk about the comet.

Then Mom got into it, for the first time she spoke. "I was so terrified that I jumped up and looked out of the window, the sky was black except for a green glow…"

"Some weird atmospheric anomaly, that's what the scientists, all the big brains are telling us over the television," Dad said.

"Dad, we can't talk about it," it was now that I looked up at him, and let my eyes move around the room hoping that he would understand not to say another word about the comet. "It's just that there's some things that we can't talk about."

He nodded his head, and I knew that he understood what had happened. Then without another word my Mom came over, and we all hugged. We must've stood there hugging, and not saying a word for what seemed the longest time, but I didn't mind, I really didn't. And when I finally got the nerve to look into my Dad's eyes I was glad that I did. There was no disappointment there; in fact he looked like he was kinda proud of me. Yeah, I was really happy that I had gone home that day.

The very next day Mom and Dad took me out and brought me a new mountain bike to go riding in the woods. I tried to call Jimmy, but he had been grounded for a month for running away from school, and all of the other junk we had to pull to stop the comet.

Both of us got suspended from school for a while, but I think that the Principle, Mister Foster wanted to do a lot more to us. My Dad went down to the school, and promised that our bad behavior was just a one time thing, and Mister Foster seemed to buy it. While on suspension I took that time to go out to the Professor's house, and hang out with Will and Kate.

Jimmy snuck out a couple of times, but when he got caught that just added more time to him being grounded.

The Professor had checked the history books, and now there was no mention of Sir Saggy or of the great witch-hunt that his disappearance had 'caused. "It seemed that Saggy had played no significant role in the history of his country," yeah, that's what the Professor said. By going back in time he had become just as insignificant as Will and Kate in the history timeline. We knew better, but for the sake of the world it was all better that it never happened.

Here in this century Will and Kate were picking up things fast, and Will's favorite food was still potato chips. They were wearing normal clothes, and looked almost like they belonged in this century. Both still had to work and learn how to do a lot of normal stuff like riding bikes and junk like that. Flynn was right about one thing, they had good teachers to show them all of that stuff. And it was almost like having an extra brother and sister to hang out with. In a little bit we thought we could bring them to school. Flynn had gotten them fake ID'S and stuff so that they could fit in and have their background checked and all. The Professor was getting use to having them around. So the story became that Will and Kate were his sister's kids who had come to stay with him while their parents were doing charity work in another part of the world. I think that that was Flynn who came up with that whopper. Oh and they had come from England, so we wouldn't have to be explaining their crazy accents.

About Flynn, we got to meet with him a couple of times. He would just show up at the Professor's place in the woods. When that happened the meetings were always moved to the outside where we felt pretty sure nobody could listen in. We were starting to trust him a little, but still were careful not to let him know where the Gravity Boxes were hidden.

416

"I don't have to know," Flynn told us, but I do need to know that I can count on the two of you if they are ever needed again."

"We'll be there," I said, "if the world ever needs saving again just call on me and Jimmy."

Both Jimmy and Flynn looked at me and smiled. We were all hoping that the world wouldn't need saving again for a long time.

EPPI-LOG

Well we're at the end of the story, and like Jimmy told me that's usually called the eppi-log. We took some of Flynn's advice, and we stopped playing with the Gravity Boxes all of the time. We learned by then just how important they could be. But that didn't stop us from taking them out for a spin every once in awhile.

When we were sure that we weren't being watched we would slip on out to the woods, and take a ride over the clouds. Jimmy also thought that it was a good idea to keep in practice just in case we should ever have another comet headed our way. When we thought it was safe we moved the Gravity Boxes back over to the Professor's place. When we were there we never spoke about them, and we only took them out when it was dark. If anyone had been listening they would not hear anything about the Gravity Boxes or the time belts, we still always went outside if we had to talk about stuff like that. Jimmy thought that that would be a good idea, just like we never talked about them over the phone or in our houses.

It was almost June before we took them up in the sky again. Having not gone up in a very long time it was exciting taking to the air, and kinda like the very first time we soared across the woods. From up there the whole world looked a lot different. Although I never talked about it with my parents, I knew that they were proud of me and understood why I had done what I had done. Way up in the sky we could keep everybody safe, up there we were the two most powerful kids in the Universe. We just had to keep that information to ourselves. If we were gonna keep the world safe we had to keep The Gravity Boxes out of the wrong hands.

As higher and higher we flew I knew that what the Professor had said was right. The only limits we had were in our heads, and whatever we could imagine we could make come true.

The End

Early Concept Art For The Gravity Box I. Book Cover

www.ingramcontent.com/pod-product-compliance
Lightning Source LLC
Chambersburg PA
CBHW060808030726
47503CB00002B/399